Praise for *Metropolis*

"[*Metropolis*] is, like New York itself, satisfyingly dense and complex."
— *The New Yorker*

"Gaffney's novel is a page-turner that exudes local color."
— Baltimore *Sun*

"A rambunctious literary novel that has it all . . . it's a glorious, satisfying treat of a book." — *Glamour*

"Ms. Gaffney is a first-time novelist of unusual distinction. . . . [She] bridges centuries and defies expectation while she fuses analysis and emotion."
— *The New York Times*

"Gaffney has crafted an engrossing fable, smoothly told, fraught with suspense, and all the more poignant for the social issues it illuminates — issues that, as the book's last lingering images suggest, must be resolved again and again by each succeeding generation." — *Elle*

"Dickens was the first novelist who really nailed life in the modern city, and Gaffney's Manhattan, with its horse carts and street urchins, is . . . recognizably Dickensian." — *Time*

"Tantalizing . . . [In] this big, busy, imaginative, atmospheric, and compulsively readable historical novel (and remarkably capable debut) . . . Gaffney evokes a world of hidden marvels. . . . [Her] tale of old New York is pure bliss." — *Booklist*

"Elizabeth Gaffney's *Metropolis* is vibrant, richly detailed, and compellingly plotted. The territory of her late-nineteenth-century underworld resembles that of *Gangs of New York* or *The Night Inspector*—but the sensibility is all her own, and her characters are unforgettable."

—ANDREA BARRETT, author of *Servants of the Map* and *Ship Fever*

"Trust the excellent Elizabeth Gaffney—in her debut novel, no less—to use the best of both history and her own considerable powers of creation to construct this compelling tale of a young immigrant's journey through the chaotic underbelly of post–Civil War New York. The star of Gaffney's dazzling show may be male, but the true heroes are the crafty, clever and resilient female cast members who, with their own nineteenth-century brand of girl-gang feminism, help to reinvent the world."

—HELEN SCHULMAN, author of *P.S.* and *The Revisionist*

"What an absorbing experience to visit Elizabeth Gaffney's imagination while it shakes, shimmers, and sizzles with extraordinary storytelling against the backdrop of history."

—ANNA DEAVERE SMITH, author of *Talk to Me*

"A towering work of brilliant imagination, as exquisitely written as it is intricately constructed. *Metropolis*, with all its brawn and brains and heart, will no doubt find its way into the skyline of the greatest of the great New York City classics."

—DAVID GRAND, author of *The Disappearing Body*

METROPOLIS

RANDOM HOUSE TRADE PAPERBACKS
NEW YORK

METROPOLIS

A NOVEL

ELIZABETH GAFFNEY

2006 Random House Trade Paperback Edition

Copyright © 2005 by Elizabeth Gaffney

Map copyright © 2005 by David Lindroth

Reading group guide copyright © 2006 by Random House, Inc.

All rights reserved.

Published in the United States by Random House Trade Paperbacks,
an imprint of The Random House Publishing Group,
a division of Random House, Inc., New York.

RANDOM HOUSE TRADE PAPERBACKS and colophon are trademarks
of Random House, Inc.

READER'S CIRCLE and colophon are trademarks of Random House, Inc.

Originally published in hardcover in the United States by Random House,
an imprint of The Random House Publishing Group,
a division of Random House, Inc., in 2005.

Library of Congress Cataloging-in-Publication Data
Gaffney, Elizabeth.
Metropolis: a novel / Elizabeth Gaffney.
p. cm.
ISBN 978-0-8129-7085-2
1. Brooklyn (New York, N.Y.)—Fiction.   2. Bridges—Design and construction—Fiction.
3. Arson—Investigation—Fiction.   4. German Americans—Fiction.   5. New York (N.Y.)—
Fiction.   6. Immigrants—Fiction.   7. Circus—Fiction.   8. Gangs—Fiction.   I. Title.

PS3607.A355M47 2005
813'.6—dc22   2004050804

www.thereaderscircle.com

Book design by Barbara M. Bachman

150116994

For my great, outrageous father

Richard Waring Gaffney

1935–1998

CONTENTS

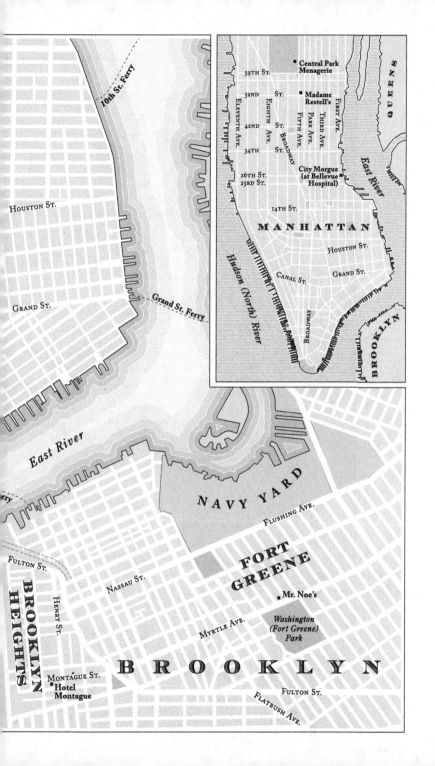

10th St. Ferry

HOUSTON ST.

GRAND ST.

Grand St. Ferry

East River

FULTON ST.

BROOKLYN HEIGHTS

HENRY ST.

NASSAU ST.

MONTAGUE ST.
Hotel Montague

Central Park Menagerie

59TH ST.

52ND ST.
Madame Restell's

ELEVENTH AVE.

EIGHTH AVE.

42ND

34TH

FIRST AVE.

THIRD AVE.

PARK AVE.

FIFTH AVE.

BROADWAY

26TH ST.
23RD ST.
**City Morgue
(at Bellevue
Hospital)**

14TH ST.

M A N H A T T A N

HOUSTON ST.

CANAL ST.

GRAND ST.

Hudson (North) River

BROADWAY

QUEENS

East River

BROOKLYN

NAVY YARD

FLUSHING AVE.

FORT GREENE

■ Mr. Noe's

MYRTLE AVE.

Washington
(Fort Greene)
Park

B R O O K L Y N

FULTON ST.

FLATBUSH AVE.

AT LARGE IN
THE CITY

1.

CASTLE GARDEN

"H ot corn, get your hot corn!"

Her voice cut through the clamor of Broadway but attracted no customers as she made her way south through the teeming crowd, bouncing her basket on her hip. When she reached the gates of the old fort known as Castle Garden, where the immigration center was, she flashed a smile at the guard, entered the premises and quickly sold her corn, several dozen ears, to the usual cast of hollow-cheeked immigrants. The stuff had been dried on the cob in the fall and had to be soaked two full days before boiling, but even so, it had tasted good to her, five years back, after the unrelenting porridge of the passage from Dublin. Here and there, ears that had been stripped clean lay discarded in the dirt, kicked up against the pillars, along with every other sort of garbage.

So she'd sold her corn, but it didn't earn her much, just pennies a piece. She didn't mind. Selling hot corn wasn't why she'd come. Hot-corn girls were notorious for rounding out their incomes by stepping into corners and lifting their skirts upon request, but that wasn't the sort of compromise Beatrice had chosen to make. She'd found another way to save up the money to bring her younger brother over, and to keep her dignity, too.

"That was fine, miss," said a boy, politely swallowing a belch. "Have you got any more?"

He was just about her brother's age. Her voice had sounded that Irish when she had first arrived. Now it was more flexible; she could show her brogue or not, depending on the situation. She let her voice lilt just enough to tell him he was at home there, too, but her answer was no, and she didn't crack a smile. She had too much to do to linger with him.

She and her friend Fiona generally hit the disembarking passengers together. They were good, the two of them, could make more money as a pair than the rest of the girls in the gang put together, not least because they had fun doing it. They'd never been arrested, not even once. The jobs they pulled brought in plenty of money, but half the take went to their boss, just for starters, and then they split the rest between them. It was better than piecework, but it was taking too long for her to save up enough for Padric's ticket. She worried about what would become of him if she didn't send for him soon. And so she had been pleased to learn that morning that Fiona was needed to help on another job, leaving Beatrice free to go out solo. A small lie or two when the gang did their weekly accounts would mean she could keep four times as much as on a usual day, bringing Padric over that much faster. The only problem was, it was also far more perilous, since it wasn't just the cops she had to worry about, but the boss as well. He would break her fingers if he ever discovered she'd kept his cut for herself.

She took a sharp breath and stashed her basket behind a vast pile of luggage. The day was raw, and she was freezing. To do what she was going to do, she needed her hands to be warm and nimble. Her fingers fluttered in the dank harbor air, then vanished into her dress, leaving the sleeves of her overcoat dangling empty. Her hands darted past cheap gabardine and worn shirting and came to nestle in the heat, the musk, the fine damp hairs of her armpits. Soon her fingers were starting to feel warm. But her arms were trussed, and all she could do, when a gust of wind worked a copper strand loose from its braid and whipped it in her face, was snort and shake her head. Through it all, she watched the steamship's tenders as they were loaded up with trunks, then passengers.

The first-class passengers had long since gone through a genteel version of immigration and customs on shipboard; their tender landed them at a well-appointed West Side terminal, not Castle Garden. Steerage would be last off, as usual. But a ship this size carried people of every level of wealth and class, and her targets, the second-class passengers, would be the first to disembark here. As the tender bumped against the pilings, Beatrice extracted her hands from her armpits, stuck them nonchalantly back through her sleeves into her pockets and began to move. Her eye followed the parade of ribboned hats and horn-handled canes that parted the crowds in the frigid brick rotunda.

"As if there weren't enough of these people already," said a woman in a high velvet toque with a nervous thrust of her chin at the crowds of steerage passengers from earlier ships. Her husband winced and nodded. They'd just spent the season in London. Before the war, they had traveled first class and never had to set foot in Castle Garden, but most of her money was Southern—which was to say diminished since the War Between the States—and they'd been forced to make concessions.

Beatrice shed her hat, let down the braids that had been twisted under it and adjusted her posture and face in subtle ways that stripped her of nearly a decade in a handful of seconds: She was suddenly quite a little girl. The second-class couple emerged at the north gate, relieved, with sighs and murmurs of "Ah, New York, so good to be home!" At the curb, while the coachman raised their trunks to his roof rack and the gentleman made to hand his lady up onto the tufted leather carriage bench, Beatrice pressed forward. With her hand outstretched, she said, "Welcome to America, sir, miss! Have you anything extra to help me and my ailing mother?"

The couple looked away—he to the side, his wife to him. That was the trick, of course: to force them to look away.

Beatrice's fingers were as fast as her eyes seemed innocent. Watches were her specialty, but this time she focused on the lady, who wore a pin on her lapel that reminded Beatrice of her mother's long-gone gold-rimmed brooch. She wasn't sure how good it was, how much it would bring, so she also grabbed the silk and suede wallet that protruded from the gentlewoman's muff, which turned out to be bulging at the seams, though some of the currency was foreign. Then Beatrice was gone, and the couple was grateful. The horse left a loamy turd steaming on the pavement as it strained against its harness. The wheels ground forward. They were halfway home before they realized what they'd lost, at which point Beatrice was just pushing through the swinging doors of Marm Mandelbaum's pawnshop, wondering what price she'd have to accept on the brooch in exchange for the old shrew's discretion.

2.

INFERNO

Asleep in the dark, with his limbs tucked up against his belly for warmth, he had made himself small, just a fetal lump in the middle of his narrow pallet. His blankets were topped by his overcoat, and he'd tucked the whole pile tightly around himself to keep it from sliding off into the night. The floor of the tack room had been strewn with hay, the wall by the bed decorated with a couple of nails from which, on warmer nights, he might have hung his clothes. The horseshoe propped upright on a cross-beam above his head was a relic of a previous tenant's superstitions. There was little in that room to suggest who he was, this stableman, except per-haps the worn cashmere and shredded silk lining of his coat—it had been a fine garment, once. And on the narrow shelf made by another beam, a bowie knife and a few whittled figurines: a bear, a gorilla and a strange hy-brid creature, like a griffin, but of his own imagining, composed of assorted parts of the exotic creatures he cared for.

It was no ordinary stable where he worked. The horse stalls were inhab-ited not by hacks but by dancing white Arabians, and there were no cows at all, but an orangutan, a giraffe, a python, a tiger. He had never expected this land of dreams to be quite so dreamlike, so uncanny. The job he had landed through the Labor Exchange was certainly not what he'd imagined doing in America when he'd left home. What he wanted to do was build cathedrals or, barring such glory, churches, houses, even roads. That was his training and, what with the constant stream of immigration to New York, he'd been sure there would be work for a man with experience in the building trades. It hadn't been so easy, though. So there he was at P. T. Barnum's American Museum, shoveling dung and hay and whiling away his few bits of spare time carving figures from odd chunks of wood he found lying about.

His other possessions included a second shirt, some extra socks, a sack of apples and a guidebook to New York with a picture postcard tucked between its pages, one side showing an elegant bath hall at Baden-Baden, the other a stamp, a postmark from a decade before, a name and address, a message. His mother had sent her love, said the weather was fine, she was feeling much better and she would be home soon: the usual. Only the name above the address was notable—for its difference from the one by which the stableman was now known, on his documents and to his employers. He didn't worry about anyone putting that together, though. Sometimes even he was incredulous at the great distance that lay between his present self and that boy who had been missed by his mother at Baden. How far was it from Germany to New York? He wasn't exactly sure. It wasn't a journey he'd ever meant to take. Things had happened to him, and he'd responded. Now he was here.

Was he happy? Not by a long shot. But not sad either. It was more that he was waiting for the next phase of his life to begin. In the meantime, his face and features were locked and shuttered like a shop at sundown, cinched tight like a burlap sack of onions with the drawstring knotted and wound around. When he was awake, he was cautiously optimistic—he'd landed on his feet more than once before. While he slept, he snored. And all around him in the stable, buzzing flies joined the noise, awakened from their quasihibernation by a warmth premature for the season and puzzlingly at odds with the weather outdoors.

That was the first alarm that something was amiss—a quiet one. The stableman was sleeping too deeply, dreaming too hard, to hear it. The clear screen of his cornea refracted the image of his optic nerve, and he saw backward into his own mind. The veins were like road maps leading to the time when he'd had a family, friends, a proper home. But that night the subject of the magic-lantern show flashing through his brain was nearer to hand: a sightseeing jaunt he'd taken on his last day off.

He'd been walking back from the Battery when he first saw the girl. She was an average young woman hawking corn from a basket. He'd just eaten. But suddenly he found he was hungry, even for one of those mushy luke-warm ears of corn. The stuff was sold on every street corner by hot-corn girls of every variety: black near Union Square and Irish at the Battery, German further north and east. Wherever he went in New York, there was always one of them singing the same song, but he'd never heard it sung so nonchalantly, so appealingly.

"*Hot corn! Get your hot corn! Here's your lily-white corn.*"

And so a woman was conjured into being while he slept, conceived from his memory of seeing Beatrice on the street and a certain strain in the position of his limbs. But then the pleasure of the dream was stymied by the same frustration he'd felt that day at the crowded corner of Broadway and Maiden Lane. There she was, hawking her corn, but just when he'd nearly caught her, she slipped away from him into the crowd. In his sleep, in the tack room, which was filling now with smoke, he thrashed. Shouldn't he get to taste her corn, if not to hold her, he wondered, at least in his dream? Something had ignited within him, just as the building he slept in so soundly was going up in fire. *Oh well, there will be other hot-corn girls*, he thought, never guessing, asleep or awake, that the skirts of his fate swished around that very hot-corn girl's ankles.

She'd disappeared on him, but the heat she brought on remained. At least he was no longer cold, he thought, middream. He was standing before a roaring fire, a marble mantelpiece, a gleaming brass fender. He was back home in Germany, a boy in his father's parlor. His mother was serving tea. But no, he'd gotten rid of his whole complicated past—or tried to. The dream flickered again.

He'd made it to the new world in steerage—no fine Meissen china any-more—and found himself a bed and a job. He was starting over. Barnum's stable was a good enough place to wait for spring, when he could go out and look for building work. He thought of Raj, the Bengal tiger, who'd lain shivering in his fourth-story cage in the museum when last the stableman made his rounds. Of all the animals he cared for, Raj was the one he most identified with—his grace and frustration, his power and imprisonment, his obvious desire to burst forth and do something grander than slouch around Barnum's. He could devour the world if he weren't chained up in that cage. The stableman felt the same way. He was aware that, cold and poor as he was, the bottom was miles below. What he didn't see, though, our stableman, was how close he lay to the edge of that abyss, how soon he was going to roll off into it.

That early March night had been frigid, so what then was this feeling that crept over him now—*heat*? Baking, burning heat. Could it be, he wondered, that he'd frozen to death? If so, he thought, Hell wasn't quite what the faithful imagined. There was no settlement, no knowledge. Ignorance of Heaven and God persisted, but more cruelly—devoid now of any suspense or hope. Nor, yet, was it the nothingness that he'd expected.

So what was going on? The smell of burning horsehair reached him next, and he glimpsed where he was: in a stable. Not Heaven, not Hell, not with the girl from his dream; but neither was this his father's house in the city or his uncle's farm. He began to identify the sounds that had roused him: animals' screams, the trumpeting of an elephant, the banging of animal bodies into metal bars and latched stall doors. He was in the circus stable of Barnum's Museum, on Broadway, in Manhattan. Yellow flames jetted up in one corner through the smoke that billowed around him. The splintery barn wall by his cot was hot against his cheek; dark wisps of smoke swirled into every orifice. Barnum's was on fire.

He knew he should fly, but he couldn't quite seem to gather his wits. He lay there propped up on his elbows and gaped. It was inappropriate, given the situation. For God's sake, the roof was about to tumble down on him. He'd always been broody, a daydreamer, a weigher of options, and a ponderous nature can be a liability, but it wasn't quite a fatal flaw. That wasn't what held him back. No, he was stupefied by the smoke. All he needed was a sip of oxygenated air.

How different everything would have been if that small, flaming beam on the far side of the room had not dislodged itself—or if it had brought on a cave-in. But instead it opened a draft that fueled both the fire and his mind, and the structural quiver that ensued from its fall sent that horseshoe spinning tips-over-nadir off the ledge through the air to land squarely with an audible *thunk* on his shin.

"*Ow!*"

In the moments it took him to go from stupefaction to pain and finally to action, two more charred rafters crashed down, forcing the flames several yards forward on every side. He sat up coughing and weeping from the smoke, clutched his covers, grabbed his boots. He considered possible escape routes and whether he'd have time to let loose the animals before the whole roof collapsed. He thought with a lurch of all Barnum's rarer monsters, who were locked up in the far upper reaches of the museum, positioned expressly to lure patrons through the myriad more pedestrian exhibits—atrocious taxidermy, apocryphal texts, fabulous paintings. "The freaks and the fauna, boy. That's what keeps them coming," Barnum had said the one time he'd met the man, to impress him with the importance of his job; but that wasn't why the stableman now chose to run into the flames. He loved the animals, and he had a humble favorite in a four-horned goat who was kept in a horse stall at the far end of the barn. It couldn't even see over its door. In the end, it was mostly the thought of that goat being smoked alive that overruled his impulse toward self-preservation.

In stocking feet but otherwise fully dressed against the bitter night, the stableman was up and running at last. Or up and crawling. At first he clutched his bedding and boots to his chest as he crouched and leapt, groped and ducked, stayed close to the ground where the air could still be breathed; but everywhere he stepped, everything he touched was searing hot, and at some point he stopped and swathed his head in the blanket, jammed his feet into his boots and draped the rest around his shoulders for protection from flying embers as he crept forward toward the stalls. Not a heroic costume or posture for an opening scene, but that was the best he could do.

What he saw from under his improvised turban just might have been Hell after all. The fire had licked its chops and slurped up everything familiar, everything he had. The room he'd just left, though nothing but a cold closet off the tack room, was his only place in the world. It had suited him to live there, adjacent to all those animal souls, normally taciturn, howling now like the dead they were soon to join. In addition to the circus creatures, Barnum's stable had a row of stalls for hackney horses. They pulled the roving wagons for the circus when it went out on the road, and when there was no road show they stayed home and plied the carriage trade, which, of course, ran all night.

But where were all the hack drivers now, he wondered. There were always a few of them hanging around, setting out late or returning early. Had they all succumbed? Had they noticed the fire early on and fled? And if so, why hadn't they thought to free the horses at least, or to rouse him, to save him? They'd never hesitated to wake him in the past when there was trouble to attend to, whether fighting dogs, drunken midgets or ailing beasts.

The air was choked with burning particles and eerie sounds, and the maze of hallways, pens and stalls confounded him, though normally he knew every turn in the dark, every beast by name and temperament, every horse by whether it liked to be scratched between or behind the ears. From where he stood, he could see the far wall glow and billow orange and black, swaying like a cobra, dancing before it strikes. *The python!* he thought. It would soon be baked behind its terrarium glass. But even if he were able to free it, where would it have to go after that but slithering off to a different death among the embers?

Just then, he heard a distant bellow, and he recognized the voice of Sedric, the rather mangy dancing bear. The stableman's urge to save the bear was checked by the recollection of the shackles, padlocks and iron bars Barnum used to prevent the theft and exaggerate the danger of his more grandiose or dangerous beasts. The panther, the gibbons, the elephants—all the carnivores and imports, in fact—were beyond his aid. He had no keys. Why should Barnum trust a nobody like him with keys?

The horses were screaming and the fire was all around, so that it seemed to be the flames that spoke in equine voices. Then a thunderclap of collapsing wood preceded the onrush of hooves; bared square teeth flattened him against the doorjamb. A roan hack caromed down the corridor, away from the fire and the door. He knew her—Alice, she pulled a fruit cart in the city, the monkey wagon on tour—and she reminded him of the one thing he could do: He marched into the heat, to the horse stalls. First came the show horses, six of them plus the pair of miniature white Arabians, then the hacks. He ran down the hallway, pausing every few steps to open two more stall doors, stopping only once to stroke the quivering nose of his goat before he drove her from her stall, shouting, "Go on, go! Get out of here!" And then he shouted it again, in German, and she went.

Saving the horses and the goat was a futile if good-hearted act. For in what way were their lives worth living anyhow? Split hooves and whippings, not pastured days, awaited most of them, even the ones that wore sequined saddle blankets seven nights a week. It took more than sugar lumps to train a stallion to juba. And when the toil and moldy oats had finally taken their toll, the soap and glue trades would pay cold cash for the honor of hauling the fallen away. But he didn't think of that. He thought of low whinnies and bristly upper lips and the grateful munching of hay. The further he strayed from the main door, the harsher grew the air, until, by the time he thought of his own escape, the fire possessed the building. He could hardly see or breathe or move. His feet hurt where he'd stepped on coals before he got his boots on, blisters rising fast; his face was black with char, his hands were scorched and seared. He'd freed perhaps a quarter of the horses, but they hurtled to and fro in terror, unable to find the door. He'd never seen so many animals rear up in a single hour, never imagined the likes of Alice would again get beyond a trot.

He had it in mind to run for the fire station next, as if he were the only man in Manhattan and there were no watchtowers, no alarm boxes, no neighbors, no hack drivers to notice the blaze that now burst through the roof in multiple places. But somehow that thought enabled him to make it, crawling, coughing and finally stumbling over the fallen lintel to the stable door. He was on his knees as he made his way into the night. The air was clear and cold, and the wind seemed to whip the smoke away from the Earth, straight to the stars. The stableman saw Orion's Belt—three lights straight as ninepins, bright and fine and reassuring—and then he heard a fire wagon pull up at the curb, saw its steam pump gushing clouds of ice that mingled with the smoke. The clanging of bells suggested that other carriages approached as well. In the fire's quavery light, a posse of men leapt forward to attack a small figure at the curb. General Tom Thumb? He wondered deliriously why they would do such a thing—unless they thought he had set the blaze? But of course it was only the fire hydrant on which the stableman had sat more than once, taking in the street scene, before the weather turned so cold. Soon a supple length of hose jerked and jumped. Water surged to its nozzle. Two men stood on either side to restrain it, like boys playing tug-of-war. They raised it toward the flaming doorway where he lay. *Salvation!* he thought, but it was a bit late for that.

The spray of water hit him like the whole North Sea, icy and powerful. He was on his knees already, and it smashed him to his belly, crashed against him like a wave on the rocks, shooting out in a horizontal geyser. He could neither advance nor retreat. Behind, the fire roared; ahead, hoses spewed. Above, the sky was high and black and dry and windy, filling fast now with low gray billows. Cinders wafted bright among the stars and a light snow fell from the spray of the hose. But he saw nothing anymore, save a white death as perilous as the red-hot one he'd escaped. Nor did the firemen see him, or the torrent relent. His eyes clamped tight, his mind shut down. How many choices did he have? How many do I? To save him from an early death here may be only to deliver him to a slow one later, a lifetime of struggle and humiliation. It might be kinder just to end it here, but now that I've taken him on, how could I?

It was Beatrice who spotted him. She wore an enormous winter shawl on top of her overcoat and for a better view of the excitement was riding on the shoulders of her friend Fiona, her feet tucked into her partner's armpits, her skirts bunched unladylike around her thighs, letting the cold air in. Beatrice was describing the scene to Fiona, who could see only snatches here and there through gaps in the milling crowd. Being pickpockets, they were always on the job, of course, but among many other things they were also girls, curious of a spectacle, and they'd long since ceased trying to work the crowd.

Beatrice thought she saw a man emerge from the doorway and struggle briefly to stand, then ball up against the rushing water and disappear from view. Everyone else was watching the horses with their tails aflame, the windows shattering, the orange roil, but she stretched herself higher to confirm her sighting. Yes, there was a man in there, and she gesticulated to no one in particular. "Stop," she shouted, "Stop!" But nobody heard. She was trying to flag down a fireman when she swayed too far sideways, and Fiona staggered and dropped her. She was too large a girl to be carried like that in the first place, even without all that flapping. She didn't hit her head or break her arm, nothing grave, just landed on her back and lay gasping for breath, her arm still jabbing the air, pointing toward the stable door. She had become a small spectacle unto herself, and finally, when she got her breath back, her cries—"There's someone alive in there, I saw someone trying to get out the door!"—at long last drew people's attention to the man whom no one else had seen.

If he'd heard her voice, he wouldn't have recognized it, regardless of how he'd dreamed of her, or how many times she'd sung her wares in his neighborhood before. A song is not a shout. Even if he'd seen her, he might not have recognized her—she didn't look exactly like the woman of his dream. The bridge of her nose had a larger bump, her eyes were deeper set, her chin was sharper. But no matter—he'd meet her again soon enough, and not find himself all that happy about it, if you must know. She couldn't see his face—it was night, there was smoke, he was black with soot—and no, she wouldn't have known him, but she'd find out who he was before long. But all that was later; this was now.

Quite a crowd had gathered, and the collective eye of all those people followed the girl's finger to the muddy figure writhing in limbo between fire and ice. Her announcement was repeated, mouth to ear, mouth to ear, until someone finally told a fireman, who told another, who briefly diverted the stream to a window above. Most in the crowd were silent with horror when they saw him; some cheered the survivor; others were more cynical, doubting aloud that he would live. Fires were common in New York— death, too.

One of the onlookers was a dirty-blond man in the front row. He knew the stableman from Barnum's, where he held some nebulous job that brought him through the stables now and then. He was talking to the boy at his side, loudly, so that anyone nearby could hear him—one of those people who seem to think everyone cares to know their opinions.

"Look at that, Jimster—isn't that the new stableboy, the German one? Jesus Christus—you think maybe he's the firebug?" He scratched his neck as they watched a fireman run up and drag the stableman to the sidelines.

"Come on, Mister U.," said the boy. "Him?" But he wasn't really paying attention; he was marveling at the water that came through the hydrant under fabulous pressure but started to freeze almost before it met the flames. It seemed the hoses were shooting snow.

"Well, somebody did it, didn't they, Jimmy? Fire doesn't light itself. Just look at it: Barnum's burning down *again*. Just look at that blaze."

"Yeah," said the boy, breathing out white puffs. "But you know what gets me? Where the Hell all that water comes from." He was thinking of the corner well where he filled a pail in the mornings. He was thinking he was thirsty.

"What, Jimmy, really? Don't you know? Croton. Travels forty miles over bridges, through tunnels, all downhill, just to get to that reservoir uptown."

But how would the boy have known that? He lived in the Fourth Ward, where the water had never been connected to the tenement flats. *Sanitation for the population!* was the cry of the social reformers, but it was just a slogan. Neither the city nor the tenement lords would pay to bring the water indoors. Meanwhile, every seven seconds one of New York's more pampered households flushed a newfangled toilet bowl full of piss-yellow Croton water, sending another tiny wave of sewage out with the ebb, into the harbor—but never far enough. For the flood tide brought it back again, and naturally it settled in the boggy lowlands abutting the slums, and the tenement wells drew a questionable brew that was much the worse for having been in high places.

The water the firemen were spewing at the blaze was the first Croton water the stableman had ever tasted, but he had no idea how clean and pure it was. There was the clanging of bells, the roar of flames, the rush of pressurized jets, and then he felt the arms of strangers lift him up and carry him away. His sodden clothes swiftly started to freeze into a stiff box around his body, and he felt the ice crack and rain down against his skin as he was packed off, shivering uncontrollably, into an official vehicle, whether ambulance or police wagon he didn't think to wonder at the time. Someone asked his name, but he couldn't respond. What did his name matter? What did his face? What did anything, when he'd lost yet again what little he had to lose? Most of Barnum's animals were certainly dead—if not burned up then suffocated, their lungs scorched beyond resuscitation. His own breath was perilously shallow.

Through the open rear doors of the coach, the stableman spotted a ghostly figure in a fourth-story window, and he thought a fireman must have ventured into the building to try to save the menagerie. Perhaps they had found the keys to the animals' shackles. The face he saw was orange and strange, which he put down to the glow of the fire—until it opened its jaws and roared. Raj the tiger was free. The big cat tapped his paws against the hot glass, crouched out of sight, then reappeared in fluid motion. He pounced straight through the windowpane and sailed through the night in an aura of flames, shards and sparks, his leg iron trailing a charred lump of timber.

His flight was magnificent. The people on the street watched silently as he landed with a thud, then they let out a collective scream. The tiger staggered, one of his legs in grave disorder, at a strange angle from his body. He looked around him, and for an instant his yellow eyes met those of the stableman in the back of the wagon. The fur along Raj's back smoldered. He grumbled from deep within, dropped to his haunches and roared. Then he ran north, at a fairly fast pace for a tiger who was dragging one leg and a four-by-four by the shackle. The onlookers scattered and the stableman had a view of the tiger's path. As Raj picked up speed, his singed fur was fanned by the wind and flames broke out across his back and down his long, pumping tail. Then the stableman heard a blast and saw the tiger recoil. Another two shots, and the animal crumpled to the icy pavement with a growl. He had been a splendid but miserable creature whose huge paws had worn a perimeter groove in the wooden floor of his small cage as he furiously paced, mouth half open in contempt, teeth bared, long white belly scruff dangling between his knees. He often sprayed urine at spectators who approached his cage too closely but had never marked the stableman, who sometimes brought him a greenish hunk of beef when the lion tamer was otherwise engaged. Had they shot him to put him out of his agony or because they considered him a threat? Had there even been a reason? Had it just been an officer's lust for heroism, satisfied at last against the wildest beast ever let loose on a New York street? A fear seized the stableman then that he and Raj were two of a kind—foreigners in this land, misfits who'd managed to escape the blaze but only after sustaining injuries that rendered them useless and possibly dangerous.

The authorities had dispatched the tiger. A man in a uniform laid a blanket over the stableman and pulled it across his face, as if he were a corpse, and he read the word POLICE woven into its border. He groaned and struggled to paw it from his eyes. Was the officer there to help him, to arrest him or just to cart him off to die? He looked for an answer in the eyes of the man standing above him, but the man's eyes looked away.

And so began his career as a suspect, a man on the edge of the law, for a second time—despite all his intentions. It was why he'd fled Germany. Now here he was in a city he'd thought was big enough to get lost in, big enough to need innumerable builders to help make it bigger yet, and he found himself in a different boat of the exact same class. How had it happened, and so fast? Was there something about him? A curse? Did his face look felonious, threatening? That's certainly not what Beatrice thought when she peered into the back of the wagon while he watched the tiger being shot.

She'd already heard the rumor flying through the crowd that the man she'd seen and saved was a disgruntled worker from the museum, that he was the one who had set the fire. Maybe, she thought, but who had ever heard of an arsonist sticking around long enough nearly to die in the fire? Barnum had enemies enough that it hardly seemed likely this stableman was responsible, at least not by himself. He looked a little too honest, too stunned. What she was thinking was that this fellow had gotten himself in over his head. Someone had set him up to take a fall.

She scanned the crowd to see if she could guess whom he was working for. When she had her answer, she began to formulate her plan. She needed a story to take back to Johnny, her boss. He would certainly want to know all about it.

3.

THE SCENE OF THE CRIME

He woke up in the Tombs, but he had no sense of being in jail. No, at first it rather seemed as if he'd died and gone to Versailles. He was lying in a soft bed, and the first thing he saw was a wheeled metal bathtub full of steaming water. His head was heavy. His eyes burned, and so did his lungs. He took account of his limbs and digits and found them all there, but they hurt. His hands and feet were scabbed and blistery and had stuck in several places to the fine Egyptian sheeting. He wondered if this was a hospital. Then a strange, grinning little man materialized from a corner and helped him soak the blisters free in a basin of water from the tub.

"What is this place?" he asked when they were done.

"Why, the Hall of Justice, sir."

He'd heard the name, but it didn't make sense. "Sir?" he said. "You mean the Tombs?"

"The very same." And then the fellow—less jailer than manservant—helped him stand and undress. He laid out a black woolen robe and directed the stableman's attention to a decanter of port, a tumbler and a tub of anesthetic salve on a small side table. Then he disappeared. Sore and coughing and still half delirious, the stableman helped himself to several glasses of port while he soaked. It was spicy and delicious. He tried not to think, because when he did, he kept seeing burning horses, the flight of the tiger, the stagger and jerk, the blood steaming red against the ice. Eventually, when the water had cooled, he rose from the tub, smeared himself with the soothing cream, crawled back under the covers and fell deeply asleep.

He dreamed. He was in the dripping marble chambers of the Roman Baths at Baden-Baden, where his father had introduced him to the rituals and rigors of manly purgation while his mother underwent one of her therapeutic regimens and the governess took his sister, Lottie, strolling through the cure park.

"This will fix anything that ails you," his father had said as they entered the front atrium of an imposing building with the air of a courthouse or museum. The doctor purchased tickets and they proceeded down a hallway and into a changing room with many cubbies and tall stacks of white towels.

"But what do I change into?" he asked when his shoes were lined up neatly under the bench and his trousers folded. On the next bench, an old man let out a cackle that set the flesh of his hairy belly a-wobble. Then his father stripped off his shorts to reveal something awful in the midst of his firm abdomen and pale, powerful thighs: a thick, red, leathery proboscis. It was quite unimaginable to the boy that he would remove his own thin drawers before these two naked men, his father—a firm, strong God—and the mocking old satyr.

"There are no ladies allowed here, son—you don't need a bathing costume." His father had slapped him on the shoulder then and made him feel a man, though in truth he was not at all sure he wanted to be one. And then they'd gone together through the alternating pools and chambers—hot and dry, cold and bracing, steamy humid, body-warm—to arrive at last in a luminous circular chamber where beds ringed the walls like spokes on a wheel and a silent attendant trussed him in a blissful cocoon of smooth sheets and soft fleece blankets.

It was, perhaps, his fondest memory of his father, the great doctor who was beloved by generations of patients and medical students, his father who had disowned him long before he reached his majority. But even it was tainted, as every thought of his father was, by what had happened after. The following day, he had awakened in a sweat, with a fever, and everything else was a sea of confused images, half hallucination, half real. It seemed that weeks passed without his seeing his parents or sister or anyone but the nurse and the visiting physician. Or then again, like just one long day. At the end, when he'd finally been given permission to get out of bed, he found a new suit of clothes laid out for him by the governess. He imagined a party of some sort and smoothed down his hair with spit until it shone, just as his mother liked, but the nurse took him to a room where his father sat alone. His father's arm didn't move when he tugged it; the man was entirely rigid, a statue. Finally, he'd blinked and looked at his son and told him where they were going and why. His mother was dead.

The nightmare ending of that dream was still playing out in his head in the Tombs when, at noon, a meal of poached eggs, white sauce, toast points and tea was brought in on a tray. There were sugar cubes. He found a jug of fresh, cool water for drinking on the table and a pitcher of hot for washing on the stand; a chamber pot as clean as a dinner plate awaited his need beneath the bed. He was further from the tack room where he'd gone to sleep the night before than he was from his lost, pampered boyhood just then, and it was only slowly that he recalled the series of events that had happened to him in between. The whole thing seemed so improbable. Perhaps there were quite a few other firstborn sons of prominent men who had been disinherited before their majority and sent to live on farms with distant relatives; surely many first wives' children were hated by their stepmothers; and probably it was the majority of new immigrants to the great city who found themselves living unexpected lives. But how many of them were mucking *elephant stalls*? How many had been falsely accused of arson? How many of those who had ended up in jail were in *this* sort of a jail? When he looked around, it seemed more of a hotel suite or guest room. Was he lucky or unlucky, he wondered. Apparently it wasn't the right question. He was both, by turns. So far, New York had not exactly offered him the fresh start he sought, but then again, it kept helping him back up every time it battered him down. Maybe that's the way it would go: He had to go under before he could rise. If that was the case, if each setback would be followed by some odd bit of good fortune, he felt sure he could make it. Maybe, with a little perseverance, he could thrive.

And so he resolved to make the best of whatever came his way for as long as it lasted. He knew from his childhood what the high life could be like and how quickly it could disappear; he also knew destitution. He'd grown up in a monarchy and come to a democracy. He'd seen firsthand that both of them required an aristocracy as well as an underclass. He had been a member of both and hadn't much liked either. Above all, perhaps, he'd learned that class distinctions were more fluid than they seemed and tragedy befell the privileged just as often as the poor. On the ship over, for instance, the rich had died the same as the likes of him in steerage. But he had survived.

"Well, buddy," said his jailer-cum-manservant later, as he carried in a pile of clean laundry, "either you're somebody—but I don't think so—or you got lucky last night." Apparently, the man had taken a closer look at the condition of his clothes.

The stableman shrugged and scooped up the last of the yolk with his toast. He was grateful for the fluke that had gotten him this bath and bed and breakfast, and he doubted it would last; still, he saw no reason to accelerate its end by saying anything at all. When the man left, he slept again, this time without dreaming—a relief.

Several hours later, an angry officer woke him abruptly by yanking the sheet from his grasp. His fingers stung and he braced himself, he knew not what for.

"Wake up, you Goddamned Irish arsonist! What do you think you're doing here?"

"What, sir? I'm not Irish. I'm German. I work at Barnum's. I was trapped in the fire. You were maybe thinking from someone else? Is the arsonist here as well, maybe not this room?"

"All right, you kraut scum bucket, how the Hell did you manage to get yourself into this particular cell?"

"I didn't manage anything, I was brought here."

But by this time he was scrambling into his clothes—he noticed buttons where there had been none, long-split seams that were joined, places where holes had been patched with a similar fabric.

"There was a bloody Astor in the drunk tank all last night and most of today," the officer spat, "all because you somehow snuck your dirty German hide in here. Who's going to pay for those toast points now, boy, tell me that? Goddamnit, you don't look the least bit like an Astor!"

"An aster?" But instead of explaining, the warden responded with a right hook to the jaw, just one solid, dizzying punch, then turned on his heel. It turned out to have been a cell reserved for criminals of the upper echelon, where all the amenities were billed home; so he was told by the comparatively benevolent warden of the squalid cell in the great hive of barred cells to which he was transferred a quarter hour later. The society wing was occupied mostly by bachelors who'd shot their rivals at supper clubs and businessmen caught consorting with the wrong kind of women at the wrong houses on the wrong nights and unlucky enough to have been rounded up in raids. The second warden smiled a little as he spoke, perhaps imagining the scenario that led to this mix-up: a comatose, vomit-encrusted millionaire wastrel scooped up half naked in an opium bust and issued prison stripes; a working stiff brought in unconscious in an overcoat that, though wet and burned, looked well enough cut to suit a gentleman. In fact, the situation was the handiwork of a skinny little anarchist desk clerk, name of Biedermann. As much as he hated all Astors, Biedermann liked the name he saw on the stableman's papers: Geiermeier. It had just as many letters as his, sounded equally foreign and was considerably more unpronounceable to an American tongue.

Georg Geiermeier was the name the stableman had bought himself in a dark Hamburg alley, in the form of a Prussian passport. He'd booked his passage on the *Leibnitz* under that name. At Castle Garden, a scrivener had copied it from the ship's register directly onto an immigration form, which a port official had stamped ENTERED AT THE PORT OF NEW-YORK, and Geiermeier it was (though a minor slip of the pen did contribute an *e* to the stableman's *Georg*). Biedermann took pleasure in assisting a countryman, especially a down-and-out one, but the truth was it could just as well have been an Irishman who benefited from his little game. He quite simply hated industrialists, and especially their dissipated scions. Biedermann, God bless him (though naturally he didn't believe), smirked through his mustache at the little subversion for most of a week—long after the stableman was back outside, staggering through the slush and snow, and the Astor had turned the episode into an anecdote. "Well, boys, here's to Herr Guy-er-meyer, that's G-*i-e-i-e-i*—" young Astor laughed, raising his glass of gin. His friends puffed their cigars and chuckled, slightly envious. "They're saying he murdered a girl and burned down Barnum's, and just think: He slept in my bed and ate my breakfast, while I had to hold my own with the convicts—and my father paid his bill, in advance. Now who says we don't treat the little man well? Maybe too well!"

It was nice of Biedermann and a big help to the stableman—I shudder to think of the oozing infections his burned hands might have suffered if not for those basins of warm, clean water, that soap, that salve—but as for this *Geiermeier* business, don't bother learning the pronunciation; the stableman won't be using that name long.

"I hope you got some good eats over in Washington Square," the second warden said, referring to the society block. Then he passed in a tin bowl of porridge and shut the gate behind him. The stableman realized he still had reason to be grateful. Even this cell was warmer than the stable. He ate the food and wondered what would happen to him next. Was there any chance they really thought he'd set the fire? Would he be able to defend himself, with no money and only his broken English? Several men shared that cell with him in the following days. At first he thought he might learn something from them—what the papers were saying about Barnum's, maybe, or at least what he ought to expect in this place—but soon enough he realized there was no camaraderie among the prisoners here, just competition for resources. The stableman had never felt so alone. Sometimes, lying on his bunk, he thought about women, and one woman in particular, a girl he had befriended on the boat. Maria.

The *Leibnitz* had been a typhoid ship. He'd not forgotten the pungent smell of her body, the sardonic twist of her smile, her fine waist or the suddenness of his own desire when he stood beside her. But on the boat, there was also death. That was what had really brought them together. It boarded the ship politely, with good manners, circulating first in a cold potato soup and then in a batch of fresh-baked pies—sweet, tart lakes of apple custard in tender crust, destined for the first-class dining room. The petri dish per se was yet to be invented, but what a petri dish custard made that day! A banker ate a piece, and a broker. Thus, on one frosty winter afternoon in the mid-Atlantic—and it wasn't even fever season—did destiny transcend the boundaries of class and power. The germs gnawed like termites, inconspicuous but hungry, wracking the insides of a few fancy people who quietly took to their staterooms and clung to their chamber pots, shaking.

Then the illness spread wider, and death came like a wrecking ball, taking everything and everyone it wanted, indiscriminate of cabin size or class. The stableman's sweat ran clammy when he saw the sick passengers, their familiar fever. He and Maria, who was working in the galley (and doing overtime in the first mate's berth) to defray the cost of transport, were among the few who weren't taken ill. They tried to help the others by distributing medicinal teas of chamomile and willow bark, but the infusions just seemed to make the people worse.

The *Leibnitz*'s passengers were no sturdier than his mother had been, his aunt, his little sister. They gasped and clawed and died like flies in their stinking bloody sheets. Maria and the stableman had helped the remaining crew to heave the mortal remains of dozens of passengers into the sea, shrouded only in their bedclothes, and watched them sink unblessed, unabsolved. He knew they would rise again, bloated, in a few days' time to be pecked at by the gulls. Through it all, Maria had worked by his side. She was perhaps fifteen, but the way she handled the plague made her seem more than that, and he, who was somewhat older, felt ancient. In other circumstances, he would have wooed her. As it was, he had bemoaned the money he'd stolen and the trouble he'd gone to to get on that boat. At first he'd thought, *Oh God, I'm next*, but then it turned to *Why don't I die?* The very death he'd been plagued by back home in Germany had tagged along, a stowaway, but somehow, in the midst of all that horror, he'd been smitten.

There in his cell in the Tombs, he lay on his bunk and pictured her face and imagined various ways he might try to track her down, assuming he ever got out of jail. It didn't seem very easy. Finally, exhausted, he pulled his bedclothes over his head and slept. His body had work to do, repairing its various breaches.

Several days later, when he descended the broad front stairs of the Tombs just past noon, he kept his eyes to his boots. He felt ashamed to be coming out of that place. Leaving implied having been there, after all, and being an inmate of the Tombs implied a good deal. He still felt congested from the smoke, too. First thing on breathing the fresh, cold outside air, he had a painful coughing fit and spat up a pink and gray object. After that his breath came easier but more raw. He was sore, exhausted and demoralized, but the thing that troubled him most was the arrest itself. Or had he ever been arrested? He wasn't sure. *Goddamn Irish arsonist*, the policeman had said. Clearly they thought he'd burned the museum down, but he was never brought before a judge or formally charged. It was all very odd. There were crimes he *had* committed, to be sure, but not this one. He had no earthly reason to do such a thing. The place was his job, his home; everyone he knew worked there, and, if you included the animals, so did his only friends.

"You have now the true incendiary, you have found him?" he had asked of the desk clerk who signed him out.

The man looked at him. "Yeah, I have him—right before mine eyes."

"But it is agreed I did not do this. I am free."

"Agreed? No, I wouldn't go that far. They ain't no charges 'cause they ain't got nothing on you. Can't keep ya without a lawyer, ain't nobody going to get you one—so you're outa here. But don't get too relaxed. We'll nab you back when we're ready. We got your address."

He had protested. He had said he preferred to stay in jail for as long as it took to clear his name, argued that it shouldn't take long at all, considering how simple it all was. He attempted to ask for the captain of police, but with his English as it was, and his anxiety about not being cleared and Tom Thumb somehow in mind, he muddled it and asked not for the captain but "the general."

"Oh sure," said the officer. "The general. Which one would you prefer, maybe Grant? Let me call him for you."

He shook his head. "No, I mean . . ."

"Just go. Go on, go, get outa here."

He left. His first plan was to find someone who *knew* him—the menagerie manager, even one of the hack drivers—someone who could vouch for his character and explain that he'd been in the building because he lived and worked there. But as he walked away from the Palace of Justice, it began to dawn on him: They were going to make an example of him, guilty or not. They hadn't even questioned him, after all. Probably they knew quite well he was innocent but had chosen to hold him since they had no other suspect. Crimes like arson just couldn't be left unsolved in New York—they were too political, too terrifying to the people of the wall-to-wall wooden-frame city. Just the month before, he'd followed the show trial of an incendiary in *Frank Leslie's Illustrated*. The man had been tried, convicted and hanged in a public spectacle. The main illustration in the issue that covered the hanging was a collage of several scenes: a sparking match and can of oil; the charred frame of the house that had burned; the bodies of the victims laid out at the morgue; a gaggle of urchins and ne'er-do-wells vying for a view of the gallows; and, in the center medallion, a vile-looking character dangling by his neck. If he didn't find some way to clear himself, he feared that could be him.

But then he had it: If all they really wanted was a hanging, perhaps he could save himself by finding the actual arsonist. Just so long as it hadn't been an accident. But the more he thought about it, the more he knew it hadn't been: the direction the heat had been moving, the dying embers in the stove, the cold, the empty coal bin. Candles weren't allowed in that part of the building at all, and lanterns were awfully safe. Were there any accidents, he wondered, or did every fire have an arsonist behind it—this one and the one that had destroyed his uncle's farm in Fürth alike? No, he thought, and then again yes. There had to be a cause; there had to be a guilty party somewhere.

And then, as he walked, another notion came into his head: The officer had said, "We got your address." But where he'd lived was gone. They only thought they had his address. He'd filled out the stable address of Barnum's in pencil on the back of his paper of naturalization, which they'd gotten from his pocket. But he'd not be sleeping there again. He was homeless, but for the moment that meant he was free. He didn't have anywhere to be, and there was nowhere anyone could find him.

He walked and walked, until he realized he smelled smoke. Then he came to a halt. The smell was strong—acrid and meaty—and the streets even there, around the corner from the building, were thickly paved with cinders and ice. Opportunistic children—a lucky few in ice skates, most glad just to have shoes—laughed, slid and sprawled across it, running for their lives to the sidewalk when the occasional carriage rumbled past. He asked himself what he was doing going back to the museum, the way a criminal returns to the scene or a man on the run stops foolishly by his old dwelling. Was it habit? Was there any way he could investigate? Did he just want to see the destruction, the remains? He wasn't sure. He was full of curiosity, nostalgia, disbelief. But yes, he thought, it did seem the only place to go if he wanted to figure out what happened.

He pressed ahead, around the curve. The wreckage was beautiful, in a way. In places, nothing remained but blackened posts and beams, whittled by the flames to delicate proportions and decked out in shimmering ice stalactites that tapered like the fingers of his uncle's beard. Where the walls still stood, they were coated with thick, even layers of ice that gleamed in the sun.

That was when the hot-corn girl saw him. She'd been peering up at a singed canvas banner fringed with icicles. You could still make out the word CURIOSITIES. Then she turned and saw him. It was eerie—she didn't even know he was out of jail, yet it seemed as if she'd known exactly when he'd appear, where he'd be standing. He felt her stare and looked at her, blinked. She was no one, just some girl, but she met his gaze. It almost seemed to him she was going to say something, and he smiled. She was pretty, despite the way she stared. But then she turned, and he felt ashamed of the loneliness that made him hope to turn every onlooker into a friend. He never heard the signal she gave to her friend, standing on the opposite side of the street, to keep him in her sights. He never saw the two detectives who had recognized him while combing through the rubble for evidence and taken note of his appearance—another bit of circumstantial evidence for the file.

He walked around the block to the back of the building and saw that the area where his room had been was largely gone, eliminating any hope of salvaging his few possessions. The only one worth saving was the *Stranger's Guide,* and that mostly because of the postcard from his mother. He certainly didn't care about the figurines. There was a tintype picture of himself he'd had taken at a photo studio on a whim on his day off. It was a novelty to be able to have a picture made so quickly and inexpensively, but the likeness had been poor, he'd thought, comparing it in his mind to the vivid daguerreotype of his mother that once sat on the mantel of his parents' house. And anyway, what need could he have for a picture of himself? It was really only the postcard he'd miss. He noticed the mare Alice, struggling to budge her load—the charred, frozen carcass of a camel—and seeing her alive made him feel slightly better. He wondered about his goat. He heard the slightly off-key strains of a hymn being sung by a high male voice, a tenor, and watched the singer emerge from the blackened interior. It was a fellow he recognized, a man who'd never driven a coach, curried a horse or lifted a pitchfork but had always seemed to think he was in charge. Now he was dragging a beam and carrying a hatchet over his shoulder. It looked like he'd been chipping in for once. Then he stepped into the winter sunlight, looked straight across the street and fixed the stableman in a glare.

It hadn't occurred to the stableman till then that people might know he'd been detained as a suspect. Now he wondered if it was possible that people who knew him believed he was guilty. Of course they did. Rumors would be flying. What he didn't guess was that this was the man who had spread the rumors and given the tip that had landed him in jail rather than the charity ward. The stableman felt a chill crawl down his back. He had an awful feeling that everyone in the vicinity recognized him and held him to blame. He turned and walked quickly away.

What he needed now was some dinner and a warm place to spend the night. Then a job, a plan for building his life back up from nothing. A few blocks north of the museum, he stopped to count his money. He had less now than when he'd stepped off the boat. Fewer possessions and less hope, too. He was sore, lonely and worried about what would happen next.

He had no idea, of course, just how much he had to fear—and from how many other people, in addition to the police. Beatrice, the hot-corn con girl, for one, was on her way, even then, to tell her boss of the stableman's release from the Tombs and his visit to the scene of the crime; the capstone of her story would be the meaningful glance he'd exchanged with his countryman, the one everyone called the Undertaker, who was supposedly one of Barnum's security guards. And the Undertaker, too, would be a problem for our man. No, he hadn't a clue, yet, about the underworld of the metropolis.

4.

W I L L

He slumped on the bench in the hiring office and sighed; it hadn't been his name called after all.

The clerk at the desk gazed out in another direction, and another man across the room inhaled loudly, straightened his cap, placed his hands on his thighs and buttressed himself to stand after long sitting. But the stableman had been there longer—all day yesterday, all day today. He watched the other man at the counter, listening, nodding, mumbling, taking pen in hand. *What can he do that I cannot?* he asked himself, and stamped a foot against the floorboards, not in a disorderly way, but he was frustrated and discouraged, and it did feel good to express it. He thumped his boots a couple more times, under the pretense of trying to drum up warmth, which was not too far-fetched in that room. Another name was called, vaguely French-sounding. At first it made him angry, but then he told himself his turn would come eventually. What he dreamed of, of course, was a job on a church or as a mason, anything working with stone, and his hope was that his long wait would be rewarded when the hiring office matched him with the perfect job. But he couldn't afford to be so choosy; for now any work would do.

Perhaps, he thought, the tongue-twisting syllables of his borrowed name were simply unpronounceable to the clerk. At Barnum's they'd called him George Jerrymerry, and he'd answered to it. He didn't much care how the name was pronounced. It wasn't really his, after all—just the name on the passport he carried, which listed physical dimensions close to his own. The stableman had given his own documents away to the identity vendor in Hamburg in partial payment for the Geiermeier papers, which meant someone else was probably now traveling as him. Who? he wondered. What was the real Geiermeier's name now? Had he passed the burden of his own terrible crimes off onto the stableman, like a curse? They both had brown hair and black eyes, stood five ten, but didn't half the world? The stableman wished he'd thought a little more about how the vowel-plagued name on his papers would be sounded out by an American tongue, but it was too late now. At least he wasn't alone. He'd sat all day listening to squashed-sounding versions of European names—Polish, Hungarian, it was hard to tell, the way they came out. There were Germans—he'd heard Schultz, Franck and Handel called—and of course plenty of English and Irish: Evans, Jones, Callahan and even two Harrises. A small squabble had broken out over that, but soon enough the second Harris had gotten his turn and set off with a letter of reference and a certain hopeful spring in his stride. That had been hours ago.

The stableman looked at the broad hands lying in his lap. Despite the burns, which were healing, they were good, honest hands. He wore his considerable physical strength as overtly as he could and concealed his foreignness and the unexpected contents of his mind with a quiet tongue. He knew he looked like a man who could work, but what good did that do, when the man who stood watch at the desk wouldn't look at him? Or was there some aura of having been in the Tombs still lingering around him? In the week since the fire, it seemed no one at all had met his eye or even looked at the wide contours of his face, which had taken on a tinge of desperation of late.

What exactly did he look like, our man? Well, with the scorching of the fire and the freezing of the weather and the chapping of his cheeks, I'm afraid his face resembled nothing so much as a scrubbed potato from the fields of the country he'd left behind, a potato that had battered around a long time in a barrel. His forehead was prominent; his eyes were dark and glimmering; his nose was straight. There was something there, beneath the tired surface of his features, that had made Beatrice take an interest in him.

A certain intelligence was revealed by the crinkles at the corners of his eyes. He had shed his name, he had grown calluses and now blisters, but the rest was still him: the soul that animated his face, the body that sustained him, the beating of his heart, the silent whirring of his mind. Yes, he looked clever, which had not helped him at the Tombs, but he didn't look half as well educated as he was, and that suited him, for now. All he wanted was a job, any job.

Time and again, whenever the clerk rose to call a name, he raised his head, eager for his chance, optimism rising, willing to do almost anything, but the clerk never called his name.

It was five days now since he'd left the Tombs, over two weeks since the fire. White flakes had just begun to filter from the clouds that morning when he'd set out from Wah Kee's flophouse on Mott Street. It was the cheapest thing anywhere—full of Chinese, Italians, sailors, drunks, bed-bugs and the likes of him. There was also a general store at the street level, but Wah Kee made most of his money selling opium in the basement to people of every background—men and women almost as broke as our hero and adventurous bon vivants as wealthy as the Astor whose cell he'd mistakenly inhabited. The stableman had watched them stumble up from the cellar room with the sweet, acrid whiff of opium on their clothes and seen the strange justice of the drug. The poppy was a great democratizer—for however divergent the quality and state of their wardrobes, they all looked the same when they left: not happy, not anxious, just blissfully blank, regardless of their station. The look implied a feeling that the stableman envied, and he'd have joined them in a moment if he'd ever had the extra money. But the remnants of his wages had gone, coin by coin, to Wah Kee for his bunk, to bowls of soup, to a plate of salty kippers, to a shave in a barber shop before heading to the hiring office, to coffee and eggs. As of noontime, when he'd eaten from a pushcart, he'd reached the very end. All of the expenditures had seemed essential, but all were fleeting, and now he didn't even have the money to sleep in the flop another night.

His timing was particularly poor. Of all recent nights, this would surely be the worst one to go without shelter. The snow had grown heavy and the day bright white as a storm settled in. By afternoon, hardly anyone was still abroad, and the stragglers were nearly hidden from sight by the white haze.

The door opened only now and then to let out a man with an assignment. As the winter sun crested and slid around fast and low, the stableman could almost feel his whiskers creeping out. There was no end to their growing, and suddenly that most trivial fact was an emergency. Tomorrow, after sleeping on the street or, with luck, in some church foyer, he'd be a bristly hedgehog, a lowlife without even the cost of a morning shave to his name. It seemed that unless he found work that afternoon, and it was waning fast, he never would.

Finally, late in the day, he felt his hope fail. No one would look at him. At least before, he had had the animals. They had known him and in just the short time he had worked for Barnum's had come to trust him. But all his gentleness, which had made them lose their skittishness around him, had done no good. He had let them die. It's better, surely, that he couldn't imagine what came next, at the soap and glue houses over by the river, where the animals' bones would fall apart from one another and sink to the bottom, their severed heads bobbing in the bubbling foam, their eyes hard-boiled.

The waiting area grew colder and emptier as dark fell, and he moved closer to the smoking stove by the clerk's counter. Soon there would be nothing left to do but knock on church doors and seek lodging for the night. Station houses offered shelter, too, but he couldn't very well imagine going there, unless he wanted to be hanged. He brooded over other possible avenues but came up only with cold alleyways. Well, it was warmer by the stove at least, and he stretched out his legs toward the heat.

He surprised himself suddenly with a twitch—he'd been asleep. He raised his head from his chest. Strange shadows flickered. The room was quiet and unfamiliar. Gaslight illuminated the counter, and orange coals glowed through the nearby grate. Something had stirred him. He looked to the far corner and saw the clerk at the desk beckon at him.

"You. Yeah, *you.*"

He had been called.

"Yes, sir." Hands on thighs, optimism rising, he stood.

"You been here all day. Didn't you sign in? Don't you realize we're closed?" He looked about and saw that the other benches sat vacant and the hall was empty but for himself and the clerk. The optimism dwindled away. The man was just kicking him out.

"Sorry. Sorry, I'll go."

"No—wait. Turns out you're lucky. See, I only let you snore because of the rotten weather, but now it seems *I'm* lucky. You noticed the snow? Well, someone at Street Cleaning only just looked out the window, and they sent a boy over here with an order for an overnight shoveling crew—just in time for closing. So what about it? Shoveling snow for the city. You want the job?"

It took him a moment to follow. "Snow, a job, shoveling," he repeated, and then he understood. "*Ja, danke, danke,*" he said.

"Is that a yes? You better stop speaking Dutch and learn some English."

He thought of the pink, tissue-thin, new-grown skin on his hands.

"Yes. Yes, sir."

"All right, good. You can start now and go till the regulars show up at six, see? Anyway, you've had your beauty sleep, and I think I can tell from looking that you ain't got evening plans." *Beauty sleep?* the stableman wondered. *Evening plans?* He wasn't sure how he should respond.

"Or don't you want a night job? You want I find some other lug?"

"A lug? No . . . or, yes. I mean, yes, I'll do it—and no, no one else."

"You'll take the job."

"I'll take it."

"Good. The thing of it is, you're the only man left. You think you're man enough to shovel the city alone?"

"The city, alone?" He thought a moment. Perhaps it was a joke. "That would take a long time, sir," he finally said. His English might have been better if only the few people who talked to him had made more sense.

"You're right, it would. So, first thing you do is round up, say, twenty men and take 'em down to the dock at Coffee House Slip, East River off of Wall Street. You'll get the carts and shovels there and sign up with the fellow at the office. The others get paid for the time they shovel, you get paid foreman's wages, starting right now."

Foreman's wages.

"What's your name?"

"Geiermeier," he said, and leaning over the clerk's ledger, he saw it written out in the beautiful Gothic script he'd learned as a boy and pointed to the entry. "I signed in this morning."

"You got to be kidding. Is that how you say that? I must have tried to call you five times today, yesterday, too. I started to think it was Chinese, all that up and down and curlicue around, no way of knowing what letters is meant. Where'd you learn to write like that anyhow? You don't know how to give yourself a leg up, do you?"

A *leg up*? Americans said much that he didn't understand. He had listened almost obsessively to the names being called. But then the clerk uttered a strange, vaguely familiar word, and it dawned on him: This was how the clerk had been pronouncing his name, with the g misinterpreted as h, the vowels collapsed, the m transmuted, and the sounds and stresses generally so different from the actual pronunciation that it hadn't even registered on him. He frowned slightly with frustration—how many opportunities had he missed in the past two days because of this?

"That's a G," he said weakly, pointing to the page. "I never realized you were calling me."

"What kind of writing is that, Greek? You ain't Greek, are you?"

"It's German."

"Aw, jeez. Now, there's plenty of Germans in New York, and they seem to get along. But where are you going to get with a name no one can read, and you can't even tell when they're trying to? It just won't do, that name. Or the handwriting either."

"But it's my name," the stableman said and then smiled faintly to himself because in fact it wasn't.

"No, no, forget it. I'm going to do you a favor here. I'm just going to put you down as . . . yeah, that'll do . . . that was my father's name, why not? And then there's the prince. Mr. William 'Willin' to Work at Night' Williams. Or Prince William of Prince Street, if you'd rather." He tittered to himself, but the man he was naming was slow on the uptake.

"Wilhelm is your father's name?"

"Yeah, but no—not *Vil-helm*. Just *Will*. See, it's a free country over here—you don't have to be a German. You can be whoever you want to be."

Will, the former stableman thought. *Will Williams. All right.* He looked up at the clerk with gratitude and was disconcerted to see the man staring straight at him. It might have been an unpleasant feeling for some men, but for him to be looked at, at all, was a rare intimacy, a comfort—certainly not an affront. This man had named him, he thought, and after his own father. This man would not forget his face. If they met again, they would trade nods of recognition, smiles even, hellos.

He was still slightly skeptical as he took the new name into his mouth— gingerly, like a bite of sausage with mustard. He let it rise to the back of his throat and his sinuses, opened his mouth a crack to let it mingle with his breath.

"Will 'Willin' to Work at Night' Williams," he said, mimicking the clerk so closely that his accent almost vanished. He had a good ear, the stableman.

The clerk raised his eyebrows and laughed. "Oh, so now you're a quick study, eh? I guess you'll do all right."

And maybe he would. At least he had a name now.

Call him Will.

5

TO SQUAT SAVES THE BACK

His luck had turned again. In fact, he realized, it had turned for the better several hours, maybe even days, before. He'd only failed to notice it, by failing to hear his name when it was called. It was a lesson he told himself to keep in mind. Now he had to get to work, but where on such a night could a man who knew no one in the whole metropolis find a handful of able-bodied men? He had no idea. It didn't matter. He would find them.

His employer was the city itself, a curious idea to him. He was to hand his documents over to the night manager at the Street Cleaning office, once he had his men—if he could assemble twenty men. The street was entirely depopulated. The city was shut down, which was at once his problem and his opportunity. Clearly he wouldn't have gotten this job if the storm hadn't worsened, if he hadn't been the last man there. And yet his assignment was made difficult by the very fact that there was no one abroad. He wished he knew where to find the men from Barnum's, even the ones who'd let him sleep while the stable burned, the ones who now suspected him. They would all be out of work, too, and needing money. He imagined being in a position to offer them work—to offer them anything, really—and wondered what it would take, exactly, to convert the weak bond of acquaintance he had with them into something stronger. But none of them had been forthcoming enough before the fire for him to know where they lived, much less where they might hole up to drink for the night. He thought of the thin German, the one with the beautiful voice, and the odd look he'd gotten from him when he saw him up at Barnum's. His name was something like Ludwig, if he remembered correctly. What he would have given, just then, for a conversation in German. Now and then he heard a female voice speaking German on the street, and he thought of Maria. If only he knew where to look for her. He had thought about going to a German church and asking, but he remembered that she wasn't religious as far as he knew. He hadn't the slightest notion where to start.

He told himself to concentrate. He was an American now, his name was Williams. There was no point searching for people in his past. He was starting over, again. He had problems to solve in the present, like how to clear himself of the arson charges and how to do this job he'd been given. To start with, he would comb the streets for as long as it took to find twenty men.

Half an hour later, he'd seen no one remotely likely to join a shoveling crew—just a gentleman in a top hat and a couple of girls out late playing in the snow. Little did he guess that the girls weren't really having a snowball fight—Beatrice and Fiona had been watching him since he showed up at the scene of the crime, monitoring everything he did. They'd found out about his new name almost as soon as he'd gotten it, but to them he was still Geiermeier. He wasn't in the least sure about his name himself. He had long since given up his real name, but suddenly the thought of his new name— his *two* new names—appalled him. If the police caught up to him again, they would surely see all this name changing as a further sign of guilt. Could a clerk in a hiring office give him an entirely new name, just like that? Was it legal? America was an insane place, he felt, a place with no sense of history or past, and it dawned on him that he still did take some pride in being a doctor's son, after all, even a down-and-out, disinherited one. At home, he had at least been secure in knowing himself to be a person of a certain class, with a certain education—truncated, yes, but he'd studied Latin, French and English. Even on his uncle's farm, where he'd been treated so unkindly, his education and his father's social position had bought him a certain respect. The clerk who'd named him couldn't make out the letters of the German Gothic alphabet—*Greek*, he'd said! *Chinese!* The stableman's Gothic script was elegant and flawless, he knew, but here everything was upside down. What was once an asset had become a liability.

He made his way up Broadway in the general direction of Mott Street, thinking that at least there were sure to be men needing work at the flophouse, if not the fittest specimens. The wind had died, and it was cold and quiet on the street; even when a horse and carriage struggled past him through the drifts, the only sounds were those of the jingling harness and the creaking springs. He walked in the middle of the street where the sparse traffic had somewhat dispersed the heavy snow. Then he turned the corner and spotted a group of figures emerging from a basement door in a cloud of smoke, hot air and laughter. There was a saloon on the lower level, he saw — Billy's, it was called. He must have passed it before but had never noticed the place.

A saloon might not be the best place to find workers, he thought, as he ventured across the street toward the doorway, but it was surely a place to find men and quite possibly a better one than an opium den. He heaved open the door. It was actually hot inside, and noisy and crowded. His cold cheeks flushed, and he took in a deep breath redolent of old sweat and sour beer. He paused there in the threshold at the sight of the barkeep, who cocked his head at him, asking in gesture what he would have. But the man whose name was now Will Williams had no money, none at all — not even enough to buy a single glass of beer — and thus, he knew, he had no right to enter.

To hesitate on the doorstep of a warm locale on such a night, to hold the door open and let in the cold air while the hot flies out — such actions can only detract from one's welcome. There was a chorus of shouts — *"Close that door, you fricken idget! In or out!"* — but he was pleased to see so many potential shovelers. Dozens and dozens of men, most still wearing their hats, stood at the bar or sat on stools or leaned against the columns down the middle of the room. Off in the corners, they crouched in small groups and threw dice. And toward the back, a few women in fancy bonnets and bright-colored dresses stood out amidst all the black and brown. Will Williams smiled at the sight of them all as the warm air rushed past him and out the open door.

The bartender, Billy himself, wiped his fingers on his white apron and said, "Leave then, why don't you, if you ain't comin' in!"

But instead, Will Williams shut the door behind him. He looked around the barroom, surveying the population, groping for a strategy. He ought simply to have slipped to the rear of the room and quietly inquired if anyone sought a job for the night. He would have gotten takers. But it was too late for that.

"All right then, now that you've ventilated the joint for us, *what'll you have?*"

He couldn't very well say *Nothing, thank you* without being evicted. His odd silence was almost as bad, but as a result of it the hubbub in the room quieted down a bit and nearly every pair of eyes glanced toward the door.

"Listen, men!" he said, surprising himself. His voice sounded strong. He felt as if he were standing on a pulpit, and he started to preach: "I'm not here to drink. I have one offer to make! I have twenty jobs for twenty men—shoveling the snow for good hourly wages. You'll be working for the city. I have all the paperwork to hire an emergency crew. I'm looking for men who want work tonight!"

Billy went purple—this guy was doing his best to rob him of his customers—and then he came out from behind the bar, white apron flying. The stableman backed up to the door. No one had risen in response to his announcement, and now Billy was plowing his way through the crowd toward him, but this was his only chance; he seized it. "The first twenty men to meet me at Coffee House Slip will have paying work this night!" he shouted, even as he half tumbled onto the street. He slammed the door behind him just an instant before Billy would have wrapped his fingers around his throat.

On the street, once he realized the bartender wasn't going to chase him down, he felt a thrill rush through him. Even if he hadn't drummed up a single worker, seeing that crowded barroom had given him an idea: He would walk over to the Bowery, where there were countless bars. From here on out, though, he'd be a little more subtle about his pitch. He would stop at as many places as it took until he'd gathered a crew.

He'd only gone a half block when he heard the door of Billy's bang open again. He glanced back and saw several men moving quickly in his direction, coats flapping open in the wind. The snow was still so thick that their brims were trimmed in white in just a few seconds. He kept walking, looking backward. Were they hoping to take up his offer of work or to carry out the wishes of the barman? He heard a shout and saw a couple of waving hands. As he watched, more emerged, running to catch up to the others. Then another cluster of overcoats stepped out into the snow. If they were angry, he was in trouble, but it looked like they were with him, in which case, he was set—there were nearly twenty already.

He kept walking, slowly, doing his best to project a feeling of confidence, and the men kept coming toward him. It worked. Despite his unimpressive dress and his foreign voice, they came to him like supplicants. He had offered money for work, no commitment, no questions asked. There were more than twenty. The bar had been full of men needing exactly what he offered, men who'd been laid off that day because of weather or earlier on other grounds, men who'd drunk up their wages, men with too many children, men who were broke or unreliable in a dozen ways. Now, on the sidewalk, they jostled one another jockeying for position, and an unanticipated problem occurred to Will: How would he decide among them? He could try to weed out the drunkest ones, or ask who had children at home and favor them. But when he looked at them, they seemed a small group in the wide, snow-filled expanse of street. The clerk had said *say, twenty,* but he guessed that if the people who'd hired him had any sense, they'd appreciate every man who could wield a shovel.

"Follow me!" And he started off.

In his pocket was the piece of paper referring him to the street-cleaning authority of the City Inspector's Office. He had no name, and only a vague idea of where Coffee House Slip was, but the men seemed to know where to go, and they steered him from behind like a rudder, south to Wall Street, east to the river, and then toward the one office with windows still aglow. When he turned to look at them, before he went in, he could no longer count how many men there were. Perhaps twice the number he'd had with him outside Billy's. He felt power and a tinge of anxiety. All those pairs of eyes. As long as they'd followed him, he was Moses, but the thread of his control was thin. If it broke, they could turn in an instant from herd to angry mob.

He gathered himself and barked out, "Make a line! Anyone not in the line when I come back won't be taken on." He entered the building.

"What the heck's going on out there?" asked the man at the desk.

"I was sent by the city hiring office to find some men—to shovel the snow." His accent made it obvious where he was from, but he spoke calmly, which was remarkable. He wasn't calm at all. He felt he was on a ledge, on the verge of something either very good or very humiliating. "They said you wanted twenty, but I found more. With such a weather, I thought maybe more is better." He pulled out the papers.

A grunt slipped from the old man's lips. It was very warm in the office, and Will found he was dripping with melting snow.

"Well, sir, I'm amazed," the old man said. "You certainly found some men, all right—I thought it was a riot. I was starting to figure there was no one left over at the hiring office by the time they got the order. I was just about to send over to the Tombs, but that wouldn't'ta been till tomorrow because jailbirds, they don't work at night. Public safety, you know—so, it warn't the ideal situation. How many you got out there, anyhow?"

"I don't know. They kept joining up with me all the way here. Quite a number."

"Well, like you say, the more the better. The first job's to free up the Broadway streetcar tracks. It'd be almost a miracle if we got it clear up to Chambers Street tonight. All right, I'll tell you how we'll do this." The old man handed Will a clipboard and a large, blunt pencil, and together they walked outside where they encountered the implausibly orderly line that had taken shape in the dockyard. To Will's surprise, there were a couple of familiar faces in the line. He'd happened to stumble into the bar that some of the stablehands frequented. He got a couple of curious looks, a couple of scowls and one warm greeting.

"Hello again," said the blond man he remembered from the stable. *Not Ludwig,* he thought, now that he got a look at him, and not a nice-looking face, either. His eyes were small and pink-rimmed, and the skin around his neck was at once flaky, oily and inflamed. Maybe his name was Martin? Considering that they had never exactly been friendly, it was odd the way the man now reached out and grasped his hand.

"I was glad to see you made it out of there the other night," he said.

Out of there? Out of where? The Tombs? Barnum's? Who was this guy exactly, and why was he suddenly making overtures? Quite frankly Will would have been inclined to warm to any such gesture on a normal day.

But then it occurred to him that he had a twofold problem: First, he didn't trust him; second, this Martin Ludwig knew him as Geiermeier. It wouldn't look good if the night manager found out *Williams* was an alias. He stepped back, nodded and moved to the next man, though he listened while the manager took this one's name. He'd been pretty close—it wasn't Martin, not Ludwig, but *Luther*. Luther Undertoe. Just seeing the name made the hackles on the back of his neck go up. He wasn't sure why, but he filed the feeling away and then continued reviewing the names.

They signed up the men in teams of ten, one horse and cart to a team, one shovel to a man, one team to each cross street from Wall to Reade. The first job of all was to clear Broadway all the way down to the streetcar tracks. After that, the crews would work east, then west, if they got to it. When the orders had all been given and the men were ready to set out, the old man looked down at Will's paper once more and then directly into his eyes.

"Well, Mr. Williams, it says here you're the foreman, which means you're responsible for all that property—shovels, horses and carts. I'm aware you been out of work yourself, from this referral, and that you just picked these men off the street and can't speak for their characters, so keep an eye out, eh?"

Responsibility. This was the opposite of being an able-bodied laborer, and he was more than ready for it. He nodded, then shouted instructions to the drivers and hopped up onto the front of a cart. The going was slow through the snowy streets, but at last they reached Broadway and Wall. He looked north and south and watched the men plod through the snow beside the carts. The driver got down from his bench, and the stableman-turned-foreman was on the verge of doing so, too, but he paused. He was the foreman, not a laborer. He didn't really like the idea of just watching other men work; he felt he ought to jump down and work alongside them; but it would hardly be possible with his hands as they were. The newly healed skin would quickly tear. He could never keep up.

Then he thought of his impromptu pulpit back at the bar. He thought of the pastor in the church in Fürth and the way his uncle had marshaled groups of hired hands to bring in the hay in the fall. Speech was a different kind of power from brawn. In every group, there was someone whose job was to talk to the others, to rouse them, to goad them. He'd gotten a taste of that back at Billy's. *He was the foreman*—the papers in his pocket said so. He looked out at the men in their dark clothes, leaning halfheartedly into their shovels, then wrenching up and flinging loads of snow in all directions. There wasn't much to say about shoveling snow. He'd done enough of it to know that.

Snow came early and fell heavy in Fürth. It held the whole world in a state of crystal beauty for a good five months, and the only means of travel from Wittold and Hedwig Diespeck's farm to town was the sleigh with its shiny metal runners and tatty bearskin lap blanket. Deep drifts gathered quickly, and when the wind was from the south snow would fill the entire yard and barricade the doors to the barn. Then he and his uncle would boost his youngest cousin up to the hayloft window to feed the cows, while the rest of the family worked to free up the doors to let the animals out to water at the trough by the well. His uncle took frequent leisurely breaks to admire their progress and smoke his pipe while he and his sister, Lottie, and Tante Hedwig and the cousins grunted and sweated and shivered, all at once. He remembered one snowbound morning in Fürth when Tante Hedwig had been especially peeved. "Get back to work yourself, Wittold, you lazy man!" she'd demanded, and Uncle Wittold did so, but not before dispensing a piece of advice that made the work go easier and faster both, advice no one asked for and no one thanked him for, except in taking it, advice that Will Williams, fugitive from Europe, suspected arsonist and foreman, repeated now for the benefit of his crew:

"Remember, to squat saves the back, men—bend at the knees, not the waist!"

The crunch of metal blades was dull. Their shovels had not yet rung against the cobbles, but the snowfall seemed lighter already and the air less raw, perhaps from the slight added warmth of so many men beginning to sweat.

"You there! Squat!" he called. "It's a long night. And throw it in the cart." But he found he couldn't give the order without earning his authority. His uncle had shoveled, too, after all, if not a lot. And so he jumped from the cart into a soft, white drift and bent at the knees himself. His hands would be good for a couple of minutes before the new pink skin blistered and tore. *To squat*, he crouched and buried his blade in the snow.

Saves, grunt, he gripped the handle of his shovel as lightly as he could. *The back*, his legs lengthened, and snow flew. A few drops of blood and fluid leaked from his blisters into the cotton lining of his gloves. He gritted his teeth but did not permit himself to grimace. The load landed cleanly on the boards. Then there were ten thuds as the crew's ten shovelfuls hit home.

"That's the way," he said.

To squat saves the back, *thwack*, to squat saves the back.

6.

LA VITA NUOVA

P eople were looking at him, up to him even, and with respect, not derision. But beware what you wish for.

For it wasn't just the men on his crew. Beatrice saw him and stared, and her interest was not benign. He had no idea of it, but she was there, in the shadows, everywhere he went that night, watching.

When she'd informed her boss, a man with ax blades embedded in his boot soles, about Geiermeier's latest activities, he said to keep the tail up all night, to find out just what the guy was up to.

"Aw, Johnny. It's freezing. Fiona and I have been on him all day already. Put someone else on him, why don't you?"

"No, I don't think so. He's your project. You've got an understanding for how he operates, and I don't want to lose track of him, so you're stuck with the job. Go on then. I want to know what he's up to by tomorrow morning."

She had to admit, she'd taken the initiative on Geiermeier. The other problem was she'd gotten Fiona into it, too. Fiona was not going to be happy to hear their tour of duty had been extended. Beatrice would have to convince her that there were opportunities here—to earn some extra cash and, above all, to gain the boss's favor.

It was worth a good deal to have Johnny on your side. When he was happy, he could be generous; when he wasn't, people suffered. He ruled the Whyo gang with a strong hand, a well-conceived master plan and a mixture of charisma and violence. Together, it worked. He'd been the uncontested boss for over five years in a city where gangsters more often had short, explosive careers. *Dandy Johnny* he was called, on account of his white teeth, red lips and how dapper he always looked, even after a fistfight or a drinking binge or a night in jail—and no one laughed at it. His dark hair was slicked back with gleaming oil, his ice-blue eyes flashed, his smile came easy. Then, too, he did love clothes—elegant clothes, the clothes of a gentleman. Johnny dressed better for housebreaking than some men did for the opera, and it wasn't just for vanity: His grooming had helped him walk away from more than one crime scene unnoticed. No, the boss was no ponce, flashy ascots and lavish use of pomade notwithstanding. He'd killed at least a dozen men and never even come under suspicion. And thanks to him the gang he led was more powerful and safer to be in than any other gang. Whyos almost never got arrested—they looked out for one another on the streets—and Johnny had earned their loyalty by spreading the wealth around more fairly than any other boss in New York.

The Whyos were a very good gang to be in, if you were going to be in a gang. They'd gotten their name decades before, from a queer call the first boys who banded together had used to communicate with one another from down the block or across the street. Sometimes it was actually *why-oo* or *who-woop* or *hey-oh*—each variation of the call had a different connotation—but *whyo* was the broadest and most essential term, being used to convey assent and greeting and to time an attack, just before converging on a victim. The whole thing amounted to a kind of song, which came to be known as whyoing. Over the years, the gang had refined those early calls to something approaching a language. A girl gang had eventually been formed within the gang, consisting mostly of sisters and girlfriends of the Whyos, but this was no ladies' auxiliary. They spoke the language and did their share of the work, too. Our hot-corn girl, Beatrice, and her friend Fiona were Why Nots, and they'd been keeping tabs on the stableman pretty much continuously for the week since the fire. They'd missed his release from the Tombs but then they caught sight of him again back at the museum, giving his silent signal to Undertoe. It was odd, that, Beatrice thought—the two were obviously still working together, despite the fact that Undertoe had turned him in to the cops. It was apparently a complicated scheme they had going. She couldn't guess exactly what it was, but clearly her man was skilled at playing roles, and she was impressed. He was operating in a manner so subtle and unexpected, with such a good cover, that his stealth rivaled the stealth of the gang that was watching him.

She knew Johnny would want a man like that either in the gang or dead—and certainly not working for Undertoe. Undertoe was a nothing compared to Johnny and the Whyos, but he was a prime snake. The way she saw it, Geiermeier's main problem was that he was new in town, didn't know the right people and consequently trusted Undertoe too much. He should have seen a double cross coming. The previous night, she'd tailed him from the hiring office back to a Chinese flophouse and spent a night on an upper bunk, scratching flea bites and watching the stableman sleep. He seemed so innocent, the way he snored, but there was no mistaking him. He was a contract firebug, was the word on the street, a new talent just arrived from overseas. The Whyos didn't do fires for money—they preferred subtler schemes—but he had talent, unorthodox methods and a certain brazenness that she knew Johnny would appreciate.

The day of the snowstorm she'd been expecting her man to go back from the hiring office to the flop, and judging by his pace through the knee-deep drifts, she'd decided she could risk letting him out of her sight for a minute to warm up by ducking into Billy's. She was confident that she could track him down again if he wandered off, and also that he was unaware of being followed, which set her up nicely to be flabbergasted when he blundered into Billy's himself. She had been sitting at the far end of the bar, nursing a hot lemon-gin, and she nearly choked on it when she saw him. Had he seen her after all? Had he seen who-all else was there, including Luther Undertoe? Or was he *still* oblivious to the setup? Did he have some plan of his own? Then he'd started his spiel from the doorway. *So much for warming up*, she thought, gulping the rest of her gin and slapping a coin on the counter. She rose to follow the crowd of job seekers out the door.

"What, you, too, Beanie? *You're* going to shovel snow?" said Billy. That was what they called her on the street: Beanie. Everyone had a nickname.

She'd just laughed and trailed the crowd to Coffee House Slip, waited in the shadows, taking note of the faces in the crowd, making sure they—

especially Undertoe—didn't see her. Then she followed Geiermeier to Wall Street, where he set his gang shoveling. Oddly enough, he really was doing the job, even throwing a few shovelfuls of snow himself, though it seemed to her he'd more than succeeded in creating a bluff without actually having to bother. As he headed off alone down Broadway to check on the work at the next intersection, she was thinking he really was just some dupe, some fool. Then he hailed the group of shovelers with a shout, and dammit, there was Undertoe again, stepping forward. She wasn't sure what they were up to, yet, but the situation seemed worthy of reporting to Johnny in person. She needed Fiona.

She stepped into a doorway and began to whistle—a strange cooing-pigeon song that at once stood out from and blended in with the sounds of the night. A minute later, she heard the owl screech that told her Fiona was in earshot and would take the watch. Then she headed over to a Whyo bar called the Morgue, wondering whether Johnny would be pleased with what she'd learned or annoyed that she hadn't yet made contact with her mark. Certainly the situation had just grown more complicated. It was illogical, improbable, this shoveling gambit—as was the entire way the man worked. But she was also starting to admire him: He'd thwarted her ability to direct people's attention where she wanted it and make them do exactly as she bid.

He was thinking of a different girl as he watched over his men, Maria of the *Leibnitz*. He thought of her more often than she warranted, that girl. But there was something about her that drew him. Possibly it was physical—her strong arms, narrow waist, flared nostrils, pale skin—but in another sense it wasn't about her. She was a woman who'd survived the disease his mother had succumbed to, as he had survived it. Dreaming of her blurred easily into a dream in which his mother still lived.

But whyever the stableman thought of Maria, it wasn't mutual. She didn't think of him, ever, especially not then, when she happened to be busy lavishing saliva on the nethers of a Pennsylvania anthracite merchant. She'd found a way to survive in the metropolis, but at considerable cost. She'd do pretty much anything, Maria—not because she liked it, mind you, but for a small extra fee. She strove to please her customers and expected ample payment in return. Maria thought of various things, to keep her mind off the chafing and the ludicrous obscenities of her clients: a pudding in the pie safe, a pair of boots she wanted, the warm loft above the kitchen of the squalid little house she'd grown up in, where she used to lie among the drying roots and herbs and daydream for hours. She was not nostalgic, Maria, not in general—it was only that she needed something to distract her while she worked. Certainly she didn't spend her time reliving the voyage of the *Leibnitz*.

But he did.

It was January when the *Leibnitz* arrived in New York harbor and moored at the quarantine station north of Sandy Hook, the decks dusted with carbolic acid. The third- and steerage-class passengers were hanging their heads, awaiting transfer to the various hospital ships and quarantine islands in the lower harbor. Some of them would be buried on Hart's Island.

"I'll take care of you," he'd said, speaking far beyond his ability to follow through. But her mother had died, she was alone, and he was smitten.

She'd looked at him with a squinted eye and half a smile on her upper lip, clearly thinking he was daft. It was her independence, her fearlessness—the very qualities that precluded her from needing him—that he liked about her. Afterward, he realized he should have put it differently: He should have asked her to marry him.

"You'll take care of me," she'd repeated, and rolled her eyes. She wanted to start over in America, not be saddled with some German boob who'd seen her at her worst, on the boat. The truth was, Maria found him annoying.

Maria and her mother had signed aboard the ship as kitchen help and scullion, and their labor reduced the price of their passage to a pittance, but for that the duties were rather broader than advertised. Maria's mother was still quite attractive—she had all her front teeth yet—and her daughter, well, her daughter was blond and shining. At the interview, in the galley, the cook had hacked chickens apart with his cleaver on the butcher block while the captain and the mate circumambulated the women.

"I suppose I'll take age and experience," the captain said to his mate after a minute or two. "You break the filly."

The first day at sea, the mate had summoned Maria away from a mountain of potatoes and she went, not exactly sure what she was in for. Her mother found her curled up like a weevil in their tiny, windowless berth some hours later, nursing a fat, ferrous lip in addition to deeper bruises. She'd put up a pretty good fight, Maria.

The next time, she hid when she heard the mate coming, but he found her and dragged her off by her arm. He seemed to enjoy the game of hide-and-seek. "Come along you little vixen, you wolverine," he laughed. Eventually, she grew accustomed to it, as one can to almost anything. The thing she couldn't stand was learning that her mother had known what she was doing when she signed them on. *Just the price of getting to a better world, schatzie, chin up,* she'd said. But Maria couldn't see ahead to a better world—she was really just a girl. She saw betrayal. When it was her mother's turn to go over the side, she didn't weep, just frowned and heaved. When our man thought he saw her clutching at her mother's skirts, he was wrong. It was just her ragged fingernail catching in the weave. She'd been thinking, *Goddamn her for dying so fast—the captain'll be after me, too, now.* It didn't happen, though, as the captain was also laid low. The epidemic was in full flower.

This is how it spread: On the second-class deck, a lady who sported a consumptive complexion came down with a fever the night of the day the ship sailed. Maria and her mother took turns tending her and bringing her meals in her berth. She needed compresses, cups of hot consommé and fresh sheets at least once a day. Then there was her chamber pot, that terrible vat. They did it all and didn't wash their hands—even less so on shipboard than normal, since fresh water was precious and must be conserved. Then they helped the cook make the vichyssoise and the apple-custard pies.

But don't blame Maria—she knew not what she did. It made no sense at all to her, the way the sickness started. She knew what caused fevers: It was stink. And so why hadn't it hit the steerage first? She opened portholes, hatches and doors wherever she could. She'd never heard of a *vector*. If you'd tried to tell her that she, Maria, could carry a disease from one person to the next, she'd have knelt and said a Hail Mary, quite from reflex.

The man we're calling Will had been born into another world, a world in which he'd learned about Anton van Leeuwenhoek and his wee animalcules, Louis Pasteur and his milk. He'd peered into a squat black micro-scope and seen the unimaginable creatures that existed in a drop of water. The father may have sent the son away after his mother died, may have al-lowed his education to falter and ignored him entirely, but he couldn't take away what the boy had seen: the laboratory, with its stone countertops, etched glass beakers and myriad fluid-filled phials, or the university stu-dent, Robert Koch, who eventually became his father's protégé in the son's stead and somehow nevertheless the son's close friend. Will had not forgot-ten Robert Koch, but Koch was lost to him. He could never make contact with any of them again.

For as innocent as he was of the crime he was wanted for in New York, he was guilty of another crime, committed back home, and he knew that in fleeing he'd as much as confessed it. So it wasn't entirely misguided of the Whyos to be interested in him. He had the capacity to scheme. We all do, and in some of us it blooms—cultured by neglect, by cruelty, by dumb fate, by loss. It was Beanie's skill—and Undertoe's, too—to be able to see that in-stinct in him from a mile off.

The first blow was his mother, of course. And then, after the funeral, he and his sister, Lottie, were packed off to their uncle's farm. Their first Christmas back, they'd brought everything home with them, expecting to stay. They had crept down to the parlor to look at their mother's daguerreo-type together, many nights, with a candle, taking turns peering into its mir-rored surface from every angle, seeking that elusive instant when her face melded with their own reflections, then returned to the clarity that was al-most sharper than life. He was nine, his sister seven. But their father had sent them back to their uncle's after all, and they didn't see him for another year. There were letters, empty, benignant letters, and the following year they were invited to arrive the day *after* Christmas. On New Year's Day their father was remarried, to a widow, a woman of noble title with children of her own. Ever after, it was the same: eleven months, including Christmas, at their uncle's farm, New Year's in town, a January full of hope, and then they were sent packing. Their Tante Hedwig gave them her own account of why: "He didn't marry the kitchen help, this time, and you'd only be an em-barrassment." She didn't have to mention the other part: that everyone knew their mother's family had been Jewish till a generation back, making her children not quite the siblings the new wife, the baroness, imagined for her own daughters.

His mind wandered over all of that and more as he shoveled through the night. All the while, one of them was watching him, Fiona or Beanie, sometimes both. The decision Johnny had made when Beanie tracked him down was not to pull him aside as long as Undertoe was near. They were to get him alone. So they waited. And all night long, as they sipped their flasks of gin, they wondered what on Earth he was thinking, what his schemes were, if he was wise to Undertoe or not, whether he would join the Whyos or defy them, making this a wasted night or worse.

If only they could have known his mind. Several times just before morning, he stopped working, stopped walking, to peer into the snowy dimness up the street or at the end of an alley. He kept thinking he saw someone, some girl. He knew there were always urchins out at that hour. Urchins, the mostly nocturnal breed of boys and girls who scavenged alongside the cats and the rats and had been known to fight four-legged rivals over choicer morsels from restaurant-kitchen bins. He kept an eye on them, half worried about the safe return of the equipment, and wondered where they'd come from, what they would become. New York had so many pits for a person to fall into, more than he could fathom, though he'd dipped his own toes into the shallows. He thought of the women he'd seen at Billy's that night, the colors they wore, slippery and bright, the jade silk shawls and scarlet-trimmed bodices that offset their hard faces. He'd read in his *Stranger's Guide* about women who only posed as prostitutes to rob the men they lured, and also about gangs of runaway girls who sold flowers or candies, stole watches and lived communally in abandoned buildings on the edge of town. Most of them apparently packed a mean punch and carried knives. But despite these notions, he never suspected that two of the urchins he watched were older than the rest, not even when he looked one of them in the eye.

She was leaning against a hitching post near the lighted doorway of Billy's when he walked by again, a short while later, and he felt a prick of desire, a yearning for a woman he could press up to on such a frigid night. That's how good she was at what she did: She could make herself an urchin one minute, then transform herself into a woman and stir up lust in a passerby, just by her posture. As for Beatrice O'Gamhna—for that was the full name of the Why Not more commonly called Beanie—she wasn't a waif at all, nor a runaway. She was nearly a woman and fairly well off and, truth be told, she wasn't even chilly, what with Billy's gin and the plan she was working out and the hustling she'd done that night to keep ahead of this man, their target: Geiermeier, Williams, whatever.

7

THE UNDERTOE

I t was Trinity Church that sustained him through the night, the way its bell tolled the hours. Every time he heard it, he paused to take stock: of the city, himself, the other men who stooped and stood and spewed out gray plumes of frost in complex syncopation. A hopeful feeling expanded in his chest with every cold lungful of air. Yes, he thought, he would rise from the ashes of Barnum's—perhaps as Will Williams, perhaps even as Geiermeier, if he could clear that name, if he could manage to find the one who'd really set the fire.

Now and then, he hacked up a rusty black mass from his lungs, and he could still taste the smoke, but his satisfaction at getting the job of foreman endured. Once, he found himself half dreaming of lying down on one of the carts and letting the men bury him under a blanket of snow, but it wasn't a gloomy fantasy, just a weary one. He listened again and again, as the hours passed, to the fading reverberations of the church's bells.

Beatrice watched him, imagining he was plotting some strange and masterful theft, some slippery way to escape the setup Undertoe appeared to have put in place, but she was wrong. He was wondering why churches toll their bells. Why keep time? To remind the faithful that God is there through the hours, perhaps, but every time he heard the peal, he thought rather of the sexton whose job it was to stay up all night and heave the heavy bell cord hourly. Then he thought of the bell itself, then the building and last of all of God. God, he thought, was spread out too thin across the world—far thinner than the great blue wasteland of an ocean where, somewhere between Bremerhaven and New York harbor, he'd lost the last vestige of his faith.

In truth, he had always been more attracted to churches as buildings. A cathedral with tall stone spires was the most transcendent thing he knew; a dim side chapel with muted stained glass the most sheltering. And so it was that with every hourly stroke of Trinity's bells, his resolve somehow to get back to working on stone grew. He would try again, maybe at that papist cathedral he'd heard was going up in the north of the city. And surely there were enough smaller churches being built that he could find a job on one of them.

At home, apprenticeship was the only way in, and since he hadn't finished his, he'd had no chance there. Here, he understood that it was different. Maybe he had bungled his chances at the Labor Exchange and just now at the hiring office, too, but this was America. There would be other opportunities. Why wait for spring? There were plenty of secular buildings under way, too, and nowadays everything going up was stone. Why wouldn't they want a man like him, who could work at heights and had all the skills? He'd managed to go from jailbird to foreman; surely in this city of nearly one million people and what seemed like one million buildings, some building crew somewhere would give him a chance to haul a few sacks of lime.

The sky had brightened when he made his last round of the crews. They'd done a lot more than the night manager had dreamed. Broadway was clear from the Battery all the way to Reade, and so were all the major side streets to the east: Wall Street, Whitehall, Fulton and Chambers—the ones that led to ferry piers. He was standing with his hands laced together over his shovel's grip, surveying one of the crews from half a block away, smiling. Undertoe's crew. Earlier, Undertoe had gotten the men singing as they shoveled. It was a good idea, and they'd kept it up most of the night, working fast and well, but they were silent now. He tried to discern which one of the ten sets of hunched shoulders was Undertoe, but he wasn't really eager to speak with him again. He didn't want to risk being called by his previous name. Then, as he watched, one man broke ranks, thrust his shovel into the snow and rooted around in his pockets for something: to-bacco. That was him. He was rolling a cigarette, lighting it, gazing off toward the river. A man had a right to take a break, Will told himself, but in fact, he was annoyed. *He* was the foreman, after all.

"Give me another round of 'Willy the Weeper,' boys," called Undertoe, and they began to sing:

> *There was a young man called Willy the Weeper,*
> *Made his living as a street sweeper.*
> *He had the hop habit—he had it bad.*
> *Listen, and I'll tell you 'bout a dream he had.*
> *He went to the Chink's the other night,*
> *Where he knew the lights would be shining bright . . .*

Get back to work, you, Williams wanted to say, but as he watched, Undertoe disappeared in the shadow of a building's entryway. When Williams approached, he heard a cough, a grunt, then a cry in a voice too high to be Undertoe's. He could hardly believe it.

"Mr. Undertoe?" he called.

A bit of rustling, a thump, and there was Undertoe, flushed, doing up his pants and wiping his hands on his thighs, reaching in his pocket for his tobacco and beginning to roll another cigarette.

"Oh, Mr. Geier—" Undertoe said, as a girl who looked twelve years old slunk out from the shadows, pulling down her skirts and daubing at her red face with her sleeve. She spat in the snow before running off. Undertoe smiled—false sheepishness—and struck a match. Williams was disgusted.

"I don't approve of that, what you just did. You ought to be working." He was wondering how much Undertoe had paid for that girl, knowing it was too little, could never be enough.

"Now, George—"

"Mr. Undertoe, it's *Williams.* Will Williams."

Undertoe laughed. "Williams? Oh, *right.* Williams. Names tell so much about people, I always say."

A man called Luther Undertoe ought to know, thought Will, though he didn't guess the half of it, not knowing Undertoe's name on the street: the Undertaker. He'd had it since his mother died, when he was fifteen. She'd just nursed him through a horrendous, humiliating case of the mumps when she suddenly took ill herself. He hadn't paid much attention to her complaints, because he was half mad with the ringing that had started in his ears when he was sick and wouldn't stop. The doctor said he'd gotten the mumps too late—he was practically a man—and that was why it happened—and why his gonads swelled up so badly, too. Possibly he would never have children. He'd been a soloist in the Newsboys' Choir before his illness, but now with the ringing in his ears his pitch was spoiled, and he had to give it up. With his mother dead, he'd moved into the Newsboys' Lodging House, but he hated it, especially now that he wasn't in the choir. Luther had been cruising the Five Points, gloomy and desperate for something easy to steal one night, when he'd stopped in a doorway to light a cigarette butt he'd found on the street, a pretty good one, with a full inch of tobacco left to be smoked. Not until his match flared had he noticed the wizened old man sleeping in the shadows. On closer inspection, he had sores on his hands and an outsized goiter. The geezer had woken and reached out to Luther, grabbed his ankle—right up under the pants cuff, horny nails and scabrous fingers touching his skin. "Penny for an old soul?" he'd begged.

It started off with just a single kick in the belly, to teach him a lesson, but Undertoe found the old man's whimpering made him angry, so he kept on kicking till there was silence. After that, it became a bit of a habit for him to nix some half-dead vagrant whenever his mood grew foul. It wasn't so much that he was murdering anyone as that he was expressing himself. The leatherheads certainly never investigated deaths like the ones he caused, but people in the Points came to know of Luther's penchant for hastening death, thus the name.

Undertoe smiled at Williams. "Oh, come on, now, let's be friends," he said, and put out his hand. Undertoe flicked his cigarette into the snow and proposed they repair to Billy's for a warm-up. Bars were closed from 6:00 A.M. to noon on Sundays, but it wasn't yet five. Will noticed that the men on Undertoe's crew had gone on to another song: "Amazing Grace."

"I can't do that. Besides, I'm the foreman." Not that he wanted to.

"Oh, the *foreman*. Is that the way you are? I thought we were going to be friends, George."

Williams felt sweat break out across his back, despite the chill, but his face remained flat, impassive. He considered whether it would be wiser to go with Undertoe, to make friends, so he could explain the change in his name, tell him he wasn't hiding from the law, just moving forward. Probably it would be, but he couldn't bring himself to do it. He just picked up his shovel. "Maybe another time—and it's Williams."

"Oh right, Williams. *Hey, boys*," Undertoe shouted over to the others on his crew. "How about we give the foreman here another round of 'Willy the Weeper'?"

Now even Undertoe cocked his shovel and dug in as he intoned the words of the ballad's first line. He was a tenor, Williams realized, but not such a pure one after all—it was somehow off-key, a half tone wrong. The other men joined him in their lower, rougher voices, and it was true that the snow flew faster all of a sudden.

The tune, however imperfect, rang out beautifully through the streets, but the *words*—it was just a song, just a popular song, the same one they'd been singing earlier, but now the name of the protagonist and reference to visiting an opium den seemed a little too close to the bone. *There's no such thing as coincidence*, Williams thought.

He let his shovel strike the ground, which was well enough shoveled now for the metal to clang on the frozen paving stones. Then he moved on to the next crew, forcibly excluding Undertoe from his thoughts.

Trinity Church, he thought as he walked back down Broadway and saw it before him again. It was nothing like the Nikolaikirche in Hamburg, which he'd worked on, nothing near as grand, and yet it had a steeple that soared. How could he have let that man off the hook for what he did to that girl? How could he just have stood by? He kicked a big chunk of snow from the curb into the middle of the street and kept punting it along until it crumbled into bits. Why had he stayed at Barnum's so long, why hadn't he had the courage, on one of his days off, to go get a job in the building trade? Instead, he'd let Barnum's burn, he'd been arrested, he'd let his name be changed to the implausibly English-sounding Will Williams, and now he'd

allowed himself to be engaged in a creepy conversation with Luther Undertoe, a man who'd never deigned to speak to him before the fire. It
seemed to him that part of it was that he didn't feel in control. He was off,
somehow. All that death. Also, how could he ever have power over his life
if he couldn't communicate properly? His English sounded pretty good, he
didn't make many mistakes, but he was always slightly misunderstanding
what people told him, and often he couldn't make his own meaning clear
enough. It had started the very day they brought him out of quarantine and
he went through Castle Garden. His rough but generally serviceable English had somehow completely failed him. His accent had been out of control, his vocabulary worse.

"Any skills? Trade?" the man at the immigration desk had asked. "Guild
memberships in the old country? What work do you do?"

He had understood the questions. He knew he should have known what
to say in response. He had prepared it. But at that moment he'd been so
overwhelmed he couldn't summon the words, the English words. "*Ich bin
Steinmetz*," he'd said, knowing it meant nothing to the man. In the absence
of official guild papers, he must at least manage to name his profession in
English, but he had faltered, failed.

"Okay, no English—but you look like a burly man. We'll put down
'able-bodied laborer,' okay? Welcome to America, Mr. Geermeer."

"No," he'd said. "I have a trade. I've done two years' apprenticeship as a
mason on Hamburg's St. Nicholas Cathedral, the third tallest church in the
world." But it came out all wrong, starting with *Nein*. It came out in German—*Steinmetz . . . Praktikum . . . Nikolaikirche . . . drittgrößte Kirche der
Welt*. It might as well have been gibberish. The man gave Will a quizzical
look and said, "All right, move along now. Next."

That was how stone was taken from him the second time.

Mason, he'd remembered a moment later. Or *stoneworker*. That was the
other term. But he'd stammered at the crucial moment. To be a stableman
again, a snow shoveler, was not why he'd crossed the Atlantic.

But in a way he could never know, it wasn't just his lack of English that
did it—it was luck, it was timing. It was how it had to be. The afternoon of
the day he got the job scooping up elephant dung, a paving contractor had
filed forms with the Labor Exchange to hire a half a hundred newly landed

men for crews that would cut and lay curb and cobbles. An hour later, and he'd have been one of them. Most of the men that were called for those jobs had never worked with stone at all. There were streets to pave in Manhattan and Brooklyn, so many they couldn't just wait around for men with experience. The fifty new men would be given jobs they could hardly botch at first. They would start out hauling loads or stoking fires under reeking tar pots and sizzling pans of broken stone, but some of them would eventually progress to greater responsibilities and higher wages. A man who clearly knew what he was doing would have stood out, risen faster. And if he'd managed to get *mason* on his papers, he'd have gotten an even better job, the job of his dreams, a position in the yard at St. Patrick's. Such were the opportunities he missed. Either would seem preferable to the fire, the incarceration, the shoveling of snow, the Undertoe.

But no. Not if we look further forward: If he'd gotten that job, on the paving crew, say, where might he have gone? Nowhere but on to other paving crews, all across the greater metropolitan area, on to a lifetime of paving but always the grunt, the lug, never the foreman, never having the freedom to think beyond the arcing rows of Belgian blocks that he'd have laid out in endless fans and herringbone patterns, depending on the volume and direction of traffic, all across the avenues of the metropolis. It would have led to cabbage and sausage three times a week, boiled too long by a wife less feisty than the Maria of his dreams but no less dour. Never to a promotion, because he was German and paving was mostly an Irish trade, because he was dark and could be taken for a Jew (there was indeed a Reb Diespeck in his family tree). Despite the two years he'd spent in Hamburg learning to carve tracery and set vast stones perfectly in place at the tops of delicate fluted spires, he would still have been roasting gravel, the lowliest of jobs, two years down the line. His life would have been uneventful and grim. And if he'd gotten that job at the cathedral, what then? He would have had the chance to put to use a bit more of what his teacher, Meister Teichold, had taught him; he'd have been the author of a pair of marvelously humorous gargoyles perched way up high, entirely out of sight except to God and roof repairmen; he'd have gotten to enjoy the thrill and danger of working at the top, insanely high, and looking out over the city and the river, the same way he'd loved to take in the harbor view in Hamburg. It looks better at first, I grant you, but no, down the road, that was not going to be a good option. It would have put him squarely on the bench of a certain mule cart, one August afternoon about a decade hence, a cart hauling statuary for a minor chapel, a cart that was just about to break an axle. And that cart would have toppled and the bowl of a basin designed to hold holy water would have bounced from the truck bed and cracked in half on its way to breaking his ribs and exploding two lobes of poor Geiermeier's lungs like wax-paper lanterns. For what we in all good faith want in this world isn't always for the best. The stableman was hapless, with a doleful past, and the city was a place of inconceivable complexity. Frankly, his chances for happiness were slim enough to start. I'd rather not lay his fate in his own burned, blistered hands—not till his English is stronger and his confidence up. For the moment, let's lay his fate with luck. For he was, in fact, a very lucky man. It just didn't always feel that way to him.

Every time he got ahead, something happened to undo his progress, so that his whole life till now was an up-and-down jig that kept moving backward no matter how many forward steps he made. When he had passed through Hamburg on his way to America, he'd been frightened to leave everything behind, fearful the police would catch him before he got away, and yet above all he'd been hopeful. He went back to the Dicke Wirtin, the bar he'd often gone to, and asked after the girl he'd spent so many nights with when he had worked on the cathedral. She'd been gone a good year, the proprietress told him.

"But where?"

"Not moved away, pet. Dead. Now what about someone else?" she asked. "I have plenty of blondes. I'll make sure you get your money's worth." He left without another word. The only other person he'd have liked to see was Meister Teichold, but given his precarious situation he didn't try to find him. Instead, the morning after he'd bought the Geiermeier papers and his ticket on the *Leibnitz*, he waited with the tourists and the schoolboys in the long line to climb the newly completed cathedral tower. At the top, he'd looked out over the city and felt dizzy. But it wasn't so much veritgo as nausea. He was simply full of grief and remorse and fear of what would become of him in New York. He'd had no idea, then, that the Hamburg skyline, with its five great church towers braced like God's daggers against the infidel sea, was so much grander and more beautiful than New York's dingy, wide, low one.

When the bells rang at five, the only thing he was sure of was what he wanted for breakfast: eggs, pancakes, bacon, toast, oatmeal with milk and sugar. And coffee. Two cups of coffee. He was ravenous and bone weary. The snow had begun to glow with the indirect light of predawn as he hopped into the cart of the crew he was with and led the men back to Coffee House Slip. When they got close, the smell from the coffee warehouse made his mouth begin to water, but then he made out the lean figure of Luther Undertoe kicked back against a lamppost near the office door. The rest of the men were waiting in the equipment shed, warming themselves by the potbelly stove. Will stepped past Undertoe into the office, where it was warm and dry.

"Good morning, *Mr. Williams.*"

At first he wasn't sure—had Undertoe betrayed him? It took him a moment to register the man's goodwill, another to return the civility. The lag would have been obvious to anyone who even suspected that Williams wasn't his name, but the night manager wasn't suspicious. He was pleased. He was smiling.

"Mr. Williams, you've done great work. Why, ordinarily it would take this department half the week to undo what nature did in a day. I've got good news for you. If you and your boys want it, there's going to be work again tonight, when the regular sweepers go home. While I make out vouchers, you can sign up the ones that are worth their salt for tomorrow."

"Vouchers," said Will. Of course. The night manager would hardly be capable of doling out so many payments in dollars and cents. But you couldn't buy breakfast or a bed on a voucher. He needed cash. His body thrummed with hunger and panic.

Meanwhile, the men of the regular sanitation corps wandered into the large equipment shed for the morning shift, joining the night crew where they waited to be paid. By the time Will and the night manager got there, the garbagemen's jackets had begun to give off a stench. It was dead hog, stale beer, rotten perch, rancid milk, moldy slops, sewer slime, night soil, you name it—a miasma theorist's nightmare and an unhappy smell even to those who didn't believe vapors spread disease.

There was less grousing about the vouchers than Will had expected. No one who was working under him that night was quite as flat broke as he; they could wait till Monday to cash their vouchers. And as for Undertoe, he had seventy beans in his blueboy. His was an easy-come-and-go economy of faro, molls, booze, poppy and hydrate of chloral—an expensive substance that was sold by the drop in glass phials but an excellent investment, since a dram could render a dozen men insensate and vulnerable. Undertoe had any number of ways of earning his daily bread, but shoveling certainly wasn't normally among them.

Undertoe went out and bought himself the breakfast our man was dreaming of. After he'd eaten, he found he was plagued by a shard of bacon lodged in his teeth. He sucked and probed, but it was firmly stuck between the upper left first molar and second bicuspid. Then he found a slip of folded paper in his pocket, used it as a toothpick and peered at the offending object. It was smaller than he expected, the particle, and so was the figure he saw written to the right of the dollar sign. Not that he needed the money, but the fact that he'd stayed up all night shoveling, just to keep his eye on Geiermeier, and that the pay was this paltry—well, it fairly made the hairs at the small of his back bristle. Add to that that the fellow was turning out to be a bit odd, a bit unpredictable, and to have an attitude to boot. First, he'd interrupted Undertoe's amusement with that girl. Then it had almost seemed like he was picking a fight, like he knew more than he ought to. Undertoe felt a bubble of discomfort in his solar plexus, the kind of pain that's indigestion, if it isn't angina. He picked the smidgen of bacon from the edge of the voucher and popped it in his mouth, then let forth a bilious ribbet. *Will Williams* was it now? Not very savvy. But if he did know more than he let on, why had he made such a point of revealing his new alias? There was something off about the man. An image flashed through Undertoe's mind: George Geiermeier, alias Will Williams, slit straight open, liver to anus. He smiled.

At which point Will was still chatting about the depth of the snow with the night manager. "Oh, at least two feet," he speculated, stomach rumbling, never guessing how Pyrrhic his small rebuke of Luther Undertoe could turn out to be, nor that his more immediate adversary, Beanie, was out on the pier, shivering and impatient, waiting.

8

EXTRA! EXTRA!

A t 7:00 A.M., though it was barely light out, a small cluster of people had already gathered at a side door of Bellevue Hospital on Twenty-fifth Street on the far east side. One of the men stepped forward and lifted the heavy bronze knocker, and when the door was opened the lamplight from within glimmered against the gilded letters carved into the lintel overhead: MORGUE.

A body had been discovered deep in the wreckage of Barnum's museum the day before, and it was in surprisingly good shape when it was found — no burns or visible injuries. The story in the *Sun* was based mostly on a brief statement made by the chief of police, so the reporter wasn't able to mention that the girl had come in frozen solid, in a slumped-over, seated position. But now she was thawed and ready to meet the press.

The morgue attendant, whose name was Louie, invited the party inside and took down their names in a large black book. Then he asked them to wait in the lobby while he went back to his office, put his feet up, and flipped through the paper. It was the usual procedure, except that this was Sunday morning, and the morgue didn't open to the public till eight. This was a special showing. Even so, Louie had learned it was advisable to make all visitors, whoever they were, sit for a while and get used to the place — its smells, its prospects — before introducing them to the bodies. It reduced the amount of swooning. Louie didn't have to read the coverage in the early edition of the *Sun* to get the story of the murder and its victim—he knew her a bit more intimately than that by now. But he was eager to know the progress of the case, and he was pleased with what he read. There it stood, in plain type, for the edification of the populace: They had a suspect. Someone would hang for this.

The group in the waiting room included an officer of the metropolitan police, half a dozen members of the press—sketch artists and reporters from the major daily and weekly papers—representatives of several institutions for social reform, a lady physician, and an employee of P. T. Barnum. The one that Louie was worried about was the lady physician, Sarah Blacksall, and the problem was that she wasn't just a woman but a real *lady*—the kind he knew tended to be squeamish. Louie needn't have worried himself. Dr. Blacksall had seen more cadavers in her courses at the Women's Medical College than the rest of that rather hard-boiled group ever would, combined—all excepting him, of course, and one other. The other was Luther Undertoe.

In his capacity as deputy security guard and general odd-job man for P. T. Barnum, Undertoe had been sent to verify whether the girl was an employee, the girlfriend of an employee, or anyone otherwise known to have frequented the museum or its stables. As they entered the dead room, he reached inside his collar and scratched the rash on his neck.

Louie pointed to the leftmost table. He pulled the sheet back—it was wet and clung to the body—exposing the girl's head and shoulders. She was young and dark haired. But the most salient fact about the cadaver had been revealed even through the sheet, by the bulge in the middle: She was pregnant.

"She ain't one of ours," said Undertoe quickly. "I don't know her."

"Nor I," tsked the matron of women from the Five Points House of Industry.

"So young," said the sketch artist from *Harper's*, as he began to draw. And then to Louie: "Can you tell me the way her hair was arranged when she came in?" Hair was crucial for a likeness.

"Are those her clothes?" asked a reporter, gesturing at the ruined gown that dangled from a hook on the wall at the head of the table.

"May I?" asked Dr. Blacksall with a glance at the sergeant. At his shrug, she approached the table and removed the sheet entirely.

She wasn't just great at the belly. She had swollen breasts and ankles like overstuffed, underdone pork pies. Pregnancy can be beautiful, if the woman's alive; in death, it is hideous. And yet there was a strange aura about the girl, something shimmering and almost invisible. She and the slightly tilted granite table she lay on were shiny wet, running with a cool, thin sheet of Croton water that spritzed onto her forehead from a nozzle above and spread out across her flesh, keeping it cool. It was a modern design that greatly postponed decomposition. Dr. Blacksall approved of it. She leaned down to the young woman's ear as if to whisper something and inspected the skin around her neck and jaw. Then she shooed the others from where they gaped at the foot of the table and asked them to wait outside. Louie cocked his head, but Sergeant Jones nodded. Permission had been arranged.

When Dr. Blacksall was alone with Louie, the sergeant and the girl, she bent the girl's right leg at the knee and peered between her thighs, almost as she would have with a living patient. She removed several articles from her bag, laid them on the table and asked for a candle. Louie assisted reluctantly. A few minutes later, when she'd completed her examination, Sarah Blacksall laid her hand on the girl's cold, wet knee. It was just 7:30, but she had already seen more than she cared to that day. She left the morgue in a state of melancholy and determination.

Luther Undertoe was in another mood entirely. He had taken courteous leave of the sergeant, an old acquaintance, and he was whistling "Willy the Weeper" as he sauntered down the street and away from the morgue, his mind idly rehearsing the words as he puckered and trilled, just a half tone out of key. He had several errands planned for that day, most of them to do with his work for Barnum, but there was also a meeting at the Central Park menagerie with a gentleman who owed him a considerable sum in cash. He was tired after the night of shoveling but looking forward to the ride uptown.

Meanwhile, Will was sitting in a coffeehouse across from the first man he'd met in years who seemed to like him and to appreciate the work he'd done.

"Eggs?" the night manager had asked. "Rasher? It's on me."

How could he say no, when his stomach was a yawning cavern that threatened to digest itself? The night manager had sensed his hunger and his poverty in the way he'd blinked at his pay voucher, and so he had invited him out for breakfast. So there he sat, eating bacon, trying to ignore the shame: shame that he had nowhere to go, shame that he needed his breakfast bought for him, shame that he had no money, shame that he'd lived on to get himself in so much trouble, when others far worthier had gone to their rewards. Shame ran in his blood, a cocktail of Protestant self-loathing with a splash of Jewish guilt, but he was not living according to his bloodline anymore, and he had determined not to let it mire him. It helped when the night manager said to him, after second cups of coffee were brought, "You're a hard worker, Williams. I like the way you supervised those men. What I'm thinking is, there could be a place for you in this department. Things are changing in New York, you know. It doesn't even matter that you're German. Do you know about the Sanitary Commission? We're trying to clean the city up—for real this time. We're expanding. Men like you are needed."

He thought of the street sweepers in that shed down at Coffee House Slip. It was the last thing he wanted, to join that wretched battalion, even as a foreman. He still had the whiff of their coats in his nose. "I'd like that," he lied. Images of stone flickered past his eyes: granite, marble, limestone, and the great teetering scaffolds it took to turn them into steeples. Could he build up to that from being a garbageman?

"Why don't you stick around tomorrow morning, after quitting. I'll get the paperwork going on my end, and I can help you fill out the forms. Now, mind you, I'm not promising anything . . . but I can offer my personal recommendation."

"Thank you," Will Williams mumbled, "thank you very much." He envisioned his future collecting horse dung and maggoty butcher's tailings and all manner of filth from the streets. But then he took a sip of coffee and got ahold of himself. For now, he needed paying work, and he could make street cleaning do, if that was what had come his way. He would not *become* a garbageman; he would simply make the best of this opportunity and move on as soon as he could, possibly very soon. He smiled at the night manager, lifted his cup, and let the last dribble of sweet black coffee fall onto his tongue. Now he just had to find a warm place to pass the day—perhaps even sleep—and he'd be able to manage the second night's work just fine. Soon, from there to something better.

They said good-bye on the street in front of the restaurant, and Will walked up Broadway, trying to look as if he had a purpose and a place to go.

He was wondering what his first step should be, in attempting to investigate the fire, and he wasn't the least bit sure. The going was hard on the sidewalk, where much of the snow from the street had been piled in great banks but not yet carted to the river, and after a block or two he decided to walk in the street. Then an omnibus approached, a team of six horses pulling two passenger cars on the streetcar tracks. He was pleased—his work had enabled the buses to run—but then he had to scramble up onto a bank of snow considerably taller than he was to get out of its way. When the mountain of snow ended, he found himself sliding down the other side on his behind, and he laughed aloud. Last night he'd been by turns too worried, too hungry, and too busy to enjoy the snow, but now he remembered that however much work and inconvenience it made, a heavy snow was also a delight. It covered the ugliness of the world, made hard things soft, and anyplace at all a playground. And then, thinking how soon such a pristine snowbank would turn gray and dirty on Broadway, he dug in his heels, got a running start and hurled himself back over the bank. He rolled all the way down the other side to where the sidewalk was still more than knee-deep in fluffy snow. He lay there smiling to himself for a moment before gathering his wits and dusting himself off. Then he did it again. The morning was still so young and the street was quiet; he was sure no one saw his display, but even if they did, what did he care?

He was wrong, of course. Undertoe may have moved on to other matters, being confident he knew where to find his man again that evening, but Beanie and Fiona were still on the job, quite frankly exasperated with how difficult it was turning out to be to corner him somewhere private and deliver Johnny's message. It's not all that easy to tail a man in a world that's blinding white. They were slightly ahead of him when he opted to jump, and they'd hurled themselves over the snowbank in the other direction to avoid coming face-to-face with him when he landed. But when he went back over, what could they do? They ran off in a mirage of snowballs and giggles. By all rights he ought to have gotten suspicious—they'd been tailing him for a little too long for him not to have noticed—but he didn't seem to find anything odd about seeing them again; he just smiled and trudged off through the powder.

Still, the girls were more careful after that. They split up, Beanie at times as much as a block ahead, Fiona lagging. From time to time they exchanged a couple of low Why Not whistles that were lost among the snow-muffled noises of the city long before they reached his ears. They stayed a little further away from him from then on but continued to follow him.

As they were heading uptown, Undertoe moved south. He was looking for a newsboy he employed on the side, a kid he knew to have deft fingers and cleverly constructed pockets in the lining of his coat. And Jimmy was always game: He'd carry out even the most unusual of errands, exactly as asked to, and afterward keep quiet about it. Undertoe was coaching him to do more. At Astor Place, he spotted him.

"*Extra! Extra!*" the boy crowed, performing a little when he saw Undertoe approach. He was hoping for a job. You could learn a lot from crooks like the Undertaker, he'd found—not so much by asking them anything (which would only shut them up) or listening to what they said (which was usually the opposite of what they meant) but by watching how they worked.

"Morning to you, Jimster," Undertoe smirked.

"Likewise, Mister U. Seen the special edition?" Undertoe had seen only the *Sun*, so he shook his head and the Jimster tossed a copy of the *Tribune* his way, catching in midair the dime Undertoe flipped back. It was a bit of a disappointment, coming from the Undertaker, even if the paper cost only two cents.

But then Undertoe pointed to the cover story and said, "I want you to look out for this Geiermeier guy. The one we saw get dragged off the other night, the stableman. And let me know if you see or hear anything." Almost as an afterthought, he reached into his pocket and brought out the voucher. He stuffed it into the Jimster's breast pocket.

"Cash that thing in at the bank in the morning, why don't you, Jimster.

I don't have the time. You want to hear something funny? I earned it my-self—ten hours of hard labor last night."

He left the Jimster puzzled but pleased and turned to the paper's head-lines.

There were several stories he was curious about, especially the murder of the girl found in the Barnum's fire, but not just that—Undertoe had any number of balls in the air. More than a normal man needed, you might say. Why wasn't he content with his day job for Barnum? Why on Earth had he spent the night shoveling snow, pushing our protagonist's buttons? Pretty much for the same reasons he'd gouged out Sheeny Mike's eye the month before in what ought to have been just an ordinary brawl, the same reasons he usually slit the throats of the whores he visited, the same reasons he'd stolen even the underclothes and shoes off that Poughkeepsie gentleman he'd rolled for his wallet a couple of weeks back and then left naked, bloody and unconscious in a dustbin. It was meanness; it was to keep the world on its toes; it was because he wanted people to fear him and to suffer, as he had, as his mother had; it was rage; it was revenge. His tactics were pecu-liar, even for the metropolis, and unpredictable, which made him hard to catch. He didn't run with a gang—he couldn't get along with people—un-less you wanted to count his newsboy pawns. There were always one or two of them doing his bidding, but even they tended not to last very long. As soon as they started to get independent or a little too familiar or to know too much, he did away with them.

Undertoe had choreographed a role for the man he knew as Geiermeier in one of his plans. He'd sized him up early on at Barnum's, long before the fire: a foreigner, utterly without connections and splendidly naïve. The guy actually tried to chat Undertoe up in *German*, a language which, though it was his mother's first, Undertoe wouldn't have deigned to speak, even if he had known how. Germans were treated like scum in America, second only to Irish, and in his opinion those who didn't manage to leave that cumbrous tongue behind them actually *were* scum. You didn't stand a chance in New York unless you could talk fast and understand everything everyone said, unless you could hustle. Why, the stableman was so daft he'd spoken to the animals at Barnum's in German. Undertoe had gotten the gist of some of the sentimental things he'd said—they were exactly the kinds of things

Undertoe's mother had cooed to her lovers and to him, as a boy, though the tone of her voice had varied with the listener.

To Undertoe, our stableman was a reminder of his Germanness, which was an embarrassment, but above all he was a tool. The guy was weak, he was accessible, he was friendless, he was penniless. He was perfect. Keeping track of him had become a little more difficult since he'd gotten out of jail—that was a hitch—but now he'd found him again. In fact, all Undertoe had really needed to do, the night before, was to put someone like the Jimster on his tail to watch him. Joining the shoveling crew had been just for kicks—he was playing with him then. Getting to know him. Learning how to make him mad. And now he knew where to find him later on.

As for Williams being predictable, his feet had led him right back up Broadway toward Barnum's. He was figuring things would be quieter now, given the hour and the storm and the passage of time. Perhaps he'd be able to poke around the rubble. Instead, there was a veritable crowd milling around in front of the ice- and char-bound museum, and not just men at work on the demolition. Too much time had passed for so many gawkers still to be thronging the site, he thought. Then he noticed that almost half the crowd consisted of police inspectors, and his stomach lurched. *We'll nab you back*, the clerk at the Tombs had warned him. What was he doing there? Could he learn anything without compromising himself? He hadn't quite decided when a kid walked up to him and looked at him strangely, as if he knew exactly who he was. It was the Jimster, and he sang out the headline tunefully, as all the newsboys did—the louder and sweeter the voice, the more scandalous the headlines, the faster the papers sold.

"Special edition—arson to murder—body of girl found in wreckage of Barnum's fire! Read all about it, only in the *Sun*—or the *Trib*." (He carried both.) Then he shifted to a speaking voice. "Paper, mister?" He was wondering if he could be this lucky, if this could really be who he thought it was.

The stableman had no money to buy a paper, but he badly wanted to read the whole story. A girl in the stable? He didn't believe it. It wasn't right. He had done his rounds, and there was no girl there. How could she have gotten in and he not known it, unless she was the girlfriend of some cabbie or other, but in that case wouldn't the cabbie have gotten her out? Then he thought of the barn doors that were not especially secure, and he thought about the bitter cold of that night. He thought of Maria. Of course it was just a fantasy, but he pictured her, proud, stubborn and in trouble of some kind, finding herself at large on the coldest night of the year, searching out a nook of her own and coming, whether by chance or design, to the very place he worked and lived. Would he now be held responsible for having needlessly allowed not just the animals but a person to burn to death? No, he was more certain than ever that it wasn't his fault, but whose was it? He had to find out, but he had no idea how.

But the Why Nots did.

"One of each, if you please, *Jimmy*," Fiona had said with an extra bit of lilt for good measure. Moments later, she was turning to the second page of the *Sun*'s front-page story, BODY OF GIRL FOUND IN BARNUM'S FIRE — ARSON TURNS TO MURDER, while across the street catty-corner Beanie leaned against a lamppost, perusing the latest number of *Frank Leslie's Illustrated*, which had a special spread on the fire investigation. There was a picture on page three, and it wasn't of the victim (those were only just going into production). No, the picture was of our stableman, and it was an odd one, if you knew the sitter, for he was smiling in it, and perhaps as a result it didn't quite resemble him. It had been drawn from that tintype photo he'd had made on his day off. Never a very good likeness, and then, too, when the cops found it in the rubble, it was partly charred.

The drawing in *Harper's* was a little closer to life, thanks to the editorializing of the artist, who had taken a flyer and given him a rather grim expression, but it was printed only on the inside continuation, not on the cover. The article was lengthy, for just then the editors were waging a clean-up-the-city campaign, continually touting some urgent social issue, praising the technical advances of the fire brigade, deploring the state of the city's sanitation or decrying the plight of the deserving poor (which they distinguished, and sharply, from the indigent, the criminal and the fallen). The body of the girl, estimated to be twenty years old, was a priceless propaganda tool: fodder for every mother's nightmare and every man's fantasy that he might have protected her from danger. (Nobody had told the papers till after press time that the girl was bursting with child and wore no ring on her finger — the cops were sitting on that little detail, wanting to get the

message out, to up the interest in the case, which they were virtually assured of solving. They would *find* someone to convict, if need be.) The editors were all over the story. They smelled a skunk and named it Phineas—
Phineas T. Barnum, that was—a fancy name for a member of the species
Mephitis malodorus, as one columnist wrote, but fitting for a showman,
even if he tended to abbreviate it. Sure, someone might have a grudge
against him. Sure, the girl was an added twist. But so was the enormity of
Barnum's fire-insurance policy. There were observers who had noted, even
before this latest incident, that every time his ticket sales diminished, his
circuses, his museums, even his domiciles flared up like hay in August.
Even before the body was recovered, the *Sun* had committed to following
the story as far as it would go. Now, with the added boost of scandal and in-
trigue, it was really having fun.

Meanwhile, the girls were no longer actually reading the papers. They'd
learned all they needed to. Beanie was holding her copy high before her
face, pretending to glance through the corset ads while she actually peered
through a hole torn in the crease. She wanted to watch what Will would do,
to stay close enough to intervene if needed. She didn't want to be seen.
She'd have given quite a lot to know just what he was thinking, but that was
one thing her street skills couldn't gain her.

He was wishing he had the pennies to buy a paper and read all about it.
And rightly so. Information changes everything. If only he'd had a paper,
he'd have known that the cops had gotten his likeness and wanted to bring
him back in, and thus that he ought to be behaving a little more covertly.
He'd also have read that the girl's hair was dark, not blond, as he was mor-
bidly imagining, and spared himself the worry that Maria was the victim.
He didn't have the pennies, but he had an idea where to start if he was
going to try to solve the crime himself. He was tired, and he was worried,
but he did not have a guilty conscience. On the contrary, he had a plan.
And he was suddenly looking forward to the rest of his day.

As he turned away from the intersection of Broadway and Spring, he
was under the observation of several people who knew exactly who he was:
Luther Undertoe, the Jimster, Beatrice and Fiona. There were a half dozen
other newsboys in earshot, all selling papers containing his description, and

some of them hawking the illustrateds with his likeness to boot. There was a reward of five hundred dollars on his head. But his oblivion was his shield, for of all the myriad New Yorkers who passed him as he set off through the snow, only the four who already knew him were able to match his face to the pictures of the villain the *Herald* had dubbed "George the Torch." And each of them had reasons for sitting on the information—at least for now.

9.

MORGUE

Undertoe hopped a streetcar heading north. It was going to be a long trip up to Central Park, what with the snow, but at least the car wasn't crowded. He found a place and spread his legs wide, taking three seats.

He'd passed a note to the police sergeant as they left the morgue, suggesting a rendezvous later in the day to discuss some important new information, including exactly where they could find their man that evening. He was looking forward to reaping the five-hundred-dollar reward for leading the cops to a killer. Undertoe slipped into a light doze. It had been a long night. He was jolted to awareness again just north of Thirty-fourth Street, when one of the streetcar's metal wheels derailed—the tracks were jammed with ice and compacted snow. The whole coach skidded sideways, threatening to topple, then righted itself. Undertoe retrieved his hat from the floor where it had fallen. The horses plodded forward. The wheels lurched back into their metal grooves.

He had been interrupted in a dream—there was a blond German girl with soft warm flesh, and he hadn't gotten to enjoy her yet. He crossed his legs and rearranged his overcoat, cleared his throat, annoyed. He was late when he got to the menagerie in Central Park, but he found the man he expected to meet exactly where they'd planned: at the cat cages, between the American panther and the African lion. The panther looked angry as it paced; the lion was listless; his customer seemed nervous.

"Would have been easier just to shoot them and stuff them, if you ask me," remarked Undertoe as he approached the lion. His tone implied that the man was a perfect stranger.

"Possibly. I'll grant you it must have taken courage to capture them alive." The man dropped a copy of the morning paper on the park bench that faced the big cats. His top hat gleamed. His collar was silk velvet, his gloves black kid. That morning, his valet had brushed his topcoat till the nap was soft and smooth. He'd made a killing in textiles during the War Between the States—all those uniforms and blankets—and now he was parlaying that income and the expertise he'd gained into the launch of an upscale haberdashers with a wholesale business on the side. His dealings with Undertoe concerned a girl, a certain Pearl Budd, known better in the Five Points as Pearl Button, whose acquaintance he'd made at a downtown bordello. She'd been his favorite escort for a period of months preceding his marriage that winter. She was a better class of working girl, Pearl, knew how to dress for the opera and kept up with the serial novels in the better periodicals. He wouldn't have taken her to dine at a society hotel, naturally, but she wasn't an embarrassment to be seen with. Such relationships were understood. She had commanded a rather high price, which he willingly paid, and thus he'd been baffled—no, disappointed—when she'd written him that winter, from a new address, complaining of *irregularity* and implying she expected something more. He regretted, then, having allowed her to play the role of wife once or twice, though it had certainly inspired her in bed. It had been stimulating for him as well, to imagine marrying a common tart. He sent sufficient money to take care of the problem and an unsigned letter saying he wanted to hear nothing more of it but suggesting as a consolation that eventually, when his new wife became indisposed with child, as he surely hoped would happen soon, he'd gladly seek her company again. Pearl did not understand his preference for an imagined child in his wife's belly over the actual one in her own. She wanted out of whoring, and she did not use the money as he had intended. On the contrary, she wrote him again, demanding a regular upkeep and threatening to appeal to his wife if he ignored her.

Unfortunately for Pearl, she had overestimated his nerves. Her gentleman had panicked and tracked down Undertoe, who had taken care of

Pearl, a simple matter of an overdose of hydrate of chloral slipped into her gin. Disposing of her body in the fire had been an afterthought. Now Undertoe was collecting his final payment.

"Can you assure me it was her?" asked the gentleman under his breath.

"You could always stop in at the morgue and see for yourself." Undertoe laughed, knowing that was hardly an option. He picked up the paper, which had a certain heft other copies of the early edition did not, and dropped a small object on the bench in its place: a pearl button. "Or, you could trust me." Then he walked off.

The entire encounter had taken about a minute, and to an outside observer it would hardly have seemed to be a detour from the ostensible purpose of Undertoe's visit uptown: a pop-in visit to the back barn of the park menagerie, where the surviving animals from Barnum's were being housed. He let himself into the barn and went directly to a horse stall that appeared, at first, to be empty.

"Lucy, Lucy, Lucy."

He clucked his tongue, and from a warm nest of hay at the back of the stall, a small goat stood up and stepped forward. Undertoe held out a cube of sugar, and after the goat had taken it in her rubbery lips, he scratched her in the space between the four horns that sprouted up, two to a side, in a manner at once freakish and sweetly appealing, which was to say absolutely perfect for Barnum's. The stableman's goat nuzzled Undertoe's palm.

The stableman had decided to commence his investigation at the morgue. If visiting the crime scene was going to pose problems, he would go and see what he could find out about the victim. Knowing who she was and exactly how she'd died ought to give him something to go on, to track down the person who had really set the fire. At Twenty-fifth Street, he admired the golden letters carved above the door. They were deeply, crisply, elegantly executed and freshly gilded, at once a piece of work he could appreciate and dreadful.

The moment he walked through the door, he had a new set of worries, however: the ledger on the front desk and the man who was obviously there to make visitors sign it. He was rightly afraid to leave the name Geiermeier. And not wanting to associate the name Williams with the fire or its victim, he searched his brain for a new name, a story, a relationship to justify the visit. It would have to be German. Anyone could hear he was German. The name he chose was that of his old friend from his father's lab: Robert Koch. It was unnoticeable, Germanic, plausible, and at least he had some connection to it, unlike Williams. Perhaps, too, the clinical air of the morgue brought to his mind the laboratory where he and Koch had first become friends, the doctor's son assisting the doctor's assistant.

In fact, *Robert Koch* was a terrible idea. Any new name would have been. For if he was really innocent, why should he feel the need to create yet another alias? It wouldn't look good if he did have to face the authorities again, but he was banking on whatever he learned here to help him enough so that it wouldn't matter.

"Yeah?" said the man sitting at the front desk. Louie had been sitting at that desk for years, and every day had been rife with tragic scenarios and macabre spectacles. Louie was long inured to grief. The main things he cared about were keeping the visitors upright and getting the bodies off his shelves before they spoiled. But he did have a heart. Whenever he could manage it, if the volume wasn't high and the weather not too hot, he'd let the unclaimed ones stay a little longer than their allotted ten days, on the off chance that someone would come in at last, see one of them, and start to cry. For Louie, a good day was when he saw someone cry, but it didn't happen often enough. Every now and then, at closing time, after a day of shrugs and sighs but no reunions, he'd wander the dead rooms alone and offer up a teardrop or two of his own. You'd never have guessed it, though, from the blank way he stared at Will.

"Well?"

The ex-stableman turned rookie detective gave a spiel about a missing sister. Louie nodded and wrote something down in his logbook, then left him. There was a vague hint of rot in the air, and something sour and antiseptic, but they hadn't even gotten to the door of the dead room when Will's knees went soft, like noodles. He felt himself blanch and go suddenly cold. He reached out for the wall and took a deep breath, but it was too late. His body collapsed in a pile on the floor, leaving his mind to hover unmoored somewhere over near the window, then venture out into the icy wind. It wove between the snow-shrouded chimneys, and somehow it found Maria. So he need not be afraid of that; it wasn't she who was dead.

No, in fact, she was nodding at the signal of a man, tucking his folded bills into the torn lining of her rabbit muff and inviting him up to her room. She was running her fingers down his rashy chest, laughing when he reached out and slapped her and commanded her to kneel. The stable-man's swoon was brief, and though it was not a dream, it was like a dream in that he mercifully forgot what he'd seen when he roused. The splay-legged, Undertoed truth about Maria evaporated swiftly, like a volatile solvent, and he came to with the domed white ceiling of the foyer above him, the marble chill of the floor in his limbs, a new pounding in his cranium. Louie was standing over him.

"Bud. Hey, bud. Get up."

Louie brought him a glass of water, then gave him his tour of the morgue: not just the one girl from the Barnum's fire—for why would the one who received the most publicity be any likelier to be his sister? Williams had said his sister was twenty years old, and there were several girls that age in residence. The thing about corpses is that, one way or other, they're disasters. They're no good anymore, except to a small group of professionals: doctors, grave diggers, police, priests. The stableman had seen death before, but somehow this was different. He thought of the body of the vagrant who had died of the flux, still lying in the barn awaiting burial when his uncle's farm had caught fire. He'd made use of that body, knowing it was wrong—bodies should not be used, they should be buried. But he had known the man bore a certain resemblance to him and hoped no one would guess the difference when the fire had done its job.

He looked at each girl's body and shook his head sadly. But then, when Louie pulled the sheet off Pearl, the stableman was overwhelmed. Who was she? he wondered. Whose baby did she carry? Why had this happened? There was no purpose this death could possibly serve. He covered his eyes, and his shoulders shook.

Louie looked at him. He'd been suspicious before. Now he felt chagrin and relief. One more identity was about to be confirmed, one more lonely body taken off the roster of those he felt obliged to mourn.

"She was found in the Barnum's fire, in the basement," he volunteered.

When our man asked him a series of quiet questions—how she had died, if she had worn any jewelry, could he look at her clothes—Louie made himself as helpful as he could be, but the truth was there wasn't much to be learned from Pearl's singed garments and bare fingers, and Undertoe had been sure to dispose of her reticule.

"So what was her name?" Louie said quietly, *kindly*, at last.

Will just shook his head. He thought, *No*—no in denial, no in despair, no in disgust at himself for coming there and prying. No at her slightly open, empty eyes. No at the soft concavity in the top of her skull and the great, dead convexity of her womb. No at her failure to procreate or to survive. No because, despite it all, he'd learned nothing he could use in his defense.

"Sir? I need her name."

He realized now that if he didn't give a name, he would make himself very suspicious. "Lottie," he said, though it tainted his sister to give her name to this pregnant girl. It was the first girl's name that came into his head. "Charlotte Koch."

"Well, I'm very sorry, sir. I'm afraid you're going to need to sit down and fill out some paperwork with me before we can release the body. Do you have an undertaker? If not, your church may know of one, or we can make a recommendation."

"I can't. I have to go. I have to tell my mother." He was reeling with the way the lies and transgressions multiplied. He didn't want to speak anymore for fear of what he would say.

"It'll just take a few minutes. . . ."

Will shook his head and backed out of the dead room. Before returning to the street he leaned over Louie's desk. He peered at the logbook, scanning the names on the two facing pages, and what he saw made all his other concerns fade: Luther Undertoe had been there.

He left the building in a hurry then. Suddenly, he was certain that Undertoe was the one. It explained a good deal. But how could he turn these bits of circumstantial evidence into a case that might convince a policeman or a judge, when he himself was surely a suspect? What he needed was information, but he couldn't even afford to buy himself a copy of the paper. He could read the paper for free, however. He could go to the public library at the Cooper Union. From the entry in his *Stranger's Guide*, he remembered that it welcomed working men and women in particular and was designed in the grandest of styles, with the intent of uplifting its constituents. He imagined the place had washrooms fit for the aristocrats that had funded its construction, and his head was suddenly filled with visions of shining silver taps with hot running water and a brightly lit reading room furnished with padded leather wing chairs, where he would sit while he found the crucial information that would lead him out of his predicament, and which would then cradle his head while he fell deliciously asleep for a few hours, to rest up for the coming night.

He passed a newsboy on his way down the block, but it wasn't just any newsboy—it was the Jimster, who on his own initiative had decided to keep the stableman under continuing surveillance. Now his ingenuity was rewarded. Undertoe would like hearing he'd been at the morgue. The Jimster had nothing in particular against the stableman—he understood that Undertoe was framing him, in fact, and he found it unpleasant—but he was an entrepreneur, just trying to keep himself fed and housed and shod. His only problem, which he was fully unaware of, was Fiona.

The stableman wasn't in the mood to frolic in the snow anymore as he walked south. He was worried he'd drawn attention to himself by fainting; he was stumped about how to use the information he'd gathered; he was exhausted. He decided his judgment had been impaired by lack of sleep and that he would put off further sleuthing for the moment. For now, he needed somewhere to rest till the night shift was due to start shoveling.

A few blocks downtown, his eye was caught by the top halves of two young boys bobbing along at a fast clip on the far side of the street, their lower bodies obscured by the snowbank. Now and then, they stopped to gather snowballs and hurl them at each other, rather fiercely. There was something enlivening about watching those boys. They seemed so innocent, the way they played. At the corner, the boy out front broke left and crossed the street, then vanished down an alley. There was some shouting that the stableman couldn't make out, and the second boy followed.

It was a trick of Fiona's that the stableman never realized she was a girl, much less the nature of her attack on the Jimster. The two seeming boys appeared to the stableman to be playing around, but in fact the Jimster was fleeing. Fiona had just offered to pry out his eyeballs, if he didn't move along. The stableman looked both ways for them at the corner. Where had they gone? Then he spotted a shoe—a boy's shoe, much worn, resting on its side on the fresh crust of snow, having flown off the wearer's foot as he rounded the corner. Certainly it belonged to one of the two who had just run past, he thought, but they weren't the kind of boys likely to have extra shoes in their closets, if they had closets at all. He thought about what he'd do if one of his shoes were lost, and wondered if it really had been a game. Now he wasn't sure. He reenvisioned the scene with the first boy running away from a bully, which was much closer to the truth, but he still wasn't able to glean that the bully was a girl, nor that she'd chased the Jimster into a basement entry and then tackled him.

"What the—" the Jimster said. Fiona had been pelting him so hard with snowballs and epithets, he hadn't even noticed losing his shoe. Now she had him pinned by his arms. She was also laughing. Then she pulled out one final snowball and shoved it down his neck. There was no sign of sharper hardware anymore. When he shouted, she leaned down and called him a Billy noodle. Then she breathed something lewder in his ear, and he broke free, and they were wrestling, and then kissing, and then they were struggling to shed just enough of their clothing to stay warm and yet to have access. Access was gained. They spent a quarter hour in the dusty base-ment—it wasn't a place that made you want to linger—and at the end of it, the Jimster didn't care anymore that he'd dropped his papers and allowed Undertoe's man to get away.

That had been the point, of course. Fiona and Beanie had decided it was time to get the Undertaker's toady off their man's tail. They'd flipped a coin to see who would do the honors, and as a result, well, the Jimster had quite a morning. (Suffice it to say, Beatrice would not have handled the job the same way.)

"See you around, Fifi," he said.

"All right then, Jimmy. See you."

While Fiona and the Jimster had their assignation, Beanie stuck to Williams. She watched him squat down and pick up the shoe the Jimster had lost.

Its laces were broken and knotted in a couple of places. The toe was scuffed, and Will pictured how the boy must drag his feet. He thought it was the loneliest, saddest shoe he'd ever seen. He hung it up on the black painted spike of a wrought-iron fence at the corner, then he crossed the street, and plowed on toward the Cooper Union.

He did the right thing, the stableman, in hanging up the shoe, the kind and helpful thing. After the Jimster took his leave of Fiona, he went back outside and searched the route they'd come, a little wobbly in the knees, puzzled about his footwear. Where had that left shoe gone? He was surprised when he found it—and it wasn't even wet, though the same could not be said for his sock. The best thing that came of the Jimster's finding his shoe, however, was that it spared him having to rob some other, weaker boy for his pair of shoes. For he was the Undertaker's boy, after all, on assignment. The better shod he was, the better off he was in general, the worse for Williams.

Will trudged south, unaware of his tail, imagining tufted leather armchairs at the library. He wasn't even thinking about reading the papers or solving the case now, just falling asleep in a chair. When at last he arrived at Cooper Square, he passed the great arched windows, approached the front door and tugged on the handle, but it didn't give. Then he saw the small printed sign that was posted in the window: 8:00 A.M. TO 9:00 P.M. MONDAY TO SATURDAY—workingmen's hours. But today was Sunday. The library was closed.

10.

PROTEUS

Their man was moving south, and they were on him. They'd ditched the Jimster, and they were ready to make their move. They just needed to follow him onto some quiet street where no one would see them approach him. But the stableman defied them. He would not be distracted. Would not be guided. Would not cooperate. Who was this man?

"Let's give him a bit longer before we do it by force," said Beatrice at last, puzzled at how difficult this was proving. Fiona nodded.

Williams turned away from the library, coughed and spat in the snow. His lungs were healing slowly but surely. It was just his luck that the library was closed, but not having a warm place to sit suddenly wasn't the obstacle it might have been a short time before. He knew whom he was after, and he was going to see him again that night. He felt warm and determined. He had overcome exhaustion. It was quite the stunt he'd just pulled, and he found himself shaking his head, nearly laughing in bleary disbelief at some of the things he'd claimed. His nerve had served him well, gotten him the information he needed. Then he laughed aloud at the image of himself lying prostrate on the marble floor with Louie leaning over him, slapping his wrist like a girl's. From there, he found he had much more to laugh at: He laughed at the name Will Williams. He laughed at the way he'd let Undertoe get to him the night before. The damned song was the least of his problems, he now saw. He laughed so hard he had to wipe the tears from his face before they froze there, and as he did he noticed that the street was more crowded than it had been, more crowded than it ought to have been in such weather. It also seemed he was suddenly obstructing the paths of innumerable somberly dressed people who were bustling around him on the narrow path between snowbanks. He felt their disapproving stares. He was still chuckling, just regaining his composure, when he overheard a woman mutter in German that madmen should be kept off the streets on Sundays at least—they profaned the Sabbath.

Of course, he thought—these were churchgoers on their way to some nearby house of worship. And if it was Sunday, he, too, could sit in a pew for an hour or two and be warm. He could use the time to think about his next move, and he wouldn't be able to get himself into any further trouble.

He followed the last few pairs of upright shoulders around the corner and through the doorway of a strange, unimposing little Lutheran church devoid of a spire or other inspirational details. It was situated in a modest brownstone row house, with just a few religious phrases carved into the lintel over the door. Organ music swelled from within, and the bell began to ring the hour. Someone was closing the door behind the congregation. It was in or out, once again, and once again he stepped in.

What kind of a flibbertigibbet was this man, you may ask, who had renounced his faith but now attended Sunday services? He asked it of himself. A cold and tired one, was the answer. Then, too, he didn't mind that the place was filled with German voices. It made it easier to atone for some of the things he regretted having done. He felt oddly at home when an usher welcomed him in his old language and escorted him to a seat. And so it was that the stableman, who was suspected of arson, murder and more, came to stand like a supplicant in a side pew. When the congregation sat, he sat, when they knelt, he knelt, and when they stood to sing, he stood and sang the hymns from memory. It was strange even to him, the way he did it after so much time, and he couldn't help but wonder if he did belong there after all. For the moment, he was happy smelling the beeswax candles, hearing the collective voice of the congregation. His fatigue had given birth to clarity of a sort. He thought, *I am who I am, and this quick-change thing is something else entirely, not an identity but a skill I've inadvertently acquired.* It wasn't inherently bad, just a way of adapting to life in the New World.

He was resolved to make it work for him, but there were a couple of pieces missing yet from his puzzle: He had failed to notice the several tails that were onto him, was oblivious to the fact that his face was in the papers and had no idea whatsoever of the storm that would soon be massing down at Coffee House Slip, where he was still planning to show up for work. He was thinking he had a surprise for Undertoe, not the inverse.

But Fifi and Beanie knew better. It was Undertoe's storm, and their mission was to make sure it didn't happen. The Whyos had other plans for Mr. Geiermeier.

When the two of them saw him duck into the church, they exchanged inaudible signals, followed him inside and slipped into a pew at the rear. As the service droned on, they watched him closely, but he remained as oblivious of them as he was of the tsking German matrons.

The truth was, he had fallen into a light doze. The cadences of the Lutheran service lulled him like the nursery rhymes his mother had read him in his earliest, happiest days. The music and the liturgy carried him home, and in that home he rested. When the time came for Communion, he contemplated whether he should take it and decided yes; in the absence of any hope for another meal that day, he would not forsake a holy lunch of bread and wine. It was the lightest of meals, the headiest of meals. It sated him better than a feast. He felt pure, restored.

A funny thing was that despite being surrounded by their common language, he didn't think of Maria just then, never wondered whether any of the congregants knew her, which they might well have. She'd quite predictably fallen in with the German-speaking community and briefly worked as a second cook to a family that attended the church. She had even gone to services there herself. Maria had no patience with religious mummery, but a job was a job and the mistress wanted churchgoing girls in her kitchen. She'd met other servants at the church, with one of whom she'd swapped her instructions for upside-down cake for an apple-tart recipe that gave her considerable trouble. She hadn't the patience for rolling out pastry. From another, she learned she ought to be receiving fatter tips from the master, who came to her room half the nights of the week. She hinted at this, was ignored, and made up her mind to seek another position.

She regretted not having the financial wherewithal to quit on the spot, in protest, but the following Sunday, she inadvertently hastened the changeover in the course of cooking supper. She killed and plucked and cleaned the goose that her mistress had chosen at market. She kneaded dough and swirled hot oil in the bottoms of pots. She rolled out dumplings like the ones once made by Will's cousins and lined them up, dusted with flour, to be popped into the gravy when the time came. From time to time, between dicing the onions, shucking the oysters and slicing the cake, she reached down her shirtwaist and gave her crotch a scratch. On top of all the rest, the man of the house had given her the crabs.

Maria had an unpleasant habit of spitting when vexed, and as she slid the bowl of undone mollusks into sizzling roux, a gob of her ill will passed between her lips and landed in the pan with a hiss. She had no idea that her latent case of typhoid was in the final throes of activity, despite her outward good health. She stirred the pan twice, tasted once—delicious, if requiring a dash more salt—then added the liquor and cream. Three minutes later, she turned the oysters out into a silver tureen, which she set on the sideboard amidst a forest of beef-tallow candles. Her spittle had melded invisibly with the broth, and the dish was so very lightly cooked that ample bacilli survived to lay half the household low for a couple of days. The master did not recover. But Maria was innocent, wasn't she? There are crimes of omission and crimes of commission, but surely there are no crimes of oblivion. Maria didn't know her gallbladder was boiling with bacilli.

But Will did not think of Maria. Didn't even feel a tingle up his spine, a half hour after church had let out, when she crossed his path a dozen yards behind. The cook at the so-called ladies' rooming house where she now worked and lived had found a mouse drowned in the milk pail in the pantry and sent Maria out in search of more. There he went, there she went, but they were out of sync. If he'd known how close he came to finding her, he'd have sat down and wept, but to what avail? It's as simple as this: When people are not meant to meet, they don't meet. His fated appointment was with two other young ladies, that day.

The snow muffled their footsteps, but their dark-clad forms stood out in stark contrast to its brightness. He never saw them. He walked down Mott

Street to the corner of Pell, just opposite Wah Kee's flophouse. He allowed himself to hope that the Chinaman would extend him a night's credit till the following morning, when he would be paid.

The shop had a bell on the door, and Wah Kee himself looked up from behind the counter when it jangled. He recognized the stableman, and he looked annoyed.

"Too early. Come back five o'clock." Wah Kee didn't want the bums scaring off his shop trade. Will had known the flop was closed during the day, but now it occurred to him that the opium smokers were allowed to languish on their couches at all hours. Tendrils of the strange, sweet smoke had filtered through the walls to the bunk room now and then, and the smell was seductive. He and Robert Koch had sipped acrid purple tinctures from his father's pharmacopoeia a couple of times, and he well remembered the pleasant buzz of the poppy.

"Wait, Mr. Kee," he said. "You see, I'd like to go upstairs, not down to the bunk room."

"Ah. Smoke the opium, yes? Very good. All day, half dollar. Good price, great pleasure."

He nodded, to show that the money was no problem—he would have it tomorrow, after all—but Wah Kee held out his hand.

He pulled out his city voucher to show he was good for it. Wah Kee laughed.

"Credit?" he said. And then he laughed again, and kept on laughing until finally Will left the store.

So dissipation was not an option. He decided he would try making the rounds of several churches, since that had worked so well for him once. He was a few blocks north of Trinity. On his way there, he passed Billy's, the bar where his luck had taken its first, brief upward spike, and he imagined someday stopping in and ordering a drink, thanking the barkeep, handing him a generous tip this time to make up for the trouble. He slowed his pace and peered in the window, curious to see what the crowd was like during the day. It was a good thing he still didn't have the price of a beer on him, for even if the barman hadn't had it out for him, Undertoe had just sat down with a couple of officers of the metropolitan police for the express purpose of talking about George "the Torch" Geiermeier—more precisely, where they could find him that night. If he'd walked in, the arrest would have happened then and there, and everything that followed would have been otherwise. But it didn't; he walked by. In the meantime, the sergeant and Undertoe had business to conduct.

"It's the price of crime, Undertoe," laughed Sergeant Jones as Undertoe grudgingly slid an envelope of money across the table. A good portion of what he'd gotten from his gentleman was in there. He'd been hoping not to have to give so much, considering the information he offered, but Jones was not going to be impressed till the firebug was back behind bars. He still hadn't made up his mind exactly what to tell the police when the sergeant called for boilermakers, "to stimulate your loquacity, my friend. And now let's get to business. When and where?"

Undertoe thought about his options. From the Jimster's latest report, Geiermeier was out making an awfully strange tour. There was no reason he should have gone to the morgue. And if Geiermeier was going to behave erratically, it might be time to draw on his backlog of stooges, most of them with records as long and outstanding charges as black and plentiful as the hairs of their girlfriends' armpits. He could try to do a switcheroo and give the cops one of those guys—a guy like the Jimster'd be to him in a couple of years. That would be safer.

"Now hold on—don't think so hard, Luther. No pissants. We want the real thing, the kraut. We got his mug in the papers, and there's no shilly-shallying now, dammit. We need an arrest, and not just any arrest. You're going to deliver him if I have to break your few remaining teeth to make it happen."

Undertoe forced a smile. It was true his teeth had some gaps. It was true he'd gone and gotten Geiermeier's name and picture into the papers. He'd gotten himself into this, and he could well appreciate that no one would be satisfied now if some measly junior safe-breaker from the Five Points rotted in prison. He had made sure that they *wanted* a nefarious German incendiary with multiple aliases, that they wanted to hang him by his neck. He'd had it all set up, but he was feeling uneasy now. He feared he had miscalculated. Given the Jimster's observations, it seemed possible Geiermeier wouldn't show up for work that night after all.

"You'll get your man," he said. But he didn't sound convincing.

"Let me be more specific, you piece of dirt. We know well enough it's a double cross, and you're in with him one way or other. You're clearly experiencing some cold feet here, Luther, but see, I don't give a fuck about your feet. There's a special election coming up, and the chief wants a Sunday bust in the Monday papers. Unless you'd rather go down yourself, you'll provide it. After all, you're German, too, if I'm not mistaken, and that could work for us, in a pinch."

"All right all right all right, goddammit, Jones, all right. . . ."

All this while, the Jimster was gamely standing guard across the street from Billy's, seeing nothing much. His head was in the clouds. He was thinking about Fiona. He stamped his feet with the thought of getting some feeling back in the toes. He'd shown up right on schedule, twenty minutes before Undertoe was supposed to meet Sergeant Jones, and delivered his freelance report on Geiermeier's peregrinations. Then Undertoe had posted him outside. Undertoe's main concern was a double cross by the cops, but truth was there was little the Jimster could do, if it came to that.

Then the Jimster heard a crash and looked up to see a cascade of snow falling to the sidewalk. So did Williams, who had just walked past the Jimster unobserved. Both of them were gawping up at the roof, wondering what caused the avalanche, when Beanie faded into a nearby doorway and Fiona approached the Jimster. She was still wearing the man's bowler she'd had on when she chased him before, but now she whipped it off and let her hair fall down as she strode up to the Jimster, hips a-swivel, lewdly calling, "Hot corn! Hot corn!" though she had nothing of the kind to offer. It was a joke of some sort, even if Fiona herself didn't quite know what made it funny. Anyway, it worked—he rolled his eyes, smiled.

"Hey again, Jimster," she said.

"I'd gladly buy a piece of corn off you, Fifi, but I don't see no sign of it, do I? What're you up to?"

"Nothing." Then she asked him would he like a kiss. He said he was too busy to let himself get beat up again, and she frowned, smiled, puckered, dodged, moved back and forth, laughing, prattling, never allowing his eye to wander from her.

"Say, Jimster, have you got a cigarette for a girl? I could use one."

He reached into his pants, pulled out his one half-smoked butt and started to light it, but Fiona winced, and the Jimster thought better.

"Yeah, all I got's this sick butt off the street. Wait, and I'll get you a fresh one."

He darted into Billy's, not at all sure what was wrong with him, to go off abandoning his post and squandering his pennies on a girl. But then again, he did know: He hadn't had a better morning, ever.

All he knew of the brief scuffle that occurred on the street as he stepped through the door was a vague peripheral glimpse of two dark figures moving against the gray-white snow. When he came back out, ears ringing from Undertoe's boxing but with a cigarette he'd begged off the policeman, Fiona was gone. That was when it dawned on him that something interesting was going on. Fiona had been doing quite a lot to distract him. He figured he probably ought to go in and tell Undertoe, but then again Undertoe had just boxed his ears. Whereas Fiona, even if she wasn't completely on the up-and-up, had just expanded his universe in a most pleasant direction. So what if she'd had an ulterior motive for tackling him; she hadn't had to take it quite where she did. No, whatever she was up to, the whole thing made him like her more.

"Well then, see ya," he said in the direction he thought she might have gone. He dug in his pocket for a match and lit the cigarette. When Undertoe asked him later, he'd say he hadn't seen a thing. After all, he hadn't.

Will Williams didn't see much either. He had still been gazing up at the snow slide when two small, stealthy figures in brown dusters and outsize bowler hats had appeared, one on either side of him. They would have preferred greater privacy, but he wasn't cooperating, so the Why Nots had made their move. No one on the street noticed anything untoward as they flanked him, pinned his arms to his sides and lifted him straight off the ground. He'd barely gotten a look at them himself. And when he did look at one of them, his abductor met his gaze with a frown and the swift jab of a fist with a metal band across the knuckles. His head snapped back. He was dazed—not quite out, but not in any condition to fight back. Before he knew it, they'd twisted his arms behind his back and were leaning hard into him, one on each side, the general effect being something between a lever and a vise. The most he could do was flex his toes, bug his eyes and blink. His feet were off the ground. He was unprepared for this. They turned in unison, ran into an alley and spirited him through a door so black with soot it was almost invisible against the filthy stone of the building it opened into. The door closed behind them, and one of them slid home a bolt, locking it.

They were in a stairwell that was dimly lit from a window far overhead. They released him in a pile in the corner, and he braced himself for another blow, but it didn't come. His kidnappers sat down together on the steps to watch while he stumbled to his knees. He was surprised to see that they were just boys. Then one of them—Beatrice—took her hat off, and red-gold braids tumbled down.

"Jesus God, that was almost too easy." She spoke in a rather gravelly voice for a girl of her size, and with a light brogue. "You want to do the talking, Fifi?"

"Oh, go ahead, you do it."

This one's voice was higher. So they were both girls. His head was swimming.

The first girl turned to Will. Her face was very young and delicate. "All right then, you bleeding idget," she said. "Tell me what the hell you was thinking of, going back into Billy's? What's your strategy here? Are you nuts?"

He wondered if it could be a dream. Why should this girl care where he went? Perhaps he'd been knocked cold by actual thugs, and this was the queer place his mind had taken him while his body once again drifted.

"Well?" she demanded. "I'm asking you."

"But I didn't go in, did I?" He was being cautious. His mouth hurt.

"No, but you nearly did, right into the arms of the police. If you were meeting the Undertaker there, all I can say is you don't know a damned thing."

"The *Undertaker*? You mean Undertoe?" It was a very strange robbery, so far.

"Jesus, Mary and Joseph, spare me! Yes, *Undertoe*. You know what, I don't care who you say you are, Mr. Jeermeer, or what your racket is. You can take it up with Johnny. As far as I'm concerned, you're an idget who don't know nothing. Less than nothing. Let's just get moving."

"Yeah, move it," said the dark one, standing up and pulling out a knife. "We're gonna be late."

"But first, there's one fact I want to inform you of: From here on out, your name's going to be Frank Harris. *Frank Harris*. Don't forget it. Don't change it. And definitely don't use any of the other names you've been using. Because although you seem to be unaware of it, you're famous city-wide by now. You're leaving a pretty wide trail—plenty too wide for the way we work. So, forget Geiermeier, Koch, Williams, whatever the Hell else you've ever called yourself. Your one and only name is Frank Harris."

"What about *Frankie*—that would be okay, wouldn't it, Beanie? He looks like a Frankie."

"Jesus, I haven't the patience. Just shut up, Fifi."

"Uh—" he began.

"Shut up, you, too."

"Fifi?" he said. "*Beanie?*"

"No, I don't think so. Not to you—it's *Beatrice* to you. Or *Miss O'Gamhna*."

"All right, but about Undertoe, I think he's—"

This time she raised her slender fist and thrust it toward his nose, stopping just a fraction of an inch away. He saw her three-knuckle ring in sharp focus, and then she tapped a trigger somewhere on the palm side, and a short, scooped blade popped up between the middle and index fingers. Its cold edge grazed his cheek, and it made him feel cold all the way through.

"This here is my *eye-gouger*, Frank Harris. I don't want to have to show you how I use it, so would you please shut up and get moving."

He nodded and swallowed a thousand questions.

She gestured toward the stairs and then, as he began to ascend, she asked him what his name was.

"You mean really? . . . Geiermeier." He stuttered: "Georg Geier—" He stopped. Was it possible they knew his *real* real name?

"No, not Geiermeier. I told you you're done with that. *Harris*. State your name, Mr. Harris."

He said it. *Frank Harris*. It sounded awfully foreign to him, but then again so had all the others, at first.

"No, not *Frahnk Hah*-ris. You sound like a fucking Prussian."

"I'm not Prussian, I'm from Göttingen."

"Oh, well, congratulations. How fascinating. Jesus Christ. Just say it right: Frank *Hair*-ris."

He said it again, carefully trying to imitate her tones, and this time he got it right.

"Oh, aye, that's better," she said. He could almost hear her smiling, though her lips maintained a scowl. "You do have a good ear, if you want to. It's a pleasure to make your acquaintance, Mr. Harris."

He stole a glance at Fiona, wondering if he was still at knifepoint. He was.

"Just keep moving," said Fiona.

He had no idea whatsoever what was happening to him as he hurried up the endless flights of stairs, but in a way it didn't matter. Being abducted by these girls was oddly enough no worse than anything else that had happened to him lately. He'd begun to grow accustomed to this life in which emergency followed close on the heels of luck and disaster alike, where catastrophe seemed to lurk in every shadow.

UNDERWORLD

11.

THE WHYOS

It wouldn't have taken long to travel overland where Beanie and Fiona were taking him, but they led him instead through an up-and-down maze of frigid stairwells, dank basements and snowbound alleys. They entered a warehouse through an unlocked window and climbed three flights to a loft full of barrels and sacks of grain. Harris was baffled by it, incredulous, really, that he had fallen into the hands of these two girls. He tried to imagine the man they were working for, Johnny. What did he want with him? He twisted his hands in his pockets and felt the silky lining split on one side, his thumb poking through to graze the facing. He thought of the small things that could be lost to such a hole, coins rattling in coattails, keys. He extracted his thumb and tried not to show he was afraid. Finally, from the top floor of the warehouse, they ascended a rickety ladder to a hatch in the ceiling. Fiona went up first, then Harris. *Harris*, he reminded himself.

Beatrice brought up the rear, and she was ready not just with her gouger but with a fish knife she kept in a sheath up her sleeve, just in case the prisoner should balk or bolt. She didn't have to use it. The stableman went along more or less quietly. When Fiona reached the top of the shaft, she unlatched the hatch and yanked it open, dumping a load of heavy snow upon them. It was startling but refreshing. He realized as it hit him that he could seize the opportunity to jump down and run, but he didn't do it. A stream of what must have been Irish curses issued from the one called Beatrice, below. He smiled and decided he would go along without a fight, at least for now. His curiosity outstripped his fear.

The rectangle of sky the stableman saw through the hatch was that amazing blue that comes in the wake of a storm. Fiona stuck her head out the opening and then hoisted herself through the hole. The man whose name was now Frank Harris followed. Up on the roof, they trudged through the crisp snow all the way to the edge, where he saw that there was a wooden conduit connecting the warehouse to another large building across the street; from the narrow gauge of it, he gathered it was used to transfer goods, not people. A slogan was painted along its length, where anyone traversing the Bowery could see it if they looked up, not that the stableman ever had: O. GEOGHEGAN'S BEST AMERICAN ALE.

"You first, Harris," Beatrice commanded.

When he turned back to look at her, eyebrows raised, he saw she had drawn the long, thin fish knife and thrust it at his nose. She gestured at Fiona, who reached into her coat and brought out her dagger.

"Get going," Beatrice said, flashing a cold smile. "We're late." But he couldn't quite be terrified. There was snow in her rust-colored hair and a certain reassuring quality to her voice, despite the knife. They were awfully young, these girl gangsters, and they were bullying him, but somehow he trusted them. And then, as if to prove him right, Fiona offered him a bit of friendly advice as he began to climb onto the narrow conduit: "It's greater than shoulder width, see, not that bad. But with the snow, you can't trust your footing—you'll want to crawl across, not walk."

Only a few notable events would not have taken place, had he slipped. The world would have managed to fill in around him just fine. The great chunks of crusted snow that fell to the street as the threesome crawled across went undetected, except by a cart horse that startled and broke its stride. No one looked up. No one saw them, not unless you count a cold brown dog that barked three times.

On the other side, the girls dug at the snow with their bowler hats until they'd uncovered a hatch. A sour steam of yeast, hops, malt and sawdust rose from below, and they descended into it. He had the feeling of being on the verge of something, and whether terrible or promising he was eager for it. He was ready.

They came into a dim room almost as large and high as the building itself and threaded their way among rows of giant copper cauldrons and hulking iron tanks studded with valves and gauges. From somewhere in the ill-defined, echoey space, the stableman thought he could make out voices murmuring behind the occasional hissing of a pressure valve. Then behind them, footsteps, coming at a run. It occurred to him that perhaps he ought to try to break away from his kidnappers after all, but before he could make up his mind to do it, they'd entered a wide-open central area where a hundred or more men and quite a few women whispered in the semidarkness.

A single lantern stood on the floor in their midst, more casting shadows than illuminating faces. Beatrice whistled slowly, sliding her notes around the musical scale in a manner that seemed to have three dimensions. A moment later, someone whistled back, short and shrill and simple, in a way that clearly addressed not just her but the entire crowd. At once, the assembly began to sit on the floor, and a man stepped forward into the lantern light while the others receded into darkness.

He looked very like an actor taking the stage. Then he leaned down and turned up the wick. His boots flashed. His black hair glistened with pomade. He held a cane in one hand, and it was clear from his posture and the absolute silence that fell over the room when he raised that cane above his head that he was in charge. *Johnny*, thought Harris. The man whistled a few more notes that seemed to draw the room's rapt attention even tighter. He looked left, then right, surveying the crowd.

Johnny, certainly. But who was Johnny? What was this group? What did they want with him?

"Anybody got a reason I shouldn't have O'Gamhna here drowned in a vat of ale for waltzing in on her own Goddamned schedule?"

No one spoke.

"Piker, if you would take care of that for me, then . . ."

A man stood up and began to come forward, but then Johnny waved him back.

"Oh well, I suppose we ought to hear her story, first. Beanie? Fifi? Why don't you floozies tell us just what the fuck's been keeping you?"

The girls rose.

"We've been on him for over a couple of days now," said Beatrice, stepping forward. "He's cagey, or he's got horse sense. He didn't make it easy to grab him without attracting notice."

It was strange to Harris suddenly to see anxiety in the face of the girl who'd been so handy with the brass knuckles and the fish knife. But she stood her ground, and her lip quivered only slightly when Dandy Johnny's cane slashed through the air toward her.

"Dammit!" he said, stopping just a hairsbreadth before he brained her. He let his arm fall, then flicked the cane in a gesture of disgust. "Is that your excuse? He didn't make it *easy*? We've had the entire membership of the Whyos waiting on you. I don't convene such meetings lightly, or hadn't you remembered that?"

"If stealth is the chief concern in any operation, not speed or bravado, then I'm quite confident you will approve of the delay. I judged the stealth of picking up our man here to outweigh the risk of keeping the assembled waiting a wee while. I mean Jesus F. Christus, Johnny, he had Undertoe and a couple of police sergeants after him, whereas I assume you all arrived here according to protocol, undetected." Her tone was confident, too confident. It was clear that Johnny didn't like her defiance, even if it did sound to Harris like the girl was right. Fiona spoke next, before her partner could anger the boss any further.

"She's right, Johnny. This here fucker, well, he's either an addle-headed idget or a genius. Anyway, he isn't normal. He's got a way about him."

"An idget or a genius, is it? Go on then, Fifi, tell us about it. I'm waiting."

"Well, for one thing he paid a visit to the morgue this morning—"

"The Morgue? Half the men in this room were at the Morgue all morning, myself included. I never saw him. Anyone else see him?" he asked of the room at large. There was no reply.

Beatrice laughed then, almost a snort. It was risky to show such attitude—she was still in striking range—but that was the way she was. Johnny just tossed his cane to the other hand, raised an eyebrow, frowned.

"You don't get it," said Beatrice. "The *morgue*—the city morgue itself, not the bar. He went down and viewed a body at the morgue—Pearl. And then he went straight to the German church and took Communion. Body and the blood."

"Oh, did he?" There was perhaps a tinge of respect in Johnny's voice.

"That's pretty brazen. And without even confessing." He looked over at the stableman for the first time, furrowed his brow and smiled slightly. The stableman got the impression that this glance was less murderous than impressed. But why? He was increasingly puzzled. Clearly, these were not nice people. Clearly, they were also under some strange misconception about who he was and what he was doing. They had followed him, seen his day's activities and deduced things that made no sense at all. Their interest in him and what they were saying made no sense. Surely there was some mistake here, but he was far from certain about the prospects of his resolving it.

"Yeah, well, it was Lutherans," she said. "I don't believe they have to confess." She turned to look at the stableman. "Do you?"

He shook his head. Why were they talking about this? Why did they care?

"Listen," said Fiona. "Beanie's making him sound clever, but I cut the other way, toward stupid. What if he's got no idea? What if he's just a dupe?" His stomach began to quiver then, and he realized this was the most dangerous thing anyone had said.

"What makes you say that, Fifi?"

"Well, for example, after church, we trailed him straight down to Billy's—"

"You met with Undertoe, today?" said Johnny, turning to Harris. "You don't know your friends from your enemies, do you?"

Harris thought it was the truest thing said of him since the gangsters' meeting began, but he just shrugged. He didn't trust himself to speak, not knowing what they wanted him to do or be.

"Step up here, Harris. I hope you like that name—we picked it special. Sounds like some day you've had. Why don't you tell me your version of it?"

"It wasn't my usual day."

As soon as he stepped into the lamplight, Harris's size and strength were obvious, especially when he stood next to Johnny, who was lean and wiry. He was confident in his body, and that showed, masking the utter unclarity of everything else. There was so much he didn't know, including that this wasn't the usual procedure for new inductees and that many of those gathered had been skeptical of him. He also couldn't sense that they liked his reticence and approved of his brawn. He could no better read the minds of the Whyo gang than they could perceive that his power and restraint stemmed from wielding a pitchfork and working with cows, not breaking into houses or defying the odds on the street, from years of disappointment, not excitement.

After an awkward silence, Johnny laughed. "Listen, Fifi here aside, we like your style. You've done some big things lately. But you see, you're working with the wrong man. Undertoe's a user. He's been trying to get someone to do that Barnum's job for him for a while now, and he was always going to turn the guy in for it. If you hadn't been so new in town, you'd have known and stayed away. He's on the inside there, you know—he's head of security. Here's the thing: Your lapse of judgment with regard to the Undertaker aside, we like your work. We think you ought to be working for us. The money's better, and we all get along, no double-crossing, no funny stuff. This little assembly of men and women calls itself the Whyos, by the way, and if you haven't heard of us, we're proud of that. No Whyo's been convicted of so much as a petty larceny in three years. The short of it is, it's the best outfit in town, and we want you to join us. That's why the girls there brought you here."

His mind raced to find words sufficiently vague to suggest that he might be the man they thought he was, a man whose villainy this gang respected enough to conscript him by force. Perhaps there was some other man called Will Williams, he thought, or some actual associate of Undertoe they had confused with him. But it was too late now for him to be anyone else. *Not* being that man would likely prove fatal. His goal for the moment was to keep them in the dark just long enough to make another escape. Missouri maybe, this time. Or Kansas.

"So," he said slowly, "which thing . . . that I did . . ." He winced inwardly, knowing his accent was too thick, his speech awkward, his tentativeness a giveaway. What would it be like, he wondered, actually to be a man whom so many others wanted to join them? He wasn't thinking about blood and crime but acceptance and honor when he felt an odd twinge of regret that he *wasn't* a sought-after criminal mastermind. He did not allow himself to wonder what had happened to his dreams of working stone and making good the promise he knew he'd once had. He couldn't take that risk right then and survive the present encounter. Then he realized they were still waiting for him to finish his sentence. He cleared his throat. "Which thing that I did did you like?"

"*Which* thing?" said Dandy Johnny. "Which *thing*? I thought you just arrived in this town. But do tell us what other capers you've been the author of, besides doing away with a nice little hooker called Pearly Button and torching Barnum's museum?"

Barnum's. The girl. So *someone* knew who she was. He couldn't plumb the connection they'd made, but it made an absurd sort of sense that the forces of the underworld and the metropolitan police had each managed separately to arrive at the same false conclusion. And somehow, Undertoe was involved in all of it.

A *strategy*, he thought, *I need a strategy.* Dandy Johnny awaited his response with a smile of anticipation on his lips, or was it a sneer? The stableman thought of the way Johnny had slashed that cane at the girl Beatrice's face, and of all the people surrounding him.

"Is that the way you see it then, I'm a firebug? You know, I don't really like fire," the stableman said. He was lucky his figure was so imposing, smart in allowing his tongue to be slow. It made him seem tougher than he was, Harris. "Why don't you forget what I've done," he said, "and tell me what you really want. That and why you're all set on calling me *Harris.*"

Dandy Johnny laughed.

"I'd say you're a firebug, a jailbreaker and generally a ruthless bastard. I'll grant you, you got a good act, what with the down-and-out stableboy routine, the pious churchgoer. What I know is, fires and murders are up since you got into town. The cops are all in a dither, thanks to you. Maybe you think that's impressive. But you're not quite stealthy enough, Mr. Harris. Because we know about you: when you came over, under what name. We know what jobs you've done for Undertoe, and we know you did them clean and neat. But you're new around here, and it turns out you signed up with the wrong man. Undertoe doesn't work with people, he tosses them to the cops. That's what he's doing with you. And about this thing with the aliases—Williams, Koch and, uh, *addle-headed idget*—" He looked over at Fiona. "Well, a name's no good if everybody knows it. The cops ain't all that stupid, especially not when Undertoe's whispering in their ear. He's setting you up for the fall."

The stableman blinked. Going along with these people might well be a terrible error, but Harris suddenly saw it as his best chance of finding out what was going on, his only chance of clearing his name.

"All right, Harris, fine. Don't say a word. Just listen then. I'll tell you about the secret of this gang's success: it's stealth. It's the most important part of any job, as even Beanie over there knows. Anytime anybody in town does a messy job, the cops have got to work overtime to make the public happy again. They don't like it; we don't like it. It's not good for anyone. Undertoe got you to do a very messy job for him, a job that didn't make a damn bit of sense, and then he went and told the cops just where to find you. I thought you were trying to ditch him at first, with the alias; now I'm not sure what you were up to. But what I can see is that you're just starting out here and that you're working for hire. You did your part right. No one would have suspected you, if Undertoe hadn't ratted. That was clever, the way you let yourself get caught in the fire. You've got some sense in an odd way. As for what we want, well, first of all I don't like Mr. Undertoe. Nor should you. But that's the least of it. We want the best men working for us, not someone else. If you want an example of how we work, look at how the girls here snatched you off the street and brought you here: broad daylight, but no one saw it. That's the kind of work we do. Being a Whyo is lucrative, safe and considerably more amusing—what with the girls and all—than working with any other gang in town."

Geiermeier. Barnum's. Undertoe. Arson. Murder. Williams. Stealth. The stableman was amazed at all they knew and all that they had somehow misunderstood or invented. In some ways it seemed they did have the right man, then again not at all.

"Undertoe's got nothing on me," he said.

"Yeah, well, whether he does or he doesn't, he was behind the warrant they've got out on you. Did you know that? Or that he told them you were more than just a stableboy, way back on the night of the fire? He doesn't need evidence, they don't care about that. The last couple days he's been working overtime to set you up, and you didn't even see it."

"Why should I trust you?"

The man called Frank Harris was learning a lot from this conversation. He was also sweating profusely with agitation. It took an enormous effort for him not to scream, *What are you talking about?* but he didn't. He didn't even let his hand tremble. He stood rigid, and though he was close to being ill, he looked strong.

"For one thing, we just saved your ass, Mr. Harris. You were about to walk into Billy's, and the joint was full of cops with warrants for your arrest in their pockets. What's your attraction to Undertoe anyway, some German thing?"

"Maybe I wasn't going in." Had they really saved him? It all seemed so improbable.

"Aw, jeez. You know your problem? You're kind of smart but you're also kind of stupid. Because you're a foreigner. Because you don't read the damn papers." Johnny reached inside his coat, extracted a folded page torn from *Harper's* and tossed it at the stableman's chest. Harris managed to catch it without fumbling. The fire story was just below the fold in large type; his own face stared back at him. He frowned. That picture. All those names.

He found his voice. "Where'd you get this new name, *Harris,* anyway?"

"Well, you ran through quite a few of them yourself. Look, man, we fig-ure you got some skill, some experience, some interesting methods, maybe some information about Undertoe we'd like to know. We want you to join us, but then you went and got notorious. You're going to need serious cover now. *Frank Harris,* well, it's ideal. It's so common a name it would be im-possible to find all the Frank Harrises in New York. And it was a cinch to get the full set of papers, and all the vitals match. But we have to make it stick. You can't be a German with that name—or with *Williams* either—and not stand out. Let's just say we're going to make it stick. You're going to become a nice Irishman, like the rest of us."

"I can't pass as an Irishman," he said, now losing hope for a positive out-come.

"You'll be surprised. You'll hole up a while, grow you a beard. We'll get you some speaking lessons, the right clothes. You'll be a needle in an Irish haystack. Don't worry about that part, because like I said, it's our specialty. Stealth. Cover. Lying low. As long as you stay in character, no one will ever notice you. Eventually, when the cops have pinned the job on someone else and Undertoe's forgotten all about it, we'll even wait and let you settle your score with the Undertaker yourself, if you like. But the idea is you'll come into business with us. We got a couple places we could use a complete unknown, a man willing to lose his identity and start over. And that's exactly what you need to do, if you don't want to hang for the Barnum's mess." Dandy Johnny smiled. It was a delicately woven web of threats and enticements in which he was trying to snare our man, and it was a strong one.

"What if I say no?"

Johnny began to toss his cane impatiently back and forth. The stableman swallowed a mouthful of nervous saliva, but he didn't look a bit timid or panicky, standing there facing a hundred crooks. Actually, the stableman wasn't half as scared as he ought to have been, considering the circle of men that had already begun inching forward, blackjacks dropping from their sleeves, eye-gougers glinting in the lantern light, brass knuckles sprouting on their fists, lead-weighted slungshots at the ready. The Whyos were prepared to swoop upon him the moment Johnny gave the signal, but there were plenty among them who admired the stableman's sangfroid. They were thinking he was holding his own damn well in the situation, whoever he was. They were thinking he was their kind of man. The room waited for Johnny to react.

"As much as I like you, Mr. Harris, you're starting to annoy me," Johnny said. "We both know you did the girl and set the fire. Problem is, the cops know it, too. You don't seem to get it, that without us you're dead in the water. Here's something else you might not know: Until you showed up in this town, no one would take on that job. Not even the stupidest goons would trust the Undertaker. He's been looking for a firebug for months now. Whether it's because he works for Barnum or because he hates him is the only question. It was stupid to take that job in the first place, Frank, but we're still interested in you. You see, to us, you're either a problem or an asset. We'd prefer an asset, naturally. And here's the thing: It's not optional. Now that you're here, well, we're not about to let you go back out and keep on causing problems, drawing attention, helping Undertoe pull off jobs."

"I thought you said he was going to double-cross me."

"Sooner or later. Listen—you need us, we like you. Why not make it easy?"

"You've got no idea what you're talking about." He was afraid as soon as he heard how it came out—somehow gutsy when what he'd wanted was just to make it clear how wrong they were in their assessment of the situation—and he hastened to add, "I'll take you up on your offer, though. Like you say, I need you and you like me. How could I not?"

How could he not? The stableman looked out at the army of dim forms, each one ready to murder him if given the slightest signal. He had no idea how to torch a building to make it burn fast. Were they going to require that of him? What was going to happen when they figured him out? He looked at the girl Beatrice across the dim space and saw a queer, skeptical expression on her face. She knew what was going on, he thought. She understood who he was in a way her boss did not. It wasn't going to last long, this reprieve. But for now Dandy Johnny was smiling.

"All right then," he said. "That's good. Now let me introduce you to the Whyos, the unofficial rulers of the city. And our lovely sisters and partners in all things, the Why Nots."

There was a profound silence, perhaps as long as a minute, before the great brewing hall began to echo with a quiet, sinuous whispering, half wind, half whistle. It was not quite a word or a call. They did not simply say the name of their gang, *Whyo*, over and over till the word became a chant. Some of them sang it and some of them seemed just to breathe those two rhythmic syllables: the initial wind of the interrogative—*why*—and the slightly elongated sigh of surprise—*oh*—or was it a sign of despair?

Why-o. The many baritone and tenor voices were set off by the counterpoint of the sopranos and mezzos in the corner. Just as he was beginning to understand that there was some sort of statement being made, an utterance in a language that suggested the existence of an entire hidden world, the sound faded and stopped. But he could still hear it in his head, and he realized it had been there for some time already. It was the eerie voice of the streets, a noise he'd been vaguely aware of and had variously attributed to the whine of swiftly spinning carriage spokes, the rustling of dusty acacia leaves or the distant screech of ferries sliding up against sodden pilings, the background noise that had defined the feel of the metropolis for him. Who were they really, he wondered, the Whyos? What were they saying? Was there any way he could escape them, when they figured out he wasn't the man they thought? And then again, who was he?

12.

ABOUT FACE

Johnny fondled the silver-headed, ruby-eyed serpent that was the knob of his cane and mentally tallied the voices, each of which was distinct and identifiable to him. He noted the degree of enthusiasm and also listened for silences—abstentions. As far as he could tell, every last man and woman, boy and girl, had joined in the welcoming of Frank Harris. He smiled. Of course, he didn't need the gang's assent to bring a new man in. Johnny could make or murder a man at will. He could do anything he damn well liked, and no question would ever be asked. But it was good politics, this voice vote. Allowing the gang members to make their wishes known in a sort of plebiscite from time to time was an effective means of shoring up their loyalty.

He whistled, bringing the gang to silence, and dismissed them. They left the brewery quietly, in twos and threes, by several exits. Ten minutes later, there were just four of them left standing in the center of the room: Johnny, Beatrice, Frank Harris and Johnny's henchman, Piker Ryan.

For Johnny's purposes, Frank Harris could have been anyone. Frank Harris was but a cog in a scheme. And if it worked, it would enrich them all beyond their wildest imaginations. Or really, Harris could have been *almost* anyone, but not quite. There were a few criteria, the most important of which was that the cog be an outsider, not a Whyo, but also not just an average citizen, not just a dupe—he had to have a fairly hardened character, a stomach for crime, and to be tough enough to win the approval of the other Whyos. So far, Johnny was pleased with what he'd seen. He'd been looking for a man like Harris for some time—perhaps about as long as Undertoe had been looking for a man to do *his* dirty work—and then Williams turned up, thanks to Beanie. The Undertoe connection was an added twist—a bit of a complication on the one hand, an added incentive on the other—for there was no man in New York whom Johnny loathed the way he loathed Luther Undertoe.

But Undertoe aside, the job Johnny wanted Harris for had been long in the planning, and it was to be the biggest heist the Whyos had ever pulled. Johnny had done well for the Whyos, enriching himself and all of them far beyond expectations, maintaining exquisite control and keeping peace among his people. The most important factor in this success was Johnny's expansion of the original whyo, a song that served the gang as a war cry, a cheer and a secret handshake, into an elaborate language. To be fair, the whole idea of expanding the whyo had been started by his predecessor, Googy Corcoran, may he rest in peace.

Johnny remembered the feeling of twisting the knife and levering it up through Corcoran's kidney, toward his lungs. He'd used that little jab and twist any number of times, but it had never felt as good as on the day he delivered it to his boss and ascended to power himself. Corcoran blew bloody foam as he whispered, "You, too, Johnny?" Then he fell to his knees, and Johnny gave him a couple of kicks before walking away. It was over. It may have been Corcoran who first began to introduce more complex sounds as signals with varying meanings, but when Johnny took over, the vocabulary contained only six or seven terms, including an owl hoot that meant *We meet up at the rendezvous in a quarter hour* and a rutting-cat howl that warned *Abort the plan, someone's watching.*

Under Johnny's reign, whyoing became a fully articulate, sophisticated means of covert communication, and with that the gang's power grew exponentially. Communication was everything. Johnny had developed a secret weapon that was far more powerful than anything in the gang's conventional arsenal of pistols, knives and blackjacks. They could communicate with one another when pulling jobs; they could post lookouts who were able to deliver detailed situation reports without blowing cover. They also found ways of distracting and misleading witnesses. Every job they pulled was a winner suddenly, and no one ever got arrested. Dandy Johnny was a gifted singer, as were many of the boys in the original Whyos. They'd all sung in the Newsboys' Choir together, back when they were kids, and Johnny's mother had been choirmistress. So it was natural to introduce elements of music into the language when they wanted to be able to say more. For a certain job, singing "Danny Boy" in C while strolling north on Mulberry Street might mean *Everyone's in place, as soon as the roundsman turns the corner, we strike*. Whereas doing it in G minor might mean *Go to plan two, the watchman is still awake*. The only hitch was, it took some musical talent to speak this new language, and so certain Whyos—guys with tin ears or no rhythm or an inability to carry a tune—were phased out. Dandy Johnny was widely known to have perfect pitch, a keen ear and great vocal technique. His ability to trace the warbling trajectories of an individual voice back to its owner was uncanny. Standing at Broadway and Houston, he could discern if a man was sending his signal from the corner of Howard and Crosby or Howard and Elm. It was the inverse of ventriloquism, an art at which the Whyos also gradually became adept, as they saw its potential for distracting witnesses, policemen and the like. By this time, some five years since Johnny had taken over, the universe of whyo terms included every sort of sound you could imagine, from creaks and sighs and whistles to songs and subvocal tones. And as a result, the Whyos and the Why Nots could easily pass information among them without anyone else even knowing they were talking at all. That was what was going on when they whyoed their approval of Frank Harris. Of course, they had no idea that Harris hadn't passed the vocal test, no idea that Johnny had a different sort of role in mind for him.

Nor did Frank Harris have the slightest idea what the whyoing had meant. He'd heard the eerie, uncanny sound. He'd glanced up at the one called Beanie as it was dying down and seen that she was staring at him coldly, taking his measure. He felt something prickle through him then, from his scalp to his groin. His chest broke out in a clammy sweat. She was at once beautiful and nasty, alluring and awful. Indeed, he found the whole situation frightening. But he didn't begin to suspect what he was messing with when he decided to speak, to blurt out the truth, now that it was just the four of them: "I'm afraid," he said, "that you waste your welcome."

What he struggled to say next, in his broken English, was: You're probably going to kill me, but I can't go along with this. You've got the wrong man and the wrong story. I'm not working with Mr. Undertoe. I didn't do the fire. I didn't kill the girl. I almost died in that fire. I'm not the one you want. Maybe Undertoe is, but I don't know anything about it. I just happened to be there, to get mixed up in it somehow. I'm not the master criminal you think I am, and frankly, I wouldn't join you even if I were.

The bottom of Beatrice's stomach seemed to open up, to drop and keep on dropping. She'd guessed something was funny about him, that his seeming wile was rooted in luck, not strategy, but he'd been playing along up till now. What in the world did it mean that the man had just come out with it? Was *this* a strategy? It was very strange, but even stranger was the powerful impulse she suddenly felt toward the man she had dubbed Frank Harris: the impulse to protect him. For reasons not entirely clear to her, she stepped between Harris and Johnny. She was not at all sure what she was about to do.

"You think we ought to kill you, eh?" said Dandy Johnny with no expression on his face as he watched Beanie reposition herself. "Why does that strike me as odd?"

Piker Ryan was smiling. "No problem, Johnny, I'll take care of it," he said, but Johnny put his arm out.

The stableman felt he heard that distant whispering again, the way it sounded when they first entered the brewery but quieter. He almost thought he made out the words *Kill him, kill him.* After all, he'd invited them to do just that. Was he mad? Was it the wind? What did the real wind sound like? he wondered, and he found he wasn't sure anymore. He wished he'd been a little less impressed by the spectacle they'd just offered him, their strange method of communication, the seriousness of their malice. Some of their information was bad, yes, but that made them only more dangerous.

Of course, Harris didn't know what was going on in the minds of the Whyos standing around him. How could he have guessed that Beatrice wanted but feared to believe him, while Johnny suspected a bluff and Piker

Ryan, being rather simple of mind, took his statement at exactly face value? How could he have known that his denial suggested a crucial Whyo agent had passed on false information? How could he know how much Johnny had at stake? For the boss could not be seen to have been duped—especially not by Undertoe. Johnny didn't want to believe it was possible, and so he was thinking, *What's this guy trying to pull? What could he have to gain from leading us astray?* Beatrice was wondering if the Jimster was in on it. Could he be cleverer than they'd thought, not a double but a triple agent? He certainly had gotten down to Billy's quickly. And as for Piker Ryan, he was just feeling that old itch in his fingers, waiting for Johnny to give him the signal.

Meantime, the face Frank Harris presented them was blank. He had been honest. He had nothing to hide anymore but his fear, and that he managed to conceal. He stood there, determined not to blink, and waited for something to happen, preferably not his own sudden loss of consciousness, which he imagined as a dull, spreading pain at the back of his skull, a blow to the back of the knees, his legs collapsing. He was acutely aware of Piker Ryan, the way his fingers undulated, unable to control their eagerness. He thought of all he would haved liked to become in his life, the man his mother had expected him to be when he grew up: someone good, someone kind, who cared about people and was cared about, someone who had done his best, whatever that might be. He hadn't managed any of that yet. It was too soon to die, but that's the way death was, killing his mother before she could raise him, his sister before she had lived. He asked himself if he would really rather die than survive by joining forces with a gang of thieves, but the question seemed wider than the sky. He couldn't answer it.

"So tell us who you really are, then," Johnny said at last.

It was almost funny, that request, it was so impossible. But Harris went ahead and gave them an accurate account of his history since landing in New York. Afterward, Johnny was still unclear on what to believe, but he decided that even if he accepted the story, he was interested in a man who claimed to be a stonecutter-turned-stableman, nothing more, and yet somehow had the guts to hold his own in front of the assembled Whyos. If it was a ruse of some sort, it was masterful. The man had a certain tact, an odd subtlety to the way he operated, and very good timing. He might not be quite fish or fowl, but Johnny was thinking he'd make an excellent man for the job at hand.

"Piker," he said. "Miss O'Gamhna. This here fellow presents us with a problem—a couple of problems. The gang liked him, but now, if we believe him, it looks like he's not quite the man we thought. I could just let Piker kill him, but how do we explain that to the others tomorrow? I don't like that scenario too much. He's kind of unpredictable, but that can be an asset. Then there's the fact that it looks like the Undertaker's up to something, and one way or other our friend here figures into it. Not to mention he's just the right man for a job I've been planning. I don't know why, but I still like him. The way I see it, it's all good. Only problem is, I think he just said he wouldn't work with us." Dandy Johnny looked at him. "Is that true, or are you willing to live, Mr. Harris?"

Harris swallowed. Johnny switched his cane to his left hand.

"I'll do what you want," Harris said.

The boss of the Whyos extended his right hand, and the man now named Frank Harris shook it.

"Beanie," said Johnny then, "is your cousin still working on the new east side sewers?"

"No, he's laying pavement."

"That's all right. That's fine. You'll be bringing Frank Harris home with you tonight. The first stage is going to be about getting him under cover."

"Johnny, they'll kick me out again if they know I'm still with the gang."

"You can tell your aunt and cousins our friend got mixed up with some bad men in Five Points, but now he wants out, wants to go clean, just like you did, and you're trying to help him. That'll explain why you've got to keep him indoors for a month or so—just till he's grown a beard and got control of that accent. I want him to come off like an Irishman. After that, I want you to see to it Liam finds him a post wherever Liam's working. I'd like to get him a bit of a job history, references and what, before we put him on the sewer job."

She wasn't in on what the sewer job was, and she wasn't happy about this assignment. "Didn't I do enough, finding him for you? Why don't you send him home with Fifi?"

"I'm sending him home with you, so shut the fuck up about it."

"What about the accent, how's that going to work?"

"You're going to coach him."

She rolled her eyes—so it wasn't a real assignment, it was being a governess.

"And now, Harris," said Dandy Johnny. "Mr. Harris?"

Harris didn't respond.

"*Harris!*" Johnny jabbed him with his cane.

"What?" said the stableman, as if he hadn't heard. He'd been asking himself if he'd just sold his soul, and anyway Harris wasn't his name.

"First thing you've got to do is learn your Goddamn name. You're going to have it easy for a while, work on your accent, your cover. But there's something I want you to remember: You agreed to something just now. You're one of us. You don't move on, you don't quit your little job that Beanie's cousin's going to get you. You don't decide to find your own place to live. You don't use your old name, ever. In fact, you don't do a damn thing unless the Whyos are in on it. Not next year, not ten years from now, never. It's for life. It's got its pleasures as well as its responsibilities, just like a marriage, and just like marriage there's no getting out. So congratulations. You're a lucky man, Frank Harris, to be marrying the Whyos. Don't ever think you're not. Your chances of longevity just went up."

And that was how Will got an alias that stuck and soon thereafter a job that was legit, and on a building crew, too. He saved himself, and he slipped through the fingers of Luther Undertoe, from whose sights he seemed simply to vanish (precipitating a serious downturn in Undertoe's fortunes, which were closely linked to satisfying Sergeant Jones). He did it by indenturing himself to a gang of murderers. They would be calling on his services to do some ill deed before long, he knew. But for now, it seemed like the best of his options. Weirdly lucky, even.

That very night, he was thrust into the middle of a family whose members lived on top of one another in a three-room tenement apartment: There was Beatrice, there was her Aunt Penelope, and then there were her cousin Liam, his wife, Colleen, and their children. It didn't take long for Harris to see how much he'd missed being a part of a family all these years. For though the O'Gamhnas weren't his family, they took him in as if they were. They ate up the story Beanie told them, of a man determined to re-deem himself, and they pledged to help.

It was every bit as crowded at the O'Gamhnas' as it had been at the flop on Mott Street. They dragged out the mattresses and blankets from the so-called bedroom at night and spread them over every inch of the front room's floor—only old Aunt Penelope actually slept in the tiny bedroom, on a real bed—but in all other ways it was different from Wah Kee's. It was clean, for example. And strangely enough, given that he'd just joined up with a gang of thieves, he was now considerably less likely to be stabbed, robbed or poisoned as he slept.

Frank Harris's first task was to learn to speak the O'Gamhnas' brand of Irish-American English. Amidst all the lies, Beatrice told her family some truths: that he was German and in trouble with both a gang and the law and that their scheme was to have him masquerade as an Irishman to get a clean start. Harris told some truths, too: that he'd apprenticed as a stoneworker on a cathedral and that what he really wanted was to go back to working on buildings. Liam immediately promised to find him a post as soon as he was ready to face the world as an Irishman. "It's not a cathedral, but it's con-struction, and it's a start." Harris could have wept—either for gratitude or for remorse at the way he was deceiving these good people—but he just smiled and said he couldn't wait, which was true.

Every member of the family was eager to help him speed along toward that day by coaching him on his English. Even the baby of the family, a four-year-old boy, felt free to quiz him, criticize him and correct him at any time of day. Since he never left the apartment except in the dark of night to use the privy, the O'Gamhnas were his only human contact, and though it was exhausting, he made faster progress than he would have imagined. Colleen and Mrs. O'Gamhna sat home all day by the window at their sewing—they did shirtsleeves for Bloomingdale's—chatting with him, yelling at the children and policing his grammar. In the evenings, when he came home from work, Liam was concerned with teaching Harris the vo-cabulary of the building trades so he wouldn't falter when he started work. Beatrice, whom the family thought was making her pennies with her hot corn alone, was particularly obsessed with eradicating his accent.

As for Dandy Johnny, Piker Ryan and the other Whyos, Harris didn't see or hear from them, and Beatrice never mentioned them nor said anything about teaching him the queer Whyo language. English was his subject. He helped with the household chores when the women would let him, but mostly he just studied and dreamt of the job on the paving crew, of chiseling out mortise joints or shallow-grooved rain gutters in bluestone sidewalk slabs. At night, he read aloud from the newspapers Beanie brought home, practicing elocution and picking up vocabulary.

Afterwards, he sat with her and she had him write out vocabulary words on the boys' slate, which had obviously been hers, since BEANIE O'G. had been crudely carved into its wooden frame. His handwriting was a sore spot. It was so obviously German, she chided, and badgered him to change it. He knew from his experience at the hiring office that she was right, but he didn't want to give it up and rarely practiced the cursive forms she told him to. In a way, though, it wasn't so much his connection to his past he wanted to keep, it was her attention. Something strange was happening to him during their lessons. He found he wanted her to put her hand over his and force his hand to make the letters curve and slide across the slate. He could feel the warmth of her body, smell the oils of her hair and the salts of her skin. They laughed at the abominable handwriting that resulted from their joint efforts, him fighting her guidance, and time and again he promised he would try harder, do his homework, learn.

It wasn't long before he understood what it was that was happening when she drilled and quizzed him, and that it wasn't so strange. The strange part was that the girl he couldn't stop thinking about was a secret gangster, that their first meeting had begun with a blow to his head and that he knew one day soon she would stop being a girl who curled her fingers over his and drew *F* after *F* after *H*—for she was adamant that at least his signature must look appropriate to an Irishman. One day soon, she would give him his orders from Johnny, and he would not have the choice to say no. They were not destined to be sweethearts but murderers. But all that seemed awfully implausible, awfully far off, and each evening he strove to please and impress her as he read and conjugated and displayed his growing knowledge of everything from idioms to prepositions. He was gratified beyond words when he managed to make her laugh. As his beard filled in, prickly at first, then gradually thickening and lengthening, he began to imagine he might never have to fulfill the commitment he'd made, might get away scot-free.

The first violence in his new life came quite unexpectedly one Sunday afternoon, some five weeks into his tenure at the tenement, when everyone else was out enjoying the unseasonably warm spring air—even Aunt Penelope, for once. Harris had been gazing out the window, seriously considering a violation of his house arrest, when someone began pounding on the door. As a rule, he didn't answer the door. He was in hiding, after all. The clamor continued for some minutes, then suddenly stopped. He heard a quiet rattle that for all the world sounded like someone was sliding the key into its hole. But who on Earth would have made such a racket if possessed of a key? The lock turned over with a *click thunk*. He was imagining Undertoe, the police, Piker Ryan, even Dandy Johnny when he picked up the chair, positioned himself behind the door, and prepared to strike. Luckily or not, depending on who you were, the chair's leg was loose, the adjacent rung popped free under the pressure of the man's skull, and the leg clattered to the floor. The intruder fell with it, but not for long. The blow had been glancing, no more.

The first thing Leon O'Gamhna saw of the man his family called Frank Harris was the throbbing blue halo around him. He rose up and launched himself at Harris, but none too lethally. He was already half in the bag, thanks to his morning cup of a clear liquid that surely wasn't water and wasn't quite rum but something harsher and meaner. It was his thirst that had gotten him kicked out of the family apartment years before, but he came back from time to time, when he was hungry or broke. The drunkard's left hook met the shut-in's right eye. Harris was to develop a plum of a shiner by the afternoon, but being bigger, younger and entirely sober, he managed to return the favor twofold. He imagined he was fighting for his life, though his assailant had struck neither first nor very hard. He was attempting to do away with Beatrice's uncle for once and for all when she came in.

"Jesus Christus, what's going on? Harris? Harris! Quit punching him. That's my Uncle Leon. He may be a drunk, but I'd really rather you let him live."

"This is your uncle?"

"Hello, Uncle Leon, you old dipsomaniac. You need something?"

"Dipso-*what*?" said Harris.

Leon was sitting on the floor looking confused.

"*Dipsomaniac.* That's *d-i-p-s-o-m-a-n-i-a-c*, meaning drunk, alcoholic or enemy of the Ladies Temperance League. Aunt Penny won't let him in the house anymore, but I never begrudge him a pork chop or a couple dollars. After all, he's my blood, not hers. What happened anyway, did he sock you?"

As Beanie talked, Leon O'Gamhna had gotten himself back on his feet. Now he reeled back and clobbered Frank Harris with the chair leg, and Harris launched into him again. Beatrice pushed the men apart and gave her uncle a handful of money and half a loaf of bread, at which point he scuttled off, cursing and wiping a trickle of blood from under his nose.

Leon hadn't remotely resembled a Whyo, a cop or Undertoe, and he hadn't done anything more threatening than unlock the door, but Harris had attacked him. He was ashamed of it, but he had felt a thrill when his fist met the old man's nose. The question thus arose in Harris's mind whether he, Harris, really was a thug, whether perhaps he genuinely belonged in a gang, rather than, say, in a nice home with a family and a proper job. Maybe he had found his level. After all, no one is born a killer, and even a bloodthirsty hit man like Johnny's henchman Piker Ryan had probably once been just a bully. He imagined a frustrated, reckless, down-and-out Irish kid who happened to learn a certain lesson along the way: Might pays. Was he any different or better? Apparently not. He'd made his pact with the Whyos to save his own skin. He'd been willing to strike first and find out later why. Soon, he'd be working for the gang, and he knew they would ask him to kill. Was he capable of it? For the first time, he realized he might be. Wordlessly, reeling with horror at himself, he turned his back on Beatrice, the broken chair, the disarray that he had caused, and left the apartment.

"Harris," she called, "stop right there," but he didn't. When he reached the ground level, there were only two ways to go: out into the courtyard to the privies or out the front door. He hadn't been outside since the day of the meeting, and he wanted nothing more than to escape into the wide world.

At that moment, he didn't particularly care that to do so would certainly lead to his arrest and eventual hanging, if not some quicker fate at the hands of an angry gang member. The manhunt was still on, and Beanie showed him articles from the paper every few days, lest he forget it. From time to time, they even reprinted his likeness. He thought of Beatrice—his jailer, but also increasingly his friend. He wanted to escape, but he didn't want to escape *her*, not exactly. Not seeing her would be a disaster, he realized. He had been running above all from himself, from the beating he'd just given her uncle, and that was simply futile. No, what he needed now was to explain himself.

He was just about to turn and go back upstairs when footsteps approached from the staircase above. He ducked into a reeking privy to hide himself—the family had kept his presence in their apartment a secret, after all—but the footsteps he'd heard had been Beatrice. She could imagine his frustration, being cooped up so long, and wanted to talk with him. Above all, she wanted to make sure he didn't do something foolish. When she found the hall empty, she shouted toward the privies, "Are you in there?"

He wanted to talk to her, desperately, but he couldn't bring himself to call back to her from the humiliating vantage of the privy. When he failed to respond, she cursed and ran out into the street.

Harris returned to the apartment to find the chair still in pieces on the floor. He dug Liam's wide canvas bag of tools out from the closet and selected the equipment he would need to make the necessary repairs. He mixed a paste of powdered glue and water, dabbed it on the ends of the rungs and gently pounded them into place. Then he strapped the legs and the seat together with a length of rope and left it upside down to dry under compression. It was satisfying to repair a thing, he thought, even if it was his own temper that had broken it. It would be stronger than before, once it had set. He would apologize to Beatrice and the others. He told himself it was possible to make a wrong thing right. As he worked, he felt the same pleasure he always did when he was building something, whether great or small, and he began to think about the job that Liam had arranged for him.

That evening, when Beatrice returned from whatever crimes were her day's work, he avoided meeting her eye, but she wouldn't let him avoid what had happened.

"You didn't go out onto the street, did you?" she asked.

"No, I was down in the privy." She frowned and then filled the family in on the afternoon's events. Amazingly, no one seemed to think ill of him at all for attacking old Leon; in fact, they found it funny that Harris might think Leon a threat. Colleen even said she was grateful to Harris for preventing Leon from raiding the pantry.

"You've been pent up too long, Harris," said Beatrice. "Maybe it's time to introduce your new self to the world."

"They're hiring laborers on my crew, nothing better at the moment, but there's a job," said Liam.

Frank Harris nodded. He was eager to get outside and on with life, but he was also nervous. What if he wasn't convincing as an Irishman? What would people think? What were the chances that someone would peg him as the suspect in the Barnum's case? It was unsettling.

That night, late, Beatrice quietly led Harris out of the building for the first time in well over a month. He imagined taking her hand and telling her they must both run away, they must never go back to that apartment or the Whyos, they could make it on their own, but the world seemed wide and overwhelming, and he was nervous about who he was. He didn't do it. Instead, he let her take him to a dark corner bar where she reached under a bench and found a cheap suitcase that Fiona had deposited there earlier in the day. They had a silent pint and then made their way back to the building, this time making plenty of noise and idle conversation.

"And what about Granny Shea?" she asked, and he went along with it: He said she died the year before but that the funeral was lovely. By the time they'd made it to the O'Gamhnas' landing, she'd also mentioned loudly that Liam would probably be able to get him a job.

To a casual observer or a tenant overhearing the conversation through the walls, it was uncontroversial: another cousin newly arrived. Liam was waiting for them with a basin of hot water, a razor and a pair of shears, and as soon as he'd loudly welcomed Cousin Frank to New York, he sat him down and undertook to reinvent his coiffure. He cropped the hair atop his head very short. He went to work on the sideburns and made a stiff brush of what had become a ragged moustache. The beard itself he trimmed and brought to a blunt curve at the bottom. Finally, he shaved Harris's cheeks and lower lip, leaving a healthy fringe of beard to cover his lower jaw. When he was finished, it was hard to recognize Will Williams in the face of Frank Harris. His forehead was freshly exposed, which made his pate seem to rise and his whole head change shape. He was no potato head, no scruffy German stableman, not anymore—he was a respectable Irish workingman, one of hundreds of thousands.

Frank Harris felt supremely self-conscious as he stared into the little hand mirror Beatrice produced from a dresser drawer. Never in his life had he scrutinized himself this hard. He thought about that morning, what he'd done, and he thought about tomorrow: strolling out the front door of the building in daylight for the first time in over a month, going to work beside Liam, laboring honestly to make the street smooth and even. Before long, he thought, with any luck, he might actually be cutting stone, even if it was only Belgian paving blocks. Whatever the Whyos threw at him later, he would figure out a way to deal with it. He wouldn't let himself do evil at the gang's behest. He wouldn't let them own him. He had not crossed over to the other side, not irrevocably, not yet. And anyway, that was all going to happen later. Tomorrow, at least, it would just be him and the world. Tomorrow, at least, was likely to be a good day.

He could feel Beatrice's eyes on him as he looked into the mirror, and he wondered what she thought of his new face. He looked over and saw her approval. What kind of smile was that, he wondered, a Why Not's or a woman's?

She reached out and touched his newly shaven cheek. "Very nice," she said, and his face, too, broke from its usual impassive mask into a smile. Then Liam started quietly laughing, then Beatrice, finally Harris.

"Well," said Beatrice. "So *that's* what Frank Harris looks like."

13.

SAND, GRAVEL, TAR

Sleeping in the same room as Beatrice had never been so difficult. It didn't matter how many mattresses away she was; he could still hear her breathing. He could glimpse the jut of her shoulder when she thrashed and turned and lay on her side. Was she awake, too? Harris lay on his mattress, fully alert in the dimness, exquisitely aware of the blood traveling through his veins all night. It wasn't till she rose around dawn and went into the kitchen with Colleen that he finally drifted off. The church bells were tolling six. When he woke again, everyone was up, and the boys were putting away the mattresses and tugging off his covers.

"Get up, Frank, you slug, aren't you going to work today?"

Harris was queasy with excitement and exhaustion, anxiety and lust, as he dressed and then took his turn at the washstand that stood before the air-shaft window. Harris's rank was fifth and last among the adults of the house-hold. Family custom permitted each person to add a bit of boiling water to the other's dregs, and no one got a fresh bowl but Aunt Penelope—it was work to haul water and cost money to heat it. Harris tipped a bit of the old gray water out the window, then splashed in just enough from the kettle to raise a thin steam from the basin. Looking out across the air shaft, he glimpsed a vaguely familiar face in the opposite window. He raised Liam's soapy shaving brush to his cheek and saw, of course, that the man in the window did likewise. He barely recognized himself, which was good, but would his disguise stand up to the scrutiny of someone who already knew him? How long before chance put him in Luther Undertoe's way, or that of someone else who remembered his face and his alleged crimes?

He took the strop to Liam's razor a couple of times and then dipped the blade in the murky basin. He'd soon be able to afford his own shaving kit again, but for now everything was still borrowed, including his name and his face. Harris had always been clean shaven before. It was more difficult to shave around the edges of his new beard than it once had been to strip his whole chin clean. He was careless with the angle of his blade as he navigated the boundaries of his new sideburns, and a thin trickle of red ran along the edge of his cheek. Lacking a styptic, he pressed the cut with wet fingers till it quit oozing. When he came into the kitchen, where the others already sat hunched over their oats, Beatrice looked up and started.

"It's just a nick," he said, reaching for his face, realizing it must still be bleeding.

"What? No—it's just I'm not used to . . ."

"Jesus, Mary and Joseph," said Colleen, standing up from her chair unexpectedly and knocking it over behind her. "It's like there's a stranger—*another* stranger—in the house."

Harris didn't quite know what to make of their reaction, and yet it was a good sign. It didn't hurt that Beatrice was smiling at him so widely again.

"No, just me—Frank Harris."

All through breakfast, Beatrice was looking at him, but differently. She was examining the man she had made, or remade, to see how good he was. She saw something in his jaw that had been hidden while his full beard grew in: strength. His newly exposed forehead looked wide, honest; the expression in his eyes seemed less obvious, more intelligent. His accent now was perfect. He was perfect. She hadn't had much hope for this project to succeed, but Harris had proven to be a good student. And now it seemed he was outwardly as well as inwardly malleable. Maybe they *could* pull this off.

If they did, there was a large bonus in it for her, which she thought would be enough, with all the money she'd been saving, to pay for Padric's passage over. Once he was there, she would devote the extra money she made with the Why Nots to sending Padric to a good Catholic high school. She wouldn't even let him know about the Whyos and Why Nots, would keep it from him the same as she did with Penelope and Colleen, but for different reasons: She didn't want him even to consider as an option the life she led. But first she had to make sure that Frank Harris paid off.

"Good luck," she said, and kissed him on the cheek. The cheek was surprisingly warm and smooth.

A short time later, Beatrice's project trailed out the door after Liam, fortified by oatmeal and black tea and that kiss, feeling close to happy. When he'd first been confined to the O'Gamhnas' building, it was the last, bitterest part of winter. The ground had been like iron, and the snow and ice of the blizzard only partly scraped away. For weeks and weeks, he'd monitored the melting and then the budding and leafing out of the scraggly trees that reached over the privy-yard wall from the lot next door. He'd felt the weather warming, but that had not prepared him for what he experienced walking out the front door of the tenement. Window watching is a world away from living life. The day was clear and dry and mild. When he stepped onto the packed-earth sidewalk in front of the O'Gamhnas' building, Frank Harris felt the ground give ever so slightly under his foot. He smelled dirt.

It would have been a joyous morning, if not for the twinge of dread, the specter of his being indoctrinated into the gang through some gruesome murder, the forethought of the noose that would take his weight if his cover failed. How long would the Whyos let him be a paver before they demanded payment in blood? The thought of Beatrice aroused and confused him. In her presence, he was hopeful and happy; away from her, he recalled that she worked for the gang. Now he wondered why he'd even bothered to leave his home country if all he could become in the New World was a manual laborer or a criminal. He could have managed that ambition well enough in the old. But then he saw the street, teeming with people, and smelled the air, sour, sooty and vibrant, and he put dread aside. For now, there was this day, this new job.

It was a fifteen-minute walk to the construction site, and though the territory was familiar, Harris saw the city in a new way. He was gazing not just at the buildings and carriages and people but for the first time at the pavement: It looked ancient and was in awful condition, muddy, rutted and strewn with debris of every sort. Under the copious garbage, most of Manhattan's streets were not so much paved as pockmarked with knobby, pothole-begetting ostrich-egg cobblestones. Nightmares of mud. They were ankle twisters, hoof and carriage-wheel devourers. This was the kind of road they would be tearing up and replacing with seamless rivers of smooth, flat stones. Looking at the mess, Harris felt excited. There was plenty of work to do. He could hardly believe there were such things as Whyos or Undertoes or gallows in the city at all—everything seemed hopeful and wonderful to him. He felt free.

Harris was, of course, anything but free. There were Whyos everywhere, watching him. They were making sure he didn't run, blow his cover or otherwise screw up a plan that no Whyo but Johnny knew the details of, except that it required an outsider, a man who was with them in spirit but didn't know their language, their culture, their enemies or their friends. For the last six weeks, ever since the meeting at Geoghegan's, every Whyo and Why Not had been aware of Harris as some sort of special agent-in-training. They knew Beanie, not Johnny, was working with him. They had heard that he was what they called *incommunicado*, meaning he couldn't whyo. They also knew Undertoe still had his net out and was itching to help the cops close the case that the Whyos had foiled when they took Harris in.

The Why Not assigned to watch him that morning was Maggie the Dove, a onetime girlfriend of Dandy Johnny's. There was a time when people said Johnny was going to make Maggie his First Girl—the Whyo version of the boss's wife, which would have made her the leader of the Why Nots—but Johnny had thrown her over one day, without any explanation, and since then had never kept exclusively to just one girlfriend. The girls kept on reporting directly to Johnny, and Maggie went back to being just another Why Not, though many of the younger girls still looked up to her. Her cover that morning was pretty standard: She was hawking corn to the road workers as well as the pedestrians on Varick Street. For Maggie, it was a bit of a vacation; her assignment was just to make sure Harris didn't run off and to keep her eyes peeled for any sign of Undertoe and his lackeys. If anyone troublesome did happen along, she would make a subtle point of distracting them and keep them at the greatest possible distance from Harris. If someone seemed to recognize him, she would raise an alarm. It was his first day, after all, and the masquerade had yet to be tested.

Beanie had instructed Harris to speak little or not at all till he got his bearings, despite his rather impressive new brogue. There was the definite possibility that his nerve would fail him when he was put on the spot, and his rolling Irish *r*s would come out in a German growl.

As for Luther Undertoe, that day he had three newsboys drawing a per diem, as usual. They prowled the city for opportunities and information, ran his errands and received a commission when they brought in substantial gains. One of the various tasks they were charged with was keeping a lookout for the man last known as either Geiermeier or Williams. It was obvious to everyone that if he was still in town at all, he would by now be going by a new alias, and so each of them carried a picture of Williams's face, ripped from one of the illustrateds, wadded up in a pocket. The Jimster was one of them, but neither he nor the others were spending much energy on the Williams case anymore. The trail was stone cold, they all felt, the man long gone to the Western Territories, which wasn't a half-bad idea, the Jimster decided. That's what he'd have liked to do, if he could only have figured out how. In the meantime, he was grubbing for Undertoe's nickels and taking Dandy Johnny's dimes—mostly for information about Undertoe—and hoping against hope that he'd someday bump into that twenty-dollar bill personified, George the Torch.

There were perhaps two dozen workmen gathered on the corner when Liam and Harris arrived and twice as many by the time work began. Wagons loaded with granite paving stones, sand, gravel and kegs of tar were arranged in such a way that traffic was impeded at either end of a two-block stretch as well as the cross street. The day began with a roll call, and just as Liam had promised, Frank Harris's name was on the list. There were pavers, chuckers, rammers and laborers. Harris signed on as a laborer, the lowest level, at the rate of $1.25 per day. The first order of business was clearing the old road surface of the copious refuse, and he joined a gang of men wielding shovels and brooms. The warm-weather equivalent of shoveling snow was considerably less pleasant, it turned out. An hour and two cartloads of fetid debris later, they switched to pickaxes and had at the cobbles.

How many feet and hooves and wheels had traversed those backbreaking round stones, and who had laid them down originally and when? Harris could hardly begin to imagine the stories, the lives, but he realized the city was older, far older, than he'd thought. His job was to chop and hack away at the past, and he embraced it, sweating freely, even when his hands began to blister. He had done all he could to jettison his own history, after all. The round, cracked stones that were loosed from the hard dirt by his pickax had seen all manner of things: black men strung up on lantern posts in the Draft Riots, soldiers slouching off to war. They'd looked up the skirt of every lady who trod on them, and they'd tripped innumerable boys. They'd paved the way for life to go on in that corner of the metropolis for a good long time: five generations, a hundred years. They were badly uneven, yes, but still remarkably firmly cemented in by the mud after all that time. Again and again, Harris swung his ax and felt the reverberation to his marrow. Then, just when he felt his bones would break if his pick landed wrong again, he was switched to the gang that was hauling off the rubble, which was even harder work. It was remarkable how many cobblestones it had taken to pave that street, how fast the five-pound stones added up to tons. Replacing the cobbles would be square granite stones, Belgian blocks, and once they were laid you'd be able to roll a marble straight from Dominick to Broome or even Watts, if your aim was true. It wasn't a cathedral, no, but Harris felt all right about the job. It was progress. It was something worth building, he thought. It also kept his mind off Beatrice.

They had a contract on a ten-block area and just a month to complete the job, which meant the work went on at a furious pace. Behind the common laborers came the graders, to establish the correct pitch of the road. They raked, scraped, filled and raked again, contouring the street so it arced slightly toward the curbs. Their foreman brought out his level, took readings, demanded a correction or two and finally gave the work his nod. Whenever Harris turned back to look at the newly graded terrain behind him, he found himself amazed. It looked like a plowed field, ready for seed, but on the contrary: The streets they worked on would be covered with stone in such a way that nothing would grow there ever again. But first the properly contoured subgrade had to be compacted with the ten-ton roller.

"What's your name?" one of the graders asked him, and he was flattered at first. Someone wanted to know him.

"Frank Harris," he said, just right, just Irish enough.

Then he learned how his name would be used: "All right then, Harris—I need twenty bags of sand on the double, before that roller gets here!" It seemed to him that after that first command, it never let up; someone was always shouting, *Harris, over here! Rake! Hammer! Chisel! Blocks! Coal! Sand! Hurry up, I ain't got all day. And do it before you eat your dinner, man. Get a move on, hustle!* He never stopped to think all day. On the second and third days, however, he began to find spare shreds of time to observe the job that was being done.

Once the underlying surface was finished, it was time for the base layer of mortar. Without it, whatever stones the pavers laid would hardly last a season of rain. Lime, clean sand and water were turned in a drum and churned to cement. Harris's arm grew sore with the constant turning of the crank handle. When the cement had cured, six inches of baked sand were strewn evenly over the concrete foundation. One of Harris's tasks was to heat the sand till it was bone-dry. Only then did the pavers begin the laying of the stone. His next job was to deliver enough blocks to keep the work flowing smoothly.

When the pavers had finished a section, it looked like it was done, but it wasn't. It was fragile. Just one man walking across the street would have gotten the stones all out of order. That was when the rammers came through with their log butts and drove the blocks down into the sand. Last came the chuckers, who filled the interstices with gravel heated (by Frank Harris, of course) to ensure no moisture was trapped within, where it could freeze in winter, spall the stones, spring the grout. Finally, they sealed the joints with bubbling tar. It was a highly modern style of road building, tested by science and specified by the Common Council of the city for all new construction. People said a road built this way ought to last several lifetimes without a single pothole. Harris liked hearing that kind of talk—he liked its optimism. It justified his toil, even if he knew he was more than qualified to do more skilled work.

The entire first week was a blur of excitement, exhaustion, jammed fingers and nasty burns from working with the coal burners and hot gravel and tar, but nonetheless he enjoyed it, knowing he was helping to build something useful, something important. At night, he fell asleep almost before he'd finished his dinner. He dreamed of high stone towers and didn't stir till

Liam kicked him awake at dawn. Lessons with Beatrice were suspended. He told her he was doing fine, and it was true. Still, it was the first time since the O'Gamhnas took him in that he had gone for more than a day without having an intimate conversation with Beatrice. She had been his full-time tutor and constant companion. He thought of her, but truly he was too tired to handle the complexities of their flirtation, to grapple with why it was happening and whether it was real. That week, he didn't think of her slim fingers wrapping around his whenever he could steal a moment; he didn't dread his future obligations to the Whyos. For the most part, he simply watched Liam and the other pavers pause in raking smooth the sand on a section of foundation. The pavers blinked impassively as they examined the grade, agreed that it was off, and out came the protractors, the tape measures, the levels. They were perfectionists, and Harris admired that. While he shoveled hot gravel, he kept his eyes on them and let himself vicariously enjoy the rapid, regular movements of their hands as they left behind row after interlocked row of evenly spaced stones, so regular, so permanent, that they already seemed to have been there forever.

The day that one of the pavers was hit in the face with a grapeshot of broiling gravel was Harris's day of days. That was the way luck worked in the metropolis—for some to win, others must lose. Cooking the gravel had become one of Harris's favorite tasks. The flames had to burn blue for an hour under each load to get it dry enough to ensure a stable grout, and the fire had to be fed continuously. He loved watching it and enjoyed the tricky job of tipping the roasting-hot stones out into cooling panniers, especially on cool spring afternoons like that one. Harris just happened to have stepped away from the fire to help another laborer unload a cart when the paver approached the fire to warm his hands. It was not his fault that some covert pocket of rainwater had just then gone to steam, exploding its stony capsule. Indeed, it might very well have been him who was hit. When he turned at the sound of the shout, the man was already on the ground. Liam called Harris over a short time later, as the man was being carted away with white bindings wrapped around his head like a blindfold.

"I told the boss you were a builder back in Ireland, you worked on churches. And that I'd vouch for you. He says do you want to fill in?"

It was Harris's break. At long last he would be the one to set the stones again. He would be one of the authors of the road they made. "I'm sorry about what happened, but I'll be glad to do it, more than glad."

By the end of the third week, he was feeling strong: tossing the big fourteen-pound blocks as lightly as apples. He could look behind him at the end of the shift and see what he had made and that it was good, that it would last. One afternoon, when clouds rolled in and the air took on a spring chill, several of the chuckers and rammers and pavers gathered around the warmth of the gravel fire while they waited for new loads of materials. They were all talking about a man named Parnell, and they were excited. He was some sort of Irish political visionary, and he was coming to New York to lecture. Harris found himself daydreaming, humming a bit of a hymn. Without thinking about it, he had come upon a way to think in German without risking his cover as a taciturn Irishman—for he did miss his language, did feel the strain of always having to be someone he wasn't: He could listen to the lyrics in his head as he hummed without pronouncing them.

"What's that hymn?" asked one of the chuckers, and Harris realized he didn't know the English name, nor had he stopped to ask himself if that song was sung in the Catholic Church. The men had been talking politics, and now it seemed that the chucker had taken offense, had read something into his abstention from their conversation, had heard the Church of England in the melody Harris hummed. He looked up, puzzling how to respond, and noticed the woman who was always hawking hot corn on the corner.

"*Lily-white corn, get your lily-white corn,*" she sang in a tune that was somewhat different from the usual hot-corn girl's. Somehow, her voice reminded him of Beatrice. He realized he'd been too absorbed by this job. He wanted to talk to Beatrice, he needed it, to smell her skin and get her reassurance, to find out if there was a chance. He could be Frank Harris, if she really wanted him to, he'd proven that. But if she didn't care, he'd rather be himself, perhaps even if it meant exposure, arrest, being held culpable for Luther Undertoe's crimes.

Now all the men were staring at him, even Liam. He shrugged. "I don't really know. I don't remember the words." He looked at his hands, still shiny and scarred in places from being burned in the fire, and he thought of his past. In fact, he remembered the words of the hymn very well, could almost hear his mother singing them in the pew beside him. But then he heard Maggie singing *"lily-white corn,"* and something told him, *No, you're Frank Harris now. You can't go back.* He jammed his hands in his pockets and went back to work. Better not to think, just to be, he told himself.

That night, he told Beatrice he needed more coaching. His cover had been effective, so far; his accent was convincing; his taciturnity was crucial. But he didn't know enough about Ireland. He didn't know what hymns a man might hum, what horses had been famous a decade before, what politicians compelled people and why. He knew the basics, naturally, about the famine, the tenant-farming system, the English landlords, the Orange-men. Everyone had heard of those things, but he didn't know enough to have an opinion, to feel passion. To be convincing, he needed to.

"That's a good idea, Harris," she said. "I'm glad you asked." He looked at her and wished he could know her mind. Did she know that what he really wanted was anything but a political education? Did she care? He couldn't tell. But it worked. For the first time in weeks they sat up at the kitchen table till late, sipping beer. He learned that Beatrice did indeed feel fervent about the cause of Irish nationalism. She told him about how her brother had marched with Parnell in Dublin, and she pulled out a bundle of his letters, from which she read to Harris terrible accounts of what the English were still doing to oppress the Irish—starving them, robbing them, arresting anyone who dared to object.

"But I really just want to bring Padric over. I'm saving every penny for that. If he stays there, he's going to get himself killed."

"How much more do you need?" He didn't have more than a few dollars to his name, but he was ready to pledge them all to her brother's cause.

"Oh," she said. "I used to send money back whenever I had it, but he spent it just living, you know. And I think he gave some of it to the cause, to buy guns. So now I'm waiting till I can buy the ticket all at once. I'm pretty nearly there."

The following week, she took him to the Cooper Union to hear Charles Parnell drumming up support from the immigrant community for those they'd left behind. They saw a couple of the men from the paving crew on the line, who nodded and smiled at Harris. The speech was rousing, infuriating, inspiring. It wasn't Harris's crisis, but he felt he would have taken to the streets even so if they'd been in Dublin or Derry, not New York. He didn't stop talking about it on the way home, and at one point he raised his voice and almost shouted that the States had taken their independence from the English by force, so maybe it was time the Irish did the same. Beatrice stepped back and looked at him queerly, as if he were some exotic creature at the zoo.

"Do you really think that, Harris, or are you acting?" she asked.

He was taken aback by the question. "I do think it," he said at last.

But Parnell's tour moved on, and Beatrice's lessons veered away from the political. She came up with topics, such as farming and shipping and cricket and the way to serve mutton, and taught him what he ought to know. She harped on the finer distinctions among prepositions, the names of songbirds, the breeds of hunting dogs, the ingredients of puddings. Harris enjoyed the lessons, but there was a barrier. She did not speak further of herself. She laughed invitingly, but she did not press her leg to his if he brushed her dress under the table. She did not gaze back into his eyes when he tried to engage her that way. She did not exactly give him what he wanted, no, but she did sit close, did take his hands in hers and show him how to gesture, did carefully groom him for and drill him on every situation she could dream up. Surely, he thought, she was doing more than Whyo duty demanded. That must mean something.

Often, when he turned in at night after one of their lessons in which he once again couldn't tell if she was flirting or not, his mind drifted to the Whyos, Undertoe, the frame-up, whether there was any way for him to clear his old name and how long he would have to go on pretending to be an Irishman. He knew that some day soon Beatrice would tap him on the shoulder and tell him it was time, instruct him to do something awful. Those thoughts gave rise to the fantasy of running away—from her, the Whyos, the cops, Undertoe, his past. The thing that stopped him was Beatrice was so oddly contradictory—jailer and crush, caring and unresponsive, always obsessive about the details of his life but often secretive about her own. One day, it was politics, and it seemed he could kiss her, if he only had the courage; the next day, she was distant and schoolmarmish as she explained what the weave of a sweater said about the woman who knit it.

What, he wondered, did she do on behalf of the Whyos when she wasn't home with him? Had she killed, betrayed, abducted someone new? Was that what drove her mood swings? He knew she worked for the gang, and he'd seen her in action—and it was scary—but somehow Harris just couldn't believe that Beatrice could be as bad as he knew she was, nor that she would really force him into a life of crime.

Perhaps it was nervous energy or a creative force within him that had been rekindled by his promotion to paving, but he resumed his old habit of whittling, to while away the time on the several nights a week when Beatrice wasn't around. He spent a dollar on a good knife and began picking up scraps of wood wherever he found them. Every week or so, he produced another figurine, sometimes boats or bears or other toys for the O'Gamhna boys, sometimes gargoyles that were exact replicas of the ones that he had worked on or had seen being carved at the Nikolaikirche, sometimes fanciful beasts of his own imagining. When he finished them, he would sweep the tailings from the floor and throw them into the grate of the stove. Except in the case of the toys, which he gave to the boys, the tailings were usually followed by the small, beautifully wrought lump of wood. It had taken him a dozen hours to find the shape within the chunk of raw wood, but he was never satisfied with what he'd done.

Harris also took to buying a paper in the evening or sometimes going to the Cooper Union after work, if he knew Beatrice was going to be out, to do the reading that was part of his ongoing education. He struggled with the temptation just to pick up and glance at the front page of the *Frankfurter Zeitung*. He knew he must not, but invariably he strayed casually toward the German-language section and scanned whatever headlines were visible at the top of the racks. The Franco-Prussian War was tearing through the country of his birth. Towns that would always be part of his mental landscape of home had been burned to the ground. He thought about his father and his friend Robert Koch and wondered if they'd read the same headlines in the same editions a couple weeks before. Or had they experienced the news more directly? Were they all right? And what was happening now? The New York papers covered the European war to a much lesser extent. But he stuck to his cover, purchased just the local illustrateds and newspapers and studied them. The more he read—about France and Prussia at war, about Ulysses S. Grant, about the latest scandal — the better. He found that English came almost naturally from between his lips now, but reading it was still work for him, and so he practiced it.

Then at the end of summer, on an evening some three months since Harris had begun working for the paving company, Beatrice came home late, reeking of cigars and ale, and gave him the message he'd been dreading: his first instruction from Dandy Johnny. Harris was to get himself fired the following day. The Whyos had something else lined up for him. There was no smile or breathy whisper to the way she delivered it, just business.

"What?" he said. "How can I? I love this job. I don't want to get fired."

She raised her eyebrows and waited for him to absorb the fact that this was not optional. Really, it wasn't a big deal, she explained, compared to lots of things they might have wanted — they didn't want him to kill anyone, after all. But Harris believed that turning this corner and beginning to do what the Whyos wanted was a kind of suicide. If she had allowed him to imagine that she loved him, perhaps he wouldn't have minded, would have gone with her to the other side, but she had not made that clear, and he balked.

"What about a little more time, just till frost, when the work dries up anyway?"

"Harris. One way or other, you've got to be done with that job by tomorrow. If you don't handle it, I will." Instead of seducing him, she bullied him.

"But why would they fire me? I work hard. I don't want to quit."

"You think this is about your happiness?" she said. "You are right about one thing, though — simply quitting won't work. Liam would be suspicious. And Johnny wants you to keep on living here, with the family. Stability's good cover. A man who changes both his job and his living quarters at once looks shifty, might have to explain himself. So somehow you need to do it without getting Liam too mad."

He looked at her. Her eyes were very bright, but he couldn't read the emotion in the rest of her face. Who was she, really? Was it remotely possible that she wanted him in the gang so they could be together at last, might she be waiting for that to let things progress? On the other hand, it seemed possible that he had wasted three months of smoldering attraction on some-one who was not even his friend.

"Pick a fight with the foreman, punch someone. Ruin something large."

He shook his head. "Liam would mind that. And anyway, I could never—"

"Then show up drunk. Really drunk. Liam won't like it, but he could forgive it. It's his own father's vice, and he still loves Leon."

"Beanie—"

But suddenly, she wasn't having the same conversation. "Harris!" she said shrilly, as if he had done the sort of thing he'd often dreamed of and never dared—as if he had touched her in some too intimate way. It was as if she'd read his mind, and it filled him with shame to realize that she knew exactly how he'd felt all that time. She had seen it but ignored it, only now to use it against him. Of course, the others had seen him falling for her, too—it was obvious from the way he mooned and huffed when she stayed out all night, the way he jumped when she said to. Her shriek had been loud enough to wake the family—it was meant to—and it could be under-stood only one way. His face grew red with embarrassment and frustration.

"What? Are you sure?" she said next. He looked at her, at once betrayed and confused. She was doing something different now. "Come on, Harris, it's been three months. You look totally different. I don't care what you say, I don't believe he recognized you. How could he have? Now listen, you've got to get ahold of yourself." There were rustlings of bedcovers from the front room. Everyone was awake, listening.

When she spoke next, it was very quietly, just for him: "Talk back," she told him. "Argue. Loudly. Then get dressed and go. I'll follow. And Harris? Just do it, no questions. If you don't, you're very likely going to be a dead man by tomorrow."

"What?" he said. "Why?"

She just looked at him. Her chin was pointy, and her eyes were un-yielding. He remembered the way she wielded her eye-gouger, that first day. He realized that he had fallen for her even way back then. She was a monster of some sort, a beautiful, seductive, duplicitous murderer, but he had always known that, and he still just wanted to take her in his arms. He wanted to be able to talk to her, freely, to know what she truly felt. As he was thinking this, she rose and came over to him. She touched his lips gently, then she hauled back and slapped him with all her might. "Get ahold of yourself, Harris!" she said.

He raised his fingers to his face and silently got up, found his coat and shoes and hat, and left the apartment. It was too much. He was at the front door when he heard her following, and he began to run. He wanted no truck with her after all, whatever she had in mind for him. He thought about going and turning himself in to the cops right then, just to get it over with. Better that than to be the pawn of this baffling woman and her gang. Better nothingness than coming close to happiness and having it rescinded. It was time to act, and to act according to some objective measure of what was right. He was finished with letting things happen to him, surviving on luck. He would not just go along anymore.

But Beatrice was, among other things, an incredibly fast runner. She caught up with him before he'd passed the pump at the corner. When he still wouldn't stop, she grabbed his coattail. When he let it rip rather than be stopped, she deployed her right leg and entwined her ankle around his. He found himself flat on the sidewalk. She was sitting on his chest, smiling. His hands stung. And there was that eye-gouger, almost as if he'd summoned it by his thoughts.

"Jesus, Harris. Just where do you think you're going? Have you lost your mind? Do I need Fiona and Piker Ryan? Do I need to strong-arm you? It's not all that bad, your fate, you know. There's no need."

"A man has to make his own choices in life. I don't choose to be a criminal in a gang, I don't choose to let you manipulate me. I'd rather be hanged, if that's the choice."

"A person's got to be damned lucky to get to choose his own life. That's rare, and you're not that lucky. But there's other things that make it worth it, Harris. There are." And she bent down and kissed him for a long minute. She breathed in deeply with her nose in his neck. She gently took his lip between her teeth. She ran her fingers through his hair. All the gestures he'd been craving and more. "Come on, Harris, I'm sorry. There's so many things I have to hide, from so many people, to make it all work. But don't you know I need you? Do it for me."

"Can you put that thing away?"

She did.

They stayed like that on the street, kissing, until they heard footsteps coming. Then she took him to an alehouse and fed him gin. He drank it. When he asked her what they wanted him to do, she said, "Don't worry about that. Right now, just drink. Until you can't stand up. I want you to stay overnight at the Sunnyside Hotel. And have another drink or two in the morning, before you go over to the site, and *don't* be on time. Make a bit of a show of it. That should do the trick."

After that, they didn't talk much. Beatrice just ordered gin upon gin. He tried to sit close to her, to kiss her again, but she wasn't having it. "Not here," she said. "Not now." When Harris was bleary and reeling and on the verge of tears, she went into his wallet, removed most of the money, then sent him off. She put a young Why Not on the job of watching out for him and headed back down to the Morgue to let Johnny know that Harris was cooperating.

Instead of the Sunnyside, Harris gravitated to his old haunt, Wah Kee's, perhaps because of the sweet, pungent odor of oblivion that he remembered wafting from the opium den. That was the scale of his defiance, in the wake of her kiss—to go to a different hotel than she told him, to crave delirium—and she'd predicted it. That was why she took his money. With what Beatrice had left him, he didn't have enough to gain entry to temporary nirvana. Wah Kee didn't even recognize him, didn't look him in the eye, just took the coin he laid on the counter and waved him into the bunk room.

The following morning, Fiona was assigned to ensure that Harris stuck to the plan, which he did. His head felt awful as he headed for the construction site, but on the way he did what she'd told him to: stopped at a saloon for the hair of the dog. He stayed for three rounds, raising his glass in turn, in three silent toasts, to Beatrice's lips, her teeth and her persistence. He didn't understand her in the least, but perhaps he didn't need to. By the time he got to the site, he was an hour late as well as half drunk. He greeted the baffled foreman with a suitably incoherent string of excuses. Liam had been prepared by Beatrice with a story about Harris having relapsed in his ways as a result of an encounter with someone he'd had trouble with before he went into hiding. He came over to intervene on Harris's behalf, but Harris made himself unhelpful. Within ten minutes, it was over. No job, no future as a minor artisan, no respect from his coworkers, no reference from the foreman. Nothing but the promise of those kisses.

As he wandered away from the site, he thought, *I'm free,* but in truth he knew better. He was the opposite of free. The Whyos wouldn't ever let him go, and he would never have the strength to say no to Beatrice. He had made the choice he told himself he wouldn't, and made it for the second time. This time there was no excuse. Harris spent the next two days slumped on the sofa in the O'Gamhnas' front room, carving his most hideous gargoyle yet. It had warts upon its very teeth, it was so foul. Beatrice made herself scarce, but on the third day she returned. She told him to get up and shave. She had gotten him another job.

"What is that?" she asked, putting her hand out for the gargoyle.

"Nothing," he said—he didn't want her job, whatever it was—and threw his creation in the stove.

Once they were out on the street, she told him that he would be cleaning sewers for his supper and spying for the Whyos on the sly. Harris had graduated from cathedrals to circuses to roads and landed finally in the gutter. It was a pretty depressing trajectory—until she slipped her hand into his. Then she escorted him to his job interview, explaining the arrangements and all the while playing little games with his fingers as they walked.

14.

DOWN THE MANHOLE

His first assignment was to learn how the Whyos could gain access to the sewers without detection and to identify several navigable tunnels and areas suitable for hiding out in or stashing loot. He was to deliver information to Beatrice in the course of their English lessons. At other times, she would accompany him to or from work, like today. To justify spending so much time together, she said, taking his arm and snugging up against him, she thought it made sense that they appear to be sweethearts. "But Harris," she added, "if you really were courting me in earnest, it wouldn't be proper for you to live with us—and Johnny wants you to stay—so don't go too far."

He nodded and took her arm, but something seemed to drop away from him with this strangely overt and highly calculated expression of what had been ineffable. And had she had to mention Johnny? This was what Harris wanted, wasn't it? He wanted her. But was it real, even now, or was it just manipulation? Would he ever know? Was it all in his head? He wasn't sure.

The office where he signed the name *Frank Harris* to a year's contract as a sewerman stank faintly of some chemical—a clean but unpleasant smell that suggested something rotten was being kept at bay. The more he considered it, the more her affection seemed false. She wasn't his sweetheart; she was on the job for the Whyos. But he resolved to take things one by one as they came, not to panic or despair. He'd gotten himself into another unfortunate situation, but as long as he was alive there was a chance things would work out. He wasn't dying of consumption or awaiting his hanging or bobbing facedown beneath a West Side pier, a knife hole in his side and eels slithering through his beard. Maybe there was hope with Beatrice. Maybe it didn't matter if she was using him, so long as she also wanted him.

In the locker room at the Sewer Division, his new boots dangled side by side like two hanged men, heels to the ceiling, long leather uppers stretching lifelessly to within a few inches of the ground, ankles cocked like broken necks where the great brass boot hooks grabbed them. They were thigh high and built of cowhide as thick as his thumb, as supple as one of the fine silk ascots that graced Dandy Johnny's throat. *Buttery* is the word for finely tanned leather goods, but it isn't butter that softens the hide. It's repeated baths in stinking solvents and acids that could chew through your skin in a minute flat. In the case of the boots assigned to Harris, the effects of the usual caustic tanning agents had been augmented by long exposure to other organic conditioners. For Harris's boots were new only to him; they'd seen years of duty in the sewers already—and this was an asset. They were the first tools of his new trade to be issued to him and would prove essential, in the coming months, in ways that even the Whyos couldn't have guessed.

Generally, sewage runs thin and gray, not half as bad as you'd think. It smells more like a damp basement than a latrine. It's only when there are problems that the brew thickens and festers and stinks like Hell. But since the sewermen spent the bulk of their time at just such trouble spots, resolving clogs and preventing blockages, their boots were basted daily in a powerful stew. It was commonly known in the department, as young as it was, that the older the boots and the longer their exposure to the dark, turbid waters, the softer they became, the more like second skin, the greater the agility they permitted their wearer, and the drier they kept his feet. Like barrel staves in whiskey, the boot seams swelled with immersion, and Frank Harris's new boots were the oldest and best maintained in the system, as soft and as pungent as a baby's butt crack on the outside, smooth with wear within. They weighed in at thirteen pounds each and were perfectly impermeable and incredibly tough. Protection meant a great deal in the low pipeways and cramped crawl spaces, where rough edges and sharp objects abounded.

Frank Harris didn't deserve such a prodigious pair of boots, not by a mile. Normally, foot size and seniority would have been the factors that determined who got a dead or retired man's boots, but Harris, on his first day of work, had acquired the most estimable boots in the division. All this he learned from Mrs. Dolan, the matron of equipment and hygiene officer, when she gave him his locker number in exchange for his signature the day before. Then she told him to put them on. He looked at his pants and blushed at the notion of taking them off in front of her.

"Go ahead. Just put them on. It's awkward. You don't want to do it the first time in front of the others, trust me."

The boots were cut slim to the top of the thigh, which made them devilishly hard to get into. He jumped and hopped and landed on his ass. His drawers were horribly twisted, and he only had one leg in. He looked at her with some desperation.

"Sit," she said, pointing to a bench, and he sat and let her show him how to bunch and fold them and roll them up his leg the way a lady dons her stockings. When he finally strapped on his suspenders, he was amazed how free and light and limber he felt, how well protected. The boots fit him like a glove.

In the following days, Harris came to learn much more about his boots—in particular, why he had gotten them. Despite their merits as boots, they were considered unlucky. None of the other men would go near them. The complete story of what had befallen their previous owner had washed out to the bottom of the harbor with the soul of Solomon McGinty, the oldest, orneriest and most experienced of all the city's sewermen, but you didn't have to know all the details. The problem with the boots was simple: McGinty had died in them. It was bad luck to wear boots a man had died in.

Long before the city even had a Sewer Division, McGinty had been a private contractor specializing in "clogs, floods and inconveniences." That was how he put it in the weekly ad he ran in the *Sun* for twenty straight years of Mondays. When the sewer maintenance unit was started, he was hired on as an expert. McGinty was the one who recommended that every sewerman be outfitted with a pair of boots similar to the ones he'd had made for himself years before, and so the boots became the sewermen's uniform. Their primary tool was a long, hooked gaff, also of McGinty's design. There was a narrow, hoelike spade at the handle end for shoveling muck, levering crotchety manhole covers and dispatching rats. When the city put in standard-gauge manhole covers, the basic-issue gaff became a kind of key, too, with a perpendicular spur that undid the bolts. The gaffs had continued to evolve over the years, and by Harris's time they were made in various sizes, long for distant reaches and short for tight spots, but the mainstay of every sewerman's arsenal remained the basic McGinty model, the Number 1, which was just a little longer than Harris's forearm. This was the tool that Harris would carry with him every day from now on, and it was formidable. The first thing that struck him as he passed his new gaff back and forth between his hands was that it was more than a tool. It was a weapon.

As for McGinty, though he'd shaped the division in essential ways in the early days, he hadn't the least bit of talent for or interest in administration, and he soon got himself returned to the field, where his seniority and legendary bad temper earned him the privilege of working alone, answering to no man, and generally doing exactly as he pleased. He was undeniably something of a genius underground, so he was often consulted on difficult problems, but he was always careful to be as unpleasant as he was helpful, with the result that he was left largely to his own devices.

There was at least one other oddity about McGinty: In addition to his remarkable attunement to the hydrodynamics of sewage, the man had an extraordinary voice. He was popularly credited as the originator and chief lyricist of a song known underground simply as the Ballad. Its numerous verses chronicled the daily drudgery, occasional excitements and perils of the work, and the refrain, "All I want is to die / With my dogs clean and dry," gave voice to every sewerman's greatest fear: perishing down in the hole.

As is common with work songs, people were always coming up with new verses based on notable incidents or characters, but only the best of them stuck, and even though he worked alone, most of those were McGinty's. The old man's presence in an adjacent tunnel would be made known to his fellows when they heard the strains of the Ballad echoing through the conduits, and they would fill their lungs with the dank air and bellow back at McGinty, repeating his lyrics as he spun them out, by turns lewd and mournful. On such days, the murky pipes rang with their gloriously, sinuously echoing call-and-response explosion of sound, loud enough that now and then on the streets above, people thought they heard a humming or a wailing sound.

There were plenty of songs being sung in the metropolis. There were the songs of God sung by evangelists and converts; there were political ditties touting candidates espoused by party men; there were the varied songs of commerce—the hot-corn girls, fruit and flower vendors, knife sharpeners and oyster shuckers—and then there were the quieter, more covert songs, the ones people couldn't quite make out, nor were they meant to. If the sound was echoing off the buildings, it was probably from a Whyo, and you'd better watch your wallet and your back; but if it was coming from a manhole cover, it was the sewermen, just easing the passage of time. It's hard to say which would have seemed less probable to the average New Yorker, a corps of subterranean city workers with a tradition of ballad singing or the elaborate secret language of the Whyo gang. People were likelier to conjure up fanciful images of unquiet ghosts of murdered slaves, early colonists or Manhattan Indians than believe in either reality.

McGinty's last day had been a cool, pleasant one in late spring, an ample month before Harris joined the brotherhood of sewer muckers, and he was working to clear a clogged pipe just south of Chambers. He was humming quietly, well out of earshot of any other men. That morning, the foreman had sent out a crew to clear accumulated silt and muck from the mains in the City Hall area, where several gutters near prominent buildings had lately begun to overflow. A fully stopped pipe junction was the most likely explanation—that could create a vacuum seal in several directions—but they hadn't been able to find one, so the problem had been attributed to what they called *systemic malaise*, meaning generally high sludge levels. McGinty dismissed that interpretation and the foreman's plan of scraping out all the major pipes in the area and disappeared down a manhole without a word of explanation. That disappearing act was one of his trademarks: No one but McGinty ever traveled further than he absolutely had to inside a tunnel—the tunnels just weren't designed for it, most being three feet or less in diameter—but he did it wherever the pipe gauge was large enough to let him pass. He enjoyed the stealth and the privacy. It also meant he knew the submetropolitan terrain like no one else.

Thanks to that knowledge, McGinty understood that the City Hall backup was most likely caused by a problem in a small culvert off the main line, and he found it fairly swiftly. He was just about to penetrate the offending clog with his Number 8 gaff—the longest of several he'd brought along—when he began to feel tightness in his ribs and a stabbing pain down his left arm. Soon, he was sweating and breathless, but he refused to be thwarted from proving his diagnosis. He grimaced and grunted and redoubled his efforts, ratcheting the gaff back and forth. Finally, a draft of ghastly air escaped with a sucking sound, and water began to flow slowly around his knees. He flared his nostrils, smiled with satisfaction, and inhaled deeply. He liked the loamy smell of fresh, clean sewage well enough—it indicated a vigorous, healthy flow—but the truth was that nothing in McGinty's world satisfied him more than the sucking, slurping and burbling of foul air and stagnant water, moving at last in opposite directions through a narrow channel of his own making. The heaviness in his chest was immense, but he plunged his gaff in again and felt the flow of fetid water begin to run faster through the chink, eroding it. Something was in there, something solid enough to have collected silt, shit and sand until the pipe was fully sealed. He'd seen cats do it, dogs, of course, and inanimate objects from a bushel basket to a burlap sack to a lady's dress. Once, a coon that was swollen up fat as a hog. He was always curious to find the culprit.

He reamed and madly reamed, but even as McGinty was restoring circulation to the sewer pipe, another smaller, more intimate clog was forming, diminishing the flow of blood to his heart to a trickle. Sweat ran down his brow and into his eyes as his heart pumped harder, straining to keep up the output volume despite the tightening vessel. A hard, greasy plaque afflicted his left anterior descending artery, or *widowmaker*, as a physician like the good Dr. Blacksall, who had examined poor Pearl at the morgue, would have called it. The coating of epithelian cells that once kept the plaque in check had failed. At the Women's Medical College, they learned to identify this pathology in their freshman anatomy lab, noting carefully in their lab books that such clogs were common in the cadavers of portly men of mature age. As McGinty's widowmaker swelled gradually shut, tiny clots were formed by the turbulence, and crumbs of the loosened plaque broke free and then were caught again, as if by a sieve, adding to the problem, cutting

off the flow a little more with each lub, each dub. When the artery was finally fully constricted, McGinty stood up straight for a moment in surprise
and hit his head on the roof of the pipe, a thing he never did. His eyes
bulged a little, and he managed to give one final tug on his gaff, freeing the
last detritus that was packed around the seed of the clog.

Like the grain of sand that turns the oyster's mother-of-pearl inwardness
to a gem, to a commodity, to a thing whose outward value is all out of order
with that of its component parts, the source of this blockage was different in
nature from the problem it engendered. Even McGinty would have marveled, if he'd recognized the thing for what it was, that the delicate skeleton
of a newborn babe could have caused so large and odious a problem. All
that remained of the baby, as McGinty died, were the bones, but it had
been a plump and proper baby when first it had been consigned to the Ann
Street culvert—big enough, anyway, to catch a sodden newspaper in its
outspread arms, and then a thousand other bits of flotsam that had flowed
up against it to lodge between its fingers and toes and the news of the day,
gradually reinforcing the dam, layer upon layer upon layer of sad papier-
mâché.

The baby, may it rest in peace, was not just any baby. She was a Why
Not—or would have been, could have been, when she'd grown up. Her
mother was none other than Maggie the Dove, the very same pickpocket,
panel thief and hit woman who'd so recently been hawking corn and spying on Harris.

Maggie had always been a maverick, even before she fell in with Dandy
Johnny and joined the Why Nots. She'd tended bar, turned a few tricks
when she needed the money, drunk whiskey moderately, danced with
whom she pleased. She met Johnny shortly after he took over from Googy
Corcoran, and she was perfect for him: just as pretty, just as tough, both of
them with wet red lips and shiny black hair. But what drew her to him were
the rumors she'd heard that the gang he ran with had some kind of re-
formist bent—suffragist, communist, something like that—meaning that
they treated their girls as equals. She hadn't imagined quite how different
the Whyos were, though. She'd hardly known how to take it when, after a
wild night of theft and drink and sex and finally the bliss of an opium pipe,
Johnny told her he wanted her to meet his mother.

"Your mother?" she'd howled. "I thought you were tough."

But he just smiled and said, "My mother's everything to me, Maggie. I introduce all the girls to her. That doesn't mean I ain't a killer."

Maggie went to see her, but she wasn't happy about it. Johnny's mother had looked Maggie over as if she were a horse and strangely enough asked her if she could sing, then sent the two of them on their way. It was a peculiar interview, to say the least. Their next disagreement was over his refusal to put her out to work the streets. "Why not, then?" she asked, incredulous. "You want to control my every move, Johnny? You worried I'll enjoy myself? You jealous?"

He'd shrugged her questions off. "No, Maggie, do it if you want, but I won't encourage it. You and I can make better money better ways."

When she'd formally joined the gang, she learned what the vocal test had been about. And then his mother gave her a talking-to, the same talk she gave to all the new girls, and the peculiar rationale behind the Whyos and their oddities emerged.

"You only hook if you want to in the Why Nots. No man, no Whyo, not even Johnny is your boss—not in that sense. If you choose to do it, you turn in a share of your take, just the same as everyone, just the same as if you'd stole the money or forged it, no difference. And you won't need a pimp to protect you. You've got Piker and Johnny and all the rest of us watching out for you at all times. The whole gang watches out for its own, and you're expected to do the same."

She'd been issued an eye-gouger, a nicer one than the average, since Johnny was so fond of her—it was brass with silver filigree—and with the aid of that device she'd come out on top of every battle she'd fought since. Maggie never hooked while she was with Dandy Johnny. She was too excited by his lean body to waste herself on sex with others, too busy working various peculiar schemes with him to find the time, too flush, thanks to their nightly hauls, to need the comparatively small change it would have brought. But Maggie was a practical woman, and after her affair with Johnny abruptly ended, she went back to the streets from time to time. At first, allowing some cad from Poughkeepsie to rough her up a little had soothed the sting of Johnny's dropping her the way he did, without explanation, when she had thought they were happy.

The baby of the culvert clog was sired by one of her johns—quite intentionally on her part. She'd wanted a boy in particular and spent a busy fortnight cruising the city for the handsomest prospects she could find. She tended to go for Johnny look-alikes with pale, smooth faces and glistening hair.

Her cohort was fairly shocked when they eventually noticed her stomach ballooning—it was well within the resources and repertoire of any Why Not to terminate a pregnancy, should the usual prophylactic measures fail. And notwithstanding the example of Johnny's sainted mother, parenthood was not considered to be the ideal condition for a Why Not. When Maggie announced she wanted to keep the thing, people whispered *syphilis*, assumed she'd lost her mind, though really she was far too young for that symptom. Actually, those months were happy ones for her. She was alone when labor came on, as she'd wanted to be. Later that night, she told the circle of Why Nots gathered around her in her flat, where she lay in bed recuperating, of the stillbirth, with dry if stinging eyes: "It came fast and sudden in the privy. I couldn't go for help." (She never mentioned how hard she fought to suppress her cries and keep silent, to keep her options open to the last.) "Landed on the filthy floor there. He was perfect, only kind of blue, and he never kicked at all, never cried. Never breathed." She looked away, to the wall. "There I was, and the baby was just dead. I was holding him, and I kissed his little eyes shut, and then I just . . ." She made a gesture of letting go, and the women blinked and looked away, each imagining a small, pale body falling down the hole and sinking in the putrid mire.

The Why Nots asked Maggie how she felt and she said, "Weakish," but it wasn't true. She felt much worse than weak. She'd told them it was a boy, but that was a lie. All of it was, except that the baby had come in the privy. The truth was, she'd gone there on purpose, when the time came, to be sure she'd deliver alone. And after she'd looked between the baby's legs and seen that there was nothing there—a girl—she'd been quick and deliberate. She stuffed her handkerchief in the gawping mouth before it managed to cry and pinched closed the nose of her perfect, red-faced, writhing girl. That was the only time she'd cried. Maggie'd been around; she knew a girl's life would never be worth living, much less a woman's, should the child have made it that far. The disaster of her own life, she felt, was not to have been born a boy. It wasn't true that she'd dumped the thing in the privy either, though that had been her plan, if the sex were wrong. She feared it might haunt her there, her baby girl, every time she had to go. It was late at night, and no one was about, and so she'd limped out and stuffed it down the gutter at the corner of her block. She'd pictured the baby riding a flood tide out to sea, and swimming with the dolphins, not sinking, not lurking for more than a year.

She wasn't entirely wrong—it just took a lot longer. No one but McGinty would ever know it, but as he finally dropped his gaff he saw the small collection of bones sweep past him out to the harbor amidst a torrent of other debris. He was more or less an apostate, but McGinty said a small prayer blessing her passage, even as he passed on himself. Out in the harbor, where the daughter of Maggie the Dove came once again to rest, there were no porpoises, just eels and barnacles and piling worms, but it was better than the sewer, where McGinty had now taken the dead baby's place.

The gust of air from the clog had extinguished his lamp. He'd crawled blindly a few yards away from the gushing culvert, back into the space under the manhole, but he never got a grip on the ladder's first rung. His head dropped back. His mouth gaped. Hours passed. A pointed, whiskered nose sniffed his collar; a naked tail switched. Six legs landed on his mottled tongue and two of them began to preen feelers. A greasy brown oval a half an inch long ascended the supple thigh of his waders. That was that. McGinty had turned in his boots.

He'd died with his feet dry after all, if down in the hole. When they discovered his gaff hook a few yards away, protruding from the clean flushed bottom of the pipe he'd unclogged, they realized that McGinty had done it again. The sudden resolution of the flooding problem at about midday had not been their doing after all. They weren't exactly surprised. That was what McGinty always did: entered a manhole no one else thought to, found a vacuum seal no one else believed existed, reamed the pipe, fixed the problem. But they were used to him coming around afterward, cackling and crowing and accusing the other foremen of incompetence. When he hadn't shown up after the clear-up, they'd figured they'd beaten him to it that time and he was off sulking. But no. He stared at them from under half-closed lids in the shaft of light from the open disk of daylight above, gloating over one last piece of brilliant work.

And so, although normally the boots of a dead sewerman were in great demand, Mrs. Dolan hadn't even asked if anyone wanted McGinty's, just filled out a report on the condition of the deceased's equipment and sent them to the stockroom to await the next new hire whose shoe size matched McGinty's: twelve.

Harris didn't know any of that when he first pulled them on, but a strange feeling of luck came over him: The boots were as comfortable as any piece of clothing he'd ever worn. He stroked the soft creases at the knees. He told himself that this job might be better than he'd thought.

The following morning, as soon as he hauled the boots out and began to suit up, there was trouble. McGinty's boots were easily recognizable. They were older and more worn than anyone else's, and there were details that marked them: the stitching, frayed threads, creases, a tarry blotch on the knee, the mended left suspender strap. Ever since McGinty's death, the other men had been waiting with a kind of malicious anticipation to see which plebe would clomp out for roll call wearing the ghost of the gutters' second skin. It was obvious to all of them that McGinty wouldn't make a benevolent ghost.

Harris's first partner was Jaimie Fergus, a lazy bully of a man with little skill or hydraulic insight, despite his five years' service, and no inclination to teach Frank Harris anything. The first thing he said when they set out to-gether was: "All right, Harris. Here's the first and only rule: I stay between you and the hole at all times. I don't want your ghost boots blocking my exit when things go wrong."

"What could go wrong?"

"*What could go wrong?* You are a fresh body, ain't you? How about flood, cave-in, gator, poison gas, explosion, mad dog, pack of rats, dead body? And they say vicious criminals hide out down here from time to time and kill whoever they comes upon—to silence 'em . . . not to mention McGinty." He smiled. "All right then, so long as we're clear. You first. Down the hatch."

Harris was worried, but only for one of the reasons Fergus had listed. He was worried Fergus could be right that some other gang was working down there, having beaten the Whyos to the idea. Beatrice wouldn't like that news, and he wanted to make her happy. It was also true that failure to bring back positive results might be bad for his long-term survival.

"All right," said Fergus. "Go on—put your weight into opening that hole."

The cover opened with some difficulty and a low, sonorous scraping noise. Harris looked for direction to the other man.

"Yeah, just as I thought," said Fergus after a quick glance below. "This hole's too narrow for me, so you're going down alone."

Fergus was indeed a large man, and Harris, assuming that a man had to fit in the sewers to hold a job as a sewerman, had been eager to watch how Fergus did it. But instead of seeing the behemoth fold himself up into a cricket as he'd imagined, Frank Harris now saw Fergus expand himself, rather like the blowfish on exhibit in the natural-history museum in Hamburg, all puffed up with hostility.

"What are you waiting for, your pal McGinty?"

Harris put a match to the wick of his miner's lantern and strapped it to his head, then backed down the ladder, gaff and bucket clanking against the rungs. Down below, he applied his knowledge of shoveling snow to the problem of the silt and muck that had accumulated in the pipe. Despite the lantern, it was very dark. He had to kneel to work in the pipe, which was only four feet high, but he didn't mind the tight quarters. A calm descended upon him. He'd seen plenty of nastiness on the farm, and in fact the wastewater here hardly smelled at all. It wasn't very deep, really, and it ran slow and steady and cool. It pressed the legs of his boots against his skin, seeming to support him. He filled his pail, moved deeper into the tunnel and made trip after trip back to the manhole with bucket after bucket full of sludge, which Fergus hauled out, until finally he'd cleared half the distance to the next manhole. He tied the bucket one last time to the rope Fergus dangled and called up, "That's halfway."

"Come on up, and we'll walk to the next hole."

But Harris had begun to feel oddly safe in the dark. He was pleased with how his labor had already improved the flow. His ability to take pleasure in a job well done, any job, was one of his saving graces. He wasn't going to mind being a sewerman, he realized. To Fergus he said, "I'll meet you there."

There was a brief silence as Fergus digested this; then he slid the manhole shut with a grinding sound. It was infinitely darker in the hole than before—the way the night was out on the Atlantic when the moon was new. Frank Harris thought about McGinty as he went. Soon, the bottom was once again thick with silt and debris. He filled his bucket and slogged it to the next hole. He saw the rusty ladder on the wall, but there was no shaft of light pouring down from the street above. Fergus should have gotten there much more quickly than he had. Could this be the wrong manhole? Could he have missed a turn in the short space of fifty feet?

The idea of being stuck down there was awful. What a fool he was, to think he knew his way, to think himself above the company of such a man as Fergus, to prefer a pair of haunted boots to a man, no matter what an ass. But he wasn't afraid. He had his gaff and his lamp. The boots held him tight. He climbed up the ladder without much hope, unhooked his gaff from his belt and rapped on the bottom of the manhole cover. He could hear the rattle of carriages rolling along the street above, but there was no response. The weak beam of his headlamp shone on the round metal lid, and he thought of how hard it had been to pry the other manhole cover open, even from above. Still, he stayed calm. He was thinking that the Whyos' idea of using the sewers as a getaway sounded better than it really was. This matter of not being able to get out from below would pose a fundamental problem. Then he tried to imagine Dandy Johnny's reaction to the depth of the water, the lack of headroom, the sludge. He was thinking that the sewers didn't have half the romantic cachet of the old brewery. If he told them the truth of it, maybe this job would end sooner than expected, and he wondered what the consequences of that would be for him. What should he tell Beatrice, he wondered, the truth or what he thought the Whyos wanted to hear?

Then he heard a strange wail: *Wooo-hooo.* At first he thought it was a whyo, and his stomach dropped, but no, not quite. It might be a man from another gang, although actually it hadn't sounded very human at all. A *creature then*, he thought, *a bird*. Perhaps a heron had gone fishing near a culvert and been trapped? It came again: *Wooo-hooo.* It was no bird. He couldn't help thinking *McGinty*, and his flesh crawled. He whipped his head around to look behind him, and the light on his forehead sputtered in the wind he had made. It was very black. He found he could not inhale; his chest seemed to be constricted by an iron hoop. In the pitch darkness, he was not so brave after all.

"Yo, Harris!" called the voice then, faintly. "You farging idiot, where are you? Christ! I'm not coming down there and let McGinty get me, too, you know."

He breathed again. Fergus's voice seemed to be coming from back in the other direction.

"I'm here," called Harris, his voice bouncing and rolling through the tunnel until it, too, sounded ghostly. "I guess I went the wrong way."

So he followed Fergus's voice to the right hole and resumed his mucking, and Fergus went back to resentfully hauling the bucket up the shaft and dropping it back down, and the day proceeded without further haunting or jibes from Fergus, who couldn't help wondering, with a lump in his esophagus, what or who Harris was. Harris and McGinty were the only two men he'd ever heard of opting for underground travel over street side.

The following week, they were given a job that required both men to be below. Frank Harris waited with his boots on by the locker room until ten past the whistle. Whatever his faults, Fergus had not been late before. Just as Harris was about to go into the office to inquire what to do, the door banged open, and Fergus emerged with a red face and a stubborn set to his jaw. He walked past Harris without a glance.

"That you, Mr. Harris?" called the division chief from behind his frosted-glass partition. It seemed Fergus had demanded a new partner. So Harris joined another team. The following day, those men refused to go out with him, too. By the end of the month, Harris was officially working alone, not hauling and evacuating as he'd done with Fergus, since that was a two-man job, but reaming out small pipes with long gaffs. Exactly the sort of solo work McGinty had always done.

In the mornings, before he set off, Harris spent time studying the lay of the system in the map room. He went to great lengths to memorize as much as he could of the underground metropolis. He never thought of McGinty with fear anymore. As he worked, he hummed the bits of the sewermen's ballad he'd picked up and occasionally dared to sing a German lied or two—for who would hear him? And yet he often felt that he was not alone there in the dark. Whether it was the old curmudgeon's ghost or just an odd family of Norway rats peering from a dark ledge, he couldn't be sure.

He didn't really mind working alone, not least because it greatly facilitated his mission of Whyo reconnaissance. He eventually came up with a way to open manhole covers from beneath, though it wasn't easy or especially safe, not knowing what might be above, and he made little maps on scraps of paper he kept tucked into his boots as he sloshed through the pipes.

All of this he shared with Beatrice in their ongoing lessons and the walks they took to and from work. She nodded and asked questions and seemed pleased beyond expectation. When he brought her something especially good—a new section of map, perhaps—she rewarded him with a squeeze of the arm or a lingering touch on the hand. They had not kissed again. They were behaving like a proper pair of sweethearts, not gangsters, and that suited Harris. But they'd come close. They were always flirting—little jokes, empty laughs about things unspoken. It was delicious, and it felt real, partly because he didn't feel used by her. She had still never asked him to do anything dangerous or illegal, to his great relief.

Then there was the fact that he was a pretty good sewerman. After two months on duty underground, Harris was on his way to becoming a kind of McGinty himself. He had a strong intuition as to where and why blockages formed, and he worked so efficiently that he usually finished his day's assignment before lunch. Things fell in line so easily for him underground that he himself half came to believe that McGinty was guiding him. The other men certainly thought so. They muttered among themselves as they left at night, after cleaning up in the sewermen's bath hall, and they shunned him. After all, McGinty had been a normal if ornery human being while he lived, but this Frank Harris was half on the other side already, clearly possessed. How else could he have survived wearing those boots or learned the trade so uncannily quickly?

Now and then Harris would be working quietly in a tunnel near enough to a crew of men to listen as they sang verse after verse of their ballad. By tacit agreement, they'd stopped singing it in his presence the very first week, not wanting to summon the ghost. But Harris's location was rarely what they thought it was, and over time he heard them often enough to pick up many verses. It was a work song, meant for a gang of voices, but he sang it to himself. Then one day he heard men singing the Ballad nearby, and quite without thinking he joined them in the refrain. Suddenly, he was singing alone. The other voices had stopped, and so had the sound of the work.

"Mary, mother of Christ—it's McGinty!" came a voice through the dark.

"Let's get the fuck out of here!"

There was clattering and banging and the ringing of hobnails on metal ladder rungs as every man on the crew tried to flee at once. The lid clanged shut behind them.

Now that, thought Frank Harris, smiling, *could come in handy for the Whyos,* and he went on singing in the dark, thinking how pleased Beanie would be with this new tunnel-clearing tactic.

15

RECONNAISSANCE

When he arrived home from work, Frank Harris was unquestionably the cleanest member of the O'Gamhna household. For while the others bathed just once a week, on Sundays, that was the only day that Harris did not take a mandatory bath. As Frank Harris sat down next to Beatrice for his supposed English lesson, he was intensely aware of the soapy freshness of his own skin mingling with the salty, tangy smell of hers. A shiver came over him when he caught that faint whiff of her. He had something good to report, and he was looking forward to seeing how she expressed her approval.

When he'd first told her he'd got trapped below, she'd chewed her thumbnail for a moment before she said, "Yeah, that sounds like a problem. Find out a way around it." He came up with a simple lever that could be rigged from two gaffs and would open almost any cover. "Clever, Harris, clever," she said, and then she touched his forehead lightly with her index finger. All that day he felt that spot as if it were more alive than the rest of his flesh, as if it were Ash Wednesday and she a priest who had blessed him. Another time, when he was telling her how few of the pipes were actually passable, with most between one and three feet high, she suggested they keep track of just the ones that were. That had been the beginning of a great mapping project, whereby they sat up at the kitchen table late at night, carefully sketching out the metropolitan street plan on an old bedsheet and then gradually adding all the large-gauge pipes that ran beneath it. It was a rough document, but it seemed clear that they would soon have enough of underground Manhattan charted to make possible whatever the Whyos planned to do. Now, when he told her the story of how he'd frightened off the men, she listened raptly and laughed with delight. "Really? So you can sing, can you? But this is good, Harris. It means we'll be a lot safer down there. That means we do whatever we like and almost without risk."·

He felt a wave of well-being wash over him, and then something better: She got up from the table and wrapped her arm around his shoulder. Then she bent down and gently laid a kiss on the side of his head, just by the ear. "Nice work," she whispered. He turned to her, but she stepped away.

"Good night, Harris."

One evening soon thereafter, he was sketching in a newly found section of tunnel on Twenty-third Street and telling her about the rules of the bath hall, which were enforced with vigor by the crotchety Mrs. Dolan. He thought he did a pretty good imitation of the old woman, but Beanie didn't laugh. He looked up at her and decided to take a small risk, to shift the conversation toward her.

"So how'd you get into the gang? Why'd you quit school? Isn't it free?"

"Oh, no," she'd said. "Don't start on that. You're the student, not me. I didn't come here to get educated, I came to get rich. At least rich enough to bring Padric over, too. And anyway, don't change the subject. You were telling me about the bath hall and Mrs. Dolan."

The last thing Harris wanted to do was push her too far, vex her, and so he resumed where he'd left off, painting the picture with all the detail he could muster, choosing his verbs and prepositions with care—this was their English lesson, after all.

Unless, like McGinty, you could conceive of the job as a calling or, like Harris, you were doing it to woo a recalcitrant girlfriend, there was really only one perk to working in the sewer: the nightly bath. What with the constant sloshing of sewage and the occasional bursts of effluvium when drains were opened or toilets flushed, there was no keeping clean down there. But then, every evening, there was Mrs. Dolan walking up and down the five gleaming, white-tiled aisles of claw-footed tubs, ten to a row, preparing for the men's ablutions. First, she threw the common valve that opened all taps, then she dumped scoops of powdered soap into every tub from a great bucket that she pushed in front of her on a dolly. The mixture, Harris explained to Beatrice, was mostly baking soda and shavings of glycerin soap but also contained pulverized dried camphor and the oils of lavender and thyme. It smelled marvelous—not too ladylike, just lovely and clean.

"I know the smell," said Beatrice. When he looked up, he could swear she was blushing, and it made him do so, too. She didn't have to say that her nose was full of that scent even then, or that for Harris to discuss, at length, his own daily ablutions was for her to imagine him naked, underwater. Her foot pressed his beneath the table.

"You were telling me about Mrs. Dolan," she said.

After she filled the tubs, the matron of baths returned to her tiled office with its window onto the bath hall, by which time the men had arranged themselves in a queue, buck naked, to await admittance. The Department of Public Works was not in the business of running a spa, as Mrs. Dolan often had occasion to remark to the men. "It's really more of a military operation," Harris said. Mrs. Dolan handed each man a sliver of soap, a washcloth and a single small, clean towel.

"Not the least bit daunted by all that male nudity, is she?" asked Beatrice.

He confirmed that she was not. Once the men were in their tubs, Mrs. Dolan retreated to her window, from which she enforced the departmental prohibition against shaving in the bath hall. It was a great temptation—when else were their beards so soft as after that warm soak? But Mrs. Dolan was busy enough with the greasy, grimy rings they left and would not tolerate the addition of fifty men's myriad fallen whiskers to her burden nor hesitate to pull the common lever, opening all fifty drains at once, the moment she spotted the suspicious lathering of a chin or the illicit brandishing of a razor. Barring violations, they had ten full minutes of bliss before she rang the warning bell and opened the drain. A great slurping could be heard as the fifty steaming sewermen rose, sedated by the warmth, reluctant to touch their toes to the cold tile floor, only the faintest tinge of unsavory odor still clinging to their skin.

"All those naked men . . ." Beatrice said. He was on the verge of rising from the table and pressing her up against the wall, crushing her with the clean, naked body beneath his clothes, when she went on: "You know, Mrs. Dolan could be useful to us, Harris." She was playing foot games again but coy ones. The heat had gone out of her voice. "You must make sure she likes you. Do you think she does?"

He shrugged, not at all sure why Mrs. Dolan mattered. For him, the whole conversation had been in code. It had been a flirtation. Mrs. Dolan was irrelevant. But once again, all the eye contact and innuendo led to nothing. Harris was so frustrated that he couldn't remain in the room with her, and he went out and drank beer at the corner bar for an hour, till he was fairly sure she would either be asleep or, more likely, gone off on some Whyo mission that would keep her out overnight. He loathed the fact that she spent so many nights elsewhere, but she had made it very clear it was none of his business where she went.

One afternoon a short time later, Harris had finished division business early and was exploring tunnels when he found a most unusual connection. He had noticed a pipe off the Nassau Street main whose flow seemed to be running clearer and a bit faster than usual. He made his way up current the distance of a block or so, until the pipe opened out into what, in the weak glow of his headlamp, seemed to be an underground grotto, a cave with a brook flowing through it and bubbling up into a wide pool. The pipe he'd followed was apparently less a sewer than a conduit to divert the flow from the natural stream. Then he saw that part of the cave was man-made: old cement and brickwork and ancient rotting timbers. There were great stones and rusted wagon wheels embedded in the concrete. Harris had no way of knowing it, but much of the material was rock from the grading of Bunker Hill, to the north. The spring he had found was once called the Maagde Paetje for the Dutch washerwomen who scrubbed linens in its sparkling waters and laid them to dry on the grassy slope to the north. What remained of it now ran beneath Maiden Lane and out to the harbor, north of Wall Street.

The space Harris found himself in was perhaps twenty yards long and high enough to stand up in, though the footing was dubious. It seemed that the stream had eroded away much of the tunnel built to contain it. A little further on, there was a long ledge about a yard in width. When he aimed the faint circle of light from his headlamp at it, he spotted a couple of whiskey bottles. How long ago had they been left there, he wondered—or how recently? There was no reason for an ordinary sewerman to go there. Just beyond the ledge, he discovered a low arch, maybe two feet high and set into the base of the foundation wall, where the irregular cement gave way to orderly brickwork. A thin stream of sewage trickled from the open-ing, and he deduced that the buried stream had been used by the builders as a natural sewer. He'd heard of such serendipitous connections but never seen one till then. He wondered just where he was in relation to the streets above. The nearest manhole cover he knew of was the one he'd come through, all the way back down that long tunnel, but surely there was a way to get into the building's cellar from beyond that arch. He would have liked to investigate, if he dallied he was liable to miss check-in and not get his bath, and he was loath to go home to Beatrice all tainted with sewage and sweat. He put off further exploration for another time, sloshed back to the manhole, then ran the whole way back, making it just in time to watch the men filing into the bath hall without him. He threw off his gear and jumped out of his boots and stepped into place, last in line. Mrs. Dolan just squinted at him. She withheld his soap and linens and waved him aside as the others stepped into their baths.

"You wait there, McGinty." He cringed at the name and shielded his privates with his hands. "I'd like to know one thing," she said. "Are you a man or a swine? Look at your gear." He had left it in a heap on the floor of the locker room in his haste, it was true. "By God, you got the best boots in the division, and you can't even hang them up to dry. It's a disgrace! Clean that up and then come back and talk to me about a bath."

It didn't take him long, but he could feel the seconds pass like minutes. He was missing most if not all of his bath. Finally, when he returned to her office door, she seemed not to see him, so he cleared his throat.

"Well, God in heaven, Harris, what are you still standing there for? The pleasure of showing your big muscles and chest hair off to me? You think you're some Adonis, do you? I'd say not! Just go take your bath!"

She was entirely unreasonable—clearly, she didn't like him—but at any rate, she had released him. The smell of fresh-run water was in the air as he entered the room, damp but clean. His heart slowed and his skin braced at the prospect of immersion. How hot would it be, how cool? How many minutes were left before she pulled the drain? He dipped his toe in, his whole foot, his leg, his other foot and finally sat down. The water was still good and hot. He only wished he might dissolve away into it, like Mrs. Dolan's powdered soap, and be carried off through the drain, away from the strange life he was leading. He slumped down, letting his feet slide over the edge of the basin and his shoulders sink beneath the waterline, until his entire head and torso were underwater, and he exhaled a complicated vapor of emotions that bubbled up in a thick stream.

Just a few moments later, as he sat up again, Mrs. Dolan appeared at her window and rang the warning bell, but rather than pulling the lever she announced a five-minute extension. The men responded to the news in stunned silence—such a thing had never happened before—and for the next several minutes there was no sound in the room but quiet, blissful splashing, no sensation but the delicious contrast of cool air alternating with warm water. Harris examined his physiognomy through the shimmering, refractory water of his tub and saw the body of his father at the baths in Baden, the genitals that had seemed so fearfully dark red, wrinkled and hairy to him then. They were built the same, exactly so, in body if in nothing more. Then Mrs. Dolan rang the bell for real, and the water drained out around him, as irretrievable as his childhood, leaving him high and dry. He was insoluble in water, after all.

On the way home, Harris wondered what sort of job the Whyos were planning and to what extent they were planning it according to what they learned from him. Why had they been so keen on having an outsider do the job he'd been assigned? Surely not just squeamishness. And he thought of Beatrice. Why was it that every time it seemed inevitable, every time they were on the verge of something—a kiss, a declaration—she withdrew? Was she playing him just to extract the maximum information for the gang, or was it real? Harris tried to imagine the sewermen's bath hall full of Whyos who'd just pulled off a heist, killed a handful of bystanders and absconded with a fortune. Each man would be naked in his tub, just like the sewermen, but the ground around them would be scattered with billies and gougers, pistols and blackjacks, slungshots and all manner of knives. Mrs. Dolan wouldn't be there to bully the Whyos into stowing their equipment neatly. The water in Piker Ryan's tub would surely run black, if not red from the blood of some victim.

Of course, Harris didn't really believe that the Whyos would gain access to the Public Works building or try to wash up in the bath hall, even if they did do a job using the sewers. The one thing he did know about the Whyos was that they were fixated on stealth, and except to Johnny himself, it didn't seem that hygiene was a Whyo priority. There was no reason for them to take such a risk. No, it was a silly notion. He was just letting his mind run free.

Harris had no idea.

16

MOTHER DOLAN AND
THE GRAND PLAN

How could Harris have guessed that Dandy Johnny's full name was John Dolan or that the matron of the sewermen's bath hall was fondly called *Mother Dolan* by Whyos and Why Nots alike? No better than he could have known the plan the Whyos had for the sewers or what a beauty old Mother Dolan had been in her day, how pure her soprano voice.

Meg Dolan was the penultimate child of a large sheep-farming clan, all but forgotten by her parents amidst the throng. The boys were the ones the family counted on; girls just did the washing. But Meg distinguished herself early as a star of the parish church choir. At sixteen, she said good-bye without many tears and made her way to Dublin to live with a cousin and pursue her singing. She was luckier than her father had predicted: She soon became a paid soloist at St. Francis Xavier. Even so, she wasn't paid much, just pin money, and she still had to scrub floors during the week to pay her rent. She dreamt of grander things. Like every singer alive, no doubt, she wanted to follow in the footsteps of Jenny Lind, the Swedish Nightingale and international sensation. She was thrifty with her money and stole a little from the collection plate every week when she was changing out of her choir robes. In a couple of years, she had enough to book her passage to America.

She'd been naïve back then, she'd freely admit, quite a little fool. Upon her arrival in New York, Meg Dolan (who never married or changed her name, despite her eventual use of *Missus*) was disappointed to find that openings for divas were few and far between. She became a servant in a wealthy house on Washington Square. She cried every night for a month, so badly did she miss Ireland, her six brothers, three sisters and, above all, the family's twenty-odd sheepdogs. In New York, too, she gravitated to the pets of the family she worked for, for solace. One evening, the master's son found her glumly scratching the neck of the house's retriever and put his arm around her shoulder. She'd been on the edge of tears, and this bit of human comfort pushed her over it. He was her age, after all, and if not for the thousand and one circumstances that put them in different worlds, he might have been her friend. Indeed, for several minutes, he seemed to be her friend. He patted her back and offered her his handkerchief, and she was glad for his sympathy. But it was what he did next that made the night a pivotal one for Meg Dolan: He let his palm slide across her breast and whispered that she could earn twice her weekly wages that night if she joined him in the loft of the carriage house at midnight. She stood and stalked off without another word, wiping her eyes on her sleeve and her nose on her apron. Then she thought it over. She kept the rendezvous but negotiated the amount. Her encounter with the master's son was not particularly pleasant, but she'd made as much money on her back in an hour as she would have in a month of twelve-hour days on her knees with a bucket. To her, it seemed a bargain.

It wasn't long before she'd forsaken the bucket altogether and taken up residence in a house of women. She was a good-looking girl, and it was a high-class establishment. She soon had several regular clients and carefully cultivated her relationship with the most attentive one. Within the year, he offered to pay her expenses in full for the privilege of exclusivity. When she told him those expenses would include a private apartment, singing lessons, season tickets to the opera and a recital gown, he chuckled and got out his checkbook. He liked her ambition. He put her in a sweet, out-of-the-way brownstone on the far West Side, met her at her box at the opera twice a month in season and bought all her clothes. He spent two nights a week in her bed, an arrangement which also suited his wife. When he died in her arms of what the coroner termed apoplexy five years later, he'd just signed over the deed to her apartment in exchange for her agreement to abort the child she was expecting. She wanted the baby, even out of wedlock, but he was unwilling to indulge his mistress there—he had a name in society to protect, after all, a wife, proper children. He was thinking of running for office eventually.

"All right," she said. "Of course I understand. And thank you for the house, pet. It's lovely of you. I'm going to show you how grateful I can be, don't worry."

He had no idea of the potency of the dappled purple foxglove that bloomed in her little brownstone's rear yard. He'd never paid much attention to it, really, and wasn't suspicious by nature; she'd never given him reason to be. He never even considered that his Meg might be the reason he began to feel iffy that evening after dinner, to see the world through a greenish haze. He put it down to a bad oyster and took to his bed. When he began to vomit, Meg had suggested they call for a doctor, but (as she well knew) his physician was his brother-in-law, which would have made things awkward. He declined. In short, it all went according to plan, and that night, while her benefactor lay dying, Meg felt the first stirring of the baby in her own belly. She called on the unsuspecting wife the following morning in tears—and at the servants' entrance, out of respect. She offered total discretion, asked for nothing. In gratitude, the widow sent a large check the following week. The death was not investigated by the police, partly because it seemed natural that a man of his years and portly stature might pass in his sleep, but largely, too, because his wife preferred to hush it up.

So suddenly Meg Dolan owned her own house and was free: two nearly impossible dreams. She was also pregnant and without work, but she had thought out the problem of how to generate a regular income to cover her living costs. She opened her rooms to a couple of women she knew from her previous lodgings, charging them in lieu of rent a percentage of the earnings they generated under her aegis. She didn't join in their toils, however, and not just because she was by then enormous with child. (There were plenty of men who would have paid extra on account of that.) No, she had decided she was getting out of the business for the sake of her baby.

Through her singing teacher, she found part-time work at the Newsboys Lodging House, where she led their choir of street-hardened, beer-drinking, pint-sized sopranos and helped out with the housekeeping. The lady lodgers stayed on, however—they were paying for Johnny's sailor suits and shiny shoes. When Johnny was five, she finally managed to parlay her connection to a regular customer of one of her lodgers into the job as housekeeper at the Department of Public Works, but she kept on leading the Newsboys Choir because she liked it. It gave her a chance to remain involved with music and to keep Johnny busy with a wholesome activity. He was one of her top soloists, and it wasn't favoritism; he was good.

They weren't wealthy by any means, but regardless of their financial situation she always bought her son the finest clothes and shoes and made sure he looked like a little gentleman, whether he was at school, at choir practice or playing stickball with his mates. The only problem was, Johnny wasn't a little gentleman; little gentlemen didn't play stickball or fraternize with newsboys or grow up fatherless in houses of ill repute. He just looked like one. At the age of seven, Johnny Dolan was already known for his temper and his tendency to break noses. He might have looked like a ponce, the way his mother dressed him, but no one dared make any remark but "Looking dandy today, Johnny." At ten, he dropped out of the Newsboys Choir. It didn't matter how Mrs. Dolan groomed him, how sweet his soprano or how respectable her present job; Johnny was drawn to the streets. He continued to dress fastidiously and to preen like an aristocrat as he grew older, but he took increasingly to fighting, to women and to drink—in short, to everything his mother had hoped to save him from. She'd compromised the means for the end, and it had backfired: She'd not even gotten the end. There were years when she wept herself to sleep every night with worry and regret.

When Johnny first fell in with Googy Corcoran and the Whyos, his mother tried to rein him in. She badgered. She slapped. She threw crockery. She yelled. She tried pecuniary and culinary rewards to keep him home at night. She failed. He was sixteen and not eager to spend time with his mother—pork chops, potatoes and battery notwithstanding. Once, she overheard the details of a job the gang was planning to pull and spilled it to the cops, hoping the lesson of it would put an end to such things for once and all. Johnny was arrested, but a few days later he was back out of jail, charges nimbly evaded, with a new friend and recruit for Googy's gang: a pure thug named Piker Ryan. Piker took to Johnny right from the start and was loyal as a sheepdog. Together, they made piles of money. They made a perfect team—brains and beauty plus brawn—and were particularly adept at using the Whyo songs to bring their plans off without detection. As a result, they got away with everything from petty larceny to murder. It wasn't long before others in the gang began to look to Johnny instead of Googy for leadership.

Johnny had been in the gang several years when his mother finally accepted that in spite of herself, she'd raised a son who would have nothing to do with the straight and narrow. From then on, she turned her efforts to ensuring that her son became the top gangster in the city. It was a brilliant stroke for her as a mother: It brought her wayward, distant son back to her. Once she'd shown him she was proud of him no matter what work he did, he stopped slamming doors and sulking entirely. Indeed, no son could have been more solicitous of his mother than Johnny or more eager to take her advice. It turned out that Meg Dolan's advice was excellent.

As for Googy Corcoran, he never saw Mrs. Dolan coming. No one did. She stayed in the shadows, just a dowdy housekeeper for a city agency, letting Johnny appear to do it all on his own. But the truth was that before long she was in on everything Piker and Johnny did, advising if not directing the action. Then came the knife fight at the Morgue bar, a spring day the Whyos would never forget. How could they, when it ended with Johnny kicking Googy's head in? Johnny had found out Googy was keeping money and information about jobs from the other guys, which made him mad to start, but the last straw was that Googy had set up one of the younger boys, a kid Johnny was friendly with, to take a fall with the cops and distract attention from himself. It so happened that the kid was shot. The cops had been expecting a hardened criminal—Googy Corcoran—not a twelve-year-old. The kid died. Johnny challenged Googy about it in the basement of the Morgue the next night, and before long they were circling, knees bent, knives drawn. At dawn, a bloody mop head and a body cast in cement were dumped off Corlear's Hook by Piker Ryan.

With Dandy Johnny in charge and his mother covertly guiding him, the Whyos thrived, becoming more effective in their heists, more secretive in their ways, more moderate in their violence, pickier about their victims. They rarely went after weaklings anymore, except odiously rich ones, and they avoided small fry altogether. Mrs. Dolan had denounced the robbing of the poor as neither moral nor profitable. Some of this happened through subtle changes, but most of it was the result of straightforward policy implementations introduced gradually but unequivocally over the course of Johnny's first year in power.

The first rule was the one against pimping. The second they called the Tithe, under which all Whyos and Why Nots were obligated to turn a portion of their earnings back to the organization. It wasn't simply a tenth, though — it was progressive, based on the amount each person had earned. In exchange for paying this tax, every Whyo and Why Not could count on a steady weekly income from the gang, with the exact amount being a function of need, merit and overall gang revenue. If a Whyo made nothing at all one week, for whatever reason, he could still always count on a minimum draw; if a Why Not hit it big, half was hers to keep. The rest went into the communal pot. And all were entitled to aid in the face of financial, legal, medical or other adversity. A few Whyos tried to make their way around the new regulations at first, accustomed as they were to living off the fat of their girlfriends' hard-won earnings. They got their noses broken. The funny thing was, the no-pimping rule brought most people's revenue up. In the very first months, the Why Nots' contributions to the till rose by 25 percent. All of them were skilled pickpockets, an occupation which was often more lucrative than whoring and far less likely to lead to dissipation, drunkenness, depression and late sleeping.

At the same time these reforms were being introduced, Dandy Johnny and his mother began working on refinements and variations on the traditional song signal, the whyo. In Googy's day, the most common deployment of the whyo had still been as a musical war cry, a signature that proudly linked the gang to the deeds it committed. Mrs. Dolan told Johnny what she thought of that: "It's idiotic." And yet she saw great potential in the whyo, if used intelligently, especially combined with the fact that most of the boys could sing. She had trained many of them herself in the Newsboys Choir. One night, as she lay in her bed thinking about how much she knew the boys loved to yodel, whyo and hoot and what a liability it was, her mind drifted to the farm in County Sligo where she'd grown up.

All those brothers, even more dogs, countless sheep. Her father'd had more than a hundred whistle patterns for the roughly two dozen dogs and pups, and all but a basic few of the commands were unique to individual dogs. The signals that told Orkney to go left, right, forward, lie down and come were each Orkney's alone. No other dog understood or would respond to them, for each had its own set of whistles, thus enabling the shepherd to choreograph the dogs' movements with exquisite precision. The dogs could be told to move the sheep exactly where the shepherd wanted them. Whenever a dog died, a new pup was named after him and trained in his commands, so that there was always an Orkney, always a Queenie, always a Hal, and every Orkney's *Sit!* was always three short, high pipes and a long trill. Lying there in her bed that night, twenty-five years since she'd last laid eyes on Ireland, Meg Dolan envisioned an ideal gang, in which the Whyos and their girls were more or less the boss's sheepdogs. They would communicate openly yet specifically—indeed, *privately.* It would shore up the boss's power on the one hand and enable the commission of nearly perfect crimes on the other.

Johnny knew all about County Sligo and the sheepdogs. His mother was not unnostalgic and had told him many stories of her youth. But in the following days, she went into greater detail than ever before and gradually broached her idea to him.

"No, we'd look like pussies on the street if we do it that way," he objected. The Whyos had always been famous as bullies; they loved their war cry.

"Who cares what you look like on the street, if you never get caught? The gang will know who you really are. You'll know. But at the same time, the cops won't. You won't ever be thrown in jail. And you're going to get rich. Besides, you've no need to worry about how you look—you always look fabulous, Johnny."

"*Ma.*"

Soon, in addition to the whistles and calls that were common in Googy Corcoran's day, some of the top Whyos and Why Nots were trying out a new style of whyoing, including the use of musical variation and various mimicked sounds of the city, from animal noises to slammed doors. It was obviously effective, and it was pure pleasure how easy it made jobs go. Everyone else wanted in on it, too, which had been the plan. But before Johnny and his mother taught a gang member the expanded language, they swore him or her to a new level of secrecy and allegiance. They dropped those they deemed untrustworthy or tone-deaf. Eventually, each Whyo and Why Not then had his or her own set of calls for conveying information to Johnny. A nuthatch mating song could be whistled repeatedly so as to represent figures—indicating, say, an amount or a street address or a time. A ditty hummed in F might indicate that a job had gone off, whereas F-sharp meant it hadn't, and G would send the message that urgent assistance was required. The great complexities that could be embedded in variations in musical key quickly led to the sidelining of less musical Whyos and the ouster of anyone whose pitch was poor.

Further refinements were introduced some years in, after Mother Dolan saw a ventriloquist perform at the Old Bowery Theater one evening. She was amazed, and she wanted to know how to do it herself, so she dragged Johnny to several courses of lectures on the subject and a seminar on mesmerism, too. It could be downright confusing to be in a room with the two of them when they were practicing. They seemed to speak from the corners of the room, without moving their lips. It was all about diverting attention. Gradually, they introduced new and ever more subtle vocalizations and techniques to the gang. Soon, the Whyos were not just in constant, covert contact with one another all across the city, they were also influencing the behavior of their victims, encouraging compliance, distracting attention, monitoring and reporting on the whereabouts and activities of potential victims, potential rivals and of course the cops.

All across Lower Manhattan, the Whyos' calls were as pervasive, as influential and as little noticed as oxygen, say, or germs. As Mother Dolan had predicted, Whyos were rarely caught in the act anymore. And yes, as Johnny feared, people on the streets said the gang was on the wane. The

Whyos developed a reputation for being just a bunch of do-nothing ex-newsboys and whores too lazy even to work. Which was just how they wanted it. It wasn't about fame or notoriety—it was about power, money and freedom. Also happiness and justice. For Mother Dolan's rules did more than just make the Whyos a richer, more elusive and effective criminal organization; she and her son had created a quasi-socialist utopia for thieves, hookers and killers. They all lived comfortably, but none lived lavishly, not wanting to arouse suspicions about their income. If the rest of the world had to suffer as a result, their feeling was *Well then, so be it.*

Part of their elusiveness came from the fact that they rarely met en masse anymore. But that didn't mean the sense of community faltered. They still had Billy's and the Morgue, where everyone hung out, but instead of gathering formally to talk about plans and jobs, the Dolans devised a system of remote check-ins, whereby a whispered code was passed from voice to voice, like the flashing lights or semaphore flags of a signal corps. Each Whyo and every Why Not had to report back to Johnny within three hours of hearing it, reiterating the code with variations particular to his or her own personal lingo and also reporting what he or she had earned that week. No Whyo or Why Not knew the rules for anyone else's variations—some changed weekly, some monthly, some with the weather or the phase of the moon—so no one could cover for anyone else. And since the code and the variations alike originated from Dandy Johnny (or rather, his mother), the Dolans' control was perfect. Only they knew everything. If anyone failed to check in, an alarm was raised, and Whyos would pour out of the woodwork, from bars, brothels, flops and even respectable homes, to comb the streets for the delinquent. If it turned out the absentee was in any trouble, it was dealt with. If the failure had resulted from drunkenness, negligence or some other oversight, a generous dose of trouble was dealt out to the offender. The check-in itself was a hassle, but not as bad as having to go to meetings that might end in busts. The gang tolerated it because it was undeniable that Johnny's system was making the members richer and keeping them safer from the police and other gangsters than they'd ever been before.

The Whyos all quite naturally assumed that in order to have invented this scheme Johnny Dolan must be the cleverest and most eloquent Whyo of them all. That, plus his charm and ruthlessness, was why they followed him. They loved his mother, whom they thought of as a kind of mascot, because she took care of them and taught them to sing, but they did not understand the scale of her role in reinventing the gang. Even though she was the one who coached them vocally, the gang believed that Johnny himself came up with all the innovations in whyoing. That was how Meg Dolan wanted it. She also kept the books; twice a week, after the check-in, she tallied all the gang members' accounts, which could then be settled at the Morgue's bar over the course of the next few days. In keeping with their policy of stealth in plain sight, the Morgue was open to the public now, and the gang no lónger openly did business there.

As for who became a Whyo or Why Not, Mother Dolan was the shadow boss on that front, too. She happened to be a far better judge of both character and voice than Johnny was. A Whyo had to be a very particular combination of baldly immoral, highly social, musically gifted and loyal to the core to gain her approval. She had often vetoed his candidates, but there was only one person she'd ever tapped to join the gang who hadn't made the cut with Johnny: Luther Undertoe.

The Dolans had known Undertoe for years—he was in the Newsboys Choir, early on, when he and Johnny were still sopranos. He'd been a brilliant singer. But around the time Johnny first joined up with Googy, Undertoe had drifted another way. Mrs. Dolan had often wondered what became of him. Then, one night shortly before Johnny became the boss, Undertoe showed up again, cheating at cards down at Billy's. He was doing it quite successfully, didn't get caught or draw attention to himself and walked off with fifty dollars. Since Johnny had joined the game at some point, some of those dollars were his. Meg Dolan was curious enough to follow Undertoe out of the bar; she watched him rob two gentlemen of their wallets without raising so much as a shout, then step into a brothel, where she discovered he was living, providing security to the madam and her girls in lieu of rent. She remembered Luther's voice; it had been pure and pretty. And he'd grown up nicely, too, she thought. In the following weeks, she observed him closely and saw that he killed easily, at only the slightest resistance, but also that he did it neatly, never falling under suspicion. He wasn't as subtle as the Whyos—he was swiftly gaining the street name of *the Undertaker* in those days—but he routinely skirted justice by bribing the police. He also seemed to have a small but loyal cadre of newsboys under his control. She was thinking he could be a useful ally and told Johnny as much.

"Forget it, Ma. He's not even Irish. Besides, it ain't up to me to bring new guys in. I'm not the boss."

"You brought in Piker."

"Well, that one was obvious. Googy liked him. And he wasn't a bloody dutchman."

She shrugged, but she didn't forget. Undertoe was a bit of a snake in the grass, a dirty fighter, gratuitously violent—in short, a good man to have on your side, a worrisome one to work against. She feared that if she couldn't convert him to a henchman, he'd eventually become a dangerous rival. She decided to approach him herself one afternoon, to test his mettle.

All of Five Points seemed to be taking in the matinee at the Old Bowery Theater—a musicale of some sort about Indians and pioneers, with plenty of scalping and shooting and interracial love to keep the theatergoers happy. She spoke to him at intermission. He seemed surprised at her approach and scratched his neck nervously at first, but there was an eagerness in his eyes. She'd known there would be. She hadn't forgotten the way Undertoe responded to mothering as a boy. His own mother had been a sideshow artist who died when he was young, and he obviously craved maternal affection. Meg Dolan knew all too well that such a yearning never goes away.

Shortly thereafter, she sent a note around to his brothel, inviting Luther for dinner on a night when she knew Johnny would be out breaking houses uptown. She served him her signature stewed mutton, cooked eighteen hours in a bed of glowing coals. Tender was not the word—it was succulent to the point of being pudding, a savory mush, and just as soothing to Undertoe's palate as it was to her Johnny's. It served her purpose: After that, Undertoe was more or less putty in her hands. Without telling Johnny, she took him under her wing. Subtly, she groomed him to be an excellent second string, spoiling him here, confusing him there, misleading him about certain facts, keeping him out of Johnny's way but also going out of her own way to make sure nothing ever got too hard for him, never letting him yearn too much, whether for food, liquor or her attention. The final test was telling him she disapproved of his flagrant and bloody style of letting off steam—he was otherwise so subtle. He passed: reined himself in and actually went a fortnight without killing anyone. She encouraged him to get out of the brothel, and that was when he got himself the job as a night watchman for Barnum.

Meg Dolan told herself that when the time came, she would forge an alliance between Johnny and Undertoe based on their shared affection for her. It was one of her few missteps. She had a soft spot for Undertoe, didn't see he had motives of his own or how her interest in another young man would froth her own son's envy. As for Undertoe, he was not the simple creature she imagined. What he saw was that Mother Dolan thrived by taking in lost souls, the same way she'd done back at the Newsboys Lodging House. Clearly she had some need for young men to love her, and he felt it could be useful with regard to handling that annoying fop Johnny Dolan somewhere down the line. Not that he didn't get a warmish feeling when she clasped him to her bosom, but that wasn't why he went along for the ride.

Then Johnny took Googy down.

"That's my Johnny-boy," she said to him the next day. "I like it that you acted in defense of one of the boys. The others will never forget that." Then she prodded him: "But what about Undertoe, Johnny? I know you don't like him, but I don't want him against you."

Normally, Johnny never disagreed with his mother, but he said no to Undertoe. "Why are you so interested, Ma? What is it about him? He's scum."

"I'm not sure," she said. "Just indulge me, Johnny."

Mrs. Dolan stewed another mutton shoulder and invited Luther over again. She didn't warn her son in advance, suspecting he would fail to show up.

When Johnny opened the door, he couldn't believe his eyes. Just that morning, he'd discovered it was Undertoe who'd fingered a Whyo trainee to the cops. Johnny didn't like stool pigeons. What he did at the threshold was haul back and punch Undertoe. Then the two of them were down, wrestling in the doorway. Johnny had Undertoe's head by the hair and was smashing it against the doorjamb and Undertoe was reaching in his waist-coat for his knife when Mrs. Dolan hurled her bucket of washing-up water at the men. They separated like dogs in the street, bits of scum and a sheen of grease adorning their hair and sodden clothes.

Undertoe's ears were ringing loudly, as they did in times of stress, but he stood up and said, "Well, if it isn't Dandy Johnny. Nice to see you. It smells good in here. Did you make your mutton again, Mother D.?"

"What?" said Johnny. "What, Ma? You invited him to dinner before?"

"Johnny," she said. This wasn't quite the scenario she had planned.

"Well that blows all." He grabbed his walking stick and hat and stormed out. Mother Dolan encouraged Luther to stay.

"You two boys never did get along, did you?" she said, like a doddering old lady with no idea of the situation. Of course, Undertoe underestimated her, too. He boggled at her naïveté as he reassured her that he was fine and he took no offense. After dinner, she sat down at the piano and sang. Undertoe listened. She asked him to join her in "Yankee Doodle Dandy." He demurred. Then "Danny Boy." He shook his head. She asked him if he had another song he liked, maybe a hymn from the old days.

"Leave off, Mother D. I don't sing no more, not since I had the mumps and got this ringing in my ears, lost my pitch. You don't want to hear it any more than I want to do it."

"Oh," she said. "Luther, I had no idea." She gave him his pudding and then hustled him out the door. That was it for Undertoe becoming a Whyo. Johnny despised him, and now it turned out he didn't have the skills. She would have to deal with the rivalry some other way. One of those ways turned out to be lowering the Whyos' profile, and Luther, like the rest of the metropolis, had had few reminders of Johnny or the Whyos since then.

By the time Frank Harris was shanghaied by Beatrice and Fiona, the Whyos' subtle dominion stretched wider across the island of Manhattan than any other gang's. They chose not to cross rivers or range too far uptown because centralized command and vocal communication were the linch-pins of their operation. Every Whyo and Why Not was fluent in their language, and the membership was stable.

Bringing in Frank Harris was an anomaly—his allegiances and vocal

skills were unclear—but in fact neither Johnny nor his mother actually
wanted to bring him into the gang. Johnny's dislike for sacrificing stooges
notwithstanding, they had a plan for which they needed someone expend-
able, someone who didn't know Mrs. Dolan. The job was big enough that
it was worth the security risk. If the man turned out to be really good, he
might make it into the gang; more likely, they would be getting rid of him
a few months down the line. Harris was perfect. And there was an added
bonus for Johnny: Removing Harris just when he was due to take a fall for
Undertoe had put Undertoe on bad footing with the cops. But that was just
the gravy.

The particular job that Harris would be helping with was a departure
for the gang, but using the sewers had been long in the planning. Ever
since she'd gotten the job at the Sewer Division, Mrs. Dolan had been fascinated by the idea that the map of Manhattan had three dimensions, not
just two. That was what had kept her there, even after Johnny's income
made it unnecessary for his mother to work. There were old tunnels, and
there were new ones going in at all times, thanks to Boss Tweed and the
Sanitary Commission. She saw the promise of covert mobility, myriad secret caches and a network of hideouts. If she was even half right, the sewer
system could turn out to be the capstone to the Whyos' control of the city,
the foaming head on their mug of Owney Geoghegan's ale. They just
needed a mole with no known connection to the hygiene matron's son. It
was a small worksite, the Sewer Division, and she didn't want to have to
fake not knowing a man; the lie could be too easily revealed, and she didn't
want to risk compromising herself if the man blew his cover or was caught.
They'd been keeping an eye out for the right person for some time. Then,
shortly before Harris turned up, Mrs. Dolan had learned a secret that
brought urgency to the idea.

She'd passed several top-hatted men entering the Public Works building
one evening as she left, but then she realized she'd forgotten her scarf and
went back to collect it. She'd never been much interested in what took
place in the office of Mr. Towle, the superintendent of the Sewer Division,
before, but she'd often heard him sneezing or exclaiming through the vent
in the wall of her office, which shared a heating duct with Towle's. That

night, when she saw those gentlemen disappear down the corridor, she'd had a feeling there was something of interest going on. She returned quietly to her office, found her scarf and then pressed her ear to the metal grate, holding her breath. The conversation she overheard changed everything, at least for Harris. It was why Beanie and Fiona had saved him from the gallows; it was why the Whyos had let him live, even when it turned out he wasn't quite the man they had imagined; it was why he was there.

17.

THE GROTTO

eatrice knew part of the Dolans' plan, not all of it, but enough to know that Harris's chances of surviving very long were slim. So she was well aware that it was foolish to grow attached to him, and yet she couldn't help herself. She liked him. He made it difficult not to. And despite the eye-gouger she'd brandished at him, despite the blasé manner she affected whenever she remembered to, despite the way she always pulled away unless she needed something from him there and then, despite the fact that Harris knew perfectly well she was reporting everything back to Dandy Johnny, he kept doing it—flirting, making eyes. If she hadn't felt anything herself, she would just have taken him to a cheap hotel, given him what he wanted and enjoyed herself. She was no prude, Beanie, and she found Harris appealing, especially the new Harris. He wasn't pretty, he didn't have a face like Johnny, but he was solid and clean and strong. That was fine. Sex would have been fine. Her problem was that despite her long experience in the gang, despite her excellent self-control in most situations and her generally sanguine manner, Beatrice had lately found she was *fond* of Frank Harris, inordinately fond. She knew she was encouraging him. She knew she should stop. It would only make the whole thing more horrible later. But he kept surprising her, kept turning out to be unexpectedly competent in ways that were different and better than the average Whyo. He was so mechanically inclined, what with that sewer-gaff lever he'd invented. And he was unexpectedly adventurous in his explorations underground. And occasionally he was quite funny, though she wasn't always sure it was intentional.

Somehow, Harris had earned her allegiance in the past months. Not many people could claim to have done that, over the years. The gang, sure, as a group, as a society—that was her home. Fiona, her partner. The O'Gamhnas, more or less. Padric. Now Harris was butting quite unbidden into that space. But however she felt about him, Beatrice had to face the reality: Harris was not a Whyo. He might have become one if he'd been who they thought he was back at the brewery, but he wasn't. She grew a bit hopeful, though, when she found out he could sing. That was a point in his favor. She'd pointed it out to Johnny when she relayed Harris's tactic for scaring off the sewermen, adding how easily he picked up popular tunes, from the Irish songs the O'Gamhnas crooned around the flat to the lullabies Colleen sang her boys at night. But the sewermen's ballad was the most impressive. He'd used music exactly as the Whyos did: to control other people, to get a thing he needed. In a certain sense, he'd reinvented the wheel, which was a fairly impressive if redundant accomplishment. She'd gone so far as to hint that Johnny ought to bring Harris in, give him a tryout, teach him the language, but Johnny generally didn't like suggestions. His eyes glazed over, and he told her to scram.

Harris had had no idea, when she started to work singing into his English lessons, that Beatrice was coaching him, that she was trying to save his life. She had him teach her songs he knew, verses of the Ballad or German hymns, the words of which he translated while she worked out harmonies; or she'd teach him an Irish song, or something else with complicated key changes that she knew would be useful for whyoing. There were times when all other activity in the household stopped, and the family applauded at the end.

It was clear to Beatrice that, sooner or later, there were only going to be two ways for Harris to go: either become a proper Whyo or face Piker Ryan in an alley. Temperamentally, she knew he wasn't Whyo material. She doubted he had the stomach for murder. Still, he worked hard. He kept coming home with promising bits of information. He'd told her of enormous tunnels eight and ten feet tall on the Upper West Side where submerged rivers sluiced out to the harbor and three men could walk abreast.

There was that spring-fed grotto. After she'd shown interest in it, he'd gone back and charted its exact location on their map of the underground city: Nassau Street and Maiden Lane. He went out of his way, going quite far up-town to scout out places of possible interest to the Whyos, in particular a supposedly dry tunnel near Twenty-third Street that Johnny was extremely curious about. Beatrice sensed it had something to do with the Dolans' big plan for the sewers. Harris hadn't found it yet, presumably because it wasn't hooked up to the system, but he'd made any number of special trips, just looking out for junctions where the drainage didn't make sense. There were days when Beatrice felt certain that if she could convince Johnny how much initiative Harris had shown on the Whyos' behalf, she could get him brought in. Then there were days she couldn't even look at Harris because all she could think was that he was doomed. Sometimes she dreamed up various ways she might help him cut and run—the fantasy would quickly devolve into a pile of limbs, an ecstasy of long-delayed requital—but she knew her gang too well to think they'd ever really make it out of the me-tropolis alive.

For a whole year, she coached him, and he worked underground, and they filled in block after block of their map. Harris found his pent-up yearn-ings coming out in unexpected ways. It started one afternoon, when he'd gone cruising in search of unsuspected trouble spots and ended up at the Ann Street culvert, which he knew was an especially finicky and influential one, capable of causing any number of collateral problems. He didn't know it was where McGinty had died. He wasn't even trying to scare the others that day, but he sang as he sloshed through the pipes without thinking about what he sang. He didn't even know how many men were in the area. He didn't care. He was daydreaming about Beatrice's ankles, a glimpse of one of which he'd gotten that morning while she laced her boots. He was remembering how slim her legs looked in those breeches she had worn the day he met her. He'd seen her wear them again, since he moved into the O'Gamhnas', when she was going out on some Whyo job. They hugged her flesh in a way that drove him close to uncontrol, to action. It would be all or nothing, yes or no, he knew. He was almost ready to take the chance. As these thoughts of legs and risks occupied his mind, his lips and lungs were producing a particularly eerie and quavering rendition of a truly lewd and gloomy verse of the Ballad. It was enough to put the terror into three separate crews who overheard him, all on one day, without his even planning it or seeing a soul. Harris heard about it at quitting time, when Fergus turned to him and said, "Harris, weren't you around City Hall today?"

"In the general area, I guess."

"Did you *hear* anything?"

"Uh, no," he said, dreading that he'd have to go home and tell Beanie his singing ruse no longer worked — he'd overused it, and the men had figured it out.

"Well, there you go," said Fergus, turning back to a couple of the other men. "It's obvious: It's those Goddamn boots — they're calling up McGinty's ghost, but somehow Harris is protected. It's unnatural."

Once a voice shouted back at Harris, "Hey, McGinty! Leave us alone! Why don't you go haunt the new man, Harris? *He's* the one going around in your boots."

"Fergus?" Harris had called in his most ghostly brogue. *"Fer-gus?"*

But the only response was that of another voice saying, "Fergus, are you daft? You don't exchange words with a hant!" and then there was the usual *slosh, clatter, bang* as the men vacated the tunnel.

Harris made a practice of haunting sewers near where he knew crews were working and testing out the Ballad. It always worked. He'd gotten so good at his job that his daily assignments barely constrained him at all, and he began conducting a little reign of underground terror on the side. He really had become McGinty, in a way. He was a loner down there, but he took a profound satisfaction in keeping New York's sewage flowing. Harris also began covertly attending to the jobs that were left undone by the men he scared away, and with the news of so many spontaneously resolving backups even the superintendent of sewers, Mr. Towle, began to wonder if work was indeed being done by some occult force. One day, he donned boots himself and went on an inspection tour. He discovered that virtually every line south of City Hall was newly scraped and free of standing water, blockage and debris. It was inexplicable to him, and he was terrified — not so much of a sewer ghost but that someone unauthorized was poking around down there, in his domain. He made a point of checking all around the Twenty-third Street area and found some pipes mucky and slow, as usual, some clean. There was no sign, however, that anyone had found the secret dry tunnel that Mrs. Dolan had (unbeknownst to him) heard him discussing with the Tammany man some months back. Relieved that the secret was undiscovered, he went home to his wife and his highball.

In the division, only Mrs. Dolan had made sense of the fact that Harris dragged in bone-tired and smiling oddly every evening. What even she didn't know was why he did it. He wasn't really a Whyo, wasn't vested, after all. She imagined he enjoyed scaring the men who'd shunned him, that he liked being good at the job, that he had guessed something of his predicament and sought to prove himself to the gang. She never saw him with Beatrice, and so she had not guessed what had evolved between them, not that it would have bothered her much. Beatrice was reliable, and she was entitled to have her fun with the sewerman, if she liked. The Whyo network was tight, and Meg Dolan had done a great deal to emancipate the Why Nots. They were grateful and loyal to the core, down to the last girl, and she trusted Beanie as much as the others. She did wish Harris would spend more of that manic energy of his focusing on her Twenty-third Street puzzle, but there was no way to urge that any more strongly without tipping her hand to Beatrice, so she just smiled and put a little extra hot in Harris's tub at night to motivate him. She felt a bit bad about what lay in store for him, but not enough to sacrifice the plan she had made or the fortune she was certain awaited them in that dry tunnel.

Harris lived for just a few things at this point in his life: the pleasure of quietly recounting his latest ruse to Beatrice while she walked him to work in the morning, or scribbling out new discoveries in his ever better English grammar on her slate at lesson times, or sketching some new detail of the underground city's architecture onto their sheet. He loved the way she looked at him when she approved of what he'd done. He hardly ever thought about cops or gallows anymore, nor of buildings. He thought of her legs or her squinty, slightly lopsided smile or the stray touches that set his skin to throbbing or the intentional ones that made him want to writhe because they never went far enough. When he saw a rat in the sewer now, he thought of it as a happy rat, as a sewer rat in love.

It was on a cold, damp day in December when he discovered the thing he hoped would make Beatrice do more than squeeze his knee: a block-long tunnel on the far West Side, four feet in diameter and perfectly clean and dry. His only hesitation was that now that he saw it, he feared she would be disappointed. This dry tunnel didn't have half the advantages of the grotto. It wasn't a very good hiding place, really, despite the apparent comfort of not actually having sewage in it, because it wasn't directly connected to the system. It had its own manhole, but just one, which he found from above ground and investigated, realizing it seemed out of place with the general scheme of manholes. Perhaps it had been built in the wrong place or with the wrong incline, he thought, since it was uphill from the nearest main and therefore was never hooked up to the adjacent storm sewers or houses. At any rate, the section of tunnel had remained entirely unused, and Harris found nothing of any interest within it.

That very night—and he was terribly eager to get home, to deliver his news to Beanie—Mr. Towle asked to see him in his office after his bath. Towle had heard Mrs. Dolan's theory about who was cleaning the sewers, but he doubted it. Harris was a new man, after all, not a lifer like McGinty, not even from a sewer family. He had neither the experience nor the motivation to do what it seemed someone was doing. But there was no one else it could have been, and Towle wanted to make sure Harris was stopped before he stumbled across the dry tunnel.

"So tell me, Harris, are you doing some extracurricular work for us, by any chance? Anything I ought to thank you for? I have an idea that perhaps a bonus is in order."

Harris denied it, but he was a terrible liar.

Towle chuckled, letting him know it could be their secret, but he was baffled. He wondered if Harris might suffer some mental imbalance that drove him to pursue this pastime. But the main thing was, he now knew it was Harris. Harris was no threat. And with a smile and a wave of relief, he told Harris he would like to reward his dedication with a special project— a job that would be perfect for an obsessed sewerman. "Now, my dear man, I gather from your application that you've laid pavements in this city and that you worked as a mason in your homeland?"

"Yes, sir." The Whyos had told him he had to have a past, whoever he was, and that the most convincing lie was the one that was closest to the truth. So that was the story he had given after Beanie dropped him off the first day.

"You'll be putting in what we call *dirt-catchers*, a new way of keeping the sewers clear. It's a personal project of mine. You must not talk about it to the other men. We want to keep quiet about it for now, till we know if they work. And there's a lady health reformer that wants to follow you around from time to time, to monitor the work. In fact, she's my niece. Quite a progressive, too, Miss Blacksall. Later, I expect that her work will help us explain to the public how beneficial the new system is. Does all this interest you, Mr. Harris? Do you think you can keep a secret?"

"Yes, sir," he said, because he knew he wasn't really being given the option, but he was worried that this assignment would constrain what he was doing for the Whyos. He didn't want to stop making Beatrice happy, not at all. In the end, she never came home that night, so he was compelled to keep it to himself as he lay awake once again, wondering what she was doing and with whom.

The following morning, when the other sewermen had set off, he lingered, and a short time later Towle introduced him to Sarah Blacksall. Harris had read Louie's register, but he didn't recall that she was the doctor who'd examined the body of Pearl Button at the morgue; Luther Undertoe's was the only other name he'd come away with, and so he had no notion of how tight the net of his life was drawn. Dr. Blacksall was interested, she told Harris, in all manner of health reforms but especially concerned with the condition of the sewers. Towle explained that she would document various sanitary indicators, from the clarity and content of the sewage to variations in the death rate per capita in the wards where the dirt-catchers were installed. Together, the three of them rode up to East Twenty-seventh Street, where they pulled up behind a sturdy cart that was hitched up behind a mule, standing at the corner. There was a black driver sitting on the bench, smoking.

"Well, Sergeant Henley!" called Towle. Harris wasn't sure to whom he was talking. "You're looking well!"

"I am well," said the cart driver, swinging down from his bench and extending his large hand to the sewer chief. They clapped each other on the shoulder. Then Sergeant Henley turned toward Dr. Blacksall, lifted his hat and bowed slightly in greeting. "Good morning, Sarah."

She took his hand and shook it quite as if he were an old friend of hers and she were a man. Harris watched, tried to absorb the situation. This Henley wasn't a sewer worker, that was for sure. To his knowledge, the division had never hired even a German (unless you counted him), much less a Negro, only Irish. On top of that, he'd never witnessed this level of amicability between the races, not once since he'd been in New York. How did they all know one another? Henley was wearing a Union Army cap whose brass gleamed in the winter sun, so perhaps he had fought for the North in the war and met the superintendent then. The cap did seem to fit the man's head exceptionally well, as if it had sat there a long time.

Harris listened closely to their banter and picked up a good deal in the next minutes: There was talk of other men with military titles, common acquaintances, apparently both black and white. As for the doctor, she knew Henley first through her uncle, but now it sounded like she helped to run a clinic near where the sergeant lived. Her partner was another lady doctor and, he gathered, a Negro.

None of the circles Harris had been in, high or low, in New York or in Germany, had included blacks or ladies with advanced degrees and jobs such as doctor. He thought of how much an outsider he was in this metropolis and was intrigued that this black man, so different physically, could be so clearly at home. He looked at this young woman and felt a squeezing in his chest. He was to have been a doctor, once. Adversity had derailed him, yes, a thousand different times, but he had let it happen. Surely a black man in this country, fighting in the War Between the States, had suffered great travails. And Sarah Blacksall must have surmounted innumerable obstacles. And what of her colleague, both female and black? He felt deeply ashamed of himself. What was his ambition? Not to save the poor from disease but to do high-quality reconnaissance for a gang—and why? To make a girl he was in love with happy, even though he suspected, no *knew*, that she was using him.

"Well, let me tell you about these dirt-catchers," Towle began, pulling out a diagram and pointing at various details. A dirt-catcher was a deep pit directly beneath a manhole cover, a catch basin that allowed grit and debris to settle out of the effluent. It could be collected by sewer workers from a platform built around the edge of the collecting pools, eliminating virtually all need for travel through the tunnels and greatly minimizing the need to use the long-handled gaffs in narrower pipes. Several of them had been installed more than a decade before, and they still worked perfectly, but there had been a miasma theorist on the Common Council who was worried that the deep pits of sewage debris would breed dangerous gases, and he had succeeded in getting the design banned. "That's why all this is being done, shall we say, *subtly*, with funds we've borrowed from other accounts. I'm convinced this design is the way of the future, but I don't want to ruffle any feathers till we've got real evidence of its public-health benefits. I must be able to rely on your discretion. Are you all with me?"

They all nodded and said, "Of course, of course," but inwardly Harris marveled. How was it that he was about to be indoctrinated into yet another covert activity? He was frankly becoming impatient with vows of secrecy and silence.

"So let's go take a look. You'll see, Harris, that it's not your usual manhole. You hardly need your boots." He handed out headlamps all around, helping his niece to fit hers on over her coiffure.

Was the lady doctor going down the manhole, too? It was the kind of thing Harris could imagine Beatrice doing, but this woman was probably thirty or even older, not a sassy girl gangster who sometimes wore trousers. These people were peculiar, he decided, and he liked them. They weren't quite as colorful as the Whyos, perhaps, but for that they were a lot less dangerous. They were not killers. They were trying to save lives through better sanitation, through medicine. They had fought in the war, for the cause of good. It was inspiring. It reminded him of Robert Koch, whom he imagined tending the wounds of dying soldiers somewhere on the Franco-Prussian front, curing their infections through some miracle research he'd done.

Sergeant Henley moved the horse cart into the street, so that the traffic was diverted around them. Harris used his gaff to open the manhole. Then they lit their lamps and climbed down one after another, Dr. Blacksall last, with her skirts rigged up in an impromptu bustle. The men averted their eyes from her ankles. The whole space was much wider and somewhat deeper than most of the sewer holes Frank Harris had seen. There was a narrow stone ledge just wide enough to stand on and a rusty iron catwalk that bridged the pool. At the bottom, in the darkness, a quiet river of sewage flowed smoothly from the pipe at the north wall into a large pool and drained into another pipe at the south side. The smell was not sewagey at all—more like a freshwater lake with just a bit of muck at the bottom.

"This is our model. It was put in in the mid-fifties," Towle said. "And I'll tell you something: It's never been serviced, ever. And it's never backed up. But even if it did, it'd be far easier to clean than the widest-gauge pipe there is. Ideally, what we'd like to do is put these babies in at regular intervals all across the city. Of course, that would cost a lot and ultimately put some men out of work, which is never popular, but I am convinced it will save both money and lives."

Harris looked around and saw that there were also rings and pulleys built into the masonry for hauling up buckets of debris. It was perfect. How many of these were there? he wondered. And where? He wasn't thinking the least bit about the sanitary consequences, though; his mind was spinning at the prospect of such large spaces that were almost entirely unknown, even by the sewermen, since they never got called on to service them. It didn't have all the space of the dry tunnel or the grotto, but in a pinch you could get out of there by any of three different routes. Maybe this assignment wouldn't be fruitless after all.

Dr. Blacksall brought out a glass phial and a pair of tongs and leaned down and submerged the phial in the water. Harris was on the verge of laughing at the tongs—after all, he spent his days crawling through much worse than this—but then something about her gesture struck him. He thought of his father and Robert Koch and the microbes they'd collected, bred and studied.

"Mr. Harris, since we'll be working together, I'd like to explain part of my research to you. I want to collect samples from the sewers on a regular basis—daily or weekly, depending, in numerous locations. Then I'll examine them under a kind of very strong magnifying glass called a microscope, to see if I can find traces of certain tiny creatures that are invisible to the naked eye but can cause disease. These are very newly discovered theories, but I assure you, it's the truth. It's modern science we're doing, Mr. Harris."

Harris winced. His pride could not tolerate allowing this woman to think him only barely able to understand her science. He was tired of being an able-bodied laborer, a criminal. He wasn't thinking about who Frank Harris was supposed to be when he spoke.

"I know all about the work of Pasteur, Dr. Blacksall," he said. "The wee animalcules of van Leeuwenhoek. I may look like a brute to you, but my father was a doctor. I worked in his lab. I'd be glad to help you collect your samples."

"Oh," said Sarah Blacksall. "Well, that's wonderful."

"Van Leeuwenhoek indeed," Towle said, thinking of the man's paperwork, trying to recall if he'd had any schooling. "I'll be damned."

Sergeant Henley just raised his eyebrows and smiled. He always liked it when a person proved to be slightly more than he appeared. But to the others, Harris's announcement was as unfathomable as it had been for Harris to see a black man in friendly acquaintance with upper-class whites. Towle couldn't help wondering if Harris had done something awful to have come down so far in the world.

There was snow the next day, when Harris finally got to tell Beatrice about the tunnel and dirt-catchers, and it gave him an eerie feeling, reminding him of the blizzard of the previous spring, when he'd first been abducted. He drew in the location of the dry tunnel's manhole on their map. He waited for his reward, but she was sitting up at the table, at rapt attention, not leaning in.

"Yes, and what about the dirt-catchers, where are they?"

He visualized the roughly traced map of downtown that Mr. Towle had drawn for them when they climbed out of the hole and marked the sheet D-C in nine places. She remained silent. He had expected excitement, laughter, the sense of common purpose, but she was somewhere else, thinking, planning. He suggested that he would pay a visit to each of them in the following days, to determine its condition and suitability for use by the gang, and finally he got what he was after: her hand on his thigh, again, her smile. He swallowed, trying not to imagine more, but when she told him she wanted him to take her on a tour, his mouth went dry.

"*What?*"

"Didn't you just tell me some stuffy lady physician went down in the catcher?"

"But it's no place—"

"Nonsense. We'll have the proper equipment, too. You're just going to have to borrow me some boots. I want to see it all: the dry tunnel and the dirt-catcher and the grotto."

"You can't go to the grotto. It's not easy to get to, and it's not even near the other tunnel. And, Beatrice, I can't just borrow a pair of boots."

"Harris." She let her finger drift a little higher up his leg than before. All the hairs of his body seemed to stand on end. "Come on, Harris. You think I'm not tough enough? But you're right about not borrowing the equipment. The boots are huge, right? They'd be awkward to drag around, and we want to do this quietly, without fuss. I think it would be better if you just got hold of the keys somehow, so we could let ourselves into the building at our leisure and take what we needed. Don't you think?"

Suffice it to say that Mrs. Dolan was in on the arrangement and more or less encouraged Harris to make off with her keys one night shortly thereafter, but Harris didn't know that. He was shaking with nerves when he spotted them dangling from the lock of a closet door adjacent to his locker. She had made a show of having misplaced the key ring and was searching for it everywhere. With trembling hands but the whisper of Beatrice echoing in his ears, he slipped the closet key from its hole, dropped the entire ring into his satchel and left the building thinking himself undetected. Mother Dolan was quite aware of what he'd done, however. She had her backup set in her desk drawer and locked up the Sewer Division that night as usual.

When Harris got home, he made sure to jingle the keys. Beanie smiled at him. A short time later she went out, but they both knew this would not be an ordinary night. They had made a plan.

After midnight, when the others were asleep, Harris rose and left the apartment. He arrived at the designated corner, two blocks from the Public Works building, at a quarter to one. She stepped out of a shadowy doorway. He handed her the keys, and she went ahead of him. She'd been watching for hours, and there was no one around. The policeman on patrol was safely ensconced in the bed of Maggie the Dove, whom Beatrice had enlisted to support this operation. A few minutes after she entered, he followed her, and they locked the door behind them.

It was difficult moving around the building in the pitch darkness. They didn't want to draw attention to themselves, and there were large windows facing onto the street. It turned out Harris was better at working with keys and operating locks in the darkness—he was used to functioning in the sewers with only minimal use of his eyesight. In the locker room, there were no windows, so they closed the door behind them and lit the gas lamp. They found headlights, gaffs and the smallest pair of boots available, which was still several sizes too large for Beatrice. Harris also found a shelf with a stack of the light breeches that the men wore under their boots and blushingly gave her a pair. She had been wearing pants the first time they met and he'd seen her wear them since, but still it was risqué. Then it became even more so, as they both needed to undress to get their boots on. At the O'Gamhnas', the men and women took turns changing in Aunt Penelope's bedroom. Harris looked around the locker room, then tried the door to the bath hall. It was locked. He tried several keys before he found the right one.

"Why don't you change in here?" he suggested, waving her through the door.

"Wow," she said, looking around. "I had no idea." In the oblique light from the locker room's gas lamp and the faint moonlight that shone through the milk-glass windows, the bath hall's white tile and marble gleamed.

"It's not bad, is it?"

He had his pants off and his boots on in a half a minute; she took considerably longer and emerged looking rumpled. The suspenders that held her boots up were badly twisted, and the tops of her breeches were bunched at the crotch.

"These damn things are worse than stockings to get on."

"Would you like some help straightening those?"

"Nice try, Harris. We've got work to do."

Then they were off. The very first manhole they passed, she stopped.

"Let's go under, shall we?"

"This isn't the right place. We'll have to do a lot more crawling. It'll take longer."

"Stealth is the thing, not speed or comfort, Harris. I want to go down."

So they went down. And he pulled the manhole cover shut on top of them. Her too-large boots were a bit of a liability, and she had to squelch a shout the first time a rat ran across her back, but she was nimble and small—two assets he didn't share—and above all, she was game. Her stomach was strong, and she was bubbling with ideas about how the Whyos could take advantage of every small feature of the sewers. It took them a good hour to crawl their way to the grotto. She showed hesitation only once, when she realized how late it was.

"We should have gone to Twenty-third Street first, Harris. It's more important."

"But we're almost there."

A short time later, they reached the grotto. Her mood shifted again when she saw the space—or saw the black emptiness beyond the range of her headlamp, really. She began to laugh. Her laugh was high and musical, and it echoed endlessly, filling the cave, until finally Harris was infected by her mirth as well.

"It's perfect. It's marvelous. We could have a *meeting* down here. We could set up offices."

"Well, keep in mind that it's not easy to get to," he said with an odd modesty, as if he were the author of the space rather than its discoverer, as if its flaws were his.

"Never mind that now. Show me the archway." She reached out her hand and let him lead her forward. When they made out the ledge, he showed her the old whiskey bottle.

"Good idea. Hang on," she said, and reached down into her left boot. A minute later, she was holding up a silver hip flask that had once belonged to a Wall Street banker. She sat down on the ledge, all sense of hurry gone, unscrewed the cap and offered the flask to him. When he passed it back to her, her fingers lingered among his for a moment. Then she took a swig. He could feel the good burn of the rye in his gullet. The water flowed and burbled past their leather-booted feet. The dark cavern glistened with moisture. They were both blinded by the other's headlamp for a moment when they turned toward each other, but they tilted their heads and closed their eyes and leaned forward. Harris tasted the whiskey on her lips, put his hand on her waist. Then he smelled singed hair. She shouted and pulled away. A tendril had escaped from the nimbus of frizz and caught fire. It was only a momentary flare-up, but he reached down to the stream, wet his fingers and ran them across the side of her head. The burned hairs were crumbly and brittle and fell apart under his touch.

"Is it out?"

"Yeah, it's out. Sorry—" He held out his hand, gesturing at nothing.

"How bad is it?"

"Not at all."

But it had ended the kiss. She put the cap back on her flask, then he showed her the space beyond the arch. There was a vast cesspool that had apparently never been emptied. Instead, its overflow drained into the grotto and was swept away by the stream. In effect, it was a giant dirt-catcher. They found a hatchway from the cesspool that opened into the subbasement of the building they suspected was the post office, but they didn't go any further. Beatrice dropped a coin on the floor outside the hatch. If the Whyo who had a day job in maintenance at the post office found it there the following day, the location would be definitively established. If not, they'd go back to their maps and reassess the situation.

They went all the way uptown to the dirt-catcher in a cab and then went over to see the dry tunnel. It was past five but still pitch-black out when they returned to the bath hall. It was nearly midwinter and the moon had set. They went back to the locker room, and Beatrice looked at herself in the small, framed mirror on the wall. She was damp and smudged, with her hair a wreck.

"I'm quite filthy, Harris," she said. "We're here in this bath hall. Shall we take a bath?"

By the time Harris had gotten into Mrs. Dolan's office and thrown the main valve, he'd worked up the courage to ask if she wanted help getting out of her boots. She laughed, and her voice echoed in the bath hall just as it had in the grotto. As Harris turned on the taps of a tub near the door, he could see his hand was trembling. He was unsure what would happen when she came up beside him, knelt down, and rinsed her hands in the warm, rushing water. She was always backing away from him at moments like this. He reached his in, too, and she caught his fingers in her grip. A moment later, they were wrestling on the tiles, still booted up but struggling to loosen the buttons of each other's shirts with their wet hands. Then there were the breeches. A couple of buttons popped free and skittered across the tiles. Their hands and mouths were all over. The crucial areas had been bared. She dove up under his shirt, and he flinched—she had his nipple in her teeth. There was simply no way they could have waited to get their boots off before doing what they did next. No, the removal of sewermen's boots required patience, and this was frenzy. The fingers that had stolen so many watches stole his breath away. The lips that had taught him to speak smiled a smile he'd never seen before, neither impish nor ironic. He dared to think that it was real.

The bath they took afterward was as rushed as the ones Mrs. Dolan oversaw—they had suddenly become aware of the approaching dawn—but otherwise it was like no other bath that had ever been had in the sewermen's bath hall. It was crowded, with both of them in there together, but the last thing he wanted was space. They washed each other's legs and backs and feet. Then they dressed, tidied up and sneaked away from the building. At the corner where they'd met, Beatrice surprised him by stopping and saying good night.

"You're not coming home?" He felt desperate at the idea of parting.

"I don't think we should just waltz in together at dawn, Harris."

He knew she was right. He wanted to ask her where she was going, but he knew she wouldn't say, so he just leaned forward to kiss her good-bye—she was so beautiful.

"*Good night,* Harris," she said, darting away, and then she was gone.

18.

RED COW

Harris went home, flopped down on his mattress without undressing, didn't even try to sleep. In less than an hour, it would be time to get up again.

He got reproachful looks when he did emerge from the front room, the last one up in the family, rubbing his eyes. The O'Gamhnas quite rightly assumed that odd nocturnal comings and goings were a sign of illicit, probably illegal, activity, and he had come to them on the pretense of going clean. As for Beatrice, it was clear to all of them that she was her own woman. So long as she didn't bring gang affairs into the house, they allowed themselves to believe she was not involved anymore. Somewhere, all of them knew the truth—she brought home ten times what a regular hot-corn girl might—but they didn't begin to imagine the extent to which she actually had brought the gang into their home, in the form of Harris himself. Still, Harris, to the O'Gamhnas, was a cause. They had undertaken to save him. They did not approve of his relapses.

"You better not lose *this* job, Harris," carped Colleen. "I don't know where you'd go from the sewer. There isn't any further down."

She was more right even than she knew, but it rolled off him. All he could think about was Beanie. Harris kept his eyes lowered, lest Colleen or Penelope see the unsuppressible grin on his face. He shaved hastily and left the flat again as quickly as possible, taking his breakfast from a coffee cart on the corner.

He met Henley on Park Row, just south of City Hall, near the vast construction site where the new *Sun* building was going up. They had excavated the pit for their first dirt-catcher around an existing sewer pipe, a four-foot, elliptical, brick-and-mortar collecting tunnel fed by numerous smaller pipes. It turned out that Henley was a specialist in blasting, which kept the work moving along, even when they encountered large boulders. They'd installed the beams that would frame the new structure. Now they had to mix the cement for the foundation. There was no need for boots and such until they opened the sewer and installed the new manhole cover, so they skipped going by the Sewer Division in the mornings. They also worked an hour later than the regular sewermen, on a schedule designed by Towle at once to shield the dirt-catcher project from common knowledge and to spare the others from contact with Frank Harris and John-Henry Henley: a bringer of ghosts and a black. That the men did not like Harris—or rather, having Harris around in McGinty's boots—was well known to Mr. Towle, and there would surely have been trouble in the ranks about John-Henry's use of the bathing facilities. This way, the other men were long gone and the steam on the tiles had almost completely evaporated by the time Harris and Henley showed up for their nightly tubs. Except for Mrs. Dolan, who had volunteered to stay late on their behalf, Harris and Henley had the place to themselves, and theirs was always a peaceful, soothing ten minutes—a far cry from the rushing and splashing of the regular crew.

Talking quietly over the lip of his enamel tub, Harris revealed more about his several lives to John-Henry than was known by anyone else alive. And it had barely been a week. John-Henry had told him stories of growing up in Boston in the household of abolitionists who'd helped his mother come north from Alabama. She had worked in a Waltham woolen mill, and they had a small apartment in the colored section of town till the summer John-Henry was seven, when his mother fell ill with yellow fever and died. That was when the Henleys, the abolitionists who had sponsored his mother, had taken him in. They raised him with their own children and gave him their name.

Their lives could not have been more different, and yet there was common ground between them, starting perhaps with that strange fluidity to both their names and extending to the early loss of their parents. They also told each other of their present lives, though Harris did edit himself. He kept silent about his incarceration and the warrant for his arrest, but he'd fully described his awkward relations with the sewermen and the tricks he'd learned to terrify the men. He taught the Ballad to John-Henry, and they sang it together sometimes when they worked. It was partly a joke, but it was also partly for the same reason men have always sung work songs: It made the time pass and kept the work moving at an even pace.

They got along well together. John-Henry appreciated Harris's deftness with bricks and stones and mortar; Harris admired the precision and control with which John-Henry set and detonated his blasts, opening exactly the space they needed to do their job, no more. By turns they served as boss and crew to each other, depending on the task at hand. They trusted each other with a stone block on a pulley overhead, which meant a lot. Harris was still taken by surprise every now and then at the ease he felt working with a black man, but the difference in their races had ceased to be an issue within a few hours on the first day.

The morning after his excursion to the grotto with Beatrice, Harris was bursting to see his new friend, brimming over with what had happened. He needed to tell it. He needed advice on how he should proceed. And since they worked alone, with only occasional visits from Dr. Blacksall, they had all day to talk. But then he couldn't figure out how to explain the circumstances, where the boundaries of the story lay. If he told him where it had happened, he would have to tell him about the gang, and he was certain that was not a good idea. It wouldn't be a favor to John-Henry to burden him with that knowledge. So he kept quiet, quieter than usual, actually. By midmorning, it was obvious to both men that Harris wasn't concentrating. He dropped things, did the exact reverse of what they'd just planned, didn't listen.

"Damn it, Harris, you been acting like a fool all morning," John-Henry finally said, and insisted that they stop early for lunch.

Harris blushed, and then, slowly, John-Henry began to laugh.

"Oh, well, I see—so it's about a girl."

Over bowls of Brunswick stew and glasses of beer at a stand-up restaurant, Harris told John-Henry he had met her when she helped him out of some trouble he'd been having with the law. He didn't say exactly what trouble, nor mention the fact that he was rooming at her family's flat. He didn't confess he'd made love with her on the bath house floor, only to be given a curt dismissal at dawn. He didn't have to. John-Henry looked at him.

"Harris. Don't you know enough to keep your pants on till you're married? Especially if you're in love with her. It's a real mess you got yourself in, boy."

"I know."

"You already made love to her. You did, didn't you? You know they got whores for that."

Harris nodded. He had been hoping John-Henry had some advice for him, but John-Henry just shook his head. The way he saw it, it was too late for advice. The girl had been spoiled, and Harris had proven himself a less than honorable man. "You've just got to let it go. It won't ever work out with that girl, not now."

That might be true for most people, but did such rules pertain to girls in gangs? Harris wondered, if he could have told him everything, what John-Henry would have said then. Probably nothing, he would have been too appalled.

That evening, as the two men headed back to the Sewer Division, Harris realized he was nervous on more than one front—not just about everything that had happened with Beatrice but also about Mrs. Dolan. Had she detected the invasion of her realm? Would she know it was he who had done it?

And just as he feared, the matron of the bath hall came in while Harris and Henley were soaking and stood over Harris's tub, hands on her hips, glaring at him.

"Yes, ma'am," he ventured, arranging his knees as modestly as he could.

"Stop in my office before you leave, McGinty," she said.

When he knocked, there was no answer, then the door opened. But it wasn't Mrs. Dolan; it was Mr. Towle. Harris realized he was going to be fired. He grew hot all over with shame, anxiety and above all the horror that without his job in the sewers he'd be useless to both Beatrice and the Whyos.

"Listen, Harris, I must be candid with you. It was you who did the extra work cleaning the pipes, wasn't it? There's no point denying it. I don't believe in ghosts."

"I'm afraid so, sir." Harris thought that this had all been settled at their first conference. His eyes strayed across Mrs. Dolan's desk and he saw an ashtray with several yellow buttons in it—the breeches buttons that he'd popped last night.

"Now, why would a man do extra work in the sewers? It puzzles me. I take it you went back down below, after hours. But why?"

He thought of Beatrice and bit his lip. Maybe she didn't really care; maybe he had spoiled it, even if she did. But he thought of that smile, of their bath, and he told himself last night had been worth it.

"That's all right, Harris, no need to say anything. You see, I think I have an idea why. You said you'd studied science, came from a medical family, back home? What sort of education do you have, Harris?"

"Not much, really, sir."

"High school?"

"No."

"Too bad. But even so, I'd like to talk further about sanitary science, about what we're doing here in the Sewer Division. Just informally, of course. Would you be willing to meet for breakfast on Sunday morning? I go to early services, so what about afterward, say, nine-thirty?" He wrote down the name and address of a coffeehouse and handed Harris the slip of paper. "I'm going to invite my niece Sarah—er, Dr. Blacksall—too, if that's all right with you. Actually, it was her idea."

"Yes, sir. Of course," Harris said, still not at all sure whether he'd been found out. But apparently he wasn't being fired. He went home and found things equally perplexing there.

Colleen and Mrs. O'Gamhna weren't talking to him, and even Beatrice avoided eye contact. It was absolutely unbearable to be in the apartment with so many people giving him the silent treatment, and so finally he took the bucket and went to the corner well. When he returned, it was worse. As soon as he entered the kitchen, Beatrice got up and left, avoiding him like a pariah, turning away when he approached. The most he could catch was a one-quarter profile: chin and cheekbone and halo of frizzy copper. He could just make out that some of the hairs were shorter where they'd been singed. At the time they usually had their lesson, he sat down in the front room with Liam's paper on his lap and waited, not very optimistically. To his surprise, Beatrice rose from the kitchen table, where she had been helping Colleen with the dinner, to join him.

"Oh, come now," said Colleen. "Mr. Harris speaks well enough by now, I think. Maybe too well. Why don't you contribute your efforts to peeling the blessed potatoes, rather than the further education of a criminal, or did you just want to make moony eyes at him?"

Harris's heart lurched. He'd been hoping for, been looking forward to, the nearness of her thigh beneath the table all day long. He couldn't stand to be deprived of it. It emboldened him.

"I don't know what you mean by moony, Colleen. I think that's quite unjust. And I'd like you to know that I wasn't doing anything wrong last night. Just out celebrating. It's really not so terrible. I've a new job now with the Sewer Division. Today I was summoned to meet with the chief of the division to discuss my promotion. I'll be involved with, uh, sanitary science. And so you see I do need these lessons—I have a whole new set of vocabulary errors I'd better not make."

Colleen huffed and sighed, but it worked. Beatrice sat down in the armchair across from him. He wished she'd sat on the couch, but this was better than before, at least. He smiled tentatively and started to tell her about his meeting with Towle. She listened, but she was all business, quizzing him on building terminology—no warmth. Even so, every time he heard her roll the *r* in *portland cement*, a tingle traveled through him. He inhaled deeply, searching the air for a hint of her tang, but then he recalled she'd taken a bath the night before, too—she was too clean for him to smell her from that distance. He tried to make eye contact, but she kept her eyes on the slate and managed not to show any sign whatsoever that anything unusual had happened last night.

"Listen, Harris," she said after a while. "Why don't you do some copying? Colleen's right about you not really needing the lessons—you got the words and the accent pretty well under your belt by now—but your handwriting's still much too German. You might have writing to do with this new job. Work on that." She scribbled something on the slate. When she passed it to him, he made a point of catching his fingers in hers, and she allowed it for just a second longer than she had to. He told himself that that was enough, for now. What he read on the slate when he looked down, however, made his heart constrict: *It's set. Sewer job Monday. J. wants you to meet the gang, go over the plan, Sunday.*

He looked at her. There was nothing in her eyes: no apology, no recollection of their night together. She had gotten the information she needed about the sewers from him; she had given herself to him. It had been just a barter. Her gaze was the cold stare of a lieutenant seeing that the commands of her chief were carried out. He tried to swallow his distress, but his mind was in wild disorder. He wanted to stand up and take her shoulders in his hands and confront her. *Was* she in love with him? Was she just his handler? Was he mad not to know? Instead, he gripped his own knees and looked down. He considered wiping away her message and writing out *Marry me, Beatrice* in his best non-Gothic script, but it was too absurd to conduct such business on a chalk slate, too hopeless. *I don't want to go through with it,* he wrote instead, and then, *Can we talk?*

She sighed, wiped the slate black with the damp rag they kept on hand. *No,* she wrote. *Be there or else.*

Apparently, more than the lesson was over.

She got up, and when she was safely back in the kitchen, discussing the relative virtues of small and large potatoes with Colleen, he wrote out a sentence in German, the declaration he wanted to make. Then he covered the slate with a chalk tangle and left it on the table, unwiped. She hadn't given him a single sign of affection or recognition. Even when his fingers had brushed hers, it had been just that, without reciprocity. He wondered if it was possible he'd really just imagined it all. No, something had happened. But perhaps that was just the way her nights always went; perhaps she was a whore as well as a thief; perhaps he had entirely imagined the emotion, the excitement. They had finally consummated their flirtation, but that didn't mean a thing. She was a Whyo.

He was angry; he was also concerned. He'd already given them all the information they needed to infiltrate the sewers. He'd shown her more places than they could possibly need and how to negotiate them. What further use could he be to them? He couldn't stop the feeling of gloom that washed over him. She'd used sex to extract information from him, and now she would lead him coldly to slaughter.

He went to the door of the kitchen and watched her: Beatrice O'Gamhna peeling potatoes and dropping them into a pot of water. Beatrice O'Gamhna laughing casually with her nephews. Beatrice O'Gamhna actually looking up and smiling at him, though emptily, without any allowance for the grunts and clutches and kisses they had traded last night. No, there was nothing at all in the eyes, and that was what made him despair. His aunt in Fürth had smiled at him often enough over the years, and now Beatrice's eyes were the same as Hedwig Diespeck's: empty, polite, cold. Fürth had been a dreadful place, but he'd learned at least one thing there: People who take you in at someone else's bidding will never love you. They'll resent you. They'll use you for what they can. It occurred to him that the Whyos and Beatrice had taken him in the same way his aunt and uncle had. Why should he now be surprised? Hadn't he learned anything for all his sorrows?

He thought with a wave of regret of the final conflict he'd had with his uncle—a memory he'd long suppressed. He'd been rifling through his uncle's desk for the key to the shed where they kept the extra tackle for the horses when he came across an unfamiliar envelope addressed to him, from his father. It had been a grim year, with another wave of fever that claimed his aunt and remaining cousins, and his uncle had grown paranoid; he'd begun locking doors though there were only the two of them. The boy that Harris had been, then, looked at the envelope, which was empty, and grew angry. It was his name on the front. Yet he hadn't received a single letter from his father since he returned from Hamburg. Then he went and confronted his uncle in the barn, where the old man was camped out in an armchair with a crate of brandy by his side, in front of the iron stove, which was pretty much where he'd been ever since the funeral. Normally, they lit that stove only on the coldest nights, to keep the animals from freezing to death.

"That's not your business," his uncle said, snatching the envelope and tossing it in the open door of the stove. "At least I never threw you out, the way your father did." Then he picked up a half-empty bottle of brandy and pitched it at his nephew, who ducked. The bottle flew, slowly, gyrating across the open air of the barn, and landed with a thud on the straw-covered ground without breaking.

That was when he'd decided to go to America. There was nothing for him in Germany; that much was clear. He went inside to pack a few belongings. He heated water for a bath in the kitchen tub. Who knew how long it would be before he had the chance to be clean again? He'd soaked in that tub until the water went cold. It must have been sometime during his bath that the fire had started.

Just because the Diespecks and now the O'Gamhnas had taken him in — and just because Beatrice had made love to him once — didn't mean they cared for him. He saw how glad Colleen would be to get him out of the crowded flat. He was certain that Beatrice wasn't even his friend, much less his lover; she was a Why Not and his keeper, no more. Except for John-Henry, who he knew would fiercely disapprove of the double life he'd been leading and whom he feared to tell the truth, he had no one he could rely on or trust — least of all the one he'd put his heart and all his stakes on: Beatrice.

It was a long week, waiting for Sunday, and on Saturday night he slept badly, his dreams indistinguishable from his restless half-waking thoughts. Sometime before sunrise, he sat up abruptly, wide awake. It was exactly the same hour of the morning as their tumultuous unrobing in the bath hall. The room was pitch-dark, but he felt her there. He knew the slow rhythms of all the O'Gamhnas' sleeping breath, especially hers. He wanted nothing but to go over and lie with her, unless it was to flee. He did neither but closed his eyes and his mind and finally fell back into a dream — an outdated one he hadn't had for half a year — the dream of finding Maria, the girl from the boat.

They spoke in German. He asked her to go west with him, to a wild, distant state — maybe Minnesota or even further, California. She smiled, but the dream faded there, as it always had. He'd never gotten to the part where he got to marry her or to be a pioneer.

In his next dream, he was on his way to a meeting (whether with Towle or the Whyos was unclear) when he was met in the road by a red cow. It lowed at him, and then, seeing that he didn't understand, it cleared its throat and spoke in English.

"Hello, brother," it said. "I never thought I'd find you again." But then it switched over to German, and he feared to be seen with it. Was it one of the cows from his uncle's farm? Was it Robert Koch? His sister? He looked away rather than respond, and the animal lowered its head. He seemed to hear Beatrice telling him, "Don't go around with cows, Frank. You're one of us now, an Irishman and a Whyo, not a beast or a German."

"An *Irishman*," he said, imitating her voice, her intonation, "and a Whyo." In the dream, his accent was perfect, and what she had said was true: He knew their language, their secrets; and she was his girl.

He took her hand and pulled her to him, and in the dream they kissed. Their arms encircled each other's bodies, and it was perfectly natural and expected. Her hair brushed his cheek, sending shivers through him. He smelled her pungent, faintly smoky smell. They were in the grotto, and they lay down together on the narrow ledge. She was beneath him, on top of him, all over him, and he was all over her. At the crucial moment, though, she began to speak German and melded back into Maria. Harris struggled to turn her back into Beatrice, only to find, when he succeeded, that he was no longer himself but Dandy Johnny.

When he woke at last, the others were all up, and Beatrice was gone. When he'd drunk his tea and had his porridge, he put on his warm scarf, his cap and his topcoat over his jacket. His first stop was the café where he was to meet Mr. Towle and Dr. Blacksall, but he had plenty of time, so he walked rather than take an omnibus. He wasn't at all sure he would keep the second meeting. *Or else*, she had written. If they were going to kill him, why should he help by walking into it?

As Harris approached the address Towle had given him, he saw a familiar sight: people streaming toward the Lutheran church. He knew it was in the same area but hadn't realized the café would be directly across the street from that church. It made him nervous. He'd avoided that block for a long time now. For over a year he'd been good, disassociating himself from all things German. Were there still police officers and other citizens who would remember the descriptions, artists' renderings and wanted notices? He feared yes. There were people, queerly enough, who followed crime. There was also Luther Undertoe. Harris considered what Beatrice would say if she found out he had gone there, after all the lengths she'd gone to to protect him from himself, but then he saw again her final words to him—*Or else*—in white chalk in his mind's eye. Why should he care about her or the stealth she'd long advocated?

He was early, and from the density of people on the street he guessed the service would begin on the half hour, at the same time he was appointed to meet with Mr. Towle. He shoved his hands into his pockets and paced up and down before the church, nervously watching the passersby and churchgoers, unable to commit to being outside or going inside the café. Only when the doors of the church finally closed did he cross the street and find a seat at a window table in the restaurant.

He sat facing outward so he could keep his eye on what was going on out the window. He pictured the congregation across the street beginning to pray and remembered the service he'd been to there. Once that idea was in his mind, he couldn't escape the liturgy. His head was full of *thous* and *thines*, *dus* and *deines*, *body* and *blood*, *Blut* and *Leib*, and he was as helpless to quiet it as if he had actually been in the church. Towle was five, then ten minutes late. Finally, to distract himself from the mental rumble of German devotions, Harris reached for a paper from the rack and began to leaf through it. The Brooklyn *Eagle*.

He read the notices first, imagining he was looking for a job, wishing he were free to take one. He noticed several paving contractors were hiring. Then his eye wandered to the LOST column. Among many items of the sort that commonly went missing—lapdogs, wallets and ladies' brooches—he saw that there were several notices for livestock. "RED COW, white spot, answers to Bella or Moo Cow. $20 reward for return. Mr. Noe, Ft. Greene." It was a large amount—another wayward heifer was valued at only fifteen dollars. Harris was thinking it was awfully cold weather for a cow to be outside for days on end, but the thing that really struck him was the description. It brought back the faded image of the cow in his dream.

Then Towle bustled in with Dr. Blacksall, apologizing that the pastor had rambled on longer than usual that morning. They were curious about

Harris's education and his knowledge of germ theory, and after interrogating him on such matters for a good half hour, they explained their project and made him a proposal.

The initial results of the doctor's experiments were in, and they were good. Now they intended to launch a publicity campaign, and they wanted to use him, a model sewer worker with a sterling work ethic and a rational understanding of science, despite his very basic education, as a common-man spokesman to help promote sanitary reform—everything from reversing the legislation banning dirt-catchers to encouraging landlords to link their buildings to the sewers. For a moment, Harris was excited, but then he realized it was impossible, even if he did survive the Whyo meeting that day. Mr. Towle wanted to have an engraving made, a likeness of Harris in his sewerman's boots, and use it for the cover of a pamphlet, perhaps a handbill, too. They wanted him to make public appearances with prominent ministers, scientists and government officials, possibly even Mayor Hall or Mr. Tweed, who was sponsoring the project. It was going to be good for the slums, they said. Harris would have loved to go along with it, but putting himself in the public eye could easily bring him back to the attention of the cops or Undertoe, and it would certainly infuriate the Whyos. It would be suicide.

While Harris sat there in the window, trying simultaneously to manage the roil of conflicting excitements and worries, to tell a coherent tale of his supposed upbringing in Ireland and to discuss microbiology and public health and the peculiar thing called *publicity* with Mr. Towle and Dr. Blacksall, a young couple approached the restaurant. They were joking and laughing and elbowing each other in mock outrage at nothing in particular. Indeed, Fiona and the Jimster were making something of a scene. Against Beatrice's advice, Fiona had taken her flirtation with the Jimster to another level—they now frequented several different basement hide-aways—all in the name of Whyo reconnaissance, of course. Fiona had assured Beanie that she didn't really care for him, could drop him like a stone in an instant if the need arose. Be that as it may, they were just then headed for a nonworking breakfast at the coffeehouse where Towle and Blacksall were interviewing Harris—whom the Jimster still knew as George the Torch, the object of Undertoe's now rather old offer of bounty.

Fiona knew Harris a lot better now, and she spotted him at once, while the Jimster walked over to an adjacent window table. Fiona was staggered. It was the day of the first big meeting in months, and there he still sat, Frank Harris, brazen as day, right across from the German church, engaging in a highly suspicious conference with people she knew he hadn't been introduced to by Beatrice: official-looking people. It appeared that Harris was betraying them. He had to be stopped, but the first problem was making sure the Jimster didn't see him. As they sat down, she noticed a crowd pouring from the heavy doors of the church across the street. *Filthy Germans,* she thought.

"Look at that," she said to the Jimster, pointing at the church, thinking on the fly. "This java joint's gonna be chockablock with God-fearing Krauts in a minute. Let's take ourselves elsewhere, what do you say, Jimmy?"

"Sure, Fiona." He'd have been pleased to let her take him wherever she liked. Pity for him she was too worried about the sewerman, on too many fronts, to dally with the Jimster any longer. Their date was over. He shouldn't have been talking to those people, Harris, and he shouldn't have been hanging out at a German coffeehouse. The two things together demanded that she file a report with Beanie—or possibly directly with Johnny—as soon as possible.

Was it possible, she wondered, that Harris was smarter than they thought, that he'd been breaking cover all along? She'd gotten the impression that Beanie trusted him, but then again she also suspected that Beanie was smitten. Perhaps her judgment was clouded. Fiona listened to the church bells ringing and figured she would probably find Beanie at the baths.

"Jimmy, I just remembered something. Sorry, but I've got to go. Come find me later tonight."

She kissed him well enough to let him know she really was sorry, and then, before the besotted smile had even fallen from his face, she was gone.

19.

D I P T Y C H

At the baths, Fiona stood in the lobby and whyoed quietly for Beatrice, but she got no response. It was no wonder, what with the many hallways and chambers and the sound of rushing water everywhere, so she paid the fee and went in herself. She hurried through most of the rooms, finding no trace of Beanie. In the steam room she did linger for a moment, though— the moist heat was lovely, especially considering how bitterly cold it had gotten—and there, though Fiona didn't know her from Adam, she sat down beside Maria. Harris's Maria. The very same.

Fiona watched the other woman's toes stretch and curl, stretch and curl—slowly, unconsciously, happily. She tried the gesture herself—stretch, curl—and it did feel good. But then she recalled the urgency of her message for Beatrice and abruptly rose to go to the next room, a cool and shallow swimming pool. A single lap rinsed off the sweaty heat of the steam room, and then she passed quickly through the rest of the rooms. Beanie wasn't anywhere. It was puzzling. And it was a problem. She had to let people know about Harris before the meeting. Fiona was still reluctant to go to Johnny—she was sure Beanie would want to handle this herself—but if she didn't find her soon, she would have to. Then, when Fiona emerged from the great damp doorway of the baths, she saw her, settled comfortably on the siamese hydrant in front of the building, apparently enjoying a small patch of sun, regardless of the cold and her wet hair.

"Beanie!" Fiona shouted, and in her haste she failed to see a package set down by a lady who was rearranging her scarf against the chill. She tripped and pitched forward in Beanie's direction. When Beatrice looked up, there was Fiona, her still-warm hair radiating steam like a medusa. First, she was annoyed—she was waiting for Harris, not Fiona, and she didn't want an entourage; then she was on the sidewalk. Fiona had knocked her over.

"Christ in heaven! What are you doing?"

"Sorry. But I got something important to tell you. It's about Harris."

Beatrice picked herself up and folded her arms, doubting that any news would merit that introduction. She still hadn't told Fiona what had happened between her and Harris. She hadn't decided quite how to present the information, but as far as she was concerned, it was for her to tell Fiona about Harris, not vice versa. Then, before either girl could speak, Beatrice saw Frank Harris. She straightened her skirts and brushed a few damp strands of hair away from her face and turned from Fiona to smile at him. She knew well enough she had put him off the day before; she wanted him to know it was just a mood, just worry, just nothing. Not that she wasn't still worried about what would happen at the meeting and after. But she had made up her mind that she was going to fight for him. Seeing him now confirmed it.

"To be honest, Fifi, your timing is bad. I don't want to hear it," she said quietly as Harris approached. "Not right now." She thrust her chin toward Harris, who had seen her too, now, but was still out of earshot. "See, I'm planning to enjoy myself a little before the meeting."

Fiona raised her eyebrows. So it had gotten that far. "Beanie, no, you can't do that. Not now. See, I think he may have cops following him. He may even have tipped them off."

"Oh, come on," said Beatrice. "Cops? It's Harris." Her concern was betraying him, not the other way around.

Fiona glared. "I've really got to talk to you, alone, now. I saw something. . . . You need to know this."

"Fine. I'll figure a way to send him off on an errand. The curtain is at two-thirty. We'll be about a block north of the theater at a quarter to. Find me and you can tell me what you want then. But now, go."

As for Harris, quite contrary to his own expectations, seeing Beatrice made him happy. No matter that he was about to let her take him back into the company of Whyos. He looked at her, and she was smiling at him; that easily, his faith in her was restored. He wondered how he could have mistrusted her. He recalled the way Maria had invaded his dreams lately, and realized he'd never really tried to find Maria, only thought about her when things were at their worst. He hadn't known her very well, after all. She was mostly just a feeling of common doom, an imaginary double, someone else alone, cursed with ill luck, who knew his landscape and his language. It had been a feeble, seasick infatuation, and as intimate as the ordeal aboard the *Leibnitz* had sometimes been, wiping up vomit and burying bodies at sea were not experiences on which to found a friendship, much less anything more. Whereas Beatrice was standing there before him, grinning, and most important not pretending anymore that nothing had happened. He knew Beanie day in, day out, in seriousness and laughter, her family and her various masquerades. He knew her body, and he spoke her language, which she'd given him. He came up to her and smiled, reached for her hand. She let him take it, and he brought it to his lips. She was clean and fresh and glowing from the alternating rigors of damp and dry heat and hot and cool baths. *Two baths in quick succession*, he thought, wishing again that she were dirtier so he could smell her.

"Hello there."

"Hello there," he said, exactly the same but an octave lower.

"I was going to say you were late, but you aren't. You're just on time."

"I wouldn't want to get us in trouble. I'm a little nervous. And I wanted to see you."

"You'll be fine. Just take my arm. You're taking me to the theater, but the show doesn't start for a while."

He didn't question, just let her lead him east and south, through the streets. And as they walked, they played at being a couple. She clenched his arm tightly and chatted, laughed and flirted about empty things, the weather. It was just as if they were out courting. There was some part of Harris—the small intestine, perhaps, or the kidney—that still suspected this promenade was just part of a covert arrival plan, but on the whole it felt real. He was there, with her, after all, her arm in his. His skin was buzzing again. After a while, they turned onto Broadway, where the sidewalks were thick with people out strolling, showing off their fur hats and muffs and cold-weather Sunday finery. Just in front of them, a man and a woman stopped walking and kissed each other, right there, in the middle of the sidewalk in plain day.

"Did you hear that?" yelled the man to the street in general, then turned and looked directly into Harris's eyes. "Did you hear that, brother—she said yes!" He gave a little yip of glee. *Brother*. The man wore a rust-colored coat, and his white shirt showed at the collar. Harris had never seen a jacket quite that color, the very red of a red cow. *You're one of us*, Beatrice had said in that dream, *an Irishman, a Whyo*.

A little further on, they came up to a table manned by white-clad suffragists passing out pamphlets and collecting signatures. They stopped to watch the ladies argue their case to the general public. Beatrice told him how the Why Nots had turned out at the voting booths at the previous mayoral election. With several Whyos assigned to man the polling place, the girls had been able to march through the doors wearing hats and pants and sign themselves in (first initials only). They had voted and been counted, while legions of proper suffragists in white dresses had picketed the voting halls ineffectively. (Not that it was ever a question that the Tammany man, Oakey Hall, would not be elected, but for the Why Nots it was a matter of principle.) Harris had no trouble picturing her doing this—in fact, he couldn't stop thinking about Beatrice in pants. If only the freedom to wear trousers and vote didn't entail her being a gangster.

"But you know," Harris said, "just because you managed to cast your vote that way doesn't mean the suffragists haven't got a point. What about the rest of the women, who aren't like you, who can't dress up like men? And do you want to have to do it that way, illegally?"

She looked at him, eyebrows up. "Any way we can do it is better than none." But they signed the ladies' petition. As Harris wrote his name, he was aware his script was still too German. He knew Beatrice was right, the other day, when she complained about it, but he was too fond of the Gothic style of writing to unlearn it.

They strolled and talked, and finally he asked her what would happen later. She told him not to worry, and he believed her. The truth was, she herself wasn't sure. When they came to a corner where a tintype photographer had a studio, they stopped and looked at the many portraits and advertising signs posted in the window. Pictures cost only five cents apiece and took just five minutes to be developed, making it a remarkably cheap and quick amusement. Beatrice looked at her pocket watch. This was the corner where Fiona was supposed to meet them. She said, "Harris, let's go up and get our picture done, what do you say?"

He grinned. He was thinking that he'd carry the picture with him all the time. She was thinking he was very handsome, and that if anything happened she didn't want to forget him the way she'd forgotten her mother's face, her brother's.

Ten minutes later, Beatrice and Harris were still waiting for their pictures to be finished and trimmed. The five minutes didn't include waiting on line. When a clock in the back room struck the three-quarter hour, Beatrice told Harris she was overwarm, what with wearing her coat in the studio, and would wait for him outside. Fiona was waiting, as promised.

"You've got two minutes. What is it?"

"Listen, you know the German church where we followed him that day? I saw Harris at the coffee place across the street, just this morning, meeting with two people I've never seen before."

"Harris? Come on." Fiona stared. "Was he in the church or the coffee shop?"

"The coffee shop, but he was meeting with two people—"

"Who were they? Were they Germans? Were they cops?"

"No, I don't think so. It was a gentleman and a lady—who was definitely not his wife—but who's to say he wasn't arranging a tail? He shouldn't have been there, today of all days."

"Have you seen anyone tailing us? I haven't—except for you."

"No, but maybe he told them where to meet him."

"He doesn't even know where we're going yet. Listen, Fiona, I'll make sure we're not followed. If we don't show up at the meeting, I realized you were right and took him somewhere else. Now get out of here. He's going to be out any second."

Fiona had expected Beatrice to be a bit more grateful, or at least a bit more angry at Harris. Was she so besotted that she had no insight? It was obvious to Fiona that Beatrice had finally capitulated to Harris's queer charm. She knew her friend too well not to be able to see that as clear as day. Normally, she'd have been amused, but it seemed to have clouded Beatrice's judgment. On top of which, Fiona had just deprived herself of an afternoon with the Jimster for nothing. But she knew enough not to try to fight Beanie when her mind was set. "All right," she said. "Just be careful. I know you wouldn't bring him if he wasn't clean." Then she slipped into the throng.

Beatrice was leaning against a lamppost, staring at the traffic, when Harris came outside with their pictures. They were good likenesses, he thought, both of them looked happy, though the process didn't have half the clarity of the old daguerreotypes. The two pictures were taken side by side, at the same instant, through two adjacent lenses, so they were almost identical, just a few degrees apart. Harris thought he saw a distinction between them, though: In one, Beatrice looked slightly older—the way she might in five years' time—and in the other he almost appeared to be laughing. He'd watched the photographer clip the images apart with his tin snips, trim the edges and insert them into two leather slipcases. He chose a black case and the older-looking picture for himself. He had the laughing one put in a red wallet for her. He was about to show them to her when she spoke.

"Frank, I have one question for you." There was something odd in her voice. She didn't usually call him that, and he noticed it.

He stopped, swallowed, looked down. He had a litany of questions he could have asked her: Would you marry me and run away? Will you forgive me if I went too far? Do you really want to be a gangster? Do you want me to be one, too? But he could tell that this was not the time.

"Just keep walking, Harris. And while you walk, I want you to explain what you were up to this morning. Fiona just told me you were at that German church and in the café across the street, holding a meeting with someone."

"What?" His stomach lurched. He didn't know whether to be outraged or chagrined. It was true that he had agreed to avoid all things German, all the time, and the café Towle had chosen was inauspiciously close to that Lutheran Church. But nothing had come of it. He had been circumspect.

He had turned down Mr. Towle and Dr. Blacksall's quite wonderful pro-posal, for the Whyos, for her. And how did she know? "Is there someone fol-lowing me all the time, then?"

"Maybe there should be."

"I never went in that church."

"Were you in the café across the street? Having coffee with people who wouldn't approve of the Whyos?"

He looked at her. Had she changed back again?

"I can see only two possible explanations for it, Harris. Maybe you're try-ing to get yourself hanged. Maybe you don't like me after all, maybe the Irish aren't good enough for you, maybe you're lonely for your own kind— your loving father, perhaps, or a countryman like Undertoe?"

"Bea—" he began, but she just went on delivering a hissed rant.

"The other possibility is that you really went and squealed to the cops. In which case, you're hoping to watch the rest of us hang. That's the inter-pretation Fiona came to, and that's why she came to find me back at the baths. Any Whyo would think the same, why shouldn't they? Harris, I do hope you're not that stupid, because if she's right, you're dead, too, mark my words. It won't be up to me. So now would you please tell me that I'm wrong on both counts? Would you tell me why you were at that café, and who that couple was?"

"I'm not hoping to hang anyone," he said, slipping both tintypes into his pocket.

And then he described his appointment with Mr. Towle and Dr. Black-sall. He'd tried to tell her the day before, but she wouldn't talk to him. He looked at her, thinking of all those things he had wanted to say, questions he had needed to ask. This conversation, the big meeting—it was all beside the point. "Beatrice, since the other night"—his face went red—"you wouldn't talk to me. Why?"

The corners of her lips drew down.

"They're going to kill me at that meeting, aren't they?" he asked. His question was not the right one, he knew that as soon as he'd uttered it. He should have worried about her, about them, not himself. He should have made a declaration, not asked a question at all. He should at least have tried.

"Don't be ridiculous. The Whyos aren't done with you yet."

As for his explanation, she found it believable. As for trusting him, she did. There was no need to worry about cops or rivals tracking them to the meeting, she felt. She reached into her shirtwaist and extracted a watch. She bit her lip and refrained from reaching out to touch his arm to reassure him. She could just imagine the sexual jolt that would spring through her, and this was not the time for that. What she wanted for herself and whether she'd be able to act on it were separate matters entirely. Partly, it depended on Harris's performance at the meeting. There was no point declaring herself now. "We're late now, let's go."

They walked on silently, Harris in a state of suspense, not at all sure how to interpret her words, until they came to the Old Bowery Theater, where a play called *The Outcast Lover* was opening that day. She told him to go buy them the cheapest orchestra tickets he could get, in back, on an aisle. He nodded and turned toward the ticket window. There, in the lobby of the theater, he felt he was very close to learning his fate. *The Whyos aren't done with you yet,* she had said. He looked back at her and thought, *She's ruthless, she's unfathomable, she's so beautiful.* He suspected he was about to give his final performance of McGinty's ballad before an audience of his own executioners. He understood, better than ever before, that however much she truly felt for him, she answered first to her gang. But he didn't think seducing him had been part of her mission.

"Whatever happens now," he said, rejoining her, reaching into his pocket and handing her the red leather case, "I want you to know that I love you."

She looked at him and slipped the picture into her reticule without looking at it. Her face was unreadable.

"Harris," she said flatly, "my God. This is neither the place nor the time for such a statement." Why couldn't he have said that out on the street, before they were there, when she could have done something? She felt she might burst into tears.

His face was very red as he looked at his feet. When he took her elbow and led her to the orchestra, they looked for all the world like what he wished they were: two average people, a couple in danger of falling in love. But they were anything but what they appeared, those two, anything but what he'd have wished for. He still had no idea where the meeting was going to be held—certainly not in this theater full of people—and yet an image formed in his mind: himself up there on the stage of the Old Bowery, limelights blazing, bucolic backdrop at his back, Piker Ryan in the wings, a slungshot ready to hand. And then the room filled with terrible, whooping whyos, and the gang descended upon him as a throng.

Their seats were indeed the worst in the house: at the very rear of the orchestra, their view of the stage interrupted by two separate columns. In short, not much for taking in the show but perfectly suited to Beatrice's purposes.

"Nice job on the seats," she said, but of course they had been prearranged.

Harris looked around, wondering which of the other audience members were Whyos, and he spotted an unexpected face passing down the aisle: Mrs. Dolan. It made him blush, to be with Beatrice and see Mrs. Dolan, it brought back the vivid memories of what had transpired on the tiled floor of the bath hall. It had been real. He knew what he felt had been real. He turned to Beatrice and whispered, "I meant that, what I said before, you know. What happens now?"

But she ignored him until finally the lights were dimmed and the curtain rose. As the room filled with shouts and applause, he felt a jab in his side, and he turned.

"Suddenly, I'm not feeling very well, Mr. Harris," said Beatrice, not too quietly, in a quavery feminine voice that didn't match her at all. "Would you be so kind as to escort me to the lounge?"

20.

BODY IN THE BROOM CLOSET

eatrice steered him down the worn, stained, red-plush-carpeted stairs to the basement, where the lounges and the bathrooms were. There were still a few latecomers hurrying to their seats. Harris wasn't at all sure whether what she did next was for their benefit or his, but at the door to the ladies' room she slipped her arms around his waist and pulled him toward her. Then, with a showy, unseemly passion, she kissed him. His heart was beating, and his lungs were pumping, and he was kissing her back as if it was real. When they broke apart, she looked straight into his eyes. He felt a surge of hope and anxiety so great it made him dizzy. Maybe they were going to make him a Whyo. Maybe they weren't going to kill him. Maybe this was love.

She leaned into him again, but what she whispered into his ear was just instructions: "The entry hall to the men's room. Wait until no one's in there but the attendant—he's one of us—then step into the utility closet to the left of the door. Close the door behind you, walk to the back and push up against the rear wall—it swings open into a stairwell. Someone will be waiting for you."

Then she kissed him again, as firmly and sweetly on the lips as if she'd just told him she loved him madly. Was it possible she *had* told him that, he wondered, with her body at least, or some silent whyo? He couldn't rule it out. And then she traipsed toward the ladies' lounge—to follow a parallel route, he presumed.

Away from her, when he faced the utility-closet door, the clammy feeling of distrust returned. But he opened it anyway, an optimist, a fool. He was so smitten with her kisses that it wasn't till he'd pushed through the rear door of the closet and found himself looking at Piker Ryan's ugly face that it occurred to him what an idiot he was; once she'd left him, he could have run back up to the lobby of the theater and out the door, onto the street. It might not have lasted, he didn't have any place of refuge in mind, but something had always turned up before. He looked at his assassin, unable to speak.

"Well, well," said Piker Ryan, "Frankie the Devil, right on schedule. Let's go." There was no sharp blow to the head, but of course that might come later. Instead, Piker turned into the darkness, and Harris followed him down the dark stairwell. He heard another door open and close in the darkness, and Piker turned and pressed his hand over Harris's mouth, stopping him dead. Harris listened, thinking it must be Beatrice, but the footsteps ringing on the stairs above were not hers. Harris knew her gait too well to be mistaken. They went down and down until it seemed to Harris they were deeper than any sewer tunnel he'd been in. The stairs finally ended in a long hallway with a single kerosene lamp hanging on the wall. After he'd passed it, he looked back and saw the glimmer of Beatrice's hair. He had been wrong to think it wasn't her, to think she wasn't capable of hiding herself from him. She'd been directly behind him all the time.

They came out into a large rehearsal room lit brightly with gas fixtures on the walls. It had a stage just like the theater above them but no seating for a real audience, just a couple of rows of chairs. The stage itself was set up with tables, as if for a banquet, and there was a savory if slightly fishy aroma wafting from some back corner. Many of the Whyos had been there before. This rehearsal room was where Dandy Johnny had been formally anointed the successor to Googy Corcoran. The Old Bowery itself was owned by an old guy named Mike Sweeney, an original Whyo who'd eagerly gone over to Johnny's side when he came to power. The place had been a frequent Whyo meeting place in the transition period, before Mother Dolan started getting strict about not holding so many meetings. It was a perfect location, completely secluded and out of the way, and in the event of a raid there were numerous stairwells they could flee up, plus two vast scenery elevators and a dumbwaiter that was used for conveying props between rehearsal rooms and the main stage. The Whyos liked it there—it was a festive space for them—and they were glad to be back.

Why Nots were setting out bowls on the tables, and Whyos were arranging chairs, stools, boxes and benches around them. They were apparently going to dine before they held their meeting. A keg of Owney Geoghegan's was tapped, and soon everyone was drinking. Harris found a seat off to the side and watched the crowd, keeping an eye out for Johnny, who had taken on a kind of vague and mythic aspect in his mind—he wondered if he'd recognize him—and, of course, for Beanie, but neither was anywhere to be seen. After what seemed a long time, two Whyos went over to the dumbwaiter and hauled out two enormous vats of stew. The nutty, saline scent of oysters wafted through the room. Harris was still looking for Beanie when people began to take seats. He was alone in the crowded room, but people seemed to know who he was and to be kindly disposed toward him. Indeed, it was hard to imagine that all these people were killers. The longer he watched them, the less he believed it. All around him, the Whyos and Why Nots slurped their soup and told stories and laughed, just like people.

Harris himself was so preoccupied with watching the scene that he'd barely tasted his stew when a singularly unattractive Why Not offered him more. (He shook his head and suspected her of being Piker Ryan's sister.) As the meal drew to a close, he found himself repeating the refrain of the sewermen's ballad over and over in his head—*All I want is to die / With my dogs clean and dry / Snoring alongside sweet Sally.* He sang it beautifully, in his mind. When the time came to perform, he wanted it to come out as a serenade to Beatrice. If only he were sitting with her, he thought, and if only he knew where he stood, he might be able to enjoy this. Maybe the Whyos weren't so bad, and he would join them after all. As he brought the last bite of his oyster stew to his lips, two fat bodies floating in the spoon, someone rose from an adjacent table, and suddenly he had a clear line of sight to where she sat, all the way across the stage from him. She was looking the other way. Just as Harris took the final oyster between his teeth, Dandy Johnny squatted down beside him and wrapped his arm around his shoulder. "Welcome to the Old Bowery, Frank Harris. I'd like to have a few words with you later on, sort out some details, eh?" Harris nodded but couldn't speak—he was choking on the oyster, going purple. Johnny had stood up and was moving on—he was just doing the rounds, not stopping long with anyone—but he paused to slap Harris on the back. Harris grunted, and the oyster dislodged and arced across the table to land, with a small, unseen splash, in the bowl of Piker Ryan's sister. All eyes in the room were on Dandy Johnny, who had crossed the stage and was now standing beside Beatrice. He tapped Fiona on the shoulder and gestured at the piano bench she was sharing with Beatrice.

"Fiona, my bat, why don't you scram." He looked down at Beatrice and smiled.

When she realized he was going to give her credit for her work using Harris as a mole, Beatrice blushed. She hadn't expected that. But she probably should have. Johnny knew just when to reward people, just when to punish them, to play them to his need. He had a certain charisma that enabled him always to seem magnanimous, handsome, desirable, and it was a great part of his ability to lead.

"Don't you look fresh and victorious tonight, Beanie," he said to her, but loudly, publicly, too, and curled his fingers around the flesh of her upper arm.

That was odd, she thought—he'd hardly ever touched her before. Johnny took his pleasure with pretty much whomever he chose; he had physically initiated almost every Why Not into the gang (and the prettier boy sopranos among the Whyo recruits, too). He took them into the back room at the Morgue, which was soundproof, and taught them their first set of personal codes and Whyo passwords. Then he did exactly as he pleased, depending on the initiate's looks and his own appetite. Invariably, the new gangster came out adjusting his or her clothes, showing off the brand-new eye-gouger Johnny gave as a token and smiling. Yet when Beanie had gone back there, he'd simply taught her what she needed to know and sent her on her way. She'd looked at him, not wanting more, but wondering.

"You're a bit scrawny for me, no thanks," was what he'd said. She would never forget it. She'd even had to buy her own eye-gouger. So it was abundantly clear that Johnny had never found her attractive, and yet there was definitely something sexual, something proprietary, in the way he now held her arm. She was a little horrified to think that after all this time she would suddenly have to prove her loyalty to him *that* way—tonight of all nights, when her head was full of Harris. But she smiled at Johnny. He was the boss.

He gave a short little whoop of a whyo that served to stop every whispered conversation in the room. He leapt up onto the table. "I'd like to propose a toast, to the lovely Beatrice O'Gamhna. She came up with the plan I'll be describing to you shortly, and she's taken excellent care of our friend and guest Mr. Harris, over there, putting him up in her aunt's home while he did a bit of spying for us and generally masterminding his efforts on our behalf. But before we get down to business, I've got a little surprise for you: After long ambivalence, I've chosen myself a First Girl."

There was a general murmuring. The boss's public selection of his consort was a popular tradition that the first Whyos, long before Googy and Johnny's day, had carried over from the gangs they started out in, the Chichesters and Dead Rabbits.

"It's not what anyone will have expected," said Johnny, "but, well, *why not?*" He laughed at his own joke. "So, let it be known: *Beatrice O'Gamhna is mine alone.*" As Johnny pronounced this ritual phrase, his grip tightened on Beatrice's arm. The murmuring turned to whyos and quite a few wolf whistles, too, bouncing off the walls. Beatrice went pale and then, slowly, her cheeks flushed bright red.

Harris couldn't believe what he'd just heard. He couldn't look at her. He watched Piker Ryan's sister pause in her cheering to take a bite of her soup. He felt nothing. After the hoopla had gone on for a minute or so, Dandy Johnny gave a loud whistle, pulled Beanie up onto the table with him and kissed her. He bent her over backwards, holding her with one arm and letting the other hand slide from her back to her shoulders to her cheek and then down her front, across her breasts. It was an act of possession. She did what she realized she had to, given the situation: She kissed him back. Then he lifted her right off her feet. She hiked her skirt, clamped her legs around him and laughed. They spun around in place several times like that, Dandy Johnny and his new First Girl. The noise in the rehearsal room just mounted and mounted.

And in this way, Beatrice became the only Why Not in the organization who was not, in fact, a free woman, not in charge of her own body or life. To be the First Girl was to trade that freedom for power, for glamour, for influence. It was not her choice, but when at last he put her down, she whyoed herself, lewdly and loudly, as if she had won a prize long lusted after. There were just a few silent voices in the room: Mrs. Dolan, who never engaged in that crass sort of whyoing herself, a couple of disappointed Why Nots and Frank Harris.

Harris had no way of knowing that Beatrice had never even kissed Dandy Johnny before, that she was as surprised as anyone there. How could he have guessed any of that, poor Harris, because there she stood, beaming? She certainly didn't looked dismayed or brokenhearted. And she wasn't, exactly.

The truth was, this was a prize no Why Not would ever turn down, even if she could have. Beatrice was stunned. She was overwhelmed. She buzzed in anticipation of all that Johnny's decision would bring her: the power, the money and Johnny himself. His arm felt good about her waist, tight but not too tight. She looked down at his boots, smooth, shiny and elegant. They glimmered at the toes where small fragments of ax blades had been embedded in the soles. The legend was that he'd cobbled his first pair himself from a rusty ax head and a pair of old boots with the soles flapping loose in front. Now there was a Whyo cobbler who made them specially, though of course Johnny rarely had to kick heads in anymore—that was what the likes of Piker Ryan were for. Beatrice wasn't thinking of Harris at all; she couldn't. She let herself relax into Johnny's arm. She felt his power flow into her. She might even learn to like it, she thought.

There were a couple of inarticulate toasts and then someone brought out a harmonica and someone else a fiddle. Beatrice and Johnny danced across the tabletops, leaping from one to the next, sending bowls, spoons and oyster crackers flying. She didn't think of Harris again until Johnny had finally concluded the celebration and began to bring the meeting to order. There was other business that night than dancing and drinking, after all.

That was why Harris was there: They were going to lay out their plan to use the sewers at last. As soon as Beatrice began to look for him, she realized how fully she'd abandoned him rather than shepherded him as she'd

intended. Earlier it might just have been that she couldn't handle his declaration of love and simultaneously make sure he made it out the other end
of the night alive. Now, with Johnny's pinkie ring snugly on her thumb, she
found she couldn't bear to look in his direction. But she forced her mind to
be practical. She put aside the eagerness she'd felt for so long to see him in
the evenings, so clean and tired. And she shelved the memory of the night
in the sewers. There was no hope for any of that now. The best she could
do was use her new power to help him to survive.

Frank Harris, meanwhile, saw the room grow bleary and unreal. He had
drunk down a pint of Owney's ale in a single gulp, and it had not agreed
with him. It seemed possible it would all come back up equally quickly.
The sick feeling reminded him of nothing so much as his father and step-
mother's wedding day, when he and his sister, Lottie, had been seated in
the first row and expected to dance and smile, curtsy and bow, though they
knew that the day was their last at home, that this event was the reason that
they were being sent away to the farm in the country. It was a feeling of dis-
placement, dispossession and lost potential that boiled down to nausea.
The one conclusion he did come to, sitting there, was that it didn't much
matter to him anymore what happened next. He wouldn't sing, he
wouldn't fight, he wouldn't struggle when Piker Ryan took him into a dark
corridor to get rid of him. He would even be grateful, perhaps. Indeed, he
was so fully absorbed by his own dismay that he didn't hear a word of the peculiar plan that Dandy Johnny was laying out.

He was startled from his trance, however, when he thought he saw Mrs.
Dolan sitting at a far table. To have run into her upstairs, in public, was one
thing, but now he doubted his own senses. Someone passed between them
then, and when the view was clear again, another woman was sitting in the
chair. He shook his head clear. But no, Harris had not been wrong. The
second woman was Maggie the Dove, and she'd quickly changed places
with Mother Dolan, who was now once again obscured from Frank Harris's
sight by a pillar.

Meg Dolan was very fond of Harris; Beanie had done good things with
him, gotten good work out of him without letting him in on much at all
about the gang; but in the end, the key fact was that he wasn't a Whyo. And
now that she'd seen his face when her Johnny had kissed Beatrice, he never

would be. It was a pity. She had always liked him, but Johnny came first, of course. She took a deep breath and drained her ale. It was difficult, running things, she thought, and she much preferred doing it from afar so as not to get overly involved.

A few minutes later, she rose, congratulated her son, whispered a few words into his ear and left the rehearsal room, otherwise unnoticed. She emerged into the lobby upstairs in time to catch the entire third act of the play—it was an operetta in which a thief attempted to seduce a good girl who resisted him and eventually managed to reform him instead, and marry him. During the heroine's final aria, Mrs. Dolan was annoyed to find her view obstructed by the reedy silhouette of someone standing up in the orchestra, several seats in front of her. And then, when the man turned to walk up the aisle, she saw that it was Luther Undertoe.

It might have been a coincidence, but it might not have. Why should Luther Undertoe be there at the Old Bowery, at this particular performance, this particular meeting? Had there been a security breach? She stood up to follow him, but the star of the show had just reached the saccharine crescendo of her song, and there was an enormously fat and engrossed theatergoer blocking Mrs. Dolan's exit from the row. He rose only reluctantly to let her pass, and by the time she'd fought her way out, the curtain had dropped. The aisles were flooded with people, and she lost sight of Undertoe in the crowd. She headed directly for the lounges downstairs, hoping at least to confirm with the Whyo on guard at the top of the hidden staircase that Undertoe hadn't somehow found his way downstairs, but she was too late—a line of women snaked from the ladies' lounge. A shiny-nosed girl was leaning up against the mirror that hung in front of the utility-closet door in the foyer, applying lip color from a tin in careful little daubs. There was no way to get back through the hidden doorway, but she satisfied herself that at least the Why Not on duty passing out towels had registered no alarm— didn't even whyo, just met her eye and smiled. Mrs. Dolan exclaimed, "Heavens, what a line," and went home in a state of some anxiety, wishing she'd somehow made contact with the men's-room attendant as well. She couldn't shake the feeling of concern that had welled up within her—first Harris unexpectedly in love with Johnny's new girl, her unreadable, then

Undertoe showing up. She would have to make sure Johnny dealt with Undertoe sooner rather than later, she decided. Harris, too, alas.

She was right that Undertoe was up to something, of course. Mrs. Dolan had excellent intuition. He'd attended the show with the plan of lifting a few wallets while taking in an afternoon of amusement (he liked the bad boy–good girl theme just as well as Mother Dolan and the rest of the crowd). He'd spied a man he knew slightly as a panel thief ducking into the bathroom just before the show began, and had loitered in the hall waiting for him to come out, thinking they might do a little teamwork. But the guy never came back out. *Odd.* All through the first half, he couldn't stop wondering where he'd gone. The only thing he could come up with was that he'd disposed of the bathroom attendant and was down there robbing every doddering theatergoer who couldn't hold his water till intermission. And the more he thought about it, the more lucrative and amusing and delightfully risky a scheme that seemed to him, until finally, just before the show ended, he got up himself, thinking he wanted in on the action. For Undertoe, it was really just a casual foray.

He didn't see his man when he got there—the bathroom was empty except for the attendant, a young Whyo named Horatio, who was unfamiliar to him but didn't look too formidable. He decided to try the idea out himself. He took a leisurely leak, and then, when Horatio had turned back to polishing the mirror, he opened the broom-closet door with the idea of pretending to have mistaken it for the exit. A wet mop leaned against the wall, and there were various buckets and dust-covered brown-glass bottles of cleanser. He reached for his blackjack and waited for the towel boy to approach him and direct him to the proper door. He certainly didn't expect the young man to be monitoring him in the mirror or to have pegged him as unfriendly from the first or to be equipped with knockout drops and a slingshot of his own under his apron. You can just imagine Undertoe's surprise when a crack on the skull was something he received rather than dealt. Horatio dragged him into the closet and dosed him liberally. When he went slack, the young Whyo stuck his head through the rear door and called for backup, then returned, whistling, to wiping down the wet sinks, rinsing the urinals and handing out towels. He was quite pleased at the development. Guard duty was rarely so eventful, and intercepting an interloper would surely bring him to the attention of Dandy Johnny. Maybe the next time he'd actually get to attend the meeting.

Back down in the basement, the feast had been eaten and the kiss conferred, but the Whyos had still not gotten down to work. It was not, you may say, the most conventional agenda, to dance and drink before doing business, but then they were a gang of ruffians. They'd chosen that existence at least in part because it allowed them to do things the wrong way round. The tables and chairs were being pushed to the sides and the dishes were mostly cleared when Dandy Johnny said a few words into Beatrice's ear, and she left his side to fetch two cups of ale. She had no trouble finding Harris in the crowd. She pulled up a chair.

"You look poorly, Harris," she said. "I hope it ain't the oysters."

He cast his eyes up at her without moving his head and smiled cynically. It made her crumple up inside. One of the things she'd always liked about him was the absence of that bitter emotion. Now she'd added it to his repertoire.

"What happened tonight—I didn't expect it," she said.

He looked at her. "If you say so. But you don't regret it."

He had her there, both of them knew. A better chance had offered itself, and she'd shut the door on Harris.

"I have no choice, Harris, so I might as well try to make the best of it. I'm sorry. Listen, this is a big night for you—Johnny's going to get you up on stage to show the boys a few things—just to get them to trust you, to show them you know your stuff, really. If they like you and if the job goes well, you'll have a lot more options. So, Harris, don't mess up."

"So, are you his wife now?"

"Oh God, Harris," she said. "I don't know. Not exactly. Maybe this will be better. Now I can make sure Johnny brings you in, instead of . . ."

She trailed off, and he could think of nothing at all to say. So they *had* been going to kill him, but now she was claiming she could help him? Her concern seemed either terribly cruel or terribly false, he wasn't sure which.

"And Harris, don't do anything rash. Don't go sign up for that sanitary campaign. You could still get picked up for Will Williams by the cops if someone recognized you. I want you alive."

"Will you be—all right—with him?" he coughed.

"You can't worry about me. I'll be fine."

He glanced at her, then looked away again.

"But Harris? Don't *not* worry."

"So what happens now?" he asked, looking at her with as much bluster as he could summon. "I take it they'll spare me till the job has gone off and all the boys know how to navigate the sewers and I'm no longer useful?"

"Harris, the sewer stuff is all my plan. I based it on having you there to guide them through the tunnels, because you're an expert. They're going to need you alive for the next time, too, don't you see? It's your ticket in."

He looked at her. She knew he was thinking he didn't want in.

"Do it for me. If the job works, then we'll be using the sewers again, and we'll need you. So make it work, Harris. At least you're not hanging by your neck at the Tombs. You would have been dead a long time ago, if Undertoe had gotten to you that day."

"Thanks a lot," he said. "But maybe it would have been for the best."

Beatrice put down her cup of ale. She glanced across the room, caught Dandy Johnny's eye, nodded to him, and then wrapped her arms around Frank Harris. She stroked his hair. It was a maternal, sisterly gesture of comfort—at least that's what she intended outwardly to convey. Meanwhile, she was whyoing subtly but hard, throwing up a cover, and when she felt it was secure, she let her fingertips move differently for a moment, roaming along his hairline and grazing the skin behind his ear, the smooth-shaven corner of his jaw. His whole body prickled.

"I fell in love with you, Harris," she said. "I didn't mean to. I shouldn't have. But I can't help that now, any more than I can all of this tonight. But at least I can protect you. If you let me. Just help me. That's the best we can do."

There was no new thought in his head, just that contact, those words and the smell of her body through her dress. There was no optimism, no resolve. But he knew he would do it: sing the song, teach the men, show them the way. Maybe he would really become a Whyo after all. It was as simple as the fact that she'd asked him to help her, whatever her reasons, and he hadn't the power to say no.

21.

THE TAMMANY JOB

The problem with Beatrice's promise was that the sewers weren't really a very good getaway route. There was no future for Harris in being a guide to the watery underworld. She'd seen that the second she went down there with him that night. The access was just too cumbersome, and soon Johnny would know it, too, from experience. In fact, he didn't have any particular illusions about the sewers. He had begun to fill her in on a few key details of tonight's plan the day before, and it turned out they were really only doing the big sewer job to create cover for another job—something Johnny was calling *the Tammany job*—and it had to do with the dry tunnel Harris had found.

"All right, boys," Johnny called at last, raising his cane. A crew of the younger Whyos emerged from the wings dragging a series of large, low, amorphous objects and deposited them at intervals on either side of where Dandy Johnny stood. There were a dozen of them, and the wavery footlights cast their shadows long and ominous across the canted stage, almost like bodies. Only the boys who had helped Dandy Johnny and Beatrice bring them there knew what they were. And, of course, Harris knew. He could have identified them at any distance. Then came a series of strange, directionless whistles and noises, and men began to step forward as if they had been called—which they had. By the time the twelve principals on the job were standing next to the twelve pairs of sewermen's boots, the rest of the crowd was watching. All twelve men stooped down and unlaced their shoes. Then they each picked up a boot and began struggling to pull it on. Having the men boot up at the meeting was something Beatrice had suggested, knowing that the Whyos had never donned sewermen's boots before. It wasn't an easy task for the uninitiated, as she well recalled, and she was thinking it would put Harris in a good light, that he did it so easily. But Harris hadn't been called forward by Johnny. He was just watching from the side, steeling his resolve for whatever came next. After several tries at his boots, Piker Ryan was just standing there panting. His feet were only halfway down the legs, and both boot shoes were laid out to the sides, like useless, broken appendages. Then Piker gave it another shot. He balanced on his right leg and yanked at the left boot, but just as he tried to settle his heel in the shoe of the left boot, caught the toe in the opening of the other boot, and lost his equilibrium. The Whyos and Why Nots watched in delight. And Piker was not alone. The others were all in various states of disarray and distress as well.

"Christ, men!" said Dandy Johnny over the laughter. This was not the opening he had intended, though he guessed now that Beanie had. "What are you, Whyos or buffoons?" She wanted evidently to make Harris look good. She had a soft spot for Harris, which he had no patience for, but perhaps it had been a good idea. "Frank Harris?" called Johnny. "Harris! Get up and give these boys some instruction in putting on their new boots."

Harris looked around the room for Beatrice, but he didn't see her. So this was it. He stepped forward and vaulted himself up onto the proscenium.

"Harris," said Johnny, who was standing off to the side. He pointed with his thumb to a spot just outside the footlights' glow, another pair of boots. Remarkably, they turned out to be his boots: McGinty's. The grain of the leather, the pattern of creases, their miraculously buttery texture were unmistakable. Had Beatrice gone back and completely raided the Sewer Division? Quite possibly. Then there was Mrs. Dolan. Perhaps he had really seen her. He was wondering what in the world she could have to do with the Whyos when he turned and looked at Dandy Johnny, and suddenly he saw the connection: It was a younger, male version of Mrs. Dolan that smiled confidently back at him from above the fancy waistcoat and yellow silk tie.

"Put your boots on, Mr. Harris," said Johnny. "Show them the way."

Harris pried off his shoes against his heels. He showed the men how to gather the leather boots in accordion folds and draw them upwards in smooth strokes. It was a marked contrast: The Whyos still fumbled, while Harris stepped into one boot, then the next, in two quick motions, extending his legs and letting the leather stretch tight against his thigh, just as if he happened to be walking in that direction anyhow and the boots were in his path. With a flick of the wrist, his suspenders were snugly affixed. He wore the heavy boots as if they had no weight. Johnny looked over at Beatrice and decided he was pleased. It had been a good idea. And even Beatrice smiled a little, unthinkingly, with pride.

"All right then," said Dandy Johnny above the rising murmur of Whyos and Why Nots. "The men with the boots are the principals, but you're all in on this job. Here's the plan: We're hitting the old p.o. tomorrow afternoon. We're going to do it during business hours, in plain sight. These twelve up here in the boots will be the ones that get away with the money, but every last one of the rest of you's going to be involved in this job, on crowd control, to ensure the getaway. The boys here will be departing via the sewers with the help of Mr. Harris, who's an expert on that subject. That's why he's here. The rest of you, your job is to sow confusion and misdirect people's attention. If you do it right, no one's going to have the slightest idea where they went, and no one's going to get hurt. The boys will just seem to have vanished with the money. Very neat, and I'll have you know this little caper promises to bring us great returns. The post office brings in over ten grand a day, and they don't empty out the cash drawers till closing time. The biggest day is Monday. Eleven of the clerks' stations are in the main hall, but it's the business window around the corner where nearly half the loot comes in. The whole place is crowded and disorganized—that's why they're putting up the new joint up at City Hall. What we're going to do is hit all twelve windows at once, right at the end of the day. We ought to get as much as we would for a bank haul—if we did crass work like breaking banks. But no, we're going to do this one with finesse."

There would be three Whyos and one Why Not assigned to each clerk, he explained, a dozen people to each quadrant of the main hall, and several floaters to take care of whatever unexpected trouble might come up.

"You boys in the boots," said Johnny, "remember, walk calmly. You'll be gone before anyone knows what happened."

There was a door marked NO EXIT that led to the basement, and that's where they would go, rather than to the roof or the side doors, where other Whyos pretending to have seen them would point. From there, they would enter the sewer. "And from there you'll get further directions from him." He waved at Harris. "If for any reason you can't get the money off your clerk by the time the others have moved on, you walk away. Don't make a scene. It's a little more ballsy than usual, but the secret of the job is still stealth. They won't know what hit them. Thanks in part to Frank Harris here. He's found us the getaway route of our dreams."

After a moment, Piker Ryan stepped forward. "Johnny, even if we get away with it, what the Hell we going to do with all the stamps? I don't know a fence in the city who deals in stamps."

There was silence.

"Cash, Piker," said Johnny. "Don't bother with the stamps, just get the cash and move. The idea is, it's just like a bank job, but since it's not a bank, there's less security."

"Oh. Just the cash. Right." Piker flashed a sheepish, gap-toothed smile.

"You're so damn dumb you're going to terrify them."

They walked through the particulars several times, until everyone knew exactly what his or her role would be. The keg was dry, and it seemed they were ready to wrap things up when Johnny called Harris and the principals to the front of the stage and instructed Harris to sing his ballad. Harris sang and then explained the way he used the song to frighten off the superstitious sewer workers. It was odd how he felt his connection to Beatrice wrenching free as he parted his lips and crooned the first words. He had been thinking before the meeting that if he had to sing, he would do it as a kind of serenade to her, but no, it turned out to be something more like his own swan song, and as far as he could see she wasn't even listening. He wasn't asked to teach the lyrics to the men. Harris would be down there with the men as their guide. If the need arose, he would be there to sing them himself.

It was at this point in the meeting that Johnny was informed about the interloper who'd been apprehended in the men's room. The senior man on watch duty had come quickly when the bathroom attendant called for help, and he recognized Undertoe. "Shit—the Undertaker," he said. They'd added a few more drops of hydrate of chloral to a cup of whiskey and poured it into Undertoe's mouth, but most of it dribbled down his shirt-front, so they administered a little more of the knockout potion directly onto his tongue. Then they made sure he was well trussed up and locked both of the broom-closet doors. Eventually, when the theater was empty and night had fallen, the meeting broke up more stealthily than it had been convened, with little clusters of men and women scurrying off at long intervals from a half a dozen different stage and service exits of the Old Bowery. Meanwhile, Johnny went upstairs to take a look at Undertoe, who was thoroughly out, and to debrief the Whyo who'd nabbed him.

"Did you whack him pretty good, then?" he asked, and Horatio nodded. "What do you think he was up to?"

"Actually, I think he was going to brain *me*. He had his hand on his shot. I don't know what for, maybe just the tips. But he was definitely alone."

"Not even a kid with him? He usually works with newsboys."

Horatio shook his head.

"Yeah, well, it wasn't the tips. That ain't enough to interest this guy, but whatever he was after, you took care of him. Good work, Horatio, good job."

Johnny was tempted to have Undertoe pitched into the river, but then he thought about the two jobs that were going off the following day. If someone saw a couple of his boys dumping a body, it would screw everything up. He needed every hand, and no complications, so he decided to take a more cautious approach to disposing of Undertoe: "Fix him up with a bunch of hot wallets and drunk-dump him somewhere the cops'll find him fast."

It was midnight and the streets were quiet when the unconscious Undertoe was walked out the stage door to a waiting hansom cab by two Whyos, who fed him the rest of the bottle of whiskey for a chaser and took him over to the West Side, where they left him in a doorway just around the corner from a police station. Undertoe was already being dragged to his floppy-fish feet by a cop who slapped him in the face but found him unwakable when Horatio and his compatriots stepped up to the bar at the Morgue to celebrate the unexpected excitement.

Frank Harris had tried to leave when the meeting first began to break up, but he was stopped by Piker Ryan. "Wait around, Harris. Someone wants to talk with you." Hours passed. He sat at a table and brooded. Eventually, to his great surprise, Beatrice approached him and invited him to walk out with her and Johnny.

"No," he said. "I need to go."

"Johnny wants you to walk out with us. Walk out with us."

They escorted him silently out the door and all the way to Fulton Ferry. It was cold waiting on the pier, and Harris was numb inside as well as out. Why, he wondered, should he be asked to stand there between the girl he'd just declared himself to and her new boyfriend, the boss of the gang, unless they were planning to pitch him in the drink? But they didn't. When the boat came, they got on and insisted on sitting outside in the wind. Harris looked out at the ice in the water as the boat cast off. The harbor was thick with slush and floating ice chunks. People were saying the harbor would freeze solid if the weather held. It didn't matter much to Harris one way or the other.

"Privacy," said Johnny, when they were on the ferry, under way. "It's hard to come by in this gang. Everybody knows everything. But I think we can assume we're alone now. I've got a job to propose to you, Harris, on top of the heist, something I don't want the others to know about."

Johnny explained to Harris what he'd told Beanie earlier: that the real point of the p.o. heist was to distract attention from another job—the cops' attention, but also the other Whyos'. Harris looked up at Johnny. He couldn't care less about the Whyos' plans. He thought about telling him that he couldn't have Beatrice. She was taken. He would have done it, too, if only she hadn't been standing next to Johnny with her arm around his waist.

"You may have noticed my mother, downstairs at the theater, Mr. Harris?"

Harris nodded, raising an eyebrow.

"She's very fond of you, you know. But here's the point: We're very excited about that dry tunnel you found. My mother found out some time ago that it existed and that it's used as a kind of secret bank vault for the Tweed ring. Meg Dolan doesn't work in the Sewer Division for nothing, Frankie, nor do you. We've long thought the underground city could have its uses, but there are uses and then there are jackpots. That tunnel was never meant to be connected. It was put in by Towle, and it's used by him and a couple other Tammany men to store money that rightfully belongs to the people of this city. Lots of it."

Harris thought about Mr. Towle and his sanitary ideals. He could not imagine him defrauding the public. His face said as much. Johnny laughed.

"Towle? That old coot? Just because he wears a silk top hat and has a do-good niece or two doesn't mean he's honest. This is how it works: First, a contractor overcharges the city for work they've done, then someone in the racket authorizes payment of the bill—someone like Towle, who's got a big construction budget. The contractor, who's in on it for a percentage, kicks back the difference, in cash of course. The word is that with the new court-house going up on Chambers, and now the new p.o. building, they're tripling all the bills and getting away with it. That money's going to be ours."

"So why do you need me at all? She knows where the tunnel is." His eyes shifted to Beatrice, but she was looking out at the water.

"That's not your problem, why I want you, but consider it a consolation prize, if you like." He glanced over at Beatrice and laughed. "For now, just listen to what you need to do. It's a change from the plan we described back at the theater. As soon as you're sure the boys are at the right place for the pickup and they're settled in and no one's onto you, you're going to come meet the two of us. It's just the three of us plus my mother on the Tammany job, understand?"

Harris nodded, wondering what Johnny would do if he refused, wondering why he didn't, knowing it all had to do with Beatrice. They took the return trip on the ferry, and when they landed on the Manhattan side Beatrice and Johnny walked off together, leaving Harris standing on the pier. He walked past Billy's and would have gone in and ordered a glass of rye, just to test his luck, but there was a sign on the door: CLOSED FOR FUNERAL. He took it as a portent and returned to the O'Gamhnas'. Beatrice, of course, didn't return at all.

Harris lay awake much of the night thinking and thrashing. He imag-ined getting up and going to the dry tunnel on his own, finding the money and then finding Beatrice and running away. He pictured them on a steamship, him with yet another new name, on the run again, but now with her at his side. They could head west to California. Except for the fact that she was with Johnny now.

But Harris was wrong there.

A short time after they left Harris, Johnny told Beatrice to go to Fiona's for the night and stay there.

"What?"

"You heard me."

"You want me to stay at Fiona's?"

Of course he followed her. Johnny was aware that Beatrice was sleeping with the sewerman. That had been her business before, but now he wanted to know what he was dealing with, to see how both of them reacted to the evening's developments. He was pleased when she went to Fiona's directly and stayed put. He was in no hurry to claim her for himself.

Harris went to work in the morning. He felt like a mechanical man, not afraid, not angry, not the master of his own action. But that was only on the inside. Outwardly, he couldn't conceal his alternating numbness and agitation from John-Henry. He was jumpy, taciturn and preoccupied. He ruined an entire barrel of mortar because he measured the lime wrong.

Finally, John-Henry said, "You having trouble with that girl again?"

Harris shrugged. But then he couldn't contain it. He told John-Henry part of what had happened: that Beatrice had taken up with a Five Points gangster. John-Henry shook his head—he'd predicted it would go badly. Harris would have liked to tell John-Henry everything, the full story. If he didn't count Beanie and the O'Gamhnas—and he didn't, anymore—John-Henry was his only friend. Who else could he talk to, if not him? But he'd never mentioned the word Whyo in John-Henry's presence before and didn't plan to start now. Knowing about the Whyos would only jeopardize his friend, not to mention their friendship. And so he found himself in the unsavory position of cooking up a story. In the afternoon, he lied to John-Henry again, telling him he wanted to leave early to see about a possible job. John-Henry had urged him before to go look for work outside of the sewers, using his masonry skills, but Harris had never done anything about it, knowing he wasn't free to leave.

"Well," said John-Henry, "it's about time. Maybe that would help your cause with your girlfriend. It's funny you say that now, though, because I've got my eye on something, too. It's good wages but dangerous: underwater blasting for the piers of the new bridge to Brooklyn. I got a connection to one of the higher-ups, a colonel I fought for in the war. The blasting's done way down, underwater—crazy world, when you can set off a blast underwater, and I don't know quite how it works—but the thing is, of course, that they're building the tower out of stone. I'll put in a good word for you, if you want to look into working on the tower."

Harris's chest opened up. The new bridge was just the kind of thing he dreamed of working on. Tonight, instead, he would help a bunch of criminals rob the government and then help two of those criminals rob their own mates of even more. On top of that, his lie to John-Henry left him feeling ungenerous. He'd asked for a favor and lied, while John-Henry had offered to help him get a job that would have been perfect.

"That sounds like a dream," Harris said. "The job I heard about's just, uh, roadwork, but I guess I still better go." Really, he could have wept as he walked away.

His first task was to ferry the dozen pairs of boots for the principals from a shed where the Whyos had deposited them late the night before to the ledge in the grotto—the place where he'd kissed Beatrice. There was a manhole right near the shed, and he set up a sawhorse to block the street and proceeded as if he were conducting normal sewer business. No one looked twice as he lowered into the hole three enormous canvas bags containing four pairs of boots each. The hard part was hauling them through the long pipeline to the grotto, but he worked quickly, and when all of them were finally laid out, he looked at the pocket watch Beatrice had handed him to use during the job—hot, of course—and saw that he was ahead of time, so he sat down on the ledge for three quarters of an hour and tried to blank out his mind. He listened to the water flowing and stared into the blackness.

When it was time, he made his way through the archway, into the p.o.'s cesspool chamber and around the edge of the putrid holding tank. His headlamp flared brighter there, thanks to the foul air. At the hatch, he paused and listened. All was quiet. He tapped once, counted to five and tapped again. A minute later, the Whyo who'd confirmed the grotto's location by finding Beanie's dime tapped back and then released the hasp on the latch. He opened it and looked in at Harris. Harris couldn't believe he was a Whyo—he was just a kid with a shiny forehead and hardly a whisker. The Whyo made a face at the stink and pushed the rusty door shut again without latching it, and they returned to waiting on either side of the metal door for the men, who were just then responding to the signal to strike in the post office above.

Harris stood on the narrow walkway along the edge of the cesspool, breathing shallowly. Raw excrement and wastewater dribbled and spurted from the pipes in the ceiling now and then. It was a hundred times stronger than the watery brew that flowed through the average sewer pipe. The cesspool had clearly been designed into the building's plans before the construction team discovered the adjacent grotto; it was the usual model, intended to be emptied out on a routine basis by night haulers, but when they linked the flow to the stream it became unnecessary. The overflow spilled out, the rest festered, and no one had to deal with it. Still, in a strange way, it was beautiful down there: In the light of his lantern, the whole chamber glowed. Hoarfrost grew from the walls and ceiling like a glittering mold, especially around the pipes, where it formed elaborate suspended sculptures of ice, some of them so large they looked dangerous. He thought through the plan yet again, with some incredulity. Apparently it was possible for a dozen men to commit a brazen crime in a crowded room and then disappear. So why then couldn't he manage to lose just one man—himself—in the vastness of the city, the world? Why couldn't he manage to flee? The truth, of course, was that he'd handily disposed of several selves. Even now, thanks to the dubious assistance of the Whyos, he was hiding in plain sight, working for a city agency, despite the fact that he was on the most-wanted list for murder and arson. He couldn't manage to feel grateful to Johnny Dolan for that, though. What he did see at last, however, was that disappearing wasn't a way to escape after all. No matter how many identities he'd shed, what remained behind was always himself, mired in his predicaments and perceptible to the naked eye.

As he waited, he tried to envision a life without disaster. He thought of the bridge across the river. He imagined two towers rising up from the harbor. A tower, no matter how large, was built of stones, each one laid by the hand of a man like himself. A tower was ambitious but plausible. But a span across all that space and water? It was almost too large and strange for him to fathom. It defied possibility.

Then came a distant commotion from beyond the hatch. Another instant and the door flew open. Harris pulled the men through one by one and pointed them toward the grotto, reminding them to hug the wall on the narrow walkway and mind the cesspool. He counted eleven. Not twelve, eleven.

"Who's missing?"

It took only a moment for the men to realize it was Piker Ryan, and they were worried. No one had seen him during the scramble downstairs. They'd all been too busy whyoing, casting their voices and the echoes of their footsteps to the opposite side of the p.o.'s great hall. Indeed, in terms of creating a sonic cover, they'd done well: Only a deaf man would have been able to detect them, the way they moved in contrary motion to their audible paths. Harris handed out headlamps, pointed the men to their boots and then crept quietly back past the icy cesspool to the hatch and listened. He heard footsteps, then voices, faint but coming closer. On the one hand, Harris needed to be there to get Piker Ryan through in a hurry if he showed up; on the other, being there meant that the police had only to open the hatch to discover him. He held his breath.

"Show me every Goddamn corner of the basement. I don't care if they were seen climbing to the roof. As far as I can tell, they probably scattered like rats, in every direction. One or two of them are liable to be here. What's back behind the boiler? Are there any other rooms, passages, other ways out of the building from down here?"

"No, sir."

"What's that there?"

"Just the hatch to the cesspool. Nowhere to hide in there. Frankly, sir, it's just a huge bucket of shit. Sorry, sir. But there is one more utility room, on the far side, there. . . ." The voices faded. Clearly they hadn't found Piker, but the detective seemed determined. Harris asked himself what he was doing there, risking his freedom for that of Piker Ryan. It wasn't going to bring him any closer to Beatrice. He had just decided to go and join the others when he heard a tap on the door. The hackles raised on his spine, and he extinguished his lamp. Either it was a lone cop or it was Piker Ryan. He stood there frozen, waiting for the second tap, but then the hinge groaned quietly as the door was drawn back. It was Piker, and he had a wild look on his face. Harris pulled him in and shut the door. The investigators' voices grew audible again, slowly coming nearer.

"Well, sir, what do you say we go back up and join the others on the roof? Not much going on down here, and all the witnesses pointed that way."

"Not so fast, my boy. It's a perfect hiding place. Just look at the alcove. You could hide a dozen men in there."

Harris and Piker stood stock-still in the blackness. Harris dared not strike up the headlamps or breathe a word, but they had to get out of there. He reached out and found Piker's arms, placed them on his own shoulder blades, and then he inched forward, hoping Piker would follow closely—a step to the right would land him in the cesspool.

Something clanged against the hatch, and they froze again. A nightstick?

"You're welcome to look inside, sir, but you'll understand if I stand back a bit—it's pretty potent in there."

The door inched open, and then there was a cry of disgust from the policeman. "Jesus, Mary and Joseph, if that's where they're hiding, I'll leave them to it."

"All right," whispered Harris a few seconds later. "Let's move."

But when Piker Ryan let go of Harris's shoulders, he stepped too wide; his right foot landed on the ice-encrusted rim of the cesspool and shot out from under him. His leg hit the mire, splattering Harris with sewage and breaking the silence. How far away was that cop? Had he heard? Harris knew he ought to run for the archway, to save himself, but he couldn't let a man fall into that mire, even Piker Ryan. He lunged for Piker, throwing every ounce of his weight into keeping him from sliding entirely into the vat. When they landed, Piker was flat on his back, legs spread, Harris on top of him like a lover. They scrambled to their feet and flew toward the arch. Stealth was not an issue anymore—if the police were anywhere near, they had already heard—there was only speed.

In another moment, they were in the grotto. The others were gone, but there was one pair of boots left behind, along with two of the money bags. Harris helped Piker on with his boots as quickly as possible, cringing at every slight noise. They were making their way toward the sewer outlet, slowly so as not to splash, when they heard a voice echoing from the cesspool and froze.

"God! It's awful in here. I don't see anything. You?"

"No, sir. You know, I think that sound could have come from a chunk of ice up above falling off into the pool."

"Maybe so. All right, let's go back upstairs."

Harris and Piker moved forward again. Some minutes later, when they were crawling through the pipe, Piker spoke.

"Thanks for that, Frankie. If you'da let me fall in there, they'da found me drowning in that shit. The whole job would be bust."

"You're welcome," said Harris. And it was strange, considering how badly he wanted to be free of the Whyos, but he felt good about having helped Piker and possibly having saved the whole job. In just that short time, he'd developed a strange bond with the men. It had been exciting and risky, and now here they were, really escaping undetected. He thought about the planned rendezvous in the dry tunnel. It was obvious from the secrecy that Johnny was somehow duping his men out of the truly grand haul. It didn't seem likely Johnny would be wanting to share all that money with him either—not as a consolation prize, not at all. He wouldn't even want him knowing about it. What would be the consequences of his knowledge? he wondered, but he had a feeling he knew.

Piker did some whyoing to communicate to the men up ahead that they should stop and wait for them. Harris sang a few verses of the Ballad to ward off any sewermen. Ten minutes later, at the first junction, they all finally met up, and Harris led them all on a long crawl to the nearest dirt-catcher. It was a relief to stand upright after the hour they'd spent in the tubes, but it was crowded with thirteen men in there. They had to stand shoulder to shoulder, pressed up against the walls, with two of them perched on the ladder that led to the manhole cover overhead. There was ice on the walls here, too, and it gleamed dully in the light of their lamps. The men began to pull money from the shoulder bags and bootlegs where they'd stashed it.

The take looked to be enormous. Piker took out a flask and toasted Harris. Then flasks and pouches came out all around, and the smoke of a dozen freshly rolled cigarettes and one cigar—Piker's—mingled with the faint smell of running sewage. It was only reluctantly that Harris told the men that Johnny didn't want him to wait for the pickup but to make his way home separate from the boys. Piker stuffed something down Harris's shirt-front: a wad of money.

"You done good, Harris, thanks," he said.

Then Harris took a last swig of rye off Piker's flask and went off down the tunnel alone. He exited the sewer in an alley and hopped a Broadway omnibus uptown.

Beatrice and Johnny were already at the rendezvous, sitting in the window of a café near the dry tunnel's manhole. Harris went ahead and silently opened the cover without making contact, but they were watching for him, and as soon as it was open they were there with him, slipping below so quickly and subtly no one could have seen them, even if the street hadn't suddenly been so empty.

The Tammany tunnel. He could see how wrong it was, now that he understood why it had been built. It was graded far too steeply for proper flow, and there were no conduits for sewage from the buildings on that block. Once they were in, Johnny instructed Harris and Beanie to inspect for loose mortar. Beatrice soon discovered a place where there seemed to be none at all, and the bricks were pried out easily enough, revealing a deep cavity stuffed with canvas sacks of money. Countless sacks of money. And there were several of these caches. To Harris, it appeared they had wanted him along purely for brawn, to help carry away the winnings, which they piled up under the manhole. It was a big pile, but Harris felt none of the pleasure or camaraderie he'd had in the dirt-catcher. There was a cold feeling in his stomach. When they were ready to leave, he preceded Beatrice up the ladder to open the manhole. He was nearly at the top when Beatrice squeezed past him. He felt her curly hair and the softness of her breast brush his cheek. He smelled that old tangy smell. With Beatrice above, Harris on the ladder and Johnny down below, they passed the bags of money up and out into the cargo area, where a cart had been parked nearby. When Johnny finally handed him the last bag, Harris began to climb out of the hole. He was fantasizing that perhaps he and Beanie could run together and leave Johnny trapped down below when he felt something heavy on his shoulder. Her boot. He looked up. Beatrice was looming over him with her eye-gouger out.

"You need to go back down there and have a few words with Johnny, Harris. I'm sorry."

"Harris," called Johnny, "where the fuck you think you're going? Get back here."

He went back down the ladder and Beatrice closed the lid above them. Johnny was approaching him, but Harris couldn't see his face for the glare of Johnny's headlamp. Johnny came closer than there was any good reason to. Harris's back was up against the ladder when Johnny reached forward. There was something in his fist. It was an eye-gouger, and he pressed it into Harris's hand. And then a thick wad of the money. And then Johnny grabbed Harris's shoulder and pulled him close. He could feel Johnny's lips graze his own, wet and hot, then his tongue. There was rye and a faint carrion smell on his breath. It seemed to Harris that Johnny sucked out his soul.

"Nothing to run from, Frankie," Johnny said. "Hell, I don't even mind you ogling my girl—so long as you keep your pants on, from now on. I like you. We'll work it all out. You're in."

Harris swallowed. He had never felt so dirty in his life.

22

NEW MOON, OLD MOON

ack up on the street, alone, after Johnny and Beatrice had driven off with the cart full of money, Harris realized he had nowhere to go again. He certainly didn't feel he could return to the O'Gamhnas'. And so he let his feet take him toward familiar territory: Wah Kee's flop. He was carrying more money on him than he'd ever had in his possession before, but that didn't mean he could go check in someplace better. They wouldn't let a tradesman like him into the lobby at a decent hotel, even if he wasn't soiled with sewage.

He had accepted Johnny's kiss, down in the tunnel, and then he had sworn his fealty. What, he wondered, did a promise made under duress mean? Not much. He was still thinking about getting out of town, disappearing. He should have done it long before. Now, at last, there was nothing left to keep him, no more hope of redeeming anything he'd started in this city. He certainly wasn't going to stand by and serve as a lackey for Beatrice and Johnny the rest of his life.

When he got to Pell Street, he saw Wah Kee's storefront. He'd never had the money to go downstairs to the opium den before. Now he did, and the choice was easy. Harris had taken his share of laudanum syrups as a boy, when he was sick, and as a young man, experimenting. Smoking it, he knew, would have a stronger effect. He could use something strong about now. Taking opium wasn't very far beyond the pale, particularly compared to the grand larceny he'd just engaged in—just an escape, just a little bit bad. Harris felt the need to be bad in some way that indulged himself rather than served the Whyos. Yes, he thought, a bit of oblivion, a night of freedom and forgetting, would be just the thing.

A red-eyed Chinese boy took his money and showed him to a couch in a smoky, windowless room lined with padded niches. It was quiet except for occasional coughing and one man's light snore. The cushions were velvet but shiny and worn through in patches. Harris picked a spot and gave the boy an extra quarter for some additional blankets, tea and a hot-water bottle. Then he hung his coat on a hook at the back of his niche and settled in. The cushions exuded a sour, sweaty smell, but he was quickly distracted from that by other sensations: the bitter flavor that bubbled up through the water of his hookah, the sweet tingling that dawned throughout his body, the miraculously smooth flow of his breath. Soon, every cell of his body— yes, every cell—was buzzing with bliss, with optimism. The change was swift but not overwhelming. His focus simply clicked over into a better place, where everything was tolerable, even beautiful. At first, his imagination turned to thoughts of the occult world of cells and queer animalcules. The microbes swimming in Sarah Blacksall's phials of sewage merged with the patterns of living color he'd seen through his father's microscope. He drew in a universe of acrid smoke through the mouthpiece of the water pipe, and worlds long shut off were opened: He thought of his mother without sorrow for the first time in years. Her face, its solid beauty; her arms, their dimpled elbows and firm embrace. Somehow, without having forgotten his woes, he'd ceased to mind them. He was full of the sensation of pleasure. How had he gone so long without it, when it was obviously essential? Why had he waited so long? He thought of Beatrice, too—not bitterly, not about the fact that she'd gone with Johnny, but ecstatically. She'd made him so entirely happy just a few days before. He remembered exactly what they'd done on the bath-hall floor. The opium transformed Wah Kee's couch into a marriage bed, and he nestled himself down in the seamy velvet cushions and dreamed. While the opium held him in its arms, everything was fine. Better than fine.

He dreamed and smoked and mused and slept for uncounted hours. He woke thirsty and queasy and confused. His situation was blurry to him. His first thought was that he wanted another pipeful of opium, badly, but there was an underbelly to that urge, a greater, lower need: to vomit. A large spittoon awaited him just by his bunk, and the truth was it was far more often puked than spat into. For who needed a plug of tobacco in his lip when euphoria itself could be sucked from the hookah's lips? But vomiting didn't put an end to Harris's distress. There was something cruel about the beautiful haze he'd been in, he realized: It wasn't real. Now the bliss was gone, and dread had returned, even worse; gravity was, if anything, greater. He remembered the facts of his life in a flash and cringed. He could imagine only one antidote, and he called out for it. The boy was at his side in a moment with a battered lacquer box. But by the time he saw the scoop of opium being leveled, Harris had remembered another fact of his life: John-Henry, who would be waiting for him at the job site if indeed, as he suspected, it was morning. John-Henry would be worried, rightly worried. Rightly annoyed, too. It was the thought of his friend that freed him from the opium's sway. That was what it was to have a friend. But to be a friend?

"Wait. I can't pay you." That was a lie. He had more money than he'd ever had before. But it stopped the boy. The scoop of opium hovered above the burner. The boy's eyes narrowed.

"No credit. Time to go."

Harris put on his coat and then went out to use the wretched old latrine in the yard, the same one he'd used as a lodger at the flophouse. Outside, it was indeed day: bright and overcast and bitter. As he voided his bladder, he considered the way Beatrice had ordered him back into the tunnel, the nature of Johnny's kiss. He had been used and used again, and he had gone along. He had acquiesced to something awful. He felt a self-loathing that was new. His first impulse was to leave town, the same way he'd left Germany. But how much of his life could he spend running?

To his surprise, when he went back inside, Harris found a cup of tea, a bowl of warm water and a small towel on a bench by his couch. It wasn't exactly the sewermen's bath hall, but the tea killed the flavor of bile in his mouth and the sponge bath helped a good deal, inwardly as well as out.

He shivered as he walked. The temperature had dropped even further. As he went, he heard a bell begin to toll and keep on going—to his dismay, twelve times. He wasn't just late, he had slept the entire morning away, and he began to run. Soon, he was warm. He was opening the collar of his coat when he felt the unfamiliar bulk in his inner vest pocket. Considering the two gifts, Piker's and Johnny's, there was a lot, possibly hundreds of dollars, in that pocket. Blood money.

"Where the Hell you been, Harris? And what the Hell have you done to yourself?"

Harris knew he looked bad—he felt bad—but he couldn't have envisioned the redness of his eyes, the slackness of his face, the plod of his gait. John-Henry sucked his teeth in disgust.

"Can I tell you later?" He could neither stomach explaining the truth nor imagine an adequate lie.

"You better have a good story when you do, boy."

They worked through the afternoon without saying more than was necessary. Clearly, John-Henry was waiting for Harris to tell him what was going on, but Harris was not up to the task. It wasn't just John-Henry he was ashamed in front of; he was worried about encountering Mrs. Dolan at quitting time. Seeing her would be tantamount to confirming that he was doing what the Whyos expected, that he was ready to begin his training whenever they called on him. Johnny had told him he would call on him soon and begin to teach him the language. But even last night, while Beatrice was fetching the cart, he had made Harris try the most basic vocabulary word, the old Whyo war cry. He didn't want to do it, but he had, and he could feel the vibration of it still, echoing in his chest. In Whyo terms, he had agreed to something irrevocable.

When they arrived back at the Sewer Division that evening, it was quiet, as usual, and the door to the bath hall was standing wide open. Mrs. Dolan stepped from her office and waved them over. Harris approached with his eyes cast down, not at all sure what to expect, not eager to acknowledge the events of last night, but there was no meaningful look from her. She proceeded to the bath hall, where she drew two steaming tubs—with considerably more hot water than was common—and handed them their towels.

"Take twenty tonight, boys." Not ten. *Twenty.*

John-Henry didn't know whether to be pleased at this mysterious generosity or vexed that Harris was inexplicably getting off scot-free for offenses that would have gotten John-Henry fired. After all, he'd failed to turn his boots in or take his mandated bath the night before, and today, since he'd had his boots out all night, he'd obviously shown up at the site without having clocked in. Harris, meanwhile, was reeling. Her voice, her face, her manner. Her bullying and her queer generosities. It was so obvious to him now that Mrs. Dolan was Dandy Johnny's mother; he couldn't believe he'd never put it together. But the worst part of it was that it meant she had never been his friend either, just another agent of the devil in disguise, using him, her every kindness an instrument.

While the two men soaked in silence, John-Henry peered at Harris, trying to see the problem, the same way he'd once read his romantic anguish so clearly from his gait and face. This was more complex, but he didn't have to know whatever it was that Harris was mixed up in to disapprove of it. But his annoyance softened as he soaked. Clearly, Harris had gotten into trouble, but he wasn't the first person in the world to do that. How bad could it be, since he'd shown up eventually, and there they were, bathing peacefully under Mrs. Dolan's unexpectedly indulgent eye. Soon John-Henry had succumbed to the steam and heat and was thinking only of the contrasting sensations of warm water and cool porcelain where the rim of the tub touched his neck. This was the warmest he'd been all day, the warmest he would be till tomorrow's bath. The papers said last night was the coldest in years, a record low, and it hadn't gotten any warmer. He wished his wife, Lila, could enjoy such a bath as he got daily, just once, just tonight. He took his bar of soap and lathered himself all over, in stages, from head to arms to underarms, belly to crotch, legs to toes. Then he submerged himself entirely and wallowed for a few seconds, rinsing and scrubbing his hair underwater with his knuckles. It did feel good. A bit of bliss. Underwater, he imagined smuggling Lila in there when no one was around, running her a bath, helping her step up over the high lip and washing her smooth, shining back, kneading suds through her braids. A lovely thought, but when he came back up, the impossibility of it riled him. Lila would never get a bath like this in her life, whereas a white man like Harris could pull all manner of nonsense and still get ten extra minutes for no reason at all. But then John-Henry stole a glance at Harris—his big, kind potato head, the regret that was so often etched on his features, especially so today, the sadness of his posture, apparent even when he was lying in the bath—and he let his anger diffuse. It leached out into the water and settled to the bottom like silt; soon it would rush through the pipes to the sewer, then the ocean—the invisible liquid systems that made the world run.

As for Harris, he was rummaging around within himself, mustering up the guts to ask John-Henry for a favor. That job on the bridge seemed so ideal. John-Henry was angry at him, he knew, and he would have to satisfy John-Henry's curiosity if he wanted his goodwill. The problem was how to do it without either lying or telling the truth. How little could he tell him without bald deceit, how much without saddling his friend with dangerous knowledge? Was it even possible to be honest and remain John-Henry's friend? Harris filled his lungs with air and let his torso slide down the back of his tub until his head was underwater and his feet stuck over the edge. He opened his eyes and looked out through the clear water at a blurry, bluish world. His thoughts floated free, and his hair swirled in tendrils around his head. He let go of thinking about Whyos, let go of Beatrice, let go of John-Henry, let go of wanting to explain himself to the world. He was just an embryo, floating guiltlessly, all options open. And this illusion seemed so real to him that when his lungs demanded oxygen, he opened his lips, let his chest expand, and his bronchioli sucked in bathwater. The quiet surface of the water exploded with Frank Harris: his thrashing arms and legs, his coughing, gasping head, his grown man's hands clutching at the lip of the tub.

The commotion brought Mrs. Dolan in from the office, but not before she'd thrown the master drain wide—always her reflex when anything out of the ordinary went on. John-Henry sprang from his tub to Harris's side, wondering if Harris could actually have been trying to drown himself—in which case he was both stupider and in worse trouble than John-Henry thought. But Harris was breathing again, if raggedly. Mrs. Dolan stood to the side.

"Everyone alive in here? I guess twenty minutes was too long." She shooed them into the locker room and went for her mop.

Harris was still sputtering slightly and clearing his throat as he and John-Henry dressed. And he was too busy fretting about what he would say to John-Henry as they made their way out of the building to notice that Mrs. Dolan had positioned herself before the door.

"I think this must have fallen out of your pocket, Mr. McGinty." She handed him an envelope, at which Harris suffered a relapse and began choking again. She strolled away, unconcerned.

Harris had not received a single letter since he'd come to America, and few enough prior to that that he remembered every one. There was the postcard from his mother with the picture of the Windbath Terrace at Haus Berghof on the back, which he'd lost in the fire at Barnum's; there were the curt paternal invitations to spend Christmas in Göttingen that came each November, in the years after his mother had died, and the letter he'd found the day he left the farm; there was the stack of letters he'd received from Robert Koch, full of enthusiasm for nature, obsession with scientific method, and always, confusingly, respect for his father. There was the suspicion of letters from his father that Wittold had never given him. But all these letters had been more or less expected, explicable. The one he'd taken from Mrs. Dolan's outstretched hand was different. No postmark or address, just clean vellum with the words *Frank Harris* written on the outside of the sealed envelope. He had not dropped it; he had never seen it before—but he knew the hand.

Harris turned back to look down the corridor where Mrs. Dolan had gone, then to John-Henry. It was obvious to both of them that he hadn't dropped the letter. John-Henry's face held a question.

"Thank you," Harris said, though Mrs. Dolan was gone, because that's what's said when something is given, whether or not it is wanted. But he wasn't grateful. He was afraid. He didn't want this letter, didn't want further instructions, didn't want to steal things or to help the Whyos steal. Above all, he didn't want ever to hear from Beatrice again. He simply wanted to be himself, alone, unentailed. He wanted a chance to build something good and useful, a structure that would stand above the ground, visible to everyone, admired and marveled at. He wanted a job on that East River bridge like nothing he'd ever wanted before. Receiving this unwanted letter sealed his determination. It might be the Whyos would come after him, but he would take the risk. He folded the letter twice and jammed it in his pocket.

"Well," said John-Henry, "what's that about?"

"I don't know," said Harris. "I really don't want to know. But I never dropped that letter."

"You're not going to read it?"

"No."

They walked out the wide front doors and down the street. It was indeed even colder than before. The night air froze the very hair in his nostrils. He pulled his scarf over his face, and John-Henry did the same. The street seemed strangely quiet, but there were people about, here and there. It was just that the wind had died—and that John-Henry was waiting for Harris to speak.

"I guess you can walk me home while you start explaining yourself," said John-Henry at last. "You sure do have me curious, Harris, vexed but curious. But if you don't explain yourself, I'm going to be more than vexed."

As they turned east toward the river and the Henleys' street, Frank Harris opted for full disclosure. They passed the import-export companies and chandleries and markets and Coffee House Slip, where Harris's job shoveling snow had begun, and he went back and forth in time, telling pretty much everything that had happened. John-Henry made the noises of listening: murmurs of acknowledgment, *ohs* of surprise, small groans of distress at the parts where Harris made unwise decisions or things turned for the worse. Then, just between the coffee warehouse and the fish market, they turned into a narrow alley lined with small storefront shops—a smithy, a cobbler, a sailmaker, an apothecary, a printer and stationer—all shuttered for the night. As they approached the tobacconist's at the far end of the block, John-Henry slowed and looked up to the second-story window. All along the block, there were lights in upper-story windows, where the shopkeepers had their living quarters.

"That's me above the smoke shop there," said John-Henry. "We rent from the tobacconist, my cousin. And though I don't keep secrets from Lila, and as cold as I am, I don't much want to take this conversation inside, not till I understand it. Let's keep walking." Harris thought it looked like a snug little place. He tried to imagine having an apartment and a wife to come home to, but he couldn't.

They walked on, and Harris began to tell the hard part of the story. He tried to tell it square. Now and then, he looked at John-Henry, who had fallen quiet, but he couldn't read his face.

"I've decided I can't do it," he concluded at last. "I still don't really know how I got into it in the first place," he said. "It was just a mistake. Now I'm going to see what happens if I walk away. I'm going to take the risk. And what I'd really like is to work on that bridge. I'd like to go down there tomorrow and apply for a job."

John-Henry remained silent, and so Harris stammered on nervously about working on the bridge, about the Nikolaikirche and the jobs he had done there. He had leapt into the void. He was even lapsing into his old German accent. He'd reached the end of his story, and the ending was that Harris was dreaming. There was no chance he could go off on his own and live a normal life, not now. The ending was that he had just asked his only friend to jeopardize himself and perhaps his wife by continued association with a man who was wanted by felons and cops alike. What could John-Henry possibly say?

As they neared the wharf, they began to see all manner of small boats standing precariously on poppets in the streets. The East River was going to freeze solid, maybe that night, and the harbor had been busy all week with people pulling at vessels of every shape and size. Most of the boats that could do so had sailed or steamed out of New York bay the day before, when the icebreakers gave up trying to keep the port open. At the edge of the wharf, Harris and John-Henry looked out at the harbor. The surface of the river was nearly solid with ice jams piled up by the incoming tide and, intermittently between them, smooth places where the ice floes had flooded and the newly risen water had frozen so quickly it still had a liquid gleam in the starlight. The boats that hadn't sailed or been pulled had thick crusts of ice at their waterlines, and some were already frozen in hard, lifted up at odd angles from the river, in danger of being stove in by the shifting ice each time the tide changed. It was an even colder day and perhaps a stranger spectacle than when Barnum's had burned, Harris thought, and he left off his nervous talk and fell silent, beholding it. The harbor was an ancient ruin, the ships and cranes and markets and warehouses its columns and temples, all marble-white with frost. John-Henry had told him the bridge office was in Brooklyn. It hadn't occurred to him before, but if the river was frozen, the ferries couldn't run. He couldn't run away to the city across the river after all.

"So what is your real name then, Harris?" John-Henry asked.

He almost had to think about it. The last man who'd known his real name was the crook who sold him Georg Geiermeier's papers, back in Hamburg. Now, slowly, Harris spoke the name his mother had given him: "Johannes." It sounded strange in his ears.

"*John?* Like *John*-Henry, like *Johnny* Dolan?"

He shrugged. He hadn't thought of that.

"I guess if I believe your gang can make themselves invisible with a secret language and some kind of mind control, accepting the fact that your name is John should be easy."

Harris half laughed. "I don't know. It's really not my name anymore."

"It doesn't fit you. You're much more of a Frank Harris."

A patchy white mist hovered low over the river and faded off in a dark haze toward Brooklyn, where the tower of the new bridge bulged from the water like the crown of a young molar—short but sturdy and promising to keep growing till it reached its destined height. As they watched, sheets of ice groaned loudly against the pilings and piers and the sides of the remaining boats. Further out, a broad stretch of water still seemed to move, but then Harris realized it was just the swirling of snow on the surface of the ice.

"It doesn't matter about the job. Forget it. You'd be better off not getting mixed up with me, and it doesn't look like we could get across tomorrow anyway, even if we wanted to."

"No, not the usual way," said John-Henry, "but if it freezes solid, we can walk. When did it happen last?"

"I don't know. But does that mean you still want to go? You don't . . . mind?"

"I wouldn't say it's up to me to mind. I don't *approve*, but I'm not going to shun you, Harris. What kind of man do you think I am?"

Harris nodded.

"Oh, Harris—now look at that." John-Henry pointed to the sky.

A cloud had just passed away from the moon, which lay low over the mouth of the ghostly white harbor, and the moon was as strangely transformed from its usual state as the waterfront itself. It seemed to be a hybrid of its two extreme phases: a brilliant, thin, up-curving fingernail paring and, cradled within it, the full moon, round-faced and wide-eyed but oddly half lit, a shadow of its usual brilliance.

"How can that be?" marveled Harris. He tried to remember what phase the moon had been in the night before. "Is it the full moon or isn't it?" It struck him as both auspicious and terribly sad.

"Haven't you ever seen that? It's the new moon holding the old moon in her arms."

He'd never even heard of it before. "But listen," Harris said, "would it be safe to go across? Won't we have trouble getting back? What if it melts?"

"Compared to your life, it'll be pretty safe, I'd say. It's the tide, not the sun, we have to think about. It's just timing. Why don't we get up early and take a look?"

Get up early, Harris thought, wondering where he'd be sleeping that night. There was Wah Kee's, but the temptation to take the door to the opium den—and more than likely sleep through the rendezvous—was too great. He would have to find another place, one that didn't make oblivion that easy.

"What time?" he asked. "I'll come by your house." He felt John-Henry's eyes on him, probing.

"Where you staying tonight, Harris? Not with your girlfriend's family anymore, I guess. Where'd you sleep last night?" That detail hadn't made it into Harris's narrative.

"Just a place I know, a flophouse."

"Which one?"

Because it seemed highly unlikely to make any difference to John-Henry, he told him.

"What! The Chinaman with the pipe-smoking room? I thought something like that might be going on this morning. No wonder you was half dead when you finally showed up. You're not going off on your own again, Harris. Not tonight. I'm not letting you. If you want to get that job on the bridge, you better come home with me. And all I can say is your gangsters better damn well steer clear of you while you're under my roof."

It took Harris a moment to realize that John-Henry's strong disapproval amounted to an invitation, an absolution, an offer of what felt like salvation. Tomorrow, they could go together and apply for new jobs, new lives.

"Thank you," Harris said. "All right." He didn't try to excuse his night at Wah Kee's, and John-Henry didn't take his reproaches any further.

"So let's get home then, why don't we? It's damn cold out here."

John-Henry laid his hand on Harris's shoulder, and Harris extracted a hand from his pocket to wrap his arm around John-Henry's shoulder. In so doing he discovered that his fingers numbly grasped a thick fold of paper.

"What's that, that letter?" asked John-Henry. "What's it say, anyway?"

Harris regarded the paper with dismay. If it had been warmer, he'd have reached out and dropped it into the drink, watched it bob and falter, grow soggy and sink. But then, if the weather could have been otherwise, what else, why stop there? Everything and anything might as well have been different. Wishing for a change in weather when so many predicaments faced him was like wishing for sausages. There were the Whyos. There was Beatrice. There was America itself, if one wanted to wish for change. There was the predicament in Germany that had driven him to flee. There was his mother—maybe that was it: He could wish that his mother hadn't died. Of all the things he regretted, that was the earliest, sorest loss, when all his misfortune began. So long as his mother had walked with and sung to him and stroked his brow, life had been fine, better than fine: lovely. Thinking of her now, he started to go red in the face and his throat closed up. What was the point of wishing anything? he wondered. He wished he wouldn't wish so much.

"Listen, Harris, I really don't need to know what it says—that's your business—but you'd better read it. You'll be better off knowing what to expect."

The wind lifted, rushing sharply through the cloth of their coats and tugging at the paper in Harris's fingers, but he tightened his grip and returned the envelope to his pocket. As they climbed the stairs to the Henleys' little apartment above the tobacconist's shop, Harris said, "I'll read it in the morning. I can't bear to tonight."

Lila Henley didn't seem in the least surprised to have Harris show up at that late hour in need of a bed. She welcomed him, put a kettle on for tea to warm the men, and laid out a nest of extra blankets by the hearth for Harris. He thought of the way Liam and Colleen's boys always laid out the sleeping pallets at the O'Gamhnas', including his and Beatrice's, regardless of whether they were home yet or not. They would have done it last night, too. What about tonight? How long would it take them to write him off? He pictured the two boys, huddled together, cold under their worn quilt, and wished he could let them know to go ahead and take his covers. He would have liked to thank the O'Gamhnas for all their help, but he wouldn't be going back there. He couldn't, which thought led him to think of Beatrice. He didn't want to think about her. Why should he? Surely she wasn't thinking of him. But it wasn't so easy for him *not* to imagine Dandy Johnny's fingers encircling her wrists, his hot lips bearing down on hers, his palms sliding across her milk-pale skin.

23

FIRST GIRL

Harris was right: Dandy Johnny did have Beatrice in his arms. But Harris couldn't have guessed, as he took off his shoes and stepped up to the Henleys' fire grate to warm his toes, that Beatrice and Dandy Johnny were talking, in the darkness that enveloped Johnny's bed, about what it could mean *not* to fall in love. He had a penthouse apartment on the roof of a six-story building on Downing Street. The windows rattled in the wind, but the stove was stoked, the heavy blue drapes were drawn and Beatrice and Johnny were sweaty and warm enough to have thrown the covers off the bed. She had never been there before. Few Whyos had, probably because the luxury of the details and furnishings and fittings belied the egalitarian myth that underpinned the Whyos' allegiance. There were actually two penthouses up there, on opposite sides of the roof, with a wide terrace between them. His mother occupied the other. Beatrice thought about Mrs. Dolan and wondered if she herself would ever bear a child. She'd actually gotten so far as to imagine having Harris's son, in those two heady days before Johnny chose her, but now, with Johnny, children didn't seem at all likely. Being First Girl was only a quasi-marriage, after all.

She had protected herself against such an eventuality with a small lemon that Maggie the Dove tossed her before leaving the Old Bowery the night before. First, she sliced it lengthwise with the little fish knife she usually used to cut buttonholes with promising fobs looped through them. She'd peeled the stem end smooth, then trimmed out most of the guts. The result was a hollow dome of rind and pith, and it didn't take much to slip it in, a bit of dexterity and a long arm was all. There were several things Beatrice knew of that could prevent a quickening if the lemon failed. Herbs and elixirs were the simplest but notoriously ineffective. Drinking oneself numb and provoking a beating from some john was known among Why Nots to be quite effective. The last resort, the most certain but dangerous way, was a visit to an extractionist. Nowadays they were increasingly calling themselves *abortionists* to conceal the nature of their business, but the name mattered little; their patients got fevers and bled to death just as often. Beatrice was perhaps a little more squeamish about extractions than the average Why Not, since she'd never gone in for the quick-cash-and-slippery-thigh trade—she made plenty doing pleasanter jobs. She'd never had one. She thought of what she'd be getting back from Dandy Johnny for the sex and risk of pregnancy, for giving up her freedom: money and power, neither of which she really needed. She frowned. Then she felt the awkward silence in the room and realized Johnny had been talking to her, talking and talking, as she mused. She hadn't heard a word of what he said. Now he was looking at her. Had he asked her a question?

"What, Johnny? I'm sorry, I didn't hear what you just said."

"You didn't *hear* me? You weren't listening?" He was scowling. But then he smiled. "That's the thing about you, Beanie. That's just the kind of thing that made me pick you. Who else would have the balls to ignore me? Who else would admit that?"

When she realized he was praising her, she laughed, and that was when the blow fell—not a palm but a fist to the side of the head. She didn't even have a chance to flinch before her head hit the bedstead. You could argue that it worked, it got her attention. At least she listened to him, this time, when he told her the arrangements he foresaw: Their union, he explained, was to be a strategic one.

"There might be some gymnastics, when I'm in the mood, but not romance. That's not what I picked you for. You're not even my type, too skinny, but I guess you know that already. What you are is a lieutenant, see?

Like Piker with tits—except not very big ones." He paused, but she didn't laugh. "See, Piker's strong, but he's dumb. You're clever. We needed that, for balance. You're gonna help me and Ma run the show."

Her temple throbbed painfully as he spoke, but her vision came back into focus. She touched her hairline and found no blood. She thought about everything that had happened since the meeting at the Old Bowery, and she felt this wasn't right, wasn't fair. He shouldn't have allowed her to go through the contortions of trying to fall in love with him. He should have told her the arrangement up front, but instead he had duped her, made her naked and vulnerable. She understood, of course, that he had done it on purpose. It put him in control. But had he really said help him *and Ma* run the show? She said, "All right, Johnny, I can do that."

He seemed to like her acquiescence. Suddenly, the gangster who didn't want romance was acting friendly again. He smiled at her through his hank of dark, shiny hair, grabbed her around the waist and pulled her to him, ready for another round. She wanted to hate him, to reject him, but he knew how to smile, Johnny. He could make a woman feel it in her marrow like a magnet, like a craving for drink or drug. It wasn't just his lips, which were as red as a woman's, or his blue stare, it was the dimples of his cheeks, the crinkles at the corners, the way they worked together. It wasn't bad at all, the way Johnny touched her, until he turned her over. Then he got selfish; there was some ripping, and there were twinges. He was the same handsome, vain, self-centered bully in bed as out. The odd thing was that as angry as she was, and even when he caused her pain, she felt a certain thrill—because of who he was, because she was alone with him, the boss of the whole gang, the highest authority she knew. When he finished, he rolled onto his back and pulled her into the crook of his armpit. The odor was strong, just tolerable, she thought. Harris had smelled so good.

"You're a scrawny little bat, aren't you, Beanie," he muttered, sitting up and poking her hip, just as she thought he'd fallen asleep.

"What's that, Johnny? I wasn't listening."

"I said, *You're a scrawny bat.* You're nothing but fucking bones. You ought to eat more."

"Pardon me, what? I didn't hear that."

"Goddamnit."

"And you're a big vain bully and a real asshole, if we're making observations."

"Listen here, Miss Beatrice O'Gamhna," he said, with a certain rigidity and a curl on his lip. She worried he was going to whack her again. Apparently he didn't want to be talked back to. "Don't try to charm me with your feisty little quips. I don't need to be charmed. You work for me. You're not in love with me. Don't bother trying to flirt. It's not a good idea."

"So what do you want to fuck me for, Johnny? I'm a bit uncertain what my role is."

"What for? Because I felt like it. That answer your question? You just do what me and Mother tell you, in your own ingenious little way, and you'll do fine. And don't be mooning around, not about me, not about Harris, no mooning. If running the Whyos was a romance, I'd still be with Maggie."

Maggie the Dove. She was so much older, fleshier, more womanly than Beatrice. No wonder he called her scrawny, if Maggie was the one he thought about. But why wasn't he with her anymore?

"If you wanted her, then why didn't you choose her? You're the boss."

"I'll tell you a story, Beanie. Something you need to know. There was a night, shortly after I took over, that I went out and got stone drunk. I was mooning over Maggie, jealous of some john she was seeing just to piss me off, you know. The result of it was, I missed check-in. Everyone was calling in to me with their figures and codes, and I was too looped to answer them, all because of love. Someone else had to cover for me."

No one should have been capable of covering for Johnny. Not only was his voice perfect, but he used various small flourishes and private codes that made his voice instantly recognizable to the others. Telling Beatrice that someone had faked his voice was an admission that that Whyo had the ability to imitate his vocal signature and the knowledge of all those codes. So this was the beginning of power, she thought, feeling wide awake: not love, not trust, *knowledge*.

"See, when I thought about Maggie, I forgot everything else. On top of missing the check-in, I botched a job. I nearly got myself and two other guys thrown in the can. You can't keep control of a gang if you're not the best and strongest member."

"I would have heard that," she protested. "Everybody would know about a thing—"

"I told you, someone covered for me," he said. "I got quite a chewing out from the one that did it, too. I'm telling you this because now you need to know how it really is, how this gang really runs. It *is* possible for someone to cover for me. And you might just have to do it one day. I'm going to teach you how."

Beatrice nodded, minding less and less that he had fucked her like a dog. This knowledge was going to bring her power of a sort she hadn't envisioned before.

"What I learned that night was that I'd go down like Googy if something like a woman could distract me from my work."

"But who covered for you, Johnny? How'd he do it? Wouldn't he have been your rival, after that? Did you kill him?" She was thinking, *Would you kill me?*

"Never mind that right now. I just want you to understand that Maggie nearly ruined everything. She sapped me, and it nearly got me killed. That's when I realized the gang mattered a Hell of a lot more than some twat. The gang's the thing. And I wanted to stay the boss a long time. I had plans. I couldn't bring them off if I was being distracted by a woman. So the next morning, I told her it was up. You should have seen her, too. Maggie was gorgeous—you'd hardly recognize her now—and damn good at picking wallets. And I came to her with a broken nose and black eye, looking like a chump—because the one that covered for me made me pay—and told her it was time to move on. I guess she never figured out why. It's a pity a man can't have it all. But that was it."

Beatrice had always admired Maggie the Dove. She somehow brought in twice the money anyone else did without ever compromising her dignity. And then there was the way she'd decided to carry that baby—that was brave—and then she hardly seemed to falter when she lost it. She was probably the toughest Why Not there was, and she was still a stunning woman. She pictured the beautiful set of brass knuckles she always wore on a loop at her waist, all tooled and engraved and inlaid. Beatrice's own eye-gouger was as plain as they got, just banged out of a mold, and she didn't really like to use it—the rings cut her fingers when she threw a punch.

It dawned on her as she thought about her own crappy set of knuckles that what she'd just heard was more than an instructive story from Johnny's past; it was also the strangest rejection she'd ever had, at once the most thoroughgoing and the most equivocal. He had just told her he would never love her, indeed that he wasn't attracted to her and had picked her largely because he knew he never would be. Really, it was quite annoying. Being First Girl tied her up, kept her back. She could have been with Harris and still worked for Johnny. Why had he done it?

"But you've got your pick of whoever you want, whenever you're in the mood. I work hard for you already. Why do you need to fuck me, Johnny, especially if you don't like my bones? What else do you want from me, exactly, why pick on me like that?"

"Christ, are you tiresome; you ask too many questions."

"You knew that before, though, didn't you? It's one thing you like about me."

He raised his eyebrow a little in admission of this point.

"Well then?"

"I like the way you put the caper together. Nobody's ever going to know how we did the p.o. job. And as for the Tammany money, the way I see it, you found it for us. You ran Harris like a pro. Being First Girl, well it's pure gravy. I guess it's just your shit luck, my dear, but you did too good a job. You made yourself essential. Proved you could get things done without drawing notice. See, if I didn't fuck you, Beanie, I'd have had to kill you along with your German boyfriend, because you knew about all the details."

"That doesn't explain this whole *scenario*. Making me your girl. *Touch her not.* You never needed that."

"Maybe I wanted it."

"So you don't like me but you want me to be your lieutenant, and you'll fuck me just to keep me in line? Is that about it?"

"That's about it. And I would like you to shut the fuck up about it right about now. You got no complaints. You'll get status, you'll get money, you'll get power. From time to time, you'll get me. It's a good deal for you, Beanie, admit it."

"Oh, thank you. Thank you for the honor."

"You'd rather go with Harris." He laughed. "I know. But I'm afraid that just wouldn't look good. It's me or nothing."

"Are you really going to bring him in?"

"Yeah, well, I'm considering the Harris problem." He smiled, knowing it made her furious. "He's a little too honest and too stuck on you, but I'd rather Piker and the boys lay low for now. We don't need bodies popping up through the ice all spring when we've just done so well for ourselves."

"Just let him go. He won't talk. If you kill him, the cops might make the connection between the sewers and the p.o. job, maybe even Geiermeier and the Barnum's fire and the gang. And if you let him live, he could come in handy. He could help us out again. Your mother's got her eye on him, after all. And he's a perfect straight man. What if you don't give him too much language, just run him like you run Geoghegan and the other semi-retireds? Special projects only."

"You like him too much. You're not helping his case."

She looked at him. "Yeah, I like him."

"No romance, Beatrice. No romance, at all. I don't want people even to wonder if my girl is carrying on with some sewer rat."

"I'm not carrying on with him."

"That's not what I've heard." He pushed her back and took her shoulders and ground his stubble against her chin, then slipped his fingers behind the small of her back and yanked her against him.

"Oh Jesus, Johnny. If you insist on pinning me every time I make you a wee bit peevish, I'm going to start thinking you do have feelings for me after all."

"You want to feel something, you want me to feel something for you?" His grip tightened and then, with no further warning, he jammed himself into her.

The starburst of pain that radiated through her was a function of the lemon rind, which in their earlier contortions had become misaligned. The angle he was coming from meant that he was jamming the edge of it into her cervix, but all Beanie knew was that every thrust felt like rending flesh. This time, she cried silently. At least he didn't have much stamina left. When he was done he said, "That's all for today. You can go now. Stay at my mother's." And then he cracked one of his gorgeous smiles and kicked her onto the floor.

It was something most Why Nots would have killed for—to be ravished and kicked out of bed by Dandy Johnny—but she was not most Why Nots. She was furious. She was wondering whether the knife in her skirt pocket was near enough to grab before he saw what she was up to and sharp enough to kill a man by throwing. But she didn't lunge for it; she just lay there on the floor thinking, gathering her dignity. She knew she couldn't kill him. The Whyos would not allow it. But could she take this? She thought so. It was only her body. And she had to agree that, as he had said, she had much to gain from the alliance. Maybe she could save Harris, for starters.

"I want to make a deal, Johnny."

He snorted.

"Excuse me?" she asked, but the snort had been only the prelude to a vast snore. He was dead asleep, the bastard. It would have been so easy to walk right up and slit his throat, even with just her small blade. The thing that made her maddest was that he wasn't even worried enough about her to stay awake. Before she dressed, she looked around for something with which to wipe the mess from between her legs. She chose a clean, pressed, monogrammed shirtfront from his dresser. Then she saw an ascot dangling from the bedpost and finished the job with that. She looked at herself in his dresser mirror. She wasn't scrawny, just slim. She was going to have quite a black eye by morning, but that was no huge surprise. No one in the gang would think twice. Johnny was famously violent in bed.

Out on the freezing terrace between the twin penthouse apartments, she thought about Harris again. He would be hating her now. She'd been smiling the other night, riding on the thrill of being chosen; she knew he had seen it, and she regretted it. She couldn't bear the idea that Harris thought she'd chosen Johnny, that she loved him. The only reason she hadn't given him more of a sign when they were cleaning out the Tammany cache was she didn't want Johnny to catch on to her feelings for him. But she'd miscalculated there. Johnny had her figured perfectly, in advance. The only person she'd deceived was Harris. She'd made him think her only interest was to use him for the gang. It had started that way, but it couldn't have been less true by the end. She would have liked to tell him the truth now, but it wouldn't be fair. It would string out his attachment. He wasn't a crook, not like the rest of them. He deserved to be free. She resolved to do one honest thing for him, whatever it cost her: to make Johnny set him free. If only she could let Harris know why she was doing it, but Harris was such a straightforward man. She knew him. He just wouldn't understand.

THE LOVE OF
HEIGHTS

24.

ON THE ICE

Harris smelled biscuits and coffee.

Certainly there had been no biscuits, no breakfast, wherever he was dreaming of being, not even porridge. He opened an eye and saw a dark room with an unfamiliar low ceiling, a rough wooden molding lit by the glowing red embers in the grate. He opened the other eye and saw John-Henry emerge from the door to the bedroom—a coat pulled over his dressing gown, boots untied—and shuffle toward the stairs.

Ah, thought Harris, knowing where he was now but torn between relief and anxiety. He was safe, for the moment. He thought about the job the Whyos had just pulled in plain sight—their vocal powers were greater than he'd realized—and wondered to what extent his beard and Irish accent could really protect him. How much of a cover had Beatrice been providing for him the past year? Was Brooklyn far enough away? It certainly wasn't California, but still it was another city, another police force, another world, and he'd never heard of Beanie or the Whyos working over there.

"Harris, get up, man," said John-Henry, returning from the privy.

And so he got up and began what he hoped was a new era in his life. It was coffee not tea, blacks not Irish, Henleys in place of O'Gamhnas. Maybe it would be Brooklyn instead of New York and towers not tunnels, an honest life in lieu of sordid gangsters' kisses and wads of stolen cash. He knew going to Brooklyn wouldn't hide him if they really looked, but he could make a try of it. He also needed a new name, another common one, he thought, using the Whyos' theory of hiding in plain sight—maybe Jones or Smith. He was going to have to decide on it today. He heard Lila Henley humming as she tapped a spoon against a pan, and the warmth of the Henleys' acceptance buoyed him up. He rose, determined to make good, to move ahead, not to let yet another surrogate family down. As soon as he was on his feet, however, John-Henry was badgering him to read Beatrice's letter.

"All right," he said, "just give me a minute to wake up," and he stuffed his bare feet into his boots, threw his coat over his shoulders and excused himself to use the outhouse. There were low fences between the yards of all the buildings on this block, each of which also had a privy and various outbuildings. The Henleys' outhouse was whitewashed and irreproachable, the privy itself so deep he didn't have to think about the pile of shit at the bottom. If he'd had the letter with him, he would have dropped it straight into the hole. He didn't want to know what it said. He felt he'd rather take his chances, let his fate surprise him in an alley one day, than know what was coming—but John-Henry had saved him from that urge by confiscating the envelope the night before.

"You ready?" asked John-Henry when he returned. Harris shrugged and shot his eyes toward Lila Henley as if to ask, *Now? In her presence?*

"Don't worry about me, Mr. Harris," she said. "Ain't no secrets 'twixt John-Henry and myself."

John-Henry went over to the corner cupboard and extracted the letter from a covered casserole. "What do you say I slit it for you?"

The sound of the paper tearing was like ripping skin. The letter slid from its wrinkled sheath into his fingers with a dry rasp. It seemed unduly heavy, like a book or a bludgeon, but he figured that was just a feeling. He pulled out the letter and saw green. More money. On the sheet of paper there were words, but they swam before his eyes. Harris couldn't make sense of them.

"Why don't you tell us, Mr. Harris," Lila Henley said. Finally, he laid the paper on the table, gesturing that someone else should look at it first, and so Lila read it aloud.

"You have done what we required. You have your independence. Keep your mouth shut, stay out of our affairs and expect no further contact."

There was no greeting and no signature, just a slash, as if to underscore the message, but after so many hours of chalkboard lessons, there was no mistaking who had written it. Harris fanned out the bills: ten twenties. It was the third time in the past two days that the Whyos had paid him off. He had never been so rich, but he didn't want this money. With Piker and the boys, they had simply been sharing the bounty of the job—that was all right, he felt. But Johnny had been trying to buy his soul, and he wished he'd thrown that money back in his face. Now Beatrice was paying him to go away. He tried to conceive of a world in which he was grateful that she had set him free, but in this world he was angry, crushed. There was no hint of loss or regret in her words, nothing.

After a moment, John-Henry began to chuckle, quietly but steadily, and eventually Mrs. Henley joined in. Their pent-up worry had turned to relief and then mirth, but if they thought Harris would join them, they were disappointed. Harris's face remained blank as he digested what the letter meant. It was complicated: The very fact that she'd taken the trouble to do this suggested that she cared for him after all, wanted him to live and even to be happy, perhaps. But she didn't care enough to want to be with him. She had made her choice, and she had chosen Johnny. Harris took a deep breath. What he felt was messy, neither happiness or gloom. This was what he'd wanted just a short time before. Now he had it, and he wished he didn't. He looked up at John-Henry and his wife and tried his hardest to smile.

After breakfast, John-Henry lent Harris a clean shirt and his razor while Mrs. Henley thoroughly brushed his coat and pants. By the time the sun was up, they were ready to leave, and the thought of the bridge had Harris feeling more optimistic. The air outside was so cold it seemed to strip both the romance and the tragedy away from Harris's situation—it was just about survival. As they neared the river's edge, they saw a man clambering up a ladder from the ice to the pier.

"How is it?" John-Henry asked.

"Solid. You won't believe it till you've been out there."

Then they stepped out onto the white ice. It was rock hard.

It was cold and hard in the drunk tank, too. Undertoe opened his mouth and let out a gust of foul, frozen breath and a groan. He tasted rotting bits of gristle that had stuck in his teeth at his last meal, two days before. His tongue was carpeted with fur, and his head was ringed with a metal band, like a whiskey barrel. Undertoe struggled to breathe, to see. He touched his chin and felt long whiskers poking through a crust of dried vomit trailing all the way down and around the back of his neck. His rash was itching fiercely. When he sat up, his forehead smacked the bunk above him. When he tried to roll over, he realized he was sharing the bunk with a couple of pathetic, snoring derelicts. And that was when he grasped where he'd spent the night and began to fume. He could taste and feel that he'd been doped, which was even worse. Little did he realize, then, but he'd been there *two* nights and days. The officers at the station had been unable to rouse him the morning before, and so they'd left him there, puking intermittently in his sleep, while the rest of the previous night's drunks went free. It wasn't quite protocol, but Undertoe was far from the first man they'd logged into their booking sheet as Rip van Winkle.

How in the world had he gotten here? he wondered, just as the aftereffects of the Whyos' hydrate of chloral once again boiled through his stomach and his mouth began to water. He gagged and spat on the floor and wiped his lips on the shirttail of the whimpering old codger beside him. Gently, he palpated his own head and found several tender regions and the grit of dried blood in his hair. So he'd been poisoned and walloped both. He rubbed his chin again, and only then, when he considered how long the stubble was, did it dawn on him that he'd lost an entire day. It had to have been a Hell of a lot of drops. That just wasn't right. That was the way that gangsters treated dupes, not one another. The right side of his lip began to twitch. He felt itchy all over now, and in his ears that faint, infuriating ringing rose up once again. He fought his way across the sea of bodies lining the floor to the barred cell door and rattled its iron frame.

"Jailer! *Jailer!*" It took several minutes of shouting for anyone to respond, and then it was the stupidest, most slothlike, least corruptible-looking officer Undertoe had ever seen. He was rosy cheeked and smiling. Undertoe was unable to contain himself and swore aloud.

"Oh, ho—Rip van Winkle wakes at last. But I must advise you, sir, your fancy vocabulary won't curry favors from me. You'll be charged by the booking officer at seven thirty, like all the rest, no two ways about it. You're lucky we let you stay this long, you know. We could have sent you straight to the morgue, you were out so cold."

"You mean I was out for a whole day?" The cop nodded. "Yeah, well, it may be too late, but I got something to report. I got information, about a job."

"Oh, do you?" The guard crossed his arms in front of his chest.

Undertoe hadn't planned it, but his tongue was an adept prevaricator, and he let it buy him time while he tried to reconstruct what exactly *had* happened to him two nights before: There was the guy he'd seen ducking into the men's room, who in retrospect wouldn't have been such a good choice for a partner in crime—he hung around with that fool Dandy Johnny and his crowd down at the Morgue. He tried to recollect the bathroom attendant. Was he one of them, too? He didn't think so. But there had been quite a number of familiar faces at the Bowery, come to think of it. Something must have been going on, something someone wanted to keep him out of, something that was hidden in the men's room, perhaps. Whatever it was, he'd nearly walked in on it, and so they'd doped him, rolled him and dumped him like a vic. He wished to Hell he'd seen the papers yesterday. With a shred or two of information, he was sure he could have gotten himself out of the slammer and back in his friend Sergeant Jones's favor. He picked a scab off his neck and felt the stickiness of blood rising—there were bedbugs in jail—and then he went for it.

"A little heist that took place yesterday?" he ventured, as if referring to a piece of common knowledge.

"What?" asked the cop. "The p.o. job? You call that *little?*"

Undertoe thrilled—the man was dumber than a woodchuck.

"Yeah, well, I know who done it. I don't mind telling you I've got it in for them. I would have come in with it before, but Hell, they knocked me out for over a day just so I wouldn't rat on them. Let me talk to your captain. Or actually, the one I really want to talk to is Jones, from the Tenth Precinct."

"Jones, eh? You mean Lieutenant Jones?"

"He knows me."

"I bet he does. What's your name, pal?"

The man walked off, returning just a few minutes later with a ring of keys in his hand. Undertoe was practically beaming as the copper led him down the hallway. His mind was spinning fast. Once again, he needed a dupe, but this time it was going to be tricky. It had to be plausible, but he didn't have much to go on. They were sticklers for plausibility, the cops, though whether it was true or not was irrelevant.

Undertoe followed the jailer down a winding course of dim stone passageways to a small interrogation room. His confidence lagged at little when he saw they weren't planning to take him straight to Jones, but he sang anyway. He didn't know a damn thing about the heist, but what he told them wasn't all that far-fetched. Life falls into certain patterns, after all, and he told a tale he'd lived out a hundred times, about a bunch of men in cahoots for the sake of a bunch of money that wasn't theirs.

It made a certain sense to the cop, at first, all except for the part about Dandy Johnny Dolan and his crowd being the toughs. And then, as Undertoe blabbed on, revealing his total ignorance of any salient details, the story began to make a very particular kind of sense to the cop. As far as the officer could tell, this guy knew nothing at all about the p.o. job. Undertoe's story was thin as water, especially in light of the collection of empty wallets that had been found on his person when they brought him in. Clearly, he was the loser of some Five Points turf battle, and now he was trying to talk his way out of trouble by pinning a job on his enemies. Sure, the department wanted to solve the case, but the police did not allow themselves to be used for the purposes of crooks and lowlifes.

Of all the drunks in the tank that morning, Undertoe was the only one who was kept behind. They booked him for the wallets (which had naturally been lifted by Why Nots passing time in the Old Bowery lobby). Then they threw him in another cell to await a hearing. He paced back and forth, thinking that someone, somehow, soon, would pay for this. He was Luther Undertoe. He didn't know who it would be yet, but he'd figure that out in time. He was going to have a lot of it on his hands.

Harris and John-Henry, by contrast, were moving quickly, crossing the river that had become an impossibly wide white road. The ice bridge was at once terrifying and joyous. It was nothing like making the river crossing on a ferry, though they followed more or less the route of the Fulton Ferry line. There were scores, maybe even hundreds of people out, scattered in groups as far up the river and down the harbor as the eye could see. The ice bridge had turned the weekday morning into a holiday. A few determined boys were out on skates, taking high, funny steps instead of gliding, because the surface of the ice was rough. A man pulled a small sled past them that was piled high with children screaming *giddyup* and laughing so hard they kept rolling off the side. John-Henry laughed, too, and turned to Harris, who was plodding along, dragging his feet, brooding.

"Lord, Frank Harris. I know you lost your girlfriend, but she sounded like nothing but trouble anyhow. Get over it, man. They're not going to mess with you anymore. You can do what you want now, work on the bridge, whatever. So snap out of it."

"The bridge office is probably closed in this weather."

John-Henry looked at him hard. "Yeah, probably is. And this ice bridge is probably going to melt right out from under us, and we'll likely drown or freeze to death, and I doubt they hire niggers, much less ex-sewerman–gangsters at the bridge, even if we do survive. Jesus Christ, Harris, where's your optimism? I'll tell you what: If they're closed, we'll try again in a day or two, and we'll have had an incredible walk. And you just got your freedom. I think you ought to appreciate that a little more. Think about it."

Harris nodded and made the effort to stand up straight. He knew John-Henry was right, but he was miserable anyway. He couldn't help it.

They continued past the stump of the bridge that stuck up from the river through a white frill of ice, and Harris got a glimpse of the masonry close-up: monumental in scale but elegant. The thought of the arches that were still to come made him crane his neck and peer up into the gray-white patch of sky they were destined to fill. The bridge would be something re-markable, far greater than any church.

On the other side, they found a place where a makeshift gangplank had been set up to help people clamber onto the pier at Fulton Street, just north of the ferry. It wasn't far to the bridge office, and it was open. They saw ten or twelve men already waiting to apply for jobs, and their hopes dropped a little, but then one after another every man came out of the office with hope in his eyes and a folded paper in his hand. It seemed there was no shortage of jobs. After an hour or so, their turn came. The clerk asked Harris several questions and gave him a form to fill out. He wrote the name Frank Harris. In his gloom, he had forgotten to come up with something new, and so a decision was made: Frank Harris he would remain. The clerk was considerably less than courteous to John-Henry until John-Henry mentioned he'd fought with Colonel Roebling's brigade and had been encouraged to apply as a blaster. The man brought out a thin ledger. He seemed surprised when he actually found John-Henry's name on a list, but he gave him the job. In about an hour, they were out on the street again with orders to report to work at 7:45 Monday morning. John-Henry's reference and experience had gotten him hired at a high level, which wasn't usual, given his race—there weren't many colored men on the bridge. Harris would be wielding a shovel at the bottom of the caisson, not working as a mason. Caisson worker was the one position for which there were always openings. The work was grueling, and the turnover was high, but Harris wasn't worried. He'd told them he had experience cutting and laying stone and working up high. Those were specialized skills that would be needed on such a big project. He was hopeful a promotion would come with time.

"Are you optimistic yet, Harris?" John-Henry asked as they walked to the river.

"I think so, yes." He was smiling again now, not widely but for real. "You know, John-Henry, the trouble with being a foreigner is you lose your people, your connections, your bearings. I have to thank you. I wouldn't have got this job on my own."

"It's the same for a lot of black folks up from the South—they've got no one. But if you're a good person, if you're honest and work hard, eventually you're going to be fine."

Harris wasn't so sure the city always treated people as justly as that, but he didn't want to contradict his friend. "Well, thanks for putting me up last night and for bringing me over here and getting me the job."

"Oh, come on—you just saw that any fool can get a job hauling dirt down in that hole. The work's probably a lot worse than putting in dirt-catchers, too. I don't want you blaming me when it turns out to be awful."

"But it's a bridge, not a sewer."

They climbed back down to the river from the ferry pier and set out across the ice. It was still solid beneath their feet, but they sensed the water rushing under it now, and from time to time the ice would boom or groan, causing people further out on the river to shout and run, afraid it was all giving way beneath them. It didn't, though, and all across the ice people seemed to be enjoying the risk of it, staying out as long as they dared. Maybe it would hold through the low tide, people said. Boys ran wildly across the wide-open expanse a bit further north, and a group of girls engaged in a snowball fight. A thin snow had begun to fall, and Harris was surprised to see, in the grayed-out, blurry distance, that someone had even brought a horse out. Then he realized the animal stood alone and, in fact, wasn't a horse at all but a cow. He remembered his dream and that ad. Red cow. White spot. Twenty dollars. He certainly didn't need the money now, but he thought about what must have happened. Probably the cow had wandered to the river looking for water after getting lost and missing its usual trough. Maybe it wasn't the same one that had been advertised, maybe it was, but what would happen to it when the ice did break up? He tried to remember the name of the cow in the ad. He opened his lips to explain his concern to John-Henry and realized it was a very odd thing he proposed to do, to chase a cow up a treacherous frozen river. His mouth hung open until his tongue grew cold.

"John-Henry. Stop a moment—do you see that cow?" He pointed north.

"Yeah, Frank," said John-Henry as if he wished he didn't. "What about it?"

John-Henry was more or less incredulous at the idea, but he indulged Harris. It was the idea of the cow being stranded on a floe that did it. When they got close enough to see that the cow did indeed, like so many other red cows, have a spot, it saw them, too, and began to walk determinedly away from them. They broke into a trot, and so did it. They stopped, and it slowed and began nosing the ice, as if in search of grass. Harris tried to remember the name.

"Bessy!" he ventured, without raising interest from the cow. "Bessybessybessy." Still no response. "Stella!" he shouted several times over, but then he remembered the name in the paper—*Bella.*

He called, but the cow still ignored them, continuing to browse the ice. There was a loud boom, and they could see a crack had formed in the ice further south, toward the mouth of the harbor. Nothing to worry about yet, he told himself.

"Harris, let's give it up. The tide's going out, and I'm cold."

"One more try," Harris said, and called out in a voice that belonged to another self, the stableman who had understood animals better than people, the person who'd been lost when Barnum's had burned—or so he had thought. He used a German phrase he hadn't uttered since he'd left his uncle's farm, and he used the same tone of voice that had once calmed his uncle's cows. More or less, what he said was: "*Moo cow, here moo cow, little moo cow, moo cow cow cow.*"

The cow looked up at him and lowed. It stepped closer.

"*Moo cow cow cow.*" He was singing it, really, in German, and for some reason it made his heart soar.

Now the cow trotted over to them. As it approached, Harris could see that it needed its people badly: Its udders were splitting and swollen and crusted with dirty, frozen milk that had seeped out under the pressure from not having been milked for days. He patted her flank and let her nuzzle his hand, and then he knelt on the ice, warmed his palms by rubbing them together, and gently broke away the crusted milk. When he began pulling in a steady rhythm, the cow lowed, and milk spurted out onto the frozen river where it made a steaming, creamy puddle, almost yellow against the snow.

"I'll be damned," said John-Henry. "You *are* a country boy, aren't you?"

"Thirsty?" Harris asked.

They took turns kneeling down and guzzling from the teats of the lost cow whose name was, perhaps, Bella. When she was close to dry, they discussed where to take her.

"Let's go back over to Brooklyn," said John-Henry. "Whether it's the cow you saw listed or not, she sure doesn't live in the Five Points." From the Brooklyn shore, they walked up to Fort Greene and knocked on the door of the first house that had a stable and yard behind it. Harris asked the cook who answered if she knew a man who'd lost a cow.

"Oh, *ja*, that old cow of Noe's. That's a nice reward you're going to collect, sir. The Noe place is just up the street. Where'd you find her?" She spoke in a thick German accent that made Harris nervous—it reminded him that he shouldn't have broken into German himself, back there on the river. Someone might have heard. Sound carried for miles across water, probably ice, too. Still, just the sound of it coming from his own mouth had comforted him profoundly.

"She was out on the ice," John-Henry said.

They found the Noe house in mourning. There was a black-ribbon wreath on the door, but clearly it had been there for some time—it was scabbed with dingy ice around the edges. Then the door was flung open with joyful exuberance and a cry of "Welcome! What great news! Come, gentlemen, come right in out of the cold." The man seemed a bit over-excited about his cow. The two friends looked at Bella and then the door and hesitated.

"Oh, yes, you're right—I don't guess Bella belongs in the parlor. Why don't you come around first to the stable and we'll put her to her bale of hay and her water, and we'll milk her." He stepped out into the yard and patted the cow on her neck, then wrapped his arms as far as they would go around her great, rough, red body. "Bella Bella Bella," he said, in a tone not dissimilar to Harris's out on the ice. The cow lowed.

25

BROOKLYN

Harris could hardly believe his fortune in finding Mr. Noe. They liked each other immediately, and after only the third time he'd stopped by to call on Mr. Noe and Bella—it wasn't all that much further a walk from the bridge site than the Hotel Montague, where he'd found a room—Mr. Noe made him a proposal: He invited him to live in the apartment over the barn, rent free, in exchange for some occasional help with the animals and around the house. "It's too empty now. I don't like it. I could use the company," he explained.

Harris's job in the caisson of the bridge was overwhelming—loud, dirty and grueling—but he liked it anyway, and he greatly liked coming home to Mr. Noe's every night. His apartment had a little potbelly stove, a chifforobe for his few clothes, a table and a bed with a great thick pile of blankets and sheets that the housekeeper changed every Monday. They were the big house's castoffs, of course, which meant that though they were somewhat worn, they were of as fine a quality as anything he'd slept under since the eiderdowned nights of his childhood. There also was a large braided rug so that when he climbed out of bed, his bare feet were spared the shock of the bone-cold floor. He had his own washtub, and in the evenings he heated himself a pan of water on his stove and had himself a splash bath. It wasn't quite the sewermen's bath hall, but it was private. And he needed a washing just as much or more: His actual work clothes he left in a cubby at the site, but even so he came home smudged with lime soot from the lamps that lit the underground excavation and splattered with river mud. Indeed, his bath was once again one of the pleasantest parts of Harris's day. When he stepped out of it and rubbed his chest dry and sat before the stove to bake the last drops of moisture from his hair, he could almost call himself happy. From here, he thought, he could manage to forge a life. Then he went downstairs and over to the kitchen for a word with the cook and a plate of something savory. Sometimes Mr. Noe would knock on his apartment door to ask how he thought the mare's coat looked or if Bella seemed well, and did he still think they should calve her this year? Then, one evening, Mr. Noe asked Harris to join him for dinner.

Mr. Noe, he learned, had been alone in the house for half a year, since the yellow-fever scourge of the previous summer had struck both his wife and son, Bobby. Harris was playing an ambiguous role as they sat at the dining-room table—not quite servant or employee, not friend or family either—but over soup they found that their initial bond was true, and they did indeed have plenty to talk about, more than just Bella. Possibly, they had too much to talk about for Harris's own good. By the end of the evening, Mr. Noe was quite clearly puzzled about just what sort of person Harris was, what class, of what education. He evaded specifying his background too fully that night, but Mr. Noe invited him again the following week. Harris tried to be obscure, but it was difficult. A mention of his father triggered questions about where he'd grown up, and he had to answer them as the Irishman Frank Harris.

Surely it would have been easier for Harris just to tell Mr. Noe the truth, but he didn't know him that well. He dared not trust him and would not burden him. He was still wanted as Will Williams, alias George the Torch, after all. John-Henry had accepted it, but Harris knew John-Henry was not an ordinary man. It simply was not a very sympathetic story. Instead, he took the principle the Whyos had taught him—use the truth to cloak your lies—and winged it, telling Mr. Noe the true fact that his father had been a doctor, but he placed him in Dublin and added that he'd died when Harris was just a boy. He didn't have to lie about his mother. That got him to his childhood on his uncle's farm—his Uncle Willie, he called him, which made him smile, giving Mr. Noe quite the wrong impression. He could hardly skip his truncated apprenticeship, since that was why he wanted to work on the bridge, so he set that in Dublin, too, despite his total ignorance of its churches. As for his history since he'd arrived in New York, he was on somewhat better footing, but he avoided giving too much detail or any names. And seeing that talking about the past could quickly grow perilous, he tried to suggest that his past was painful to him, a subject best avoided. At least that was honest.

Mr. Noe listened, not so much gullible as trusting. He had no reason to doubt the man who'd refused a reward for returning his cow. He told Harris his own stories about growing up in Fort Greene when it was just a country village and the Noe house was still a pig and dairy farm. As different as the quality of their lives had been, both of them fondly remembered certain things about rural life, such as how the years were divided less into months than seasons: times for sowing, tilling, reaping, threshing, cheese making, slaughtering, sausage making, tanning. Because of their pigs, the Noes had spent the quiet winter months making the pig-bristle brushes that had later become their manufacturing specialty, once the land became too valuable to farm. Mr. Noe had sold off much of it to developers, regretfully, but all the other farmers were doing the same.

Mr. Noe was a down-to-earth, funny, kind man. And odd. For one thing, his commitment to boar-bristle brushes was extreme. "It's a great business, Frank, let me tell you. If you ever want to get out of bridges, I recommend it. We've got jobs, we're always expanding. I ask you, what other toilet accoutrement is so beautiful, so utilitarian, so essential to every self-respecting person's wardrobe—gentlewoman and Bowery boy alike—and so impervious to the whims of fashion and the conventions of social class? Hmmn? The brush is the one. And nothing but boar bristle, my boy—that's the top of the line." As Mr. Noe saw it, whoever one was, whatever one wore, one's clothing had to be natty and fresh and free of lint or pill. Yes, he told Harris, brushes were a grand, thriving business. He'd never regretted going into them. His company bought the bristles as by-products from farms and slaughterhouses now, rather than raising the pigs. Harris had to suppress a laugh, Mr. Noe's rhapsody on brushes went on so long.

The day after that dinner, Harris found a small box wrapped in paper on the bench by his door. It was a fine brush with a walnut handle and black bristles, and beginning that day he used it daily to keep his rather shabby wardrobe in the best shape possible.

Soon, it was twice a week that Harris sat down to bone china and silver and the household cook's good meats and gravies. Over a turkey stew, Mr. Noe told the story of the snowy February afternoon in his youth when he first saw the exorbitant prices a Manhattan haberdasher was asking for the brushes Mr. Noe's family made. The handles were a particular shape, there were details that the maker knew without doubt. "I loved making the brushes, and I had loved seeing a crate of my perfectly made brushes, ready to go to the merchants' warehouse. But that day I saw that there was more than just the craft—it could be a good living. Markup, my boy, it's all about who gets the markup."

After hearing several of Mr. Noe's ruminations on making money as a small manufacturer (there were other disquisitions during which it was "all about distribution") and also a short monologue on the contentment that came from making good and useful things, Harris took a risk and told his landlord an anecdote from his own life, the story of how he came to choose his apprenticeship. He had set out for a walk one fall day after the harvest was in on his uncle's farm and noticed a remote section of a stone wall and its gateway that had fallen into disrepair. He'd spent whatever free time he found in the following week tinkering with mortar and stones, and after begging a favor of the village blacksmith he eventually had not just the wall back together but the iron gate swinging smoothly shut on its weighted hinges after it was opened. The project was modest, but it had required dedication for him to fit it in between his lessons from the village priest and his duties on the farm. Only when he'd gotten the whole fence in top shape did he tell his uncle. He could still hear the reply: "Yes, well, there was always a fence there, wasn't there, boy? What have you got to be so boastful about?" He had known then that he really was just an orphan, but he'd taken great solace in the work itself and continued repairing fences, not for his uncle but for the cows, for himself, for the mere pleasure of doing it. It took longer to find a way to turn building stone walls into a trade.

"How did you get your apprenticeship, then?" asked Mr. Noe, and Harris regretted his candor. He'd launched into the dangerous land of details, necessitating lies he didn't want to tell. Mr. Noe went on to ask about his master. Harris renamed Meister Teichold *Mr. Tynan* but otherwise stayed true to the man who had been his first and only mentor. He allowed himself to relive the pleasures of learning the craft and to describe the ways that different types of stone responded to the tools. Shyly, he spoke of the gratification of being told he had talent, and finally he spared no detail of the episode when he was hauled back to the farm for nonpayment of apprenticeship fees, despite his master's objections.

"Yes, it must have been a marvelous thing, to work up on the spires," Mr. Noe mused. "I've seen pictures of the Dublin cathedral. What sort of stone is it, marble?"

Harris's stomach dropped. He had no idea what the cathedral looked like, much less what stone it was made of. "It was wonderful up there," he said, awkwardly avoiding an answer. "That's what I'm hoping to feel again. I'm going to work my way right on up—from the sewers and the streets to the caisson to the bridge itself. It's going to be hundreds of feet high, just imagine!"

Mr. Noe looked at him, noticing the evasion, smiling at the dream, not knowing if it was realistic or not, then called for more wine.

Their conversations were constantly marred by such moments, or by tangents Harris wanted to go off on but couldn't, as he couldn't assimilate them into his Irish story. When an outbreak of smallpox was described in the *Eagle* and half of New York was staying home in fear, he'd have liked to bring up Robert Koch, who had been studying traditional vaccines when Harris last had heard from him, trying to determine if the cause of cowpox and smallpox was the same. But how could he explain the existence of the friend who was his father's protégé when his father was supposed to be dead? Or open up the question of hospitals and laboratories when he had no idea what the names of the Irish ones were, much less if such research had ever been done there or if Mr. Noe might somehow be familiar with epidemiology? He'd learned from Sarah Blacksall that it was becoming quite well known. Harris had been thinking a lot about Koch lately. He'd even begun a letter to him, only to tear it up. How could he explain what had become of him, what he had done to get away? How could he begin to explain where he had landed? Koch would be a proper doctor by now, a professor, had quite possibly made important discoveries. Meanwhile, Harris was a laborer, a fugitive.

It was a relief, therefore, to spend time with the Henleys, who at least knew who he really was. They often had him over for Sunday supper, and all week long he would look forward to Lila's good stews and the feeling that was almost like that of coming home. He frequently retold the Henleys the same stories he'd told Mr. Noe, but the Henleys got the true, unedited versions. It was as if Harris had to get the right version out, to correct the lies he'd spun for Mr. Noe. Unless, of course, they had other guests—Sarah Blacksall or her young partner, Susan Smith, who was black, or commonly both of them, since their clinic was just down the block. On those nights, Harris found he listened more than talked, and when he did speak he stuck to the present.

At first, Harris doubted he could keep the sham existence up indefinitely, but when the warm weather came his life was still stable. With Mr. Noe to vouch for him, he had even opened a bank account, where he deposited his wages and the money Piker Ryan had given him. The money from Johnny and Beatrice he had given away, some to the Henleys to put on a new roof, but most of it to the Women's Medical College. He had been so taken by the idea of those two improbable doctors: the white woman with her phials and microscopes and her dream of curing disease in the slums, and the black woman whose passion was bringing free care to the indigent, especially women. Sometimes Harris wished he were a woman so he could have gone to the Women's Medical College—it seemed such a visionary place. But he was not, he knew, a scientist. He was a builder, and the thing that made his day, every morning, was seeing how much taller the tower had crept since the day before. Even if they weren't his stones up top, it was resting on his foundation, he felt.

The foundation he and John-Henry were helping to bring down to bedrock was a vast, sturdy, hollow, rectangular form, built something like a ship's hull, but its walls were many times thicker. When they began construction on the bridge, the first step had been to sink the caisson carefully into position on the river bottom, open end down. Then the water within it was pumped out with pressurized air, creating an underwater bubble where dozens of men would toil, working around the clock to excavate the river-bed, except for Sundays. Often they encountered boulders under one edge of the caisson, and that was where John-Henry's talents came in: blasting the impediment to kingdom come—or to gravel, really. To provide such a tall tower with a stable base, they would have to keep digging till there was nothing but solid rock beneath. Two inches a day was a brisk pace, but eventually they would get there—perhaps, Harris speculated over coffee and Lila's cobbler, in a year.

"At which point," said John-Henry, "they'll fill up the hole we work in with cement, and the two of us will be out of a job."

"There's always the second tower—but I plan to work *on top* of that one, not under it."

The technology of the air pumps, the mechanically ingenious chutes they used to take the refuse away, the painful illness that afflicted some of the men, the strange way lantern lights blazed in the unnatural air of that cavern—all this made for good dinner conversation, but often, while he and John-Henry were explaining some curious facet of the project, Harris felt himself growing remote from the group. There was so much in his mind that he could not share with anyone but the Henleys. He would have liked to feel he really knew Sarah Blacksall and Susan Smith, to feel they knew him. But he was constrained by his situation to keep his talk painfully impersonal.

The best part of his days now were the mornings, when he and John-Henry visited before the start of work. They met at the doughnut cart just outside the site. The doughnut girl, Lorraine, was a friend of John-Henry's—she lived on his block, too—and she always had their coffee ready by the time they stepped up: John-Henry's light, Harris's black with sugar. Standing around eating crullers and leaning up against the construction fence, Harris and John-Henry would talk for a half an hour or so about what really mattered to them. Harris fantasized about proving his innocence in the Barnum's arson case, mused about his old life in Germany, fretted over flaws in the fabric of the self he presented to Susan and Sarah and Mr. Noe. John-Henry talked about wanting a family, but then sometimes he said he thought it would be better not to bring children into a world where even in the North, even in New York, even after that whole damned war, blacks were still barely thought of as men. The racism of the mostly Irish caisson workers was inescapable, and although John-Henry was a foreman and in charge of all the blasting down below, nearly every day he faced some new insult from one of the men, some rudeness or act of insubordination.

"You know," he said, "I'm glad you're not a real Irishman. The Irish are pigs."

"Germans are no better."

"I guess that's true. I even know some Negroes who can be pretty awful, time to time."

"And what about women?" But Harris was thinking of just one woman: Beatrice.

"And half this country was fighting the Negro vote, despite the war, despite the Fourteenth Amendment."

"People are pigs," said Harris.

"Ah, *humanity.* Now let's get to work, what do you say?"

One morning in the spring, when the air was frothy with the scent of crab-apple blossoms and underlain with the rich scent of mud, John-Henry gave Harris the news that he and Lila were expecting a baby. He was excited, delighted, proud—not thinking of Negro suffrage now. Harris laughed and congratulated him, but later in the day, down in the caisson, he realized the news had made him sad. He imagined the Henleys would be preoccupied with just their little family when the child came and he would see less of them. It reminded him sharply of how alone he was, really, how far he was from having a family of his own. He had mistaken something awful for the emotion of love, once; he doubted he could ever find his way to feeling so strongly again. And a really intimate relationship didn't seem possible so long as he had to lie to the world about his life.

No one had yet uncovered his masquerade or come to arrest or murder him, but there were times Harris felt an eerie chill beneath his collar and found himself looking over his shoulder, fearing that someone was watching him suspiciously, looking at him strangely—someone who wished him no good. He thought increasingly about trying to clear his name—or his aliases, rather—but he couldn't fathom how to do it. He didn't want to lose what peace and community he'd found.

He was right that he was being followed. Fiona had been making occasional trips across the river to check up on him, on Mother Dolan's instructions, ever since Beanie was promoted. What she saw wasn't very interesting. Harris's life was entirely regular, week in, week out, as far as she could tell. Fiona, on Mother Dolan's instruction and her own intuition, had not told Beatrice what she was doing. She knew well enough that Beatrice was still in love with Harris. It wouldn't help her to hear that he was still being monitored by the Dolans, which suggested to Fiona that he might not really be as free as Beanie thought. And it would only depress her, Fiona thought, to hear that the fruit of her sacrifice for Harris was a grim and dreary workaday existence.

That was how Fiona saw his life. Of course, she never felt the lurch of his heart when a blast was ignited in the caisson, deep below the river. She didn't duck the flying debris or hear the roar. She didn't watch men crumple with the agony of the caisson disease, which no one could cure, or know the lurking anxiety that he or John-Henry might fall victim to it next, for it seemed a robust constitution was no protection. Harris, to himself, was a shade more complex: There were days when he felt morose; there were also times he was actually optimistic. As time passed, he was gaining a bit of distance on the Beatrice affair. He felt puzzled now rather than bitter, at the queer blend of luck and misfortune that had marked his life. There was much he was grateful for, even including the way that Beatrice had set him free. He even thought of her wistfully, now and then, when he was tired or his mind wandered, but he couldn't sustain the fantasy of being in love with her anymore. He didn't have any doubt that he was better off living with Mr. Noe and working on the bridge than he would have been working for the gang, hopelessly smitten with the boss's girlfriend, but there was something missing, something like love. He went to the Pilgrim church with Mr. Noe most Sunday mornings, partly in the hope of meeting a young woman. Mr. Noe was aggressive in introducing his lodger to the ladies of Brooklyn Heights and Fort Greene at the coffee hour, but realistically there wasn't much hope for Harris. He was too much of a hybrid. None of those girls was likely to join herself to a Irishman whose job was shoveling mud, even if he was well-spoken and attractive. He might be connected with a wealthy merchant, but he wasn't his son.

It seemed to rain every afternoon that spring, and the drops would cool his sweat and wash the black grime from his face and forearms in tiny rivulets. Harris's name was on a list of those whose skills might bring them above sea level, but there were very few openings, and he was not by any means at the top of this list. And so he and John-Henry and their fellow workers dug and blasted and hacked away at the riverbed under the caisson, lowering it inch by inch, while the tower grew above their heads, stone upon stone, every day or so another row. Tuesday never seemed much mightier than Monday, but May was a jutting promontory compared to February's bulwark. Harris never tired of watching the men up above do their work when he was standing around in the yard, waiting to go down below.

Most days, Harris was on a shovel, moving gravel and mud, but whenever John-Henry needed helpers he pulled Harris off of his usual crew. Harris had an uncanny sense of the stone and an intuition for how it would react. He could say after just a few taps and pings with his hammer where the fault lines lay in a gigantic erratic boulder that was lodged beneath the caisson's shoe and thus how the stone would break. Never in John-Henry's experience, not even in the tunnels of the railroad lines where he'd first learned how to set charges into rock, had the precision of the blasting been so essential. They were working far beneath the bottom of the river now. If they blew out a piece of rock much larger than planned, leaving the caisson askew, the pressurized air they relied on might be blown out through the blast hole, along with debris, allowing the harbor in and drowning the men trapped below. Every time they detonated a charge, the life of every man below was put at risk. He felt grateful and honored to be working with a man he so trusted and who, despite everything, trusted him.

They had stood by him, John-Henry and Lila, and they also inspired him. John-Henry had taken great risks to fight in the war, leaving Boston, where he was safe, to go south, where blacks faced the distinct possibility of being captured and enslaved, in addition to the usual military hazards of rifle fire and bayonet thrust, dysentery and gangrene. When he thought of John-Henry fighting in the war, he would think of Robert Koch following the Prussian army, healing the soldiers fallen in fighting the French. Koch had once told him that the best laboratory was on the nearest front, wherever the fever outbreaks were worst and doctors were needed most. The two men he had counted as close friends in his life were both heroes, in their ways, whereas all he'd ever done by way of taking risks was to mix himself up with a gang.

One Sunday evening that summer, the lady doctors were there for supper, and Sarah Blacksall delivered a piece of news that was for her both personal and political. She knew it would interest John-Henry and Harris, too. Her uncle, Superintendent Towle, had been sacked and the dirt-catcher project suspended, despite its brilliant results. Harris figured the mayor and Boss Tweed would not have been pleased, not at all, when they requested their next withdrawal from the tunnel and it turned out the caches were empty. They would have suspected a traitor in their ranks, namely, Towle. It was not right or fair.

"The whole program was shut down?" he said, frustrated that he could not say what he knew about why Towle had really been canned. He had felt there was something Robin Hoodish about the Tammany job—they were stealing money from the rich, after all—but now he saw that his reconnaissance for the Whyos had brought down the sanitary-hygiene project. What he had done was even worse than he thought. "All that work," he said, "for naught."

"That's not true, Harris," said John-Henry. "We put in three of those dirt-catchers. At least those three are keeping the sewage flowing, keeping the people who live near them healthy."

"I suppose."

That night, as he walked to the ferry terminal, Harris had that creeping feeling down his neck again. He turned to look behind him, but as usual the street was empty. Just a couple of mongrels scrapping in the dust. He imagined it was just his growing anxiety, his low mood, but in fact it was Fiona—and the Jimster. They'd been keeping pace with him for a block before he felt their presence. It wasn't quite proper for Fiona to have the Jimster along when she was watching Harris—the Jimster had once worked for Undertoe, after all. But Undertoe had been sent upriver after the p.o. job, and Jimmy had sworn to her he hated the guy. In fact, Fiona had been trying to bring Johnny and Beanie around to tapping the Jimster for the Whyos. She liked him too well to let him wander back to working for some other gang or, God forbid, Undertoe, who would be getting out before long. As they tailed Harris, the Jimster quite oblivious to the identity of their mark, they passed a Whyo-controlled building where the cellar was used for both storage and as a route to the other side of the block. Fiona happened to know it would be empty at the moment. She mentioned it to Jimmy. They ducked inside, and in no time skirts and suspender straps were flying. She wrapped her arms around his neck, and he lifted her up by the ass while her booted feet climbed the doorjamb. In short, they lost track of Harris. Not that it mattered much, as far as Fiona could see. For as long as she'd been watching him, Harris had never yet done anything unpredictable.

The funny thing was, though, Harris still had that eerie feeling, even after they'd left him. The ferry was quick to come and quick to pull away, and he thought about whether it was even necessary, the crazy, enormous structure he was employed in building. Sure, when the harbor froze it would be helpful, but that was at most a couple of days a year. Otherwise, traffic flowed swiftly between the cities already. If a person wanted to go to Manhattan, he could do it from a dozen different places without waiting more than a few minutes, whatever the hour. It was cheap and convenient and democratic, for every sort of person rode the ferry: magnates, match girls and the likes of him, all of them together in the salons and at the rails. There wasn't a first-class section because there wasn't time to sort out such distinctions; that's how fast the crossing was. That evening, it was him and a bunch of elegant ladies, one of them with a couple of expensive-looking oriental dogs, no noses to speak of, prancing at the ends of long silk leads.

As Harris's boat rode across the current that last Sunday of August, angling downstream of its true destination to outwit the flooding tide, another ferry passed it, going to Manhattan. As usual, they crossed closely enough for the two ferry captains to wave hello, close enough for the passengers of the *Robert Fulton* to get a look inside the windows of the *Abraham Lincoln*, glimpse the faces of the people going the other way. And on that other boat, there sat a man whom Harris knew. Luther Undertoe was only recently down from Sing Sing, and he was looking out across the water, staring idly in the direction of the *Robert Fulton*, thinking about how best to restart his career. Harris was on his mind again. Actually, the whole of the Barnum's snafu was irking him, and the man on his mind was still known to him only

•

as Will Williams and George Geiermeier. Undertoe didn't realize he'd seen him from afar, but facial recognition is something primal, deep, inarticulate. Undertoe had looked into the lighted cabin of the *Robert Fulton*, Harris's face flashed past him, and suddenly he was mad all over again about the way the Barnum's fire had gone down.

That had been the first thing to go wrong in what had turned out to be an abysmal couple of years. He'd had a run of rotten luck during which it seemed he couldn't get anything going without getting busted and thrown in the lockup. Now he was back, but they'd gotten wise to him at police headquarters. And he'd quickly seen he could no longer count on the boys he'd had working for him before. The Jimster had grown up and gotten independent while Undertoe was in the can. It was bad, he thought, when even your toadies abandoned you. It was partly his doing—he hadn't been thinking straight that day in the precinct house, that was for sure, especially not when he'd tried to pin that big job on Johnny Dolan. But someone had put him there. There was someone else to blame. And now that he'd thought of Barnum's, he thought of Williams and wondered if possibly *he'd* been involved. Williams had turned out to be cleverer than he'd expected. It was no mean feat to vanish the way he had. And of course the guy would have it in for him, once he realized Undertoe had set him up. Yes, it seemed disturbingly likely to him now that it was his old dupe the German stableman who'd laid him low and gotten him sent upstate. He determined to renew his search for him and, if he found him, to make things even.

Harris himself was just that moment indulging in a bit of nostalgia, the corollary, perhaps, to Undertoe's ruminations: He was recalling the moment Piker Ryan had passed him his flask, wondering if he could have made it as a gangster after all. He was thinking fondly and unwisely of the bad old times. He was wondering if he could ever fall in love with a girl who didn't know he'd done those things. They were part of him, for better or worse. The truth was, working for the Whyos was the most interesting job he'd ever done, aside from his apprenticeship. The work he did now down in the caisson was arduous and repetitive. He'd had autonomy in the sewers, thanks to McGinty's boots and his secret criminal mission. He didn't approve of killing and stealing, and he felt bad about the fate of the dirt-catcher project, but there had been something vital about it, something that he missed. He wondered what jobs the gang was pulling now.

The two ferries pulled up at nearly the same time to the two ferry piers on the two Fulton Streets of the two cities. Harris had a short walk to get home, up the hill and then a mile or so. Undertoe didn't have a destination at all—he would wander till he found a target. He'd been over in Brooklyn to examine the district on the Heights where he'd heard there was plenty of money just waiting to be liberated and hardly any cops. He'd seen it that night, and it was ideal. As he'd walked along Montague Street, peering into restaurants, the grocery and the butcher shop, Undertoe had thought of two fine things he'd had his sights on last winter, before he got laid out: a certain fur-lined coat that had called to him from the window of a haberdasher's and the Union Army pistol that he'd put good green money on with Marm Mandelbaum, a pawnbroker. He'd paid more than half what she was asking, but he knew the way she worked: no weekly payment, you lose your claim. All of it had been forfeited when he landed in the can. If he'd had that gun, Undertoe thought, he'd never have gotten rolled that night at the Bowery. Just thinking about it filled him with rage, made him furious at every creature and every thing he saw, and as he disembarked he kicked the sidewall of the pilothouse so hard he dented the metal. There was a crushing pain in his right great toe. A hematoma destined to bloat to the size of a marble before he needled it, two days later, was beginning to form at the tip. A man in a ferry uniform put his head out the door, looked at Undertoe, then drew the door closed behind him and locked it. *If I had that gun,* Undertoe thought, *that mate would be dead.* Undertoe limped a little as he walked west on Fulton Street, but when the ferry had delivered him to the Brooklyn side a couple of hours earlier, he'd been sauntering. He'd been feeling good as he veered off in the direction that most of the passengers didn't, over to a side street with just a few large houses further up the hill. When a suitable bush presented itself, he'd stepped into its shadow and waited for someone to come along. He passed up any number of servant girls with baskets on their arms before he spied a gentleman walking up the hill with a buoyant foolishness, like he had had a good day or thought he was some sort of jaunty country squire. He wore a yellow checked vest and a straw boater and was whistling "Willy the Weeper." Bile rose up in Undertoe's gullet. He'd never liked that song. He coiled his energy in his legs and then, when the angle and distance were right, he pounced. The man was unprepared to defend himself. He just gasped in disbelief, gurgled and slid into the shrubbery. Never even uttered a complaint. It was a wide jugular gash, and most of his five mortal quarts had spilled onto the dirt before Undertoe finished harvesting his jewelry. Then he sorted the man's money into his own wallet and proceeded up the hill.

26

THE WAY OF ALL FLESH

That winter, John-Henry and Lila finally had themselves a daughter, healthy, wriggling and minute. They called her Liza. Harris paid the baby a visit when she was six days old. He brought a roast chicken from the cook at the Noe house all the way across on the ferry and joined them in an impromptu meal. Lila was propped up on the couch, still recovering, and it was John-Henry who moved about the kitchen and brought out plates, all the while rhapsodizing over his daughter's marvelous fingers and toes, their tiny nails, the delicate whorls of her ears. Harris took the baby on his knee when she woke and dandled her. He smiled at her and praised her infant loveliness, but somehow all he could think was that she was about the size of a cat, and she mewled like a cat. Why do we bother to reproduce ourselves? he wondered. What good is it? He was thinking the way John-Henry had before the pregnancy, and he couldn't imagine wanting to bring another person into this difficult world. The baby seemed to feel his anxiety— she fussed and cried in his arms, and he was glad to hand her back to her mother.

That night, Harris didn't sleep at all, just lay there restless, brooding, sometimes starting from a half slumber only to lie wide awake again for another hour. He knew it was awful of him, he disapproved of his own feelings, but seeing John-Henry's tired, happy little family had made him miserable. It pointed up all that he himself did not have and had no prospects of ever getting. He'd been throwing all his energy into moving the riverbed out from under the caisson. It was all he had done for months and months. He'd told himself that working on the bridge in any capacity was a grand thing, but the truth was that working in the caisson wasn't enough. It wasn't a life. Every day, he watched the hoisting of great stone blocks from the yard and the careful positioning of the stones up above, but the part of the bridge where Harris worked had been invisible virtually from the start. People talked about the bridge incessantly these days, but few ever thought about the men who toiled in the box of soot and smoke and mud and risk down at the bottom of the river. Or if they did, it was with mild horror, and then they quickly turned their minds to prettier heroics. He'd been on the bridge most of a year, and he was beginning to doubt there'd ever be a promotion from the caisson to the tower.

Finally, when he couldn't stand lying there, he pulled his pants on and went over to the big house, to the cellar, and drew himself a pitcher of beer. It took the edge off, but it didn't give him rest, just turned him maudlin. He was overcome with nostalgia—for his mother tongue, his mother, his sister, Koch, even his father. For the man—the men—he used to be. The only one not entirely lost to him was Koch, who had taken what should have been his place in his father's lab. They could so easily have hated each other, but they didn't. Somehow he had never even resented Koch. He didn't really want the lab job himself, after all, just his father's approval. The two young men had spent a lot of time together and discussed all manner of subjects at length, in person and in letters—everything from the haughtiness of Harris's stepsisters to the origins of igneous rock to war to all kinds of issues in biology. As the years passed, Harris spent less and less time in school, while Koch advanced in his university studies and rose from apprentice to assistant in the laboratory of his father, the great doctor, but they shared a voracity to understand and shape the worlds they knew. Then there was their shared taste for *Weissbier*, their common need to defy his father—for it was clear to both boys from their earliest days of acquaintance that the doctor disapproved of their friendship. Harris reconsidered his old decision to break with everyone and everything from his past and wondered if it had really been necessary. It had seemed to him then that he had no other choice. Now it seemed foolish.

He got out the folder with the stationery he'd used in his first abortive attempt to write Koch. He wasn't sure what he had to say, but he started with the salutation: *Lieber Koch.* From there he proceeded cautiously, enjoying the flow of the German through his pen and skipping over the difficult parts, such as why he'd left. He described his departure and the trip over and explained his use of the name Frank Harris. Soon, he'd filled a page.

An hour writing, and he had several pages. Then he went back to the cellar to fetch more beer. He started out intending to sketch a lightly sanitized account of his misadventures in New York, but before long he was just dreaming on paper. The epistolary Harris was on the verge of success, becoming acknowledged in America for his stoneworking skills; he worked as a foreman on the tower of the bridge. He also wrote that he had met a girl, a daughter of one of the engineers, and hoped to marry her. At which point his writing hand began to cramp up, half from being so long unaccustomed to holding a pen, half with chagrin at the fantastic nature of what he'd written. He left the letter in midsentence and went to bed; this time, he slept.

The next morning, he was exhausted. On the table he saw a seven-page missive. Foreman of a tower crew indeed. Did he really still need to impress his father so badly? It was a simple leap to think that anything he wrote to Koch would reach his father's ears. Hadn't he given up on that when he left? Maybe, but he'd grown so accustomed to leading multiple lives, he began to wonder if truth was no longer one of his options. Experience had taught him that he could be whoever he or someone else wanted him to be. Now he was addicted to it. He considered burning the thing, but then he finished the last sentence and signed the letter two ways: *Johannes* and then, in parentheses, *Frank.*

On his way to work, Harris stopped at the post office and sent the letter off in care of the medical school where Koch had studied with his father. He put no return address on the envelope, but he had written Mr. Noe's address on the last page, beneath his name. It gave him a quavery feeling, seeing that letter dropped by the clerk into a box marked TRANSATLANTIC. Soon, the version of himself he'd invented the night before would take the reverse journey from the one he'd made on the *Leibnitz.* If only it were as simple for him to return. He asked himself if he would do it, if he could, if it had been an enormous mistake for him to come here, and whether he had gained anything at all in all his mishaps. The one thing was hope, he decided. He hadn't had much of that left in Germany. He had it now. A man cannot live without hope, but lately he'd subsisted on little else, it seemed, and his hopes seemed absurdly unrealistic. Loneliness was filling in fast from behind.

Then he saw John-Henry waiting for him at the doughnut cart and heard him shout hello. He was glad to see him, as he always was. He saw now that just because John-Henry had a family didn't mean he would be less of a friend. It probably had been a mistake, sending that wild letter, but he couldn't do much about that now. And his life was here. They stood in line for the pressurized air lock, through which just six men could enter the caisson at a time. When the door was screwed shut behind them, the loud clatter of the air pump commenced, and then, when the pressure in the lock equaled that below, a hatch in the floor dropped open. The men climbed through it and down the ladder in the central shaft to the dark, smoky din of the caisson. That shaft was their umbilical cord to the world above, containing the pressurized-air tubes that kept them alive and dry. Parallel to it was the chute through which the debris was removed. Harris waved to John-Henry, who was working in a different sector, and then went and attacked a pile of sand and clay at the edge of the caisson with his shovel.

Around lunchtime, some of the men encountered a huge mass of sandstone obstructing the descent of the caisson along its western bulkhead, and John-Henry called Harris over to assess it for blasting. Against the walls, wherever men were digging, limelights fizzled and flared in sconces, and here and there a candle lantern had been nailed up, to much lesser effect. Many of the men also wore headlamps much like the ones worn by sewer crews. Harris and John-Henry discussed the proper position of the charges to blast through the sandstone, but both of them were worried about an uneven layer of basalt that ran through the boulder. It wouldn't be the biggest rock they'd blown, but it was sizable and complicated. John-Henry took a torch from the wall to examine the fault more closely, while Harris dug down a little further without finding the bottom of either the boulder or the vein. They tapped at the stone with their pickaxes, listening and feeling for vibrations. It was the sort of problem they dealt with every day, though this time it was fairly interesting. Harris told himself to remember this later on, when his pessimistic gloom descended again. It was engaging, important work they were doing—difficult enough to be satisfying.

They formulated a plan based on Harris's understanding of the basalt vein, drilled some holes and went topside to get the explosives. Then they returned to lay the charges, but before they could set them off it was time for Harris and John-Henry to go on break. They discussed having one of the foremen, a fellow named Waugh who had just come off break, set off the charges for them, but after they talked to him John-Henry had second thoughts. They agreed they'd show him exactly how they did it after the break, and then he could do the next one by himself.

As usual, on break, Harris and John-Henry took the opportunity to visit the coffee cart. It was a warm day and a very low tide, and they could smell the fishiness of the river as they drained the last dregs from Lorraine's tin cups. Then the bell rang again, and they lined up for the air lock. As they waited, John-Henry turned to Harris and said, "Let's do that blast in two stages. That way, if the basalt section's bigger than you thought, we won't risk a blowout. What with the tide as low as it is, it seems safer."

Harris nodded—it was a good idea. But just as they got below, they both saw a flare coming from the direction of the boulder. Their boulder. Waugh, determined to prove himself, had gone ahead and lit the charges without them. Harris and John-Henry looked at each other wordlessly—it was too late to change anything now—and waited by the shaft to see how it came out. The bang was normal, and when the smoke cleared they smiled in relief. Then a second boom echoed through the great chamber below the bottom of the river and there came a roaring and a rush of air and water. All the lamps and candles went dark, and a flood of river and mud swept Harris off his feet and sucked him under.

When he got his head above water again, everything was black. He could hear the shouts and screams of the forty-odd men on duty as well as sobbing and prayers being said. When he tried to stand, he found that the water was just over his waist, but he could feel that it was rising.

"John-Henry!"

Someone was shouting, "I can't swim, oh Jesus, I can't swim," and Harris called back: "Stand up, it's not that deep." But the truth was, all of them were all going to drown pretty soon if the water didn't stop flooding into the caisson.

"John-Henry!"

"I'm over here by the shaft. I'm still holding on to the steps. Follow my voice. Maybe we can get out this way, or at least stay higher."

"What about Waugh? Waugh!"

But there was no answer, and Harris went the other direction, away from John-Henry and the shaft, half swimming, half wading into the current of the water flooding the caisson. That was where Waugh would be, somewhere near the boulder, probably knocked out but not necessarily dead.

"Waugh!" he called, reaching wide with his arms and skimming the surface of the water, hoping and fearing to encounter Waugh's floating body.

"*Waugh!*"

"He was right there," said a voice. "He was right there when it blew."

"He must be down. Help me find him."

Harris sloshed around in the water a few more paces and noticed it was coming in more slowly now, a good sign. He dove under, groping his way along the edge of the floor where it met the bulkhead until he felt a ledge of stone open onto a deep cavern that seemed to extend outside the caisson, into the riverbed. So now he knew: The vein of basalt had run all the way through the boulder. This hole was his fault. He reached his arm into the hollow space. It was large, certainly large enough for a man to pass through. He went up again for air, then dove again, this time worming his way into the cave. He blindly felt around him. The space was about as large as the air lock and perfectly clean of the rubble and blast debris. Everything had been blown free, blown outside the caisson by the blast. Waugh had been sucked out of the caisson like a turd from a newfangled toilet.

Harris needed air. *Waugh*, he mouthed as he worked his way back out of the cavity toward the caisson. Bubbles floated invisibly up from his lips in the black water; he could feel them sliding like feathers against his face. It was harder getting out than it had been going forward, when his lungs were full of air and hope, but finally he got his shoulders through the hole, and then the rest of him followed. His head broke the surface a second later and he gasped for air. The first thing he heard was John-Henry shouting his name. All he could think was that his decision was at fault. He had killed a man. Not by being a gangster or anything exciting like that, but by incompetence.

"Waugh's gone," he choked.

After a thorough head count, they determined no one else to be missing, but the mood was grim. Several of the men climbed up the ladder and tried to operate the air-lock door from beneath, but it wouldn't give. Somebody said what they were all thinking: "He died fast. We're going to go slow."

Harris was thinking that the air compressors ought still to be able to function, but there was no sign of that—it was quieter in the caisson than it had ever been before. The water had stopped flooding in, suggesting the caisson had settled, but there were a hundred ways that their escape route might have been permanently cut off: shaft cracked with the torque of the blow, compressors damaged, some inconceivable mayhem above. Perhaps the tower itself had collapsed above them, in which case the shaft would be entirely gone and any number of men dead. Harris considered the possibility that there would be no bridge at all now, just a vast common grave.

What seemed like an endless time later, bubbles began percolating through the water from the central tubes. John-Henry laughed. "Do you hear that?" And soon they all did: Water was flowing up and out through the debris chute. Another hour later, they were just ankle deep, and they heard banging on the other side of the air lock. At last, the jammed hatch fell open, and down came five figures with lamps strapped to their foreheads, casting light on the flooded caisson. The stranded men put up a shout, and the rescuers began distributing blankets, pouring hot coffee from a large kettle and handing out torches. The most shocking thing to Harris when torches were lit was that the space looked hardly different than usual. It had always been wet down there; now it was more so, but really the only other difference was the disarray of the tools and the disturbing half-moon pool at the bulkhead where the blowout had occurred: the ghost of the boulder, the grave of Waugh.

Aboveground, Harris and the others were seen by a doctor. There were several broken bones and lots of cuts and abrasions. Harris was fine, except for his hearing. He was deaf in one ear. The doctor shouted into his other ear (though it was perfectly fine) that it was likely temporary, but the explosion might have damaged his eardrum. Then he patted his arm and sent him on his way with a week's paid leave. How was it, Harris wondered, that now that he'd actually murdered a man, no one bothered to arrest him? On the contrary, he'd been given a vacation.

"Why don't you come stay with us tonight?" John-Henry offered, but Harris felt too awful to tolerate solace or company of any sort. He knew Mr. Noe would be concerned, but he couldn't bring himself to return to Fort Greene either. Instead, he went across to Manhattan by himself and stopped at the first bar he came to. He downed several whiskeys, which made him feel better for a while. He told the rapt bartender and cluster of other men the story of how a man had been killed on the bridge that day, and the barkeep poured his glass full again, on the house. The men toasted Waugh and clapped Harris on the back consolingly, but it did no good. Waugh was dead, gone, floating free in the river with the fishes and the slime.

In fact, however, Waugh had not been shot free into the river. The air that escaped the caisson had sent up a small geyser of debris, but a man's body was a large thing, too large. Waugh had been caught in the bubble that briefly gaped between the great outside wall of the caisson and the riverbed—the blowhole Harris had visited, but larger. Then most of it closed up again, an instant later, and the enormous pressures involved had rendered Waugh a smear, his belt buckle up near what had been his left ear.

Eventually, the bartender told Harris to go home and sleep it off, and he left. Suddenly, Harris was very tired and wanted to go to bed. As he crossed the street, the traffic seemed overwhelming. It had something to do with only being able to hear on one side, perhaps, something to do with how much he had drunk. Harris was distinctly off-kilter.

He was crossing Broadway when he looked up and beheld the carriage looming: a black city ambulance tipped up on its side wheels, threatening to topple over, recklessly whipping around the corner in its mad rush to rescue. The red insignia of the ambulance corps was bearing down on him, but he thought only, *Someone, somewhere, is dying.* The ambulance's horse team reared up to avoid him, very nearly trampling him nonetheless. He saw their yellow teeth, enthroned by their black and pink lips and a white fury of spittle. They were close upon him, and yet their hooves were so quiet on the pavement it seemed he couldn't possibly be in danger. He heard no grinding of wheels, hardly any sound at all. They must be further off than they appeared, he thought, but then he could smell the horses' breath, their hair. A black flank filled his field of vision, a rear hoof reached out to his rib cage. He was about to be crushed by the shoulder-high carriage wheels when he finally flung himself clear. He flew backward. He landed, and his head snapped back and clonked against a cast-iron hitching post set into the curb.

The breath had been driven from his lungs, and his lips could not draw air; his heart raced; his vision swam. He felt a warm liquid trickle slowly down his neck. Then Harris realized there was a terrible clamor all around, like the world rushing in one last time before leaving him finally behind, even louder than the din in the caisson.

People converged upon him—arms and noses, hats and canes—as if they could help, as if he were not about to die, as if his death might be a sight worth seeing. Spectacles and eyes, bulging and shining, all gawking at Harris. A man in a beaver coat reached out his hand to him, and a girl in a gaudy dress kneeled down. He squeezed shut his eyes to hide from the throbbing, demanding voices. "Are you all right, sir? Can you breathe? Move? Stand? Move your fingers? Toes? Give me your hand now. Someone call the police or an ambulance. Wasn't that an ambulance that hit him? Did you see?"

He was limp with shock as the man and the girl and various others struggled to drag him from the street. There was something familiar about that girl. He looked around, trying to remember who these people were, where he was, what had happened. And then he grasped it. That girl leaning over him in the gaudy dress was *Maria*. She was holding his hand in hers, looking right at him.

"Maria—?" She blinked in surprise to hear her name—a name she'd stopped using some time ago. He smiled. And then she smiled back, in recognition. If he'd said any more, it would have been in German, all risks and bans forgotten, but he was speechless.

"*Bist doch der vom Schiff,*" she said. *You're the one from the ship.* Had he heard right? Was it real? He touched his fingers to his ear and they came away wet. When he examined them he expected to see red, but it was just water, released from his ear canal by the impact of landing. Then he looked back up at Maria.

She looked worried, and it was wonderful.

He had never been so happy to see the pout of German words on a pair of lips. It amazed him that he had ever given up hope of finding her. She was blond and lovely, and there was a strange look of jubilation in her eye. It made him recall that life was worth living, just for the surprises. It made him think, *My God.* All the time he'd squandered on an infatuation with a gangster's moll and, lately, being melancholic. Maria furrowed her brow, and he felt a little swoonish. It was the same kind of dizzy he had been in the morgue that day, when he thought she was dead. But this time it brought him to his feet rather than knocking them from under him.

"You were on the *Leibnitz*, weren't you?" she asked.

Yes, he nodded, raising himself up to stand, if shakily, not really thinking through the implications of the swiftness and ease with which she'd recognized him. *Ja*, he said, he was the one from the boat.

27.

DREAMS AND
RESPONSIBILITIES

There was a Whyo in the crowd—or, to be precise, a Why Not. How could there not be, in that part of town? Harris had gotten himself nearly run over in a place where Whyos ran rampant. He was lucky, though, because it was Fiona, who'd gone over to Brooklyn as soon as she'd got wind of disaster at the bridge, knowing Beanie would want to hear about it if anything grave had happened to Harris.

The Jimster was there, too. He'd just run into Fiona on his way out of Billy's, where he'd had a meeting with Undertoe and told him he wasn't working for him any longer. He'd decided the Undertaker was a loser, still looking for his old dupe Williams. At least Jimmy wasn't looking at Harris as he thought that—he was too busy looking at Fiona. Fiona was the one with her eyes glued to Harris.

She'd been worried he was dead until he sat up and started talking to a girl. She had been relieved by that—until she realized they were speaking German.

"What's your name again?" Maria asked him, not that Fiona understood it.

"I've changed it so many times since I knew you, it hardly matters."

Maria laughed at that, musically, in a way Harris didn't remember from before. It seemed she knew exactly what he meant, as if they were old friends, which in some sense they were: She may have forgotten his name, but she knew things that trumped names entirely. He was going backward as fast as he could, thinking he'd at long last discovered his point of divergence from the path that led to happiness. Yes, clearly, his mistake had occurred when he got off the boat and lost sight of her.

But then he realized the mistake he was making right then by talking to her in German. Their conversation shrieked with consonants and umlauts. Harris was drunk and dazed and weirdly euphoric, but he wasn't a total fool. For better or worse, he remembered that his very existence hung upon maintaining the identity bestowed on him by the Whyos. He shouldn't be speaking German, not with a street full of people's attention centered on him. Hoping to God her English was good enough to slide from one language to the other without fuss, he focused his eyes intently on hers and broke away from the language she'd just returned to him. He said, in English, that he thought he was all right, just bruised. He held his breath, willing her to respond in kind, but she looked at him in puzzlement for a moment, as if she hadn't understood him. Then she smiled.

She spoke a broken and accented but swift-flowing English. Her pitch and fall were steeper than the rolling brogue that Harris had grown proficient in. In short, she spoke just the way any recent German immigrant could be expected to speak if they hadn't been heavily coached. And rather like a meal of spätzle and bratwurst and beer at one of the many German restaurants around Five Points and the Lower East Side, her English still reminded Harris of home.

Fiona had observed it all. Harris had corrected himself quickly, she thought, but was it quickly enough? It remained to be seen how much the Jimster had noticed.

"Let's get out of here, eh?" she said.

As Jimmy and Fiona headed across the street, Jimmy turned to whisper some bit of freshness in her ear, and as he turned the Jimster caught a profile view of Frank Harris standing up. There was something familiar about that man, he thought, the tone of voice, the boxer's nose and potato face, the black eyes.

"You know," he said, "isn't that the guy we were tailing the other day? I recognize him from somewhere."

So Harris had blown his cover. It was just what she'd wanted to avoid. "Who cares about him?" she said, kissing Jimmy hard and slipping her hand inside his coat.

"Yeah, you're right. . . . Never mind."

Fiona asked the Jimster if he would take her out to lunch, and he said sure, anywhere but Billy's, as he didn't want to run into Undertoe. *That's good*, thought Fiona, *that's just the right answer*. She was thinking it was time to push Beatrice to introduce the Jimster personally to Johnny, try to get him brought in. It would certainly make her life easier.

Maria was much as Harris had remembered, a bit better fed and better dressed, which he was happy to see. But then he thought about how she had recognized him, and he grew more worried. He looked around, knowing it was not a good idea for him to be with her. He walked a few paces down the block with her, then stopped and put his hand out to shake hers in parting. She looked at him, clearly disappointed. Had she been thinking of him, too, all that time? he wondered. Had his crush been mutual? He looked around him, saw an oyster house, and smiled noncommittally. Perhaps it was just his yearning to forget what had happened earlier that day that made him do something so risky, so foolish.

"Why don't you take me there, to dinner?" she asked.

"Dinner. Yes, all right, if you care to." Immediately, she moved closer to him. Too close, he thought. He looked at her again, taking an inventory of her face: her lips, the same shape he remembered but now artificially pink; her skin, dusted with powder where it had once been fresh and translucent, so that she resembled a china doll his sister had had, the head and hands and feet of which were cold molded porcelain with painted details, the rest of the body being stuffed tubes of mattress ticking. Maria's hair was as yellow as ever, but it was done up in a complicated fashion now. Her eyes were just as blue, but less angry and more calculating, perhaps. The thing that cinched it was her dress—too shiny, too opulent. Harris was a man; he had lived in the world; he understood. Maria's changes were far more understandable, really, than his own.

"Oh, um, well." He felt an urgent desire to go home and reassure Mr. Noe that he had made it out of the caisson safely. To take this woman he barely knew and who he now realized was a prostitute out to dinner—that was not what he wanted to do. A man he worked with had just died. It was no time for sleazy self-indulgence. "Maybe I'll call on you another time? If I may." He didn't plan to. He just wanted to get away. On top of the rest, it was such a disappointment that this was who she was.

"Don't go. I promise to make it a pleasant reunion." She smiled in a way that made him go red, not quite with shame but a corollary of shame, the thing that precedes it. She quoted her price by the hour and for all night. It wasn't much either way. "Come on, *schatzie*. Let me cheer you up."

Harris did need cheering. Drinking hadn't worked. He had definitely been thinking too much about women lately, yearning for their company, their touch. His romantic prospects were terrible. Maybe this was what he needed. Maybe this was all he was going to get. He put the idea of going home aside, took a deep breath and slipped his arm around her waist.

Harris led her across the street, where he swallowed a plate of oysters almost without noticing them. He would have liked to talk to her, to find out how she'd fared since they both landed, to tell her his own stories. But now that he knew what she was, he could think of nothing to say. Finally, he asked, "Do you have a room?" She did, and they went there.

Across the air shaft, in the opposite window, an old woman sat with a candle at her side, sewing, and when Maria lit her kerosene lamp, she looked up. Maria pulled the curtain, but Harris heard the woman's muffled voice call out, "Mend your ways, Magdalene. I can get you piecework. God has hope."

He sat on the bed and took in the room: the gray of the sheets, the gray of the curtains, the gray of the old porcelain basin on its wooden stand—all slightly different tones, all gray. He thought of Waugh. But then he looked up at Maria as she shed her clothing in the yellow light, and she wasn't gray at all. She was pink and yellow like some candy, and she was stepping out of a dress that was bright, bright blue. When she spoke it was in German. Nothing smutty—she could always tell what a customer wanted—just sweet nothings, and he rose to the lovely rasp of her voice as much as to her nakedness or the way she knelt between his legs and unbuttoned his pants.

"Keep talking," he said, but talk was not the commodity she sold. So he lay back, listening to the creaks of the house and the bed and the squelching of her cheeks. His nose was full of the oily smell of her sheets. After a while, she stuck a finger up his ass, and he came abruptly, almost unpleasantly.

"Really," she said after spitting into the spittoon by the bedpost. "It's like you're dead."

No, he wasn't. Waugh was.

"Just hold me," he said.

She put her arms around him. As they lay there, he thought back to his last Christmas in Göttingen, when he'd fallen unexpectedly and inappropriately in love with his stepsister, Tatianna. She was two years younger but had suddenly grown up. It had been mutual. From the moment he and Lottie arrived that year, the previously uninterested and prissy-seeming Tatianna was friendly to him—more than friendly, flirtatious. In the past, the main good thing about those awkward winter visits had been hanging around the lab or going off with Robert Koch. But that year, Koch had a girl he was courting—the one he later married—and so the doctor's son devoted himself to Tati. She wasn't *really* his sister, after all. They stayed up late talking, laughing. She was funnier and prettier and cleverer than any girl he knew. She wore all the latest fashions, knew the daughters and sons of the local barons and viscounts, with whom she went to balls and the opera, and she had traveled as far as England. Certainly she bore no comparison to any of the girls in Fürth.

On New Year's Eve, the last day of his visit, after all the others had retired, Tati had begun to mope. "Why must you leave?" she wanted to know. Of course, he couldn't answer that. She had said she wanted to go outside and look at the stars, and he was glad for the change. Once they were out in the bitter cold, the greenhouse across the garden beckoned to them. How beautiful it had looked, lit faintly from within, the glass all spangled with frost and glowing green to the slender wooden rafters. Inside, there were many common ornamental plants in pots, but near the stove, in a large glassed-in case, were the most exquisite specimens, the orchids and other tropicals, with their frightening blossoms and smooth, leathery leaves.

They finished a bottle of champagne they'd taken from the sideboard, passing it between them and drinking directly from its mouth. When the wine dribbled down his cheek, she brought her fingers to his lips, and he licked the spilled drops from her skin. He had kissed girls before, and there was no uncertainty about her invitation. His fingers probed her shirtwaist, but finding it impenetrable he reached lower, for her skirt hem. In between them were yards of fabric, but after a flurry of rustling silk, he found the strap of her stocking. Her legs nearly undid him, they were so smooth and unexpectedly strong. He kissed her inner thigh and nosed tentatively higher. But he had gone too far. She pushed his head down and reeled back. When he'd gotten free of her dress, he tried to formulate an apology, an appeal. She listened to him stammer for just a moment, slapped him and never talked to him again.

Eventually, Maria sat up beside Harris, and he opened his eyes and looked at her. He saw something he hadn't before: The filthy, irregular pattern of stains on her sheets continued as bruises and welt marks across her torso.

"My God, are you all right?"

She swiftly pulled the sheet up to cover herself.

"Are you all right, Maria?" he asked. "This is no life."

"What's it to you? You got what you paid for."

She didn't want help or friendship. She had recognized in him a business opportunity; he hadn't exactly hoped for love—he had known it was a temporary escape—but this was the very opposite of love; it was commerce. He dressed and left quickly, in a flurry of dollar bills and shame.

That night, back in his room at Mr. Noe's, Harris dreamed he heard whyoing and woke with a start, as if from a nightmare. He saw that it was near dawn. It could have been the howling of a dog that triggered it, but quite possibly he really had heard whyoing that evening. Maria's sordid little room was in the Five Points, not so far from the Bend or the O'Gamhnas. It occurred to him then with a retrospective amazement—how could he not have noticed it before?—that he'd heard such sounds many times, many nights, while he lived with the O'Gamhnas: eerie noises in the distance at certain times of the evening. And he'd never heard them in Brooklyn. Brooklyn was blissfully quiet. He rolled over and went back to sleep, since he didn't have to go to work. He woke again much later and once again decided to stay in bed. Around noon, Mr. Noe knocked on his door.

"May I come in, Frank?" he asked. "I was worried yesterday. How are you?"

Harris was wishing his housing arrangements were less encumbered and that Mr. Noe would just leave him alone, but then, when he looked up, he saw a concern that was genuine, and it touched him. This was what he needed, wasn't it, someone who cared what happened to him? Harris sat up, swung his feet to the floor and put the kettle on the stove, to which he added a small log. Then he apologized for vanishing and letting his friend worry about him.

Mr. Noe didn't know what his troubles were, but he knew there was something amiss, something more than just the blowout. And yet he didn't press Harris, just set a plate from the cook—biscuits and some sliced meat and gravy—on the table and waited quietly while Harris fussed ineptly with the tea. Perhaps it was that patience that led Harris to start talking. He opened his lips, once the tea was made, and gave Mr. Noe a more honest accounting of his life than he'd done with anyone but John-Henry to date. He started with the story of the blowout and how responsible he felt he was, and from there he went backward. It wasn't quite the full truth—he didn't use names—but he told Mr. Noe about his involvement with the gang, about his loss of Beatrice, even about his encounter with Maria. Mr. Noe showed no sign of being scandalized or angry, he just nodded and said he was glad to hear about all this at last. He'd suspected some trouble. He understood grief, Mr. Noe, he understood guilt, and he understood how a man could go astray. Then he asked Harris if he wanted to eat his lunch. And when Harris had done so, Mr. Noe delivered a surprise of his own.

"You know, you got some mail, Frank. In fact, two letters in one day, and one of them looks to be from Germany."

"Really?"

"Really. Your timing is good. You were going to have to explain that one."

The first letter was a short note from John-Henry, urging Harris to join the Henleys for supper that night. The other letter was from Koch, and when he said he wanted to open it alone, Mr. Noe seemed to understand.

"Just let me know if I can do anything for you, my boy. Anything at all."

Under the whiteness of the February sky, Harris wandered up to the Heights, past the thorny, leafless rugosas, to Montague Street, once again a letter burning in his pocket that he did not dare to open. Several times, he took the letter out and looked at it, its envelope addressed in Koch's pared-down Gothic script, and then returned it again to his pocket. He dreaded reading his old friend's reaction to the mass of lies he'd sent him. Why couldn't he have started that letter over and told something closer to the truth?

It was perhaps the fourth time that he stopped and paused to consider the envelope that he looked up to see a familiar face, a girl's, staring straight at him from the doorway of a butcher shop, beckoning. Fiona.

He dropped the letter in surprise. She stepped forward, picked it up, then receded into the shop. Cautiously, he followed her inside and saw that she was buying a ham steak. He got in line behind her and cleared his throat, but she didn't acknowledge him. Harris looked around at the skinned rabbits and plucked geese hanging in the window, the side of beef on its hook in the back. Then Fiona took her paper package under her arm and left, without turning back to look at Harris again.

"Yes, sir?" said the butcher.

But Harris turned and left the shop in pursuit of Fiona. She was loitering at the corner, waiting for him.

"Just look straight ahead of you, listen and walk," she said. "I have a message for you: You've been getting careless. First of all, don't go sleeping with German hussies. It doesn't look good, and all you'll get is the clap. But your main problem is that the Undertaker's back in town."

Harris hadn't even known the man had gone anywhere. He could hardly believe that the Whyos were still following him. He looked behind him, imagining Beatrice might be there, too. He wasn't sure if he wanted her to be.

"A few bad things have happened to Luther lately, thanks to us, but I'm afraid he thinks it's you—thinks you were after revenge, and now he wants some of his own."

"But—"

"Whether it's true doesn't matter, Mr. Harris. He's a problem for you, always will be, and since you've worked with us, if he finds you, that would make both of you *our* problem. See? We don't want problems. You very nearly walked into his arms the other day, what with your jabbering in German. You were on his turf. His boys are all around. Have some sense, Harris. Don't break your cover. All right? Because you don't get another chance."

Harris opened his mouth.

"Shut up, Mr. Harris."

It was just the way Beatrice had said it the day they abducted him, and he felt it in his gut like a wire. She held out his letter, he grabbed it dumbly, and then Fiona was gone. She just seemed to vanish. He turned in place on the bluestone sidewalk, but there was no one in sight who could have been her. Once, the Whyos had wanted him to join them; once, they had saved him from both Undertoe and the police; later, they'd respected him enough to let him walk away. They were still helping him, watching over him, but why? Did they still want something from him? He wasn't sure he liked that idea, but for the first time in a long time he felt grateful to them.

Then he went over to the Henleys' with his letter. They had helped him deal with the last letter he'd gotten, and he figured he would let them do the same with this one, if they were willing. When he got there, it was a little early for dinner, but there was a large pot of stew bubbling on the stove, and he could see that they were expecting more company than just himself.

"Oh, Harris, I'm glad you did come after all," said Lila. "John-Henry got a couple of rabbits. The lady doctors are coming over, too."

"A party, today?" He looked at John-Henry. Harris was not in any mood for a party.

"Now come on, we didn't plan it. It just came together."

Harris cringed at the idea of having to see people. He had been looking forward to the comfort of the Henleys' company, not socializing with a couple of do-gooders. He didn't want to have to retell the story of Waugh's death, and their presence would prevent him from discussing his German problem.

"Listen, John-Henry, before they get here, I got another letter I can't stand to open. It's from home. Germany."

"Your father? How'd he find you?"

"Not my father."

Looking at the letter, Harris had no idea what to expect, knew nothing except that he must have been mad to write Koch in the first place. As Fiona had just made clear to him, it was a grave risk he had taken with his new identity and therefore his life. What had made him think that telling a man an ocean away a pack of lies about himself would ameliorate his solitude?

"Well, go sit in the bedroom by yourself and read it. Then come tell us what it says. Go on."

The letter itself was several pages long, but even before he began to read the greeting overwhelmed him. His very name looked foreign to him. There followed long paragraphs of Koch's fine, elegant Gothic script. "As you are well, you will hardly be able to imagine what we believed befell you in 1868." Koch went on to describe the fire at the Diespeck farm. "Now I realize that second man who died must have been a laborer, hired on after you left, but perhaps you can understand how we all came to believe what we did." So it had all gone off exactly as he had planned back then, except for the toll his faked death had exacted on Koch. Clearly, it had caused Koch grief, although now Koch expressed only joy at the mix-up, relief at learning of his friend's survival. He had no sense of having been tricked or abandoned. Koch wrote of his own life, too: the hardships of the war between Germany and France, the survival rate of his patients at the typhoid hospital in Neufchâteau, his work with cowpox and anthrax, and his personal difficulties in the past years—two of his children had died.

Reading his friend's words, Harris saw the war raging across his homeland in a way he never had from reading the newspapers, and he tried to imagine towns he knew as battlefields and entire valleys being swept by typhoid on a scale greater than the scourges of his childhood. Finally, he reached the part where Koch responded directly to what he had written, and he grew embarrassed. The New York–to–Brooklyn bridge was famous even in Europe, and Koch congratulated him on finding such worthy employment. He congratulated him on his fictional engagement. At the end, tentatively, Koch gave news of his father. He suffered arthritis but was otherwise still healthy, still working on mapping the microstructures of the kidney. Koch said he would not betray his whereabouts to his father, knowing of their old estrangement, but urged him to write his father himself.

"He would derive great happiness from hearing that you thrive, if a world away." Harris found that unlikely, but Koch said his father had regretted their estrangement more and more as time passed.

When he'd finished reading, Harris folded the letter back into the envelope. He looked up and saw John-Henry and Lila in the doorway, staring at him.

"Well?"

"It's better than I thought, except I wish I hadn't lied so much in my own letter."

Then the two doctors arrived, and the topic of Harris's letter was put aside in favor of Liza's daily antics, the bridge disaster, the horrible diseases afflicting the prostitutes the doctors had seen as patients. Hearing the doctors talk about their cases, he wished he could send Maria to their clinic, but he wouldn't be seeing Maria again. The evening did not draw on late, but Harris was glad when the ladies got up to go, so that he could, too, without being rude. He was exhausted by the past two days' ups and downs, and he felt nervous on the way home, as if everyone he encountered might be Undertoe or a Whyo, watching him.

The following week, he and John-Henry met early at Lorraine's cart. There was quite a crowd of them gathered there, shivering in the wind while drinking coffee and eating pastries—in fact, everyone who had been down there when Waugh was lost. It was their first day back.

"I don't feel much like going back down, you?" one man asked Harris.

"No, me neither," he said. Then the whistle blew and they filed through the gate.

But before Harris got a chance to go down, a man in a black frock coat called him over to the office. "Mr. Harris! You're the same Harris who was working with the nigger on that boulder last week, before the blowout, is that right?" He wanted to cover his face with his hands. "Come into the office a moment, Harris."

He glanced around for John-Henry, but he was already down below.

"Now, Mr. Harris, you'll be glad to hear we're changing some of the safety rules around here, given what happened. But that doesn't help that poor bastard, Waugh, does it now?"

"No." Harris had the feeling the man wanted him to laugh ironically, but he just couldn't muster it. He was about to be sacked, and apparently this was how they let you down: with morbid ruminations. He thought about the street-paving crew. That job had been all right. They were putting in pavement all across Brooklyn, it seemed. Surely he could get that kind of work again. "I'll just pack up my tools and clothes and things and go."

"What? No, no, Mr. Harris. You *are* going to need a new set of tools, but don't go off on us. You've got your transfer topside, starting today—even if it's not the finest weather for it. This is the time of year we lose the tower workers, see. Damn cold up there. People in the company were impressed with the way you went after Waugh, tried to save him. That took some courage, showed dedication. And you do have experience with heights, I believe? We figure you could use a change, Mr. Harris. Welcome back aboveground."

Harris looked at the sky, which had started to throw down something approaching sleet. Now he did manage the quiet, ironic laugh he couldn't get out before.

Harris shook the supervisor's hand. He wasn't going to have to go down below anymore. It was like a miracle. Instead of digging down he'd be looking up at the dizzying sky, craning his neck, reaching overhead. He stood up straighter already at the prospect.

Topside didn't mean the top of the tower, though, and it didn't mean he was cutting stone. He was assigned to a crew that worked the derricks and cranes to raise the enormous blocks to the top of the tower. All day, he fastened the straps and wires and buckles that held the big stones. He hauled in and let out guylines as they were raised, up and up and up, to the top, where another crew laid the cement and did final trimming and set the great stones down perfectly in place. Harris wasn't cutting stone, and the blocks were larger and the rigs more complex than the ones he remembered from the Nikolaikirche, but the activity was a lot like what had gone on in Hamburg. He was full of awe and wonder and hope.

The following morning, a mild itch he'd been trying not to scratch since his visit to Maria blossomed into a terrible, florid case of what he hoped were only crabs. Harris was forced to see an apothecary, who gave him a stinking oily salve and a fine comb. When he stopped in to tell Mr. Noe about his promotion, his landlord raised a hand and sniffed the air exaggeratedly.

"Harris, my boy, I'm afraid I know that perfume . . . all too well. Terribly sorry."

They had a brief laugh over the costs and complications entailed by encounters such as Harris's with Maria.

"What you need, my boy, is a wife, hmmn?"

Harris didn't have an answer to that, so he told Mr. Noe about the job. Mr. Noe was delighted—half proud father, half enthusiastic friend.

So Harris was doing almost the job he'd dreamt of, living in relative calm with a couple of loyal friends. At least some of the lies he'd written to Koch had serendipitously come true. Perhaps it was good to envision fresh starts.

28

THE WESTFIELD

"Beanie, I saw him."

"Who?"

Fiona looked at her.

"Harris? Where? How did he look?"

"Actually, he was half drunk and nearly got himself run over the other day, so not too good, I'd say. But that's not the point. This time it's—"

" 'The other day'? 'This time'?"

At Fiona's request, the two Why Nots had met at the zoological garden in the park uptown. The newly planted cherry trees were still barren, the fields that were to become lawns were unseeded and muddy. They were standing in front of a cage where a family of cold-looking monkeys sat picking one another's nits. Down the path, a nervous-looking pair of zebras looked on. Otherwise, it was deserted. In a month or two, the crowds of people peering into the cages would make it well worth the time it took to get up there, from a pickpocket's point of view, but in early March the park was a place to go not to be seen or overheard.

"Yeah, there's a couple things I haven't told you. I've been keeping an eye on him as a favor to Mother D. I was under orders not to tell you. Plus, I didn't think it would do you any good to hear about it anyway. There was never really anything to report before."

"You've been watching him all this time? Working for Johnny, and I was kept out? What the Hell is the plan?"

The monkeys began to cackle, and Beatrice found it infuriating. She turned away and walked toward the zebras. She had been working her ass off for the Whyos in the past months, coming up with jobs, going out on jobs, keeping all the girls in line and making sure they were happy, adjudicating Why Not disputes. On top of which she had to play accountant at check-in. Every Tuesday at 2:00 P.M., everyone reported their earnings, and Johnny had taught her to record the information in a giant logbook; by 6:00, the tithings had been deposited at the till of the Morgue; her job was to calculate the account balance and credit line of every Whyo and Why Not to reflect their cut of the grand total. To be honest, she didn't know how he'd had time for it all before. It wasn't very glamorous, but the one thing she'd liked was that she thought she knew now pretty much everything that was going on. Apparently, she didn't. It made her angry, and she kicked a bench so hard it hurt her toe, despite the steel tips in her boots— a First Girl perk. Her chest felt wide open, empty. She didn't want Fiona to see her eyes well up, her face turn red, but Fiona followed her.

"Wait, come on. Don't go off. I need to talk to you."

"Why tell me now? Why ever tell me? Why not just let them fuck me over?"

"Beanie."

"All right then, *what* is going on? Why was I kept out? Am I the First fucking Girl, or are you?"

Fiona looked at her feet. "I don't really know what the plan is. She never told me. But I don't think Johnny's in on this. Mother Dolan just wanted me to keep an eye out and make sure he didn't rat us out. Maybe she, uh— I think she wanted to be sure you weren't seeing him. Harris, you know? But she also mentioned that it would good for us to know ahead of time if Undertoe did track him down, which I agreed with. Sorry." Fiona could barely maintain eye contact. She knew it sounded awful. It was awful. She had betrayed her friend.

"So if I had seen him, you would have reported me?"

"I don't know, I think I would have told you not to."

"Dammit, we told him he was free to go. I can't believe you."

"I'm sorry. But listen, the reason I'm telling you now is something's happened. Harris was in an accident at the bridge. And then he got hit by a carriage in the street. It's kind of like he was trying to get himself killed. And then, well, it was quite a spectacle. Everyone was staring, and Jimmy was there. And Harris spoke German to some hooker who recognized him. I think Jimmy recognized him, too, almost—he just couldn't quite place him. And since then he keeps saying he's sure he'll remember who it was, like it's eating him."

"So Harris's cover's wrecked? Shit. But the Jimster hasn't gone to Undertoe yet? What does he want? What's he going to do? I can get my hands on a lot of money, Fiona."

"First of all, Jimmy hasn't quite put it together yet. And I don't think we need money, really. The thing is, Jimmy's turned against Undertoe. He might not mind getting that bounty, but we'd be able to trust him if we brought him in. Can't you convince Johnny to try him out? He's a good guy."

Fiona and Beatrice decided to bring Jimmy into contact with Johnny, casually, at first, to plant the seed. It wasn't easy to arrange the outing—Johnny wasn't much for outings or dates—and in the meantime Beatrice considered confronting Mrs. Dolan, but she doubted it would gain her anything.

Instead, she made a point of eavesdropping on Johnny's audiences with his mother. She heard quite a lot—including that they were still skimming money from the gang revenue, though she didn't see any need for it, much less how they did it or where it came from. They said nothing at all about Harris, so far as she could learn, but she herself was one of their topics. Apparently, Mrs. Dolan wanted Johnny to marry her. Beatrice recoiled at the idea. Being First Girl had turned out not to be a romance at all, and she had to admit Johnny had been right that they weren't suited to each other in that way. He hadn't touched her in an age, and she was grateful. She didn't think she could brook the charade of a wedding to legitimize a business arrangement, especially when it just didn't seem necessary. Why would Mother Dolan want that? She'd always thought of her as such a feminist. She was the one who'd always insisted the Why Nots weren't chattel, after all; that this was America, and women should be free. The awful thing was, Beatrice found herself compelled to go out of her way to be sweet to Johnny, to butter him up, the very night she heard that, since she wanted him to join her and Fiona and Jimmy on an outing. She told herself as she half flirted with and half provoked him—for she'd learned that that was what he liked—that she was doing it for Harris's sake. It was essential that Johnny get to know Jimmy so Jimmy wouldn't jump back to Undertoe's camp. That night, she traded flesh and prostration and a few degrading remarks for Johnny's agreement to come to Coney Island on a little jaunt a fortnight hence. Not that Johnny knew the bargain worked that way—he was just feeling magnanimous—and not that there was any guarantee he would keep it.

In the meantime, Fiona's assignment was at once the same and much better: to cling to Jimmy's side, to do everything she could to make sure he didn't have a chance to think about that face and somehow suddenly remember that bounty and put the two together. It wasn't too difficult for her; the man she was manipulating with her wiles was also the man she wanted. She was mad about him, especially his arms, his muscled abdomen, his way of goofing off. She managed to distract him pretty well, she thought. She certainly exhausted herself.

It was a Sunday, just after the first spring buds had let loose, when the foursome finally took the ferry across to Brooklyn and then the train to Coney Island. It was before the season, but quite a few places were already open. They ate lobster at a little shack, then ventured down to the sand— just like regular people, not even working the crowd, not like gangsters at all. Beanie had told Johnny that the Jimster had feuded with Undertoe, setting the stage for Johnny's interest. It worked. They all had a good time, and the Jimster, though he was in the dark about it all, happened to say a couple of things that made his enmity for Undertoe obvious. Johnny thought it was a good idea the following week when Beatrice suggested that they take in an operetta at the Old Bowery as a group. Afterward, as they strolled, Jimmy and Johnny got to singing one of the bawdier tunes from the show, and together the two of them were considerably better than what they'd heard onstage. Johnny was obviously pleased. Beatrice and Fiona exchanged glances: It was almost too good. After serenading Five Points for a while, the foursome parted ways at the door of the Morgue. It was the start of the workday for all of them: Beatrice and Johnny started out at the bar, overseeing the settling of accounts. Fiona was headed out to roam the streets in search of her evening's mark, preferring to go by intuition rather than plan. As for the Jimster, he had a few ideas for how to kill the night, maybe try to get a faro game going. The Jimster had no real idea of how big the Whyos were, how much brighter his nightly prospects might soon be, or what exactly it might entail to work side by side with Fiona. He had no idea even that an interview had taken place, much less that Beatrice and Fiona had arranged it.

Undertoe was doing a bit of research of his own that night: He was over in Brooklyn again, taking in the sights at Barnum's latest venue, a three-ring circus under a tent that had just opened and was apparently meant to tide Barnum over till construction on his next museum was complete. Under-toe had to laugh at the idea of a tent—it was a uniquely, laughably inflam-mable sort of structure, in an ideal location for his purposes. He had not enjoyed the unceremonious way the Barnum's organization let him go, im-plying his security work was lax, when the American Museum wreckage was finally cleared away. He didn't even get an audience with the boss, which was just the latest in a long list of slights that bastard Barnum had perpetrated against him. Since his pesky friend Geiermeier was still elud-ing him and he was eager for a taste of vengeance, Undertoe had decided that Barnum's tent might be a nice opportunity to make things even again.

The night was humid, which was merciful on his eczema, and unsea-sonably warm, which was not. He scratched his neck gingerly with his long nails as he thought about who the dupe ought to be this time. He wasn't going to haul in a stranger again, that was for sure. Geiermeier was still a thorn he was hoping to pry out of his hide, but until that time he had no wish to repeat his mistake. Also, there was no question that he'd been wrong; he had entirely misjudged the man. From now on, he would stick to people he knew a little better. Appearances could be so deceiving. He took in the acrobatics and the animal shows, and they weren't half bad— though as usual none of them could compare to the brilliance of his mother's soprano-contortionist act, back in the day. He thought about the pride and happiness it had brought him as a boy to hear the Fabulous Lola

Unterzeh sing Mozart arias while standing on her hands with her legs entwined in the air, all decked out in red velvet sequinned jodhpurs. She'd been incomparable, had never been surpassed. Nowadays, all Barnum could manage was a fat lady who pierced her cheeks with nails and a boy who jumped between the backs of two trotting horses, as if anyone wanted to see that junk. The real art of it, of course, was to combine the high and the low, culture and acrobatics, but apparently such multitalented performers were rare. When the circus shut down for the night, Undertoe took a final stroll around, casing the periphery, then caught a hansom cab back to the ferry pier. As he boarded the *Robert Fulton*, an idea came to him. *The Jimster*. He'd more than once noticed him down around Fulton Ferry, meeting a Five Points girl who had apparently moved to Brooklyn. Undertoe had a bad feeling toward the kid. He had distanced himself ever since Undertoe had graduated Sing Sing, as if he were too good to work with his old pal now. The Jimster would deserve whatever he got. First, he thought he'd put a little pressure on the wench and get her in on it, against Jimmy — it shouldn't be too difficult, with some decent money and a threat or two, just to be sure. She didn't look all too pure. From there, it would be a cinch, and in the end he could dump the girl, too, just for neatness. Yes, thought Undertoe, it was just about time for the Jimster to go.

When he looked into it, however, he encountered certain unexpected twists. Following the girl around Brooklyn took him to the Noe house, but she clearly didn't live there. (The only female in residence was the crone who worked in the kitchen.) In fact, it seemed she was there for reasons akin to his own: surveillance. But of what, exactly? Undertoe was puzzled. The house wasn't wealthy enough to merit such close scrutiny. Perhaps the girl wasn't in love with the Jimster at all but the stableboy who lived in the barn, he thought. Or possibly she was the illegitimate daughter of the house's master, plotting her blackmail. At any rate, he tailed her home to Manhattan one night, and that was how he learned she was associated with Johnny Dolan. As he watched her go up to the top-floor apartment, he scowled, raked a scab on his neck and dabbed it with his fingers when it bled. This made the whole idea of setting them up more appealing, more pressing, but also more delicate.

Harris was having a lovely summer, working on the floating pier that surrounded the Brooklyn tower. Even when the streets were hot and stank of rotting trash, the river was glorious and breezy. On the most sweltering days, the men would jump in for a swim at the end of their shifts. All day long, Harris stood in the wind, moving great stone blocks on flatcars from the delivery scow to the hoisting station, fitting the edges into the wire harness for lifting or working the controls of the boom derricks. He was fascinated by the workings of the various steam-driven engines and boom rigs. Everything was vastly more modern and mechanized than what had been used on the Nikolaikirche, but he was a fast learner, a good worker, and at the end of summer he was tapped to work at the top of the tower.

The day that he first picked his way across the catwalk that stretched thrillingly far out over the river, the tower itself was shrouded in fog and low-lying clouds, so that the space seemed almost walled in, as if one could walk upon the lead-colored ocean of air that surrounded the tower. By midday, however, it had burned off, and the two cities and their river reappeared. Harris and his fellow workmen were standing as high as any man yet had ever stood above New York harbor, or for that matter anyplace in the world. When he saw that view, his exultation was almost suicidal—he had to fight the urge to see if he could fly. But of course he didn't do it. His depression had long since lifted. The glorious act of watching the tower rise above the city, a bit higher and farther away from Five Points every day, saved him from himself.

The Saturday following his promotion, Harris made plans for a celebratory excursion to the country with the Henleys. The weather was brutally hot, and the Irish had rioted in the streets the day before—refighting the Battle of Boyne, as Beanie might have said. Sometimes Harris's Irish identity was harder for him to own than others. He wondered if the Whyos had gotten mixed up in it. At any rate, he and the Henleys had decided to go to the beach on Staten Island to get away from it all and cool off. When he arrived at their house, he was only slightly surprised to see Susan Smith and Sarah Blacksall. He had grown used to finding them there almost every time he came, but of late he had begun to feel awkward in front of Dr. Blacksall. She was slightly too curious about him, pressed him from time to time to detail his family background, to share his own scientific coming-of-age stories and to explain why he had forsaken the family profession.

"It wasn't the family profession, just my father's, and he was not an easy man to follow."

"Oh," she said, backing off. "I'm sorry."

But it wasn't long before the topic of her sewage-testing project came up—she was hoping to start it up again, unofficially, just by going down and taking samples on her own—and she encouraged him to join forces with her.

Harris blinked. He was not eager to go back there and revisit that world. But Sarah Blacksall wanted only to conduct a study, to collect knowledge to help people. It would be different than before. He had told himself he wanted to do something to make good, and this might be it. It was odd, the idea of a friendship with a woman, but he liked Dr. Blacksall. She had a large straight nose with just a small aristocratic bump at the bridge, a wide intelligent smile, a high furrowed brow. And she was a doctor, like his father. When he envisioned the two of them going down a manhole, it summoned uncontrollable thoughts of Beatrice in the grotto and he went quite red, but finally he stammered yes, he would do it.

"Well," said Lila, "everything ready, ladies? Let's go, I want to get out on the water!"

The plan was to take the ferry across the harbor and spend the day on one of the white-sand beaches of Staten Island. Harris hadn't been there since his first outing, so long ago, when he was still working at Barnum's, surviving on his own, before the fire and prison, the Whyos and Beatrice, the bridge and Mr. Noe. He'd enjoyed the wide beaches and grassy dunes so much, so innocently then, even though it was winter, and he'd meant to return again as soon as the weather was warm. Now years had passed, but at last the time had come. Harris imagined hot sand, spicy beach flowers sprawling on gray-green foliage across the dunes, the constant, quiet-noisy crashing of the ocean, umbrellas and boardwalks across the dunes.

They all walked down to Whitehall Street together, Harris beside Sarah Blacksall. He asked her more about her study and thought about whether he could ever tell her who he was, ever mention Robert Koch and his father. Probably not, for that would also entail telling her the dark side of his own history. Then, with her impeccable conversational politeness, she asked him about the work he was doing now on the bridge. He told just the usual repertoire of stories of antics and benign mishaps, some of which she'd heard before—a lady who'd gone up the catwalk to the tower and been too frightened to walk back down; a hammer dropped from the top that narrowly missed a man below. Harris was scrupulous about not diverging from his safe set of characters and anecdotes. If he was tempted to say more, he just had to remember Fiona and the possibility that he was being observed at that very moment, and his lust for such things faded.

They weren't the only New Yorkers with the idea of beating the heat that day. There was a crowd waiting at the terminal to board the next boat. When the iron sides of the steam ferry *Westfield* squealed against the pilings and the crewmen threw the hawser and hauled the gangway into place, the disembarking passengers surged forward. There was nothing unusual about such a throng, given the weather—nothing unusual at all, except for the fact that suddenly Harris saw a face within it. Ruddy cheeks and coppery hair and a rather grim frown on her lips. He blinked, but it was still Beatrice.

"John-Henry!" Harris had entirely forgotten the existence of Sarah Blacksall, though she stood beside him, following his eyes.

"Hmmn?"

"Look. It's her. Right there." Harris whispered in the way that makes it louder.

"What, now? Who?"

Harris just stared, didn't answer.

"Oh, no, not her, not that girl. Harris, you're done with her, man."

"No, I'm not." He entirely missed Sarah Blacksall's pinched smile because now he was staring at Dandy Johnny. The Whyos' boss was looking especially dapper in a white suit and a boater with a dark-blue ribbon. Harris couldn't have hated the sight of him any more even if he had known that John Dolan had just been married to Beatrice O'Gamhna by the priest of a small Catholic church on Staten Island, in a secret ceremony attended only by Mrs. Dolan, Fiona and the sexton.

Mrs. Dolan had the bee in her bonnet, and she'd prevailed. She always did. The explanation? She had decided she wanted a grandson. The Dolans had money enough now that Johnny's child would be able to live a life of leisure, not crime, and she didn't want her grandchild saddled with being a bastard. It had been lethal for Johnny—that was how she thought of the chain of causality, at least. She didn't tell him of her notions, but she had badgered and badgered until Johnny had acquiesced. Beatrice had had damn little choice in the matter. She was miserable. It was something she had been determined not to do since she'd first heard the plan, and yet it had been unavoidable, and now there she was, a bride.

Early that morning, before she knew Mother Dolan's plan for the day, Johnny had awakened her, horny. He was stroking her cheek gently, kissing her neck, pulling her up from the mattress and tugging at her bedclothes. Soon, he was grinding himself against her thigh, and she found that she responded. She wanted it, too. If he was going to be nice, maybe she could even enjoy it. And he was. At least he wasn't rough like usual. His hands had ranged widely and gently across her body. She hardly knew what to think, it was so unexpected. She felt a slight twinge within her, on the left, just before he put himself inside her. She told herself to relax. She imagined the small pain was an anticipation of the frequent twinges whenever he fucked her, either from him or the lemon rind. But this time there was no lemon.

Beatrice could have no idea of it, of course, but what she had felt was an egg being spat into play by her ovary. She pushed against his push, bent her knees, raised up. They writhed and turned, and he let her get on top of him. But not for long. Suddenly, he flipped her over, and he was on top again, and there was nothing slow about it anymore. His eyes seemed glazed over, but he didn't strike her once or insult her. She had no idea what she was feeling, but it wasn't pain. Then it peaked—not much of a peak for Beatrice, but still a peak—and afterward they slept, like regular lovers. So that when he woke her and told her to get dressed nicely, they were going on an outing and getting married, she was won over enough not to argue.

Now she was married to him. She didn't like the legality of it, and frankly she'd been called *Mrs. Dolan* several times too many on the ferry ride back. She had told herself over and over again that it wasn't markedly different than before. Her life wouldn't change. She certainly didn't expect things to go on being nice, like that morning. That had obviously been a rhetorical move, a seduction, like the first night, and she felt like a sucker, which was part of why she was in such a bad mood.

Then, as the ferry docked and the crowd lurched forward, she looked up at an apparition: Harris, gawping at her. *Harris?* She didn't believe it. It was just a reaction to the emotions she was feeling, she thought, but she looked again. He wasn't an apparition. What was he doing there? She didn't want to see him. Not then.

"Beatrice," Harris said, not loudly, across the wide space of the pier. But she heard. Her squinty eyes looked straight at him. She didn't smile or acknowledge him, except that her mouth dropped open and the scowl fell away from her features, leaving them empty, blank.

She pushed forward through the crowd, ahead of Johnny and his mother, eyes fixed on Harris. Then she stopped right next to him, said nothing, looked down, rooted around in her handbag.

"Harris, look the other way," she said. "What are you doing here? No, don't look at me, look away."

So Harris looked out, into the crowd. He saw Dandy Johnny standing by the rail, letting people pass him, but he didn't know that Johnny was waiting for his mother to get through the crowd. Beatrice did. She had just a few seconds to talk to him in semiprivacy.

"Harris, how are you? Are you all right?"

That was when the trembling began. It started with a hard little rock of mineral deposit that blocked a crucial valve of the *Westfield's* tremendous boiler. Things would have gone better had a sloppily soldered seam in the coupling that joined the main boiler to the intake valve not been repaired just the week before. But it had been. The system was tight. Too tight. And not redundant enough. There was no backup valve. The pressure mounted and mounted, and soon the copper pipes that interlinked the tanks began to gyrate, straining against their fittings. The main tank was humming ominously a song it had never sung. The glass shield on a pressure gauge cracked, releasing a thin jet of steam, but it was not enough.

Mrs. Dolan would have been overjoyed if she had known that Johnny's sperm was just then merging with Beatrice's ovum. Two gametes fused; a zygote was born; Beanie's X met Johnny's Y. Meg Dolan had no idea how well her little plan had worked—how *promptly*—to produce an heir. She was thinking of another baby while the pressure in the engine mounted, recalling how lovely an infant her Johnny-boy had been. She was musing on how handsome he'd looked that morning at the altar. Meg Dolan was delighted in all the most conventional ways that morning. Her dreams for her son had come true, if not quite in the ways she might once have planned. She was feeling more religious than she had in years. She had enjoyed the wedding immensely. She was feeling grateful to God. So she barely noticed the vibrations at first, what with the throng of passengers and the usual thrumming of the ferryboat engine beneath the deck. But then came the first loud bang, and it was definitely not normal. Then a jolt. Her head jerked, and she looked in front of her and caught a brief and baffling glimpse of Beatrice and none other than Frank Harris, staring into one another's eyes like lovers. *Frank Harris.* It had to be a mistake. The crease between her eyebrows deepened.

Then came the shrieking sound of metal and the blast that shattered windows all across the harbor and resounded up the two rivers, into Brooklyn and New Jersey, and as far north as Twenty-third Street. The fireball itself consumed everything within a fifty-foot circle. Mrs. Dolan was gone. Johnny was just far away enough to be hurtled forward by the blast, and he went somersaulting through the air, ax-blade boots over boater. He landed against a railing on the pier and found he couldn't see. Blood was dripping into his eyes. He could not stand.

"Mother!"

Beatrice was facing the other way, looking at Harris, when the screeching of metal began. She never saw Mrs. Dolan's end nor Johnny's flight, but Harris had seen it all.

"Harris!" she shrieked, turning around, pressing into him. He couldn't actually hear her voice through the blast, but he saw her mouth his name. Then hot soot filled the air, and they were moved forward by the undulations of the panicking crowd. Harris grasped her around the waist and she clung to him, and they strove together just to remain upright, not to be trampled.

When the air began to clear, he looked down at her, then back at the boat. The ferry was sinking fast, what remained of it, and there were still passengers clinging to the rails. Some of them would soon be sucked under by the *Westfield's* pull. Others were so badly burned it was irrelevant. Plenty were already dead. Maybe, Harris thought, Johnny would be one of those. Harris had entirely forgotten the rest of his outing party: the Henleys, Susan Smith, Sarah Blacksall. There were screams and cries and groans in the air, and soon one of them singled itself out from the others: a full-throated, musical, undisguised whyo of the unsubtle kind the boys used back in Googy Corcoran's day, except sadder, more desperate, and somehow more beautiful. Then Johnny called out again, in English: *"Beanie!"*

Then Harris saw him: Johnny was staggering, grasping a rail. His face was bloody. Behind him, Harris could see the stern of the boat tipping up and slowly sinking from sight. Johnny's light summer suit was all black and red and seemed to be getting redder as he stood there, blindly crying Beanie's name into the crowd. Perhaps he was dying, thought Harris with an unexpected pity as Johnny bellowed. But he was not, alas. In the end, Johnny's only permanent physical mark from the accident would be a shallow, curved scar that followed the contour of his eyebrow and stretched toward his cheekbone.

"Harris, I'm so sorry about everything," he heard Beanie say. She was very pale. "I *was* in love with you. But now I have to go." Then she stepped away from him and ran to her husband, who was now bellowing, *"Mother!"*

Harris watched her go. He saw that the spreading stain on Johnny's suit was not his own blood. It came from something he was holding: an arm. It was all that was left of her. The rest of Meg Dolan's body was in bits.

Harris thought of all the baths she had drawn for him, of the letter she had given him that had stayed his execution. He looked back at Johnny and saw Beatrice was with him. They cradled the arm in an unholy pietà. Harris was crying for so many reasons.

Some time later, John-Henry found him. "There you are. Let's get out of here, Harris. You can't do anything. And your girlfriend, she's got her own people now. Come on."

"What about Sarah? And Lila and Susan and Liza?"

"Sarah's helping people. She's a doctor. She'll be fine."

29

SANCTUARY

Undertoe sat down to peruse the sheet of newspaper his breakfast had come wrapped in. It was greasy from the meat pie, but he was pleased enough to have gotten the front page and curious to learn the details of the weekend's disaster. The death toll had been said, on the street, to be in the hundreds, but he saw that it was actually just in the dozens. So far, only twenty-six had officially been declared dead, with roughly the same number predicted soon to expire from their injuries. It was nothing, really, compared to the number that had died the day before in the riot, which had the added advantage of taking out mostly Micks. Still, he was curious and read on. When he saw that the engineer on the boat had been a Negro, he snorted. The only wonder was that the man had worked for the ferry line so long—thirteen years, the paper said—without prior mishap. And naturally, the Negro had lived. Undertoe scanned the list of names of the dead. When he saw *Margaret Dolan*, he felt a flutter in his chest—sorrow? Or glee? Had old Mother Dolan really been exploded? There were probably any number of Margaret Dolans in New York, but he took note of the location and time of the funeral, later that evening. In this heat, there was no time to spare. As for the services not scheduled till the following week, he realized those were the cases where nothing was left and gave a little laugh. Then he balled up the sheet of newsprint and swallowed the last of his beer. He flagged down the barmaid and ordered two cups of sweet black coffee and a shot of rye.

"You know we don't sell coffee here, Mr. U.," she said. But both of them had been through this routine before.

"Go buy it for me, come on." He flipped her a quarter and then, when she sneered at it, another.

The whiskey-and-coffee combination was one of his usual remedies for turning down the volume of the ringing in his ears, which had just started up again, but that day Undertoe's cure came too late. The ringing just got louder. On another day, he might have checked into Wah Kee's when it got this loud or at least bought himself a phial of laudanum and holed up in his room till it waned, but he wanted to attend the Dolan funeral.

All that day, in the wake of the accident, Harris thought not of Beatrice, not of Mrs. Dolan, but of his mother. He didn't understand why he kept seeing her face, but it wasn't unwelcome, despite the fact that the clearest image he'd retained of her came not from life but from the daguerreotype that had dominated the mantelpiece, draped in a length of black crepe, the year after she died. She looked a bit strict—as if she'd just seen him do something naughty—dramatic and terribly elegant. The photograph had been made in her hotel room at Baden-Baden, he knew, because he recognized the gleaming mahogany pineapple ornament on the back of the chair she sat in. He'd sat on her lap in that chair during his very last visit with her, and to his lasting regret he'd looked more at the pineapples than her face. He'd squirmed and jumped down and run off to play and never seen her again. It was only years later, on a Christmas visit to his father's, that he understood the picture's eerie sharpness, a function of its subject's perfect stillness for the long exposure: It was posthumous. The lights had been arranged so as to cast her closed eyes in shadow—that gave the feeling of drama to her otherwise slack features. And once you understood the context, the odd drape of her gown confirmed that the image had been captured with the subject lying down, the chair laid flat on the floor so the image read correctly when displayed at ninety degrees from the truth.

And so, when Harris made up his mind to go to Mother Dolan's funeral, he told himself it was all about grieving for his own mother, whose funeral he'd missed so long ago, being too ill himself even to know she had died.

He was not going to the funeral for Mother Dolan. He was not going to see Beatrice. That's what he told himself, at least.

The church that night was packed. People of all sorts turned out, even people who never knew her, simply because the accident and the time of the service had been in the news. The whole metropolis was grieving, and the same was true for a dozen other victims at a dozen other churches that day. The aisles were full of people searching the overflowing pews for places to sit, and he let himself be swept along with the tide of mourners past the chancel. The coffin was closed, which was unusual for the Irish. Harris tried not to think about what was in it or how light it would be. When he'd circled almost to the exit again without finding a seat anywhere, he availed himself of the small stairway at the back up to the balcony.

Just as Harris went upstairs, Luther Undertoe arrived, and he walked the same circuit, eventually ending up in the balcony, too, but on the other side, directly opposite Harris. Harris did not see him, but a short time after he felt a sudden urge to leave. He looked up, wondering if it were just a commonsense nervousness that had descended on him. He knew it was not entirely wise for him to thrust himself into a Whyo affair. Looking up, he caught the eye of a man he recognized: not Undertoe but Piker Ryan. Piker was staring at him, and it was not a welcoming look. It was slightly painful to Harris, after their warm encounter in the dirt-catcher, but it seemed clear that Piker was telling him to go. He was not wanted there. He probably shouldn't have come in the first place. Reluctantly, he rose and made his way to the back of the balcony, toward the stairs. Before he left, though, he turned back once more—one last chance to catch a glimpse of Beatrice, but she was nowhere. What he saw instead was Piker again, who was now staring across the nave at a blond head in the far balcony. Undertoe. So Piker had not just been ejecting him; he'd been trying to keep him from Undertoe's line of sight. Harris felt a surge of affection for the gangster he'd once thought would be the one to kill him. Piker Ryan was saving his skin. Harris bowed his head, half to hide himself, half in a gesture of wordless prayer to Mrs. Dolan, before he went downstairs.

As for Piker and the other Whyos, managing this crowd was more difficult than even the p.o. job. First of all, they were emotional, not at the top of their form. Johnny in particular was a basket case, leaving them rudderless. And the whole situation—the concentration of Whyos, the size of the crowd, the limited number of escape routes—was inadvisable. It had been problematic even before both Undertoe and Harris had arrived. It was an outright violation of the basic Whyo strategy of stealth. They were there only because Johnny had demanded it. But Johnny wasn't helping with the crowd control. Beatrice did her best to orchestrate the efforts of the whole gang alone, but it wasn't easy. There were police officers in the congregation, and then there was Undertoe upstairs, not to mention Harris. As far as she could tell, Piker was doing his boneheaded best to set them up to meet each other on the stairs, which was the opposite of what they wanted. She did what she could, but she didn't have as elaborate a vocabulary as Johnny. No one had that. That was why he was the boss.

Harris looked back as the organ struck up "Nearer, My God, to Thee," and the congregation rose. He saw Beatrice now, proceeding down the center aisle with the monsignor and Johnny, and it made him feel ready to go. He shot a last furtive glance across to check on Undertoe, but now Undertoe was gone. Had he seen him, too? Harris dared not go, dared not stay. He scanned the corridor and saw a low doorway at the end of the hall, so low it seemed child-size. There were doors like that leading off the balconies of the Nikolaikirche. They led to back stairwells that enabled clergy and sextons to navigate the church quietly and unobtrusively. The knob didn't turn, but there was no keyhole either, and it had a familiar feel. Harris lifted the knob and raised the door slightly, over a catch. It slid smoothly to the right on a runner—a clever ecclesiastical design that allowed quick access with a minimum of key rattling during services. A rush of cool, musty air hit him. Harris was blind at first, but it didn't take long for his eyes to adjust to the small amount of light let in by the narrow, slotlike window set high in the tower wall. Spiral stairs led down; above, a ladder ascended in darkness to the belfry. Harris left footprints in the dust on the treads and kicked up divots of matted dust as he tiptoed his way down, around and around.

Undertoe had indeed also received an ill-timed subvocal suggestion from Piker. If both men had followed Piker's guidance, they certainly would have met on the stair. But Undertoe was too ornery to respond to Piker's urgings. He fought the uncontrollable twitching in his legs and the confusing impulse to leave the building, which seemed bafflingly, for all the world, to come from himself, although he knew he wanted to stay. He looked around as the music swelled and thought about who was there and why. It occurred to him there were an awful lot of former newsboys there, other men whose faces were vaguely familiar from the Five Points, men with knife scars and no jobs. Had they all been in the choir? Was that how they knew Mrs. Dolan? Then he noticed another face, just across from him, that was curiously familiar. He wasn't a Five Points native or an ex-newsboy, of that Undertoe was fairly certain. He was agitated, and his skin was crawling, and his ears were ringing. He was feeling pretty awful, really, and wondered if that meat pie had been bad. What was it that was keeping him from placing the man's face? He had seen him somewhere before. He took a couple of deep breaths and then reached down to rake an un-quellable itch on his ankle. As he leaned down into the darkness, the man's face materialized for him. Those black eyes, that beard. If only he could see him from another angle, he was sure he'd have known who he was. He sat back up and looked over to examine his face again.

Harris was just standing up, and as he navigated the aisle his jaw was briefly obscured by a lady's hat. Undertoe blinked in astonishment. He had it: The beard was new. But the rest of it—the nose and the black eyes and the broad, bulging brow—all belonged to George the Torch Geiermeier, alias Will Williams, the elusive dupe who'd caused him so much trouble. Undertoe forgot his queasiness and the death of Mother Dolan entirely. A thrill was surging through him. Finding George Geiermeier could turn his fortunes entirely around. It could bring him back into favor with the cops and earn him a pile of money. Above all, it would give him a chance at pay-back. He had much to be paid for: the humiliation of looking like a fool in front of Lieutenant Jones, the unsporting way he had been rolled and drugged and set up and sent upriver, a crime for which he was now more certain than ever that the stableman was responsible. But then another shiver of recognition went through him: If the German stableman was at Mother Dolan's funeral, then he must somehow be in cahoots with Johnny Dolan. Were they both to blame for doping him and getting him locked up? He touched the knife in his ankle holster and then stood up. He also looked around the room with fresh eyes, searching for familiar faces, that bathroom attendant, that elusive guy from the Bowery. Were they all in on it then, that whole lame group of guys that drank at the Morgue and called themselves the Whyos? The face that surprised him was the Jimster's. He had no reason to be there, none at all, not unless he was with them, too.

Undertoe felt a wave of nausea—partly his own horror, but partly what the Whyos were doing to him. Piker had seen him notice Harris and realized the blunder. Now he was using every power he had to keep Undertoe seated. But Undertoe had at last realized that the Whyos were something larger than he'd thought. He realized he was deep in hostile terrain. Beatrice had been watching him and working on him, too. She saw the moment when his face changed. *Goddamnit*, she thought, he had identified Harris. He was peering around the room with a panicked air. How much else did he know? They were going to have to do something about him and fast, but the priest was just taking the pulpit. Now was a very bad time.

Undertoe broke free of their control and left his seat. He felt the saliva flowing fast, and he doubted he could contain the contents of his stomach till he got outside. *That Goddamned meat pie*, he thought, though in truth the pie was innocent. His gut heaved as he galloped down the stairs and into the entryway. Just outside the church doors, he spit up some sour flecks of bread and chum. His gut was writhing, and he knew he had probably lost the trail of Geiermeier for the moment, but dry heaves and bile were nothing in the face of Undertoe's rising glee, the pleasure and power of understanding. Undertoe took some trouble to walk the streets surrounding the church on the off chance of finding Geiermeier again, but he had no luck. He was in a fine temper nonetheless. Now that he knew the guy was still in New York and in the Whyo circle and wore a beard, and now that he'd realized the Whyos were up to more than met the eye, he was confident he would find him again without much trouble. On a deserted street, a few minutes south of the church, he actually stepped over a passed-out drunk of the sort he was famous for prematurely putting down. He had no desire to gut him at all—he was in too good a mood. Beatrice had hastily sent a Why Not out to follow him, but he didn't do much, and she didn't learn anything. Everything of interest with regard to Luther Undertoe was going on inside his skull.

Harris, meanwhile, hadn't left the building after all. From the stairwell, he found a passageway that led back behind the altar, and once he determined that Undertoe hadn't followed him and no one was after him, he allowed himself to listen to the funeral mass from there. The acoustics were such that the collective murmur of the churchful of voices reverberated through his body, and he found the sensation greatly soothing. Not being able to see made it only more so. After the recessional had ended, he waited almost an hour, just to be sure he wouldn't see anyone he ought not to, and then left the church through a back exit, life and limb quite intact, at least for the time being.

30.

THE LIONESS

eatrice gave Johnny a fried egg on a biscuit and a boilermaker when they got home from the funeral. He ate and drank with his shoulders stooped, ignoring a thin mix of mucus and tears that was dripping from his nose. He was still like that an hour later, when she pulled off his clothes and led him to bed. She was too weary to cry, herself. The funeral had very nearly been a disaster. She could have killed Harris for coming, and yet it had been the only bright instant in the day when she looked up and saw him. If only he could have managed to be there in a way less likely to get himself hanged and all of them locked up. But then, she thought, he wouldn't have been Harris.

Johnny called her over to him some time later and asked her to lie beside him. She put her arms around him as he cried, and somewhat to her amazement she finally did, too, very quietly. It had been grotesque, the explosion, unreal, even more so in the context of meeting Harris on the pier. She cried for any number of reasons, not just for Mother Dolan's death, not least because she was left with Johnny as her husband while the one person who had wanted them married was gone. Finally, he fell asleep, but she lay awake a long time, horrified, hating her life, wondering how she'd come to this. She'd started out with the best intentions, hadn't she? Even when she'd joined the Why Nots, she had been thinking of Padric above all.

She had sent more than enough money back for him to join her by now, but he gave it all to the Fenians, the Nationalists, Parnell. When she'd sent a ticket instead of money once, he'd sold it back to the steamship line at a loss. Recently, he'd written to her to say that he was a patriot and he was never coming over. She was alone. And the justification she had given herself for leading the life she did was gone. She let her mind wander to their mum, knowing she had let her down. She hadn't had much of a life, really—just thirty years, too short to raise her children right. Her da got a little longer, but he was more of a barfly than a homebody. She and Padric had been alone a lot at the end. It had seemed the best chance for both of them, after Da died, for her to use every last dime of their money for the passage across the Atlantic. She'd felt guilty, but she'd thought Padric would be following her soon. Instead, the cousins who took him in had dumped Padric with the Catholic brothers soon thereafter, and then in America money was harder to come by and life more expensive than she could have imagined. By the time she had the money, Padric had committed himself to his cause.

America was what her parents had left her, she thought—the insurance money, the pin. She had invested their legacy the best she knew how, but they wouldn't have been happy with the results. She had split up with her brother. She had taken up with criminals. She *was* a criminal. It wasn't anyone's American dream. The only thing about her life her mother would have approved of was that she was married at last, though that was a sham. Still, it was all she had. She slipped her arms around Johnny Dolan, her husband, and tried to sleep. She told herself that she would find a way, that there was hope.

It was bright outside when Beatrice sat up again. She heard bells tolling in the two nearby church towers—the Catholic one was always just a few seconds later than the Lutheran, and so there was a kind of echo to the time. She counted the strokes: twelve. She shook Johnny awake.

"The report, Johnny. It's noon. It's Tuesday. You've got to get up and do the report or people're going to wonder."

He opened an eye and closed it, then just lay there flat on his back and breathed. He didn't speak. Beatrice went and brewed a pot of tea and brought it to him, but he ignored her. Such grief was to be expected in a normal man. But this was Johnny Dolan, the boss. There was a gang to run.

It wouldn't take long for the entire system to crumble if the accounts weren't logged and the take collected and disbursed. But Beatrice couldn't do it herself.

"Johnny," she urged.

"Leave me alone."

"You can't sleep this off like a hangover. There's a lot of people working for you, and you're not going to stay their boss for long if you act like this."

After a long time, he propped himself up on his elbows. He looked awful.

"I can do the books for you, Johnny, but you have to talk to them. You're the one with the voice."

"I told you once that she covered for me."

So it was his mother who'd covered for him—and given him the broken nose.

"No," she said. "You never told me that. Not that it was her. You only told me that someone did."

"She did it more than once."

"What are you saying?" Beatrice was trying to picture Mother Dolan whyoing in Johnny's voice, and to her surprise, she could: She was his mother, she had taught him to sing, he had her throat.

"Just what I said. It was really her gig. Sharing the profits, the secret codes, all that. Everything. I don't really give a shit about any of it anymore. We've got enough money."

Beatrice felt light-headed, as if she were seeing him from a distance. It was suddenly so obvious and yet totally shocking: The whole Five Points commune idea, the whole vision of the Whyos in the era since Googy Corcoran had not been Johnny's, had never been Johnny's. That wasn't the kind of guy he was.

"All right, Johnny," she said, struggling not to show her alarm. She had to find a way to keep Johnny from ruining it all, not just for her but for all of them, especially the girls. Then she thought of Harris, and it occurred to her the dissolution of the Whyos wouldn't be the worst thing in the world. It might even be better. But it wouldn't be so easy for her, it wouldn't be over. She wouldn't just be free, and it wouldn't be as simple as the gang and all it entailed vanishing overnight. There would be knife fights, turf battles, pistols fired, old feuds resumed, unfinished business to conclude. If Johnny wasn't boss, someone else would be, at least for a while. What would her status be then? And what about her girls? A post-Dolan gang wasn't likely to maintain such progressive policies regarding the Why Nots for long. And on the other hand, unbreakable vows would not be lightly dissolved. Nobody would want anybody who knew what the gang had done going straight. "But you can't let the whole system collapse just because you're not interested anymore. It's a responsibility. Teach someone else how to run it, then you can retire. But don't let it end just because your mother's dead."

He got out of bed, and at first she was encouraged; then he lunged for her. He struck the side of her head, not powerfully, but she was off guard. She stumbled and fell against the bedstead. She touched the underside of her chin and found a wet, numb flap. Her fingers were smudged red.

"Don't ever say that, Beanie. Don't say *dead*. I don't like that word."

He sounded full of rage, and she gathered herself as quickly as she could, not knowing how bad this might get. Just in case, she wanted to have something to defend herself with, something like a poker. Her knife was all the way across the room, in the drawer by the bed, inaccessible. A brass-handled walking stick in the corner was the nearest weapon. Her mind filled with dark visions of both the future and the next few minutes—how the Whyos would collapse, how she would leap up and grab for the cane and strike—but then Johnny knelt down and spoke softly.

"I'm sorry," he said. "I didn't mean to do that. I need you, as much as I needed Mother. It's only, just don't say anything disrespectful, all right?"

"It's not disrespect, Johnny. I couldn't be sorrier. But she *is* dea—"

He grabbed her by the face before she could finish the word, his fingers pinching her nose and his palm across her lips. She could feel the ripped flap of skin under her chin being stretched painfully as he turned her face to his. But the thing that mattered was the lack of breath. She felt her eyes bug, her face turn red. She struggled, but he squeezed so hard in response that she quit resisting.

He spoke slowly. Clearly, he wasn't going to let her draw a breath until he'd said his piece. "I know she's gone. I know it too well. But I won't have it put crudely, not that way. You will say *she is in Heaven* or *she passed away* if you must mention it at all, which I wish you wouldn't."

It almost made her happy, hating him. Partly it was just the delirium of hypoxia, but it was also true that his threatening manner, his irrationality and his violence all triggered the same awful thrill she'd had down at the Bowery that first night. He was still a nasty gangster, despite crying for his dead mother, and there was something terribly erotic about that. When he let go, she fell back gasping, but then, as soon as she'd caught her breath, she turned angry. She wheeled herself around toward him, arm cocked, wanting to get a return blow in even if it meant he broke her nose in response, but then her arm floated back down to her side. He had crumpled again, collapsed like a pudding from the oven. His shoulders were hunched, and he rubbed his eyes like a child. She squinted at him, weighing pity and caution against practical concerns.

"What you're going to do, Johnny," she said, "is just a sort of minimal check-in tonight, not a full report, which should be fine, considering. But you have to do something. We'll figure it out from there."

A little while later, he actually went over to the window, took a deep breath and began to whistle and warble and sing bits of songs—it was the signature call he used to begin the report, but he wasn't projecting much at all. No one would be able to hear it more than a block away. Then his breath failed entirely.

"I can't," he said. "We were going to train you to do it. We should have done that."

"Well, train me now. It's her legacy—you have to keep it up somehow." To Beanie, it was much more than Mrs. Dolan's legacy; it was two dozen girls' freedom.

"All right." He was a wreck, but not as pathetic as she'd thought.

Everyone in the gang thought Johnny's voice was special, uniquely capable of switching keys and jumping octaves rapidly, creating complex messages in counterpoint. Now she learned it wasn't really his voice that was the key. It was an extra layer of hidden meaning embedded within the common vocabulary of whyoing. Mrs. Dolan had been the private voice coach of every new initiate, and she'd trained them like the sheepdogs that were her inspiration: to perform flawlessly without ever knowing the larger picture. Johnny was the front man, but the problem was that Johnny hadn't ever entirely mastered his mother's repertoire. He had always let her prompt him, coach him, and he couldn't do it alone. On the streets he might be king, but the bookkeeping, the accounts and the complex personal codes she'd devised were all her bailiwick.

"Did she keep a record of any sort, with notes about the codes?"

She did, and they found it, which meant they had something to fall back on.

"You know the script better than you think, I'd guess," she said. She hoped so anyway. "The rest we'll figure out. But what about Maggie the Dove? Does she know? Or Piker? Isn't there anyone else who can help?" She was really thinking, *Who else knows? Is there a rival out there, a challenger?*

"Maggie never did have the mind for it—or the voice. She's just a beautiful, wonderful whore, not a schemer. And mother wouldn't hear of bringing Piker in."

And so Johnny roused himself sufficiently to start the check-in. They went out onto the terrace and he made contact with the gang, all the while looking things up in the ledger to double-check the notes and stopping to explain to Beanie what it all meant. He did know it, in a muscle-memory way, and the ledger contained enough information to remind him of the things his mother used to think of for him. But clearly he didn't like doing it alone—that is, with Beatrice rather than his mother. For some of the easier signals, he had her practice quietly till she got it right, and then she called it out herself. She was a quick study. Her ear was good.

That night, people said Johnny sounded awful (and whether it was Johnny or Beatrice imitating him, they were right), but the performance was written off to grief. Within a week, Beatrice was pretty much there, vocally. He had to prompt her on the scripts, the codes, what to sing or whistle or say, and they both did a lot of scrambling though the codebook. More difficult calls she practiced first in the tiled bathroom, which was mostly soundproof. It soon became clear that Beatrice both had the voice for it and excelled at the mnemonic acrobatics required. Within a couple of weeks, her imitation of Johnny was nearly flawless. The last thing he taught her was about the existence of a double accounting system. There were extra rounds of calculations she'd never been privy to before, leaving the Dolan take considerably higher than anyone had ever guessed. The collective wasn't half as egalitarian as it had seemed. The excess was kept in a couple of hidden cabinets in his mother's apartment, as well as in safe-deposit boxes at different banks around the city. She didn't approve of it, but she reveled in the feeling of control and the completeness of her knowledge.

For Johnny, the ascension of Beatrice to his mother's role meant he could focus on lying on the couch and drinking rye, which were the only things he really cared about anymore. For two weeks, he barely left the apartment nor let anyone but her into it, not even Piker Ryan. She struggled to come up with excuses that somehow would not compromise his leadership, but people were talking, doubting him. Finally, she told him he had to make an appearance.

She helped him on with his suit and matching armband and ascot of black watered silk. Then she slicked back his hair with a dollop of pomade. He took a cane from the umbrella stand and a large swig of gin as a booster. He was pale as the moon and his eyes were as red as his lips, giving him a rather vampiric air. His temper was foul and short. He terrorized the Five Points that evening, brandishing his cane, growling at people who stammered their condolences and breaking a couple of noses. Then he went and drank himself numb at the Morgue, and Piker Ryan had to carry him home. After that, people said maybe it'd be better if he didn't come out again before he was ready.

And so, while Johnny lay in bed moping, started drinking at noon and occasionally smoked sticky balls of opium that she procured for him from Wah Kee's, Beatrice began doing the report all on her own. There were no big jobs going on at first, but people were working, and revenue was flowing in and out. Beatrice made sure people were getting the same pay or better than before, as a result of which people thought things were going on as usual, except for Johnny's seclusion.

It was increasingly clear to Beatrice that Johnny had only ever been the nominal head of the Whyos. With his mother gone and Johnny always half drunk or stoned, that meant Beatrice was now in charge. She'd gone from pickpocket and hot-corn girl to king in under a year. *King,* that was how she thought it, not queen.

Just as Beatrice was getting used to it all, she realized something was wrong: She was ill. And late. Then more than late. There was no denying it: As sure as the sewers ran beneath the streets, she was pregnant.

It could only have happened that one morning, just before the wedding, just before the explosion. Though Johnny had been clear at the outset that he didn't want her getting knocked up, she feared he would feel differently now. He might see it as a connection to his mother, who had clearly hoped for grandchildren. For Beatrice, though, the timing was disastrous. She had nothing left over for a baby, not if she was going to have to do Johnny's job. And she did have to — the fate of the Why Nots was in her hands. She didn't tell Fiona about this development, the way she would have before. She didn't have much time to spend with Fiona now, and she felt estranged from her by the enormity of her secret power.

She knew she had spent too long not noticing, and it was close to being too late, but she took a set of powders she had on hand in some tea, hoping she could still put an end to the situation. They made her feel wretched all morning, but two days later she still hadn't bled. She bought more and took a double dose. Nothing. She considered a visit to any of an easy dozen "hygienic advisers" and purveyors of "cures for ladies' ailments," but they were death shops, and there was no privacy possible there. Anyplace she went, the Why Nots would hear, and she feared the rumor would move across town so fast that Johnny would hear about it, shut-in or not, before she even got her legs up in the loops. It was going to be awful enough already; she didn't want to have to contend with his histrionics or his rage.

And so she looked for another solution. Thinking that there must be places where ladies from other parts of town went, she took herself to the Cooper Union reading room and looked through the dailies for discreetly worded advertisements. *Ladies' physician guarantees results to Unfortunates in just one interview. . . . A necessary preventive for married women. . . . For the postponement of a too rapid expansion of family. . . . A mild cure for the stoppage of monthly turns.*

Among the myriad, one stood out because the address was all the way uptown at Fifty-second Street, well outside the area where Whyos ranged. The following day, after the books were tallied, she made sure Johnny had some lunch and a bottle of rye available and went out without saying where or why. He didn't greatly care about her comings or goings, so it was simple, but still she took as many back stairwells, hidden doorways and forgotten passages as possible on her way to Twenty-third Street, the outer edge of Whyo territory, just in case anyone spotted her. From there, she caught an omnibus up to Fifty-second, at which latitude the city was entirely different from the dense, low, wooden downtown. The buildings tended more toward manor houses or farmsteads and the occasional stone mansion. The house she sought was at the corner of Fifth Avenue, and it was enormous, taking up most of a block, including its walled garden.

It was nothing like the places she had known to do this type of work, and she checked the address again; it was correct. Hoping she had enough cash and wondering at the architecture, she climbed the wide stairway to the parlor-floor entrance. As she rang the bell, a group of schoolchildren ran past, shouting, "Madame La Mort!" So now she knew it was the right address. But the servant who answered waved her back downstairs, where there was a business entrance so subtly marked that she had missed it.

The offices were opulent, with dark wood and velvet, and the interview was far from what Beatrice expected. The lady told her she was mistaken. She did not extract babies for any price. Heavens, no. Did her client know the dangers, both mortal and legal, of the operation she sought? She had medicine, she said, a powder of ergot and tansy, which she offered at no more than the cost of their manufacture. Otherwise, she was there only to advise.

"I know those powders. I could have bought them downtown, too. Actually, I did buy them downtown, and they didn't work. Surely given the size of your advertisement, you offer something stronger."

"I seek to advise girls such as yourself, because I know the dangers of extraction. It's easier to rupture yourself with a corset stay than you may know. Don't let someone who knows nothing do it for you and leave you to bleed and die."

"Madame Restell, do you offer a cure?"

The lady put an envelope heavy with powder on the desk between them and shrugged. "Five dollars." It would have cost one downtown.

Beatrice pulled out a thick wad of cash—roughly a week's revenue—and put it on the table. "I have a rather larger budget to work with."

Madame Restell looked more closely at Beatrice's dress to see if she'd misjudged her. She hadn't, but what she saw on the table was a considerable sum. She asked herself if the girl was likely to be an agent of the government, trying to entrap her. She didn't think so, but she was cautious. "I can, however, arrange a visit to a most healthful spa in the Catskill Mountains, where you'll surely find yourself feeling better in no time. Five hundred for the week. But I'm afraid you'll really need a different frock to fit in there, my dear. The company expects something a bit more . . . elegant?"

Five hundred dollars was a fortune, but Beatrice thought about the safe-deposit boxes. The problem wasn't the price but that she couldn't get *away*. She walked away from Madame Restell's disappointed. She'd expected to leave in a state of agony, but not till the following day and with her problem behind her. Her belly didn't show yet; it hadn't quickened, but it would soon. What if she didn't get rid of it? She'd felt very good in her limbs, in her flesh, the past weeks. She had thought it was just the power, at first, but now she understood that her body was happy about what was happening within it. If she hadn't understood just how short-lived that happiness would be once the baby was born, she'd have drunk dark beer and eaten well and slept as late as she could, fattening herself up into a mother. It might be lovely to be a mother, the caregiver of an innocent life, if only there weren't so much to do to keep her gang of guilty men and women alive, the girls safe—and if only the father weren't Johnny Dolan.

She wanted more than ever to tell Fiona her trouble, and the following day she bumped into her on Astor Place. They went into a little place called the Lioness, which was almost empty, and Beatrice drank two sweet gins in quick, silent succession. Fiona was watching her closely. Finally, she asked if something was wrong. Beatrice decided on candor. After all, Fiona's betrayal had been small compared to what she was up to now. It was she who'd grown secretive, she who was now participating in a scheme that daily defrauded the rest of the gang. She could trust Fiona.

"Goddamned Johnny," she said. "He knocked me up. Caught me off guard. And now, with his mother gone, I'm afraid he'll want it."

Fiona was suitably horrified and offered to go with her to the extractionist.

"No, just think about it: There's nowhere I can go without people finding out. He'd kill me."

They both sat in silence for a while. Then Fiona spoke.

"There's something I've heard about lately, Beanie—a Chinese needle doctor. He's not an extractionist—he does it some Chinese way. It's not even illegal, and no one would know a thing." The Jimster, she explained, had heard about Dr. Zhang from a girl he used to know who'd gone and married one of the Chinamen on Mott Street.

"What, a *white* girl?"

"I think she's English."

They both agreed it was a very strange thing for an English girl to up and marry a Chinaman, but for Beanie's purposes this Chinese cure sounded worth trying.

"It's like this, he told me: You have to tell the English wife your predicament because he only talks Chinese, then you lie on a table and he sticks pins in your belly. Then you go home and drink plenty of gin for two days, and then you have your curse."

"The pins go all the way into your belly, do they? They kill it?"

"I guess so. But how much worse can it be than the other way? I'd try it."

Beatrice said she would think about it.

When they parted, she got on an omnibus heading downtown. She found her way to Mott Street and wandered several blocks in search of a sign with the Chinaman's name. Finally, she stepped into a corner saloon. It was full of Chinese and whites both, but not another woman anywhere. The sweetish-sour smell of opium wafted from the rear, but she had little interest in that just then. She stepped up to the bar and asked for a sweet gin.

"A double. And by the way, can you direct me to the shop of Dr. Zhang?"

31.

SOMETHING LONG AND THIN

On the day of Beatrice's visit to Madame Restell, there were 368 women in New York who were actively considering abortions; something less than half of them would go through with it; and one of every ten women who did would encounter grave complications leading to death. Usually, it was uncontrolled hemorrhage or infection that got her. As to the demographics of extraction, they matched those of the city as a whole: more poor women than rich women, more Irish than Germans, more Germans than Italians, more Italians than Chinese, more whites than blacks, and so on. But it was all quite proportional. If you looked at the denominators—and any good scientific study must account for the denominators— you'd come up with fairly consistent numbers. It shouldn't come as a surprise that everyone was having sex, regardless of their bank accounts. Where statistics did diverge was in the survival rates: Those who could pony up to go to Madame Restell's resort in the Catskills were far likelier to live out the year and also to bear future children to term. Only half of the enceinte were unmarried, but fully a third of those girls either didn't know who the father was or had opted not to tell him. They were making their decisions on their own—not that they weren't used to that. One member of that group was Beatrice, and there's at least one other we know of: Her hair was yellow and her German accent thick and her clothes a little tawdry, so that anyone who cared to could have guessed what she was (for that was the point of such clothes).

Maria was a little further along than Beatrice. Like Beatrice, she usually used lemons, and she always bathed after a man had visited her room. There had been a time, a couple months back, when she'd known it was high time to swap out the lemon, but lemons had been astronomical at the market, and she was strapped for rent. She couldn't see spending so very much, especially since swapping required taking a day off. You had to wait an entire day after the last time a man had been in you before you took it out. That was why a lot of girls took Sundays off. But Maria was struggling to make it as an independent operator—she'd be damned if she'd go into one of those houses where the madam took half what you made and entirely ran your life. She'd had interested customers the past two Sundays and simply hadn't been able to refuse. When she'd finally reached up inside herself, what she found was not good. The rind had gone soft, like a custard. Her finger poked right through it. The rest came away in scraps and pieces that smelled less lemony than rank.

Her flux came, and she was relieved, but it was light, and the next one failed her entirely. She took the usual array of powders, without results. Finally, she realized she had to do something about it. If she didn't, she'd soon be visibly pregnant and unable to attract any customers but the weirdos. But it wasn't so easy as just deciding; the procedure was not inexpensive. So she went out noon and night to raise the money, rarely took a break between strolls, gladly charged extra for unorthodox requests. All the while she was hoping that so much activity might somehow dislodge her problem, but Maria was not that lucky. When she finally had the money, she asked a few girls she knew for a recommendation. None of them had a good story to tell. Apparently, every extractionist was a butcher. So Maria took to scanning the sheets of newspaper that were used to wrap the meat pies and cheese and vegetables she bought from the vendors at Washington Market. She would ask specially for a classified page, and there were always a few ads directed toward members of the gentler sex. At the end of a week, she had committed three addresses to memory.

It was just as Beatrice bumped into Fiona and stepped into the Lioness that day that Maria was finally gathering her dollars and steeling her nerve.

She put on the rather conservative hat she wore on Sundays—no feathers at all—left off the rouge, and set out on a stroll quite unlike her usual ones. She had eyes only for the pavement. She didn't want offers, lest she not have the mettle to refuse them. As she neared the first of the addresses, she smelled the fish market and the bitter aroma of coffee mingled with rotten brine. It was a small street just up from Coffee House Slip, one block long and narrow, and every building seemed to have a modest shop on the ground level with an apartment above. She peered into the shop windows as she went, and what she saw puzzled her. Blacks. Not that blacks were startling in themselves—she'd gotten quite used to them since she'd been here—but on this street it seemed there was nothing but blacks: black girls in front of *and* behind the counter in the little corner restaurant, blacks in the market, a black man in the window of the tobacconist's. There were no whites at all in view. It didn't occur to Maria that this was a respectable middle-class enclave or that she was safer in that street than anywhere in a ten-block radius of where she lived. To her, blacks seemed as beastly as their recent enslavement implied, and she certainly didn't want some big black woman to touch her *there*. It was a line she drew in her work as well. One had to have standards, after all. She spotted the number from the ad—an apothecary shop—peered in and saw more blacks. She straightened her skirts and walked on. Thank goodness, she thought, that she'd gotten more than one address.

It was a pity. The place she passed up, the clinic of doctors Smith and Blacksall, was as clean and efficient as they got. Smith and Blacksall were generalists, not just abortionists (though they quietly and safely did that work, too). They were outspoken advocates of modern birth control and hygiene. They were also social progressives: If a patient seemed hard up, they charged nothing for their services. They absolutely didn't want a girl like Maria to have to go on a binge to pay for this procedure. They did their best to advertise their mission by word of mouth, though abortion and birth control were both strictly illegal. The apothecary shop that housed their clinic belonged to Dr. Smith's uncle, who was glad to have doctors in his upper story because of the trade their patients brought in. The two women generally worked together but allowed the patient's race to determine which doctor was her physician and which assisted. They saw Negro women Mondays and Tuesdays, whites Wednesday through Friday. Not a single woman had ever died in their care.

The next address on Maria's list was further downtown and all the way west, in the basement rooms of an old Irishwoman. MRS. MULLIN, LISENSED PERVAYER OF CURES was painted on the door, and not very neatly. Maria turned the knob. First, she paid a princely sum of forty dollars to her *pervayer*. Next, she was issued a small dose of laudanum mixed into a pint glass of rum. She left her stockings, pants and petticoats on a hook in a changing closet and took her place on a bench to wait her turn. Actually, it felt rather good to have just her skirt about her legs for once, nothing in between.

The Irishwoman's implement of choice differed very little from the one Dr. Blacksall would have used. Whalebone corset stay or gynecologic probe, something long and thin and slightly flexible was what was needed. And it ought to be clean. Mrs. Mullin washed hers well with carbolic soap between customers. That afternoon was busy, however, and the rheumatism had seized her ankles again, and she just couldn't bear to walk to the corner well with the bucket, which was dry. So the bone was rinsed in a basin of water that had already seen her breakfast dishes. A tiny clot of egg yolk clung to the long, curved, off-white spike when she lifted it from the pan. She wiped it clean on a towel before she turned to face the patient, whose ankles were splayed and raised in two rope loops that dangled from the ceiling. With Maria's skirts up around her middle, neither woman could see the other's face, which both preferred.

Mrs. Mullin installed the cold metal duckbill speculum without forewarning, cranked it open and proceeded with the aid of a miner's lamp to size up Maria's cervix: none too pretty. It was mottled and spotted, irregularly swollen and tagged, thanks to a variety of slow, pernicious diseases caused by an array of microbes yet unclassified by science. Smith and Blacksall would have had a few things to say to a woman whose insides looked like that, even an option or two for treatment. To the Irishwoman, though, it all looked pretty normal. Mrs. Mullin didn't have to know that the small hole in the middle of the cervix was referred to by doctors, in Latin, as the *os* to traverse it with the whalebone stay. Slowly, carefully, she pushed until she hit resistance, then she went a little further. She arced her instrument up and down and back and forth, out again and in, scrambling all that lay in its path. Actually, she did her job fairly humanely—whenever Maria flinched, she paused. There was blood on the table, but that was to be expected.

When it was over, Maria gulped down another glass of rum with a black medicinal brew stirred into it, then hunkered down on an oilcloth-covered cot for an hour, till she felt she could walk. She took a cab home. Mrs. Mullin had told her she'd have to push the remains out herself and gave her a paper package of tea—mostly tansy—to bring on the contractions. She was to keep at the gin, too, and the laudanum, for pain. She lost the awful little rabbit in a flood that pretty much ruined her mattress some twelve hours later. She wouldn't have said it didn't hurt, because it did, but a strangely pleasant delirium settled over her late that night. She saw the walls give way to ocean swells, and oddly enough there was her mother. Her mother opened her lips and mouthed a word.

Maria had lost a fair amount of blood, but her real problem was the shivering. And the microscopic devils—those wee animalcules—that had got into her and begun to multiply where the baby had been. Her body threw a fever to fight them off. *What, Mutti, what did you say?* She saw her mother's lips open again, and this time she made out the message: "Forgive me." And why not? What would it cost her now, forgiveness? Maria cried as she hadn't since the day her mother let the first mate of the *Leibnitz* drag her off, not that you could have told it from looking at her, the way the tears ran in with the sweat that rolled from every pore. She was flat on her back, barely stirring, pale as water, all her ruddiness drained and puddled in her sheets. At a certain point, it seemed to her she was flying, actually flying through the air and over the ocean and all the way home to the unheard-of town in northernmost Schleswig-Holstein, where she had been born. God, it was so much more beautiful now, in her mind's eye, than it ever had been when she lived there as a girl. How had she never seen the loveliness of the hills, the fields?

As Maria flew, so did Beatrice. She lay on her back on another table some twenty blocks away, arms and feet splayed like a corpse, eyes closed, heart beating steady and hard. Her dress and skirts lay in the corner in a grand hump nearly as big as she was, even without her in them. She was nearly naked, in just her petticoat, and even that was partway undone, revealing her belly. For all the world, it felt like her body was tipping or being tipped right off the tabletop, first one way, then the other. First, she had seemed to be rising, and finally she felt herself soaring through space. The sensation was delightful. She forgot the dim room she was in, despite the dreadful stink from a cauldron sitting on the potbelly stove. She even forgot why she was there.

Beatrice had liked Amy Zhang as soon as she saw her. Perhaps it was just because the girl had smiled so warmly and said, "Oh, hi, come in," just as if they knew each other and Beatrice was expected. Beatrice was curious to find out how this white girl had ended up marrying a Chinese, but they had only got as far as trading names and where they were from when the doctor came in. He was tall, with his black hair pulled back in a pigtail, like many of the Chinese one saw downtown, but he wore a western suit. Amy asked Beatrice why she was there, and then, to Beatrice's amazement, she conveyed some version of the story to the doctor in his own language. He nodded, and Amy told Beatrice to stick out her tongue. Dr. Zhang peered at it, then took her wrists, one after the other, and prodded them with his smooth fingers. Finally, after she had lain down on the table in the center of the room, he walked around her, pressing various spots on her arms, neck, legs and feet, many of which were oddly tender, as if she had bruises in exactly those places, though as far as she knew she did not. When she flinched, he nodded and smiled. Eventually, he spoke, and Amy translated while giving Beatrice a sponge bath with a warm, damp towel.

"There are reasons for a woman not to bleed. Are you having a baby?"

Beatrice was silent. She had thought that was obvious. Perhaps it was like Madame Restell, and they wouldn't do it for fear of the laws that forbade women from meddling with their own bodies.

"Do you *want* to have a baby?" Amy asked.

"I'm not married."

"Yes, but are you very sure you don't want a baby?"

"I'm sure," Beatrice blurted, and covered her face with her hands. Amy looked away. Beatrice wondered if she'd borne her husband children yet and what they would look like—half yellow, half white, queer eyes. She couldn't imagine.

"There are things he can do so a baby is not welcome in your body. You must lie very still. The needles don't hurt—or maybe just a little—and they don't go very deep at all, just beneath the skin. But they stay there for a while. You must lie still and try to sleep, and on no account get up till I come for you. Otherwise, you could hurt yourself."

And then the doctor made a pincushion of her. By the time he was through, there were more needles sticking up from her flesh than Beatrice could count: in her ears, her arms, her shins, her feet, her head and—the only ones that had hurt—her belly. Those went slightly deeper than the others, and at first she feared Dr. Zhang really would press them in until they reached her womb. Finally, the doctor pinched little balls of clay onto the ends of a couple of the needles and set them alight with a candle. They smoked rather than burned, and she felt warmth radiate through the metal pins into her stomach. She was surrounded by a haze of incense that was nothing like what they swung on censers on Sundays in church.

It was that heavy odor that had somehow seemed to lift her into the air. And so it was that, despite being quite literally pinned on her back, Beatrice felt she flew. She swooped by faces and ideas that were only half born. She saw colors flash and heard free-floating words. Her breath came clear and deep. It might have been a day or a minute later when Amy Zhang returned and plucked out the needles, one by one. Beatrice's flesh seemed to grip some of them tightly, as if it wanted to keep them, and when it finally gave up it ached slightly, resenting the loss.

"Can I see one of those?" asked Beatrice. She hadn't gotten a look when they went in, laid out on her back the way she was, eyes closed tight.

The girl held out a flat dish full of extraordinary pins, long and slender, some with elaborate glass or metal beads for their heads.

"Now, this is important," said Amy Zhang. "You must come back again in two days. Don't wait any longer, if you want it to work."

Beatrice felt good and calm all that day and the following, but the morning after, just a few hours before she planned to return to Chinatown, a barrage of emergency reports began to come in from the gang. Piker had gotten himself arrested for brawling. Not only that, but when they searched his coat they found a freshly severed human ear wrapped in a pocket hand-kerchief. This was the kind of proof sometimes taken by contract killers to demonstrate they'd done their job, a job equally outrageous to Beatrice as to the police, for contract killing was not part of the Whyo scheme. It was not subtle. Things were getting out of hand, and she feared this might be the end.

No victim had been identified, but Piker was being held on suspicion of murder. Getting in a bar fight with such a thing in his possession was the sort of idiocy that Johnny would have kept in check if only he hadn't been lying in bed, staring wide-eyed at the wall. Beatrice took some solace in the fact that Piker was remarkably good at disposal—the cops were very unlikely to find the rest of his victim—but it was infuriating that he was doing that sort of job and ridiculous that he hadn't just ditched the evidence out the police wagon's window. Now they were all going to suffer, for a murder investigation surrounding a Whyo could potentially bring anyone associated with Piker under scrutiny, including Johnny. It was precisely the kind of thing they had gone out of their way to avoid with Harris.

Beatrice spent most of the day dealing with the situation herself: She sent a couple of boys over to the Tombs to stand around the coffee cart that parked out front and listen to the cops gossip. They returned with a precise description of the evidence, at which point she had Fiona canvass the membership for a Whyo with wiry black ear hair and a simian lobe. They found one, and after an interview with Johnny, who was suddenly enjoying himself, she noticed, the man made the sacrifice: his left outer ear. Johnny did the honors with an oyster knife, the same weapon Piker had used. It fairly sickened Beanie to see how it cheered Johnny up. On the other hand, it had been her idea. They cauterized the wound with an iron to stop the blood and to make it harder to match the edges, and the next day they sent the martyr around to the station house, where he reported the attack but declined to press charges.

It was a brilliant bit of work, a victory really. Piker was released and the entire inquiry dropped. People in the Five Points went back to laughing that anyone had thought a bumbler like Piker Ryan could manage a murder— he was just a brawler, after all. But all Beatrice could think, as she rushed back to Dr. Zhang's late that afternoon, was that it had all taken too long. The acupuncturist's shop was going to be closed. She had botched the treatment. She was right—they were closed. But they were there. They lived upstairs, and Amy Zhang had been watching for her.

"I'm sorry it's so late. I got into some trouble today."

"I'm glad you came." Amy Zhang gave her a cup of revolting tea from the cauldron in the corner, and this time there were even more needles than before. The flight felt different, too: uncontrolled and dangerous. They sent her home with a jar containing more of the awful-tasting brew. That night, just as Amy had predicted, she began to feel twinges. In the morning, when she rose from bed, she knew she was bleeding heavily. It wasn't that much worse than the pain of the usual month, but she was overwhelmed and sad and stayed in bed feigning a fever all day, trying not to let Johnny know that she'd been crying.

Now that it was too late to change her mind, she began to imagine what kind of a creature the baby would have been. There wasn't any reason it had to turn into a Johnny Dolan, handsome but bad. It might even have been a girl, she thought. She might have found some way to raise it properly, away from Whyos and Why Nots. Not likely, though. And when she thought of all that could befall a girl in the Five Points, of all the things that had been taken from her in her nearly twenty years, she collapsed facedown into her pillow. It was better this way. The following day, she went to see Fiona and told her what she had done. Fiona nodded and laid a hand on her shoulder. What was there to say?

Beatrice probably wouldn't have returned for the third visit if Amy hadn't so accurately predicted what she felt. "You'll think it's over, but you'll be tired, sick, crying, not well. You have to come the third time, for balance, or you won't get over it." So she went back one last time, with Fiona along to watch Dr. Zhang stick her. She didn't fly this time, but by the end she did feel a slight rising within her.

Over the week that followed, she felt a little more normal. And for better or worse, Johnny was up and around, too. It seemed the Piker-ear affair had been the tonic he needed to break his melancholy. He was still floating an oily layer of gin on top of his first cup of coffee in the morning, and he couldn't be bothered even to let her tell him about the accounts, but his ascots flowed dashingly from his open collar again and his famously shiny hair had its old gleam, though his childhood cowlicks had reasserted themselves.

There was a time not so long before when Beatrice would have slipped docilely back into their old routine, not dared to tell him what she thought, but now she touched the numb spot beneath her chin, fingered the slight knot on the bridge of her nose, thought about the chunky period that had contained his child. She'd been running his show single-handedly for more than two months, long enough to know how things were done and care that they were done properly. She was on top of the money, bringing it in, counting it, distributing it. She didn't want him to take back control, but her far more pressing concern in the short term was that he'd somehow reveal how out of the loop he really was, make himself an inadvertent fool, lose standing with the boys. She needed him as a front man, the same way his mother had, but he didn't grant her quite the respect he had his mother.

One evening, before he went out, she told him she wanted to talk. He rolled his eyes and poured himself some cold coffee with a splash of whiskey.

"You're drinking too much, Johnny. The eleven o'clock boilermakers are getting out of hand. You're out of touch. You can't just go out and party with the gang if you don't know who's done what and how much they've brought in or not. You need to go over the accounts first. We need to come up with something larger, some scheme, to keep them working together."

"Don't tell me how to run the Whyos, eh, Beanie? Just fuck off."

"I don't care about your shiny buttons and your posturing. If you want to stay the boss, you have to act like the boss. And you're a pathetic excuse for a boss at the moment."

"Listen to me," he said. He picked up his cane and thrust its carved-ivory snake head in her direction. Then he threw it, but she dodged, and it glanced off the table a yard to her right and clattered on the floor. He grabbed another cane from the stand, and she was afraid for a moment, but she needn't have been. He slammed the door behind him.

When he was gone, she returned to the kitchen and began to pack a basket of food. Colleen and her Aunt Penelope had written her off entirely when they realized how she was living, but not Liam. They sometimes met for an ale for a half hour at a certain pub on Friday evenings, and Beatrice would give him a parcel of such luxuries as he might have purchased on his way home on payday if only he'd made three dollars more a week and never spent a dime of his earnings on whiskey. It was usually ham or butter or oranges and a nice cheese or a piece of chocolate, and sometimes several bottles of Inca soda or ginger ale for the kids. But it couldn't be too lavish, or Colleen would put it together and reject the gifts.

The worst thing about this life of hers since she became First Girl was the way it had cut her off from her family and friends, not just the O'Gamhnas but Frank Harris and even Fiona. She'd been able to have a sort of double life before, and she hadn't realized how ideal it was.

Now, in exchange for all that, she'd gotten Johnny—some prize.

32

THE MONKEY-HEADED CANES

ell, if it isn't the Jimster," said a voice from across the barroom. "Haven't seen much of you lately."

"Morning, Luther." Jimmy looked back down at his beer, not interested in talking. It was the first time he'd ever called Undertoe by his given name, and Undertoe noticed it, found it disrespectful. Jimmy was wearing a bowler hat, as if he thought he was a big man now. Undertoe reached out and knocked it off his head.

"That's still *Mister Undertoe* to you."

"Fuck you, Undertaker," said Jimmy before stooping to recover his hat. He'd like to have punched him in the head, but he'd recently been indoctrinated in the Whyo theory of stealth, had learned how seeming not tough could enable one to get away with murder. Jimmy had done well in his trial period. He'd yet to formally enter the gang and he still didn't know the complexities of the language, but he was very close to being made a full member. All he needed was some job, some heist, to prove himself. Probably, he thought, he shouldn't have called him *Luther*. The last thing he needed at this point was a conflict with Undertoe.

Undertoe had never managed to torch that tent in Brooklyn over the summer. The new security chief seemed to be always around, and there were any number of watchmen. The venue had been too intimate, the time not opportune, but that had left him only hungrier. Now he had his eye on something grander, Barnum's new Hippodrome. He wasn't asked to head up the effort this time around, what with having been at Sing Sing, but he'd gotten a job working the crowds, apprehending pickpockets and keeping the peace. It was the perfect position, as it allowed him total access to the facility.

"You've been doing all right for yourself, I guess, Jimmy."

The Jimster put his hat on and stood up to go.

"Oh, don't be a sorehead. You're an old pal, can't you take a joke? Because I'm glad I saw you. Been hoping to. Wondering if you'd care to join forces on a little project. Two-man job, split fifty-fifty, not like the old days. Going to be a beaut."

Jimmy was thinking, *Not for a million dollars*, but what he said was "Maybe. Buy me a gin."

Johnny and Fiona were both interested in Undertoe, he knew, so he listened. It was pretty obviously a setup, and on top of that he doubted that Barnum had really contracted for another torch job, the way Undertoe said. It was going to look awfully suspicious to the insurers, the third of his properties to burn in a decade. That night, Jimmy told Fiona what he'd heard, and Fiona thought it was precisely the right opportunity. If Jimmy could get on this job and double-cross the Undertaker, it would go quite a distance to clearing Harris, which would resolve one of the Whyos' ongoing liabilities. And Beanie would like it.

Now Fiona decided she had to talk to Beatrice alone. Maybe this job was the way to get both women's projects taken care of: protect Harris and bring Jimmy in. Johnny had started going out again lately, so Fiona spent the morning lurking around the stairwell of the Dolan building waiting for him to leave. On the basement level of the Dolan place, there was a bottle-collecting operation for Owney Geoghegan's. The rest of the floors, except for the roof, were all empty warehouse space, so no one used it but Johnny and Beanie now. When Johnny came down at last, hair slicked back, a purple ascot blazing at his throat, wielding one of his signature canes—a bald-eagle design made of ivory and alabaster—Fiona let him think that she'd just arrived to visit Beanie and happened to cross his path. He waved her up, and Fiona quickly climbed the five flights. As she opened the door onto the snow-scattered rooftop, a bell rang automatically in the kitchen, where

Beatrice was sitting over the account books. She quickly closed them and slid them into a concealed cabinet. She hoped it wasn't Johnny coming back. Then she heard Fiona's voice and relaxed.

"So," said Fiona, "he's out for a while?"

Beatrice shrugged, and they went into the large parlor, where Beatrice opened the door of the cast-iron stove and tossed in a log, and they sat down to talk. Fiona told Beatrice of Undertoe's plan. Then she explained her own idea. Beatrice squinted into the fire, thinking about what would be entailed by making the Jimster a full Whyo. There was a reason they hadn't brought Jimmy all the way in yet. She wondered if she was ready to train him. She thought she was.

"It'll be good for Harris, Beanie."

"Forget Harris. It's Johnny we have to think about. But I like the Hippodrome idea—it pretty much lets Undertoe undermine himself, so we don't have to. Maybe Johnny'll go for it, because it's not a hit."

The Hippodrome. Offering every delight from horse racing to opera, from dinner theater to menageries, from cabinets of curiosities to the strange abominations—some pickled, some still walking—for which Barnum was above all famous. It had opened just two weeks before and quickly become the most popular destination in town. Everyone went there, *everyone*. Pierreponts and Livingstons and Astors in ascots and velvet coats, shopkeepers with their aprons still on beneath their coats, charwomen in skirts they'd brushed and brushed but that still smelled of soot. Bakers' wives and printers' apprentices wandered the galleries alongside urchins and newsboys just learning how to live on nearly nothing in New York. These were the boys who would grow up into Jimsters, Piker Ryans, Dandy Johnnys, Undertoes.

Undertoe, yes—he was there, too, on the job. He paced the floor with eyes peeled, making sure the souvenirs stayed out of urchins' pockets and no one caused any trouble, but he also kept tabs on Barnum himself—he coveted a nod hello from the great impresario, who had once again allowed Undertoe to be hired onto his security staff. It would have been puzzling if there weren't so much history between them. Indeed, it was puzzling still, for Undertoe was the greatest threat to security there was. As he walked the halls and stalls, his gaze was caught by lamp fixtures and sawdust bags for spreading on the floor. He had to remind himself to spare a glance from time to time for the throngs of people who were there to see the outrageous animals, the wax figures, the elaborately laid-out vitrines. He was passing through the large hall known as the Grand Emporium and doing just that when he happened to notice the Jimster, walking in step with Dandy Johnny, followed by both their girls. He ducked briefly behind a column to let them pass and smiled to see that his boy was on the job.

Visitors had to cross the Great Emporium to reach the theater or the upper floors. The place was a maze of stalls stocked with costly exotic and imitation-exotic items, as well as miniature replicas of the various wonders and horrors on view elsewhere in the Hippodrome, all overhung by banners proclaiming attractions above. Beatrice, Johnny, Fiona and the Jimster were on their way to the theater, where a minstrel show was soon to begin— their outing was turning out to be part work and part enjoyment, as how could it not be in such a place? They wouldn't have paused in the Emporium at all had Johnny's eye not been drawn to a corner stall with a remarkable display of canes and umbrellas. There were walking sticks with compasses set in their handles, umbrellas that unscrewed to reveal bayonets, a cane that was also a light rifle and several that had been fashioned from single pieces of scrimshaw. There were any number of canes with wooden heads of Indians or alabaster busts of famous men or gleaming brass and silver beasts as handles.

"Oh," said Dandy Johnny, and he began to fondle the canes and to pluck appealing models from the buckets to feel their heft. "Look at that one," he said, pointing to a pale George Washington, but it was a little short for Johnny, and he passed it to the Jimster to try for size. Then he pulled out an ebony-stemmed number with a large silver knob that was worked into a monkey's head. And a vicious-looking monkey it was, too, the way it bared its teeth and squinted its eyes. It was heavy enough that it would do for a weapon, handsome enough to satisfy his taste. He tossed it from one hand to the other and back; it was perfectly balanced.

"How much for this one here?" he asked.

When they took their seats in the theater, Johnny was sporting the monkey head and the Jimster the Washington. Johnny had sprung for both of them. He often gave a new Whyo something as a sign of his approval, and he'd decided that morning that the Jimster was solid. He was in. He'd complete the initiation later on that night, when the ladies weren't around. It was a delicate matter, involving dominance and submission and a first introduction to certain secret codes. Beatrice would take the vocal training over from there. In the theater, Johnny put his arm around Jimmy and smiled. It had been too long since they'd brought a new boy in. He adjusted his trousers and stowed the cane beneath his seat. Then the curtain rose and the show began. The crowd roared.

Out in the Emporium, another group had wandered over to the cane stall, having seen the playbill and made up their minds to skip the show: a bearded young Irishman in the company of a woman and a black couple with a toddler daughter.

"John-Henry," said Harris when they came to the cane and umbrella stall, "take a look at these. Do you think they're too outlandish for Mr. Noe? He dropped his walking stick while he was crossing the street last week, and it was run over by an omnibus."

Sarah Blacksall and Lila continued after Liza, who zigzagged from one booth to the next, looking at the thousand and one strange things for sale.

"I don't know," John-Henry said, looking at a cane with a brass cobra flaring its hood and red ruby eyes. "I think he'd like some of them, not all of them."

The whole atmosphere of the place brought Harris back to the job he'd done at Barnum's American Museum, but he tried not to think about that. He picked up a bronze elephant head on a mahogany stem, but it wasn't very comfortable in the hand, what with the ears. There was a bear that looked like a dog, a rabbit that was far too ladylike. Then he saw the laughing monkey, its head a large, silver knob, its expression almost gleeful, its eyes radiating mirth, its lips pulled back into a tooth-flashing grin. But it was the elegant proportions of the silver head atop the slim black stick that made it so suitable as a gentleman's accoutrement. He tossed it from hand to hand — the balance was perfect.

"How much for this monkey-headed cane, sir?"

They walked on. They saw the sea lion, which was housed, awkwardly enough, in a two-foot-deep pool on the fourth floor. It barked and waved its ragged flipper for fish. There was a bear that performed tricks gloomily, chained to its bars. Harris thought of Sedric, trapped in the blaze. There was a new tiger, pacing hard. Harris remembered Raj's grooved floor, his leap, his execution. The American Museum hadn't been a wonderful place, even before the fire, he realized, and this one was worse, because grander: It made even more of a spectacle of a greater number of creatures. But Liza was excited by the animals, laughing, shrieking, hiding under her mother's skirt, and for her sake they continued on to see the camels, the elephants and, along the way, a row of a dozen jars containing fetuses of two-headed pigs. Eventually, they reached the Hall of Living Dioramas, where, behind metal rails and velvet ropes, were two small stages, side by side. On the first, a family of three blue-black Negroes, pure Africans it seemed, squatted half naked in the dust beside the false front of a thatched hut. The walls were painted to suggest a jungle clearing. The Africans wore mangy grass skirts, and their faces were painted with colorful streaks and lines. The woman's breasts were bare. The girl had a cough so constant and unproductive it was clearly tubercular. There was no private space in the diorama, and after Harris and the Henleys had been watching for a minute or two, the girl stood up and went to the corner, where she squatted over a chamber pot in full view of the spectators, though she turned to face the rear wall. Her parents sat listlessly on the floor. Had they freely chosen or been tricked into this job? Did they know they didn't have to do this? This was the 1870s, after all — blacks were not slaves, nor had they been in New York for half a century. Next door, a group of Indians squatted in their own microcosm, dressed in feathers and beaded leather. Their set included a teepee and a background painting of a western landscape in which a cavalry troop was galloping over a rise, rifles shouldered, presumably preparing to release these wretched savages from their misery. Behind Harris, a small boy called out in a loud, high voice: "Look, Injuns, Pop! I'd sure like to shoot 'em dead!"

They didn't leave right away, but sooner than they'd planned. Nothing they saw in the wake of those sad dioramas managed to take their fancy. Back on the street, Harris took his leave of Sarah and the Henleys and made his way to the ferry. He spent the short ride across outside on the deck, thinking about whether John-Henry and Lila were trying to set him up with Sarah Blacksall. He ought to be flattered, perhaps. He admired her greatly. But he wasn't interested.

Mr. Noe seemed touched by the gift and captivated by the monkey head, and he invited Harris into the big house, where they sat in front of the fire in the small parlor and drank wine and coffee alternately, till it was dinnertime and the cook served them one of her excellent chicken pies. Harris compared Mr. Noe's warmth to the distrust his own father had shown him, and he marveled that he had made out so well. He was lucky to have such a friend, who had embraced him like no man, neither father nor uncle, ever had. But he was struggling with a question that seemed increasingly urgent the more settled he became: whether he should contact his father. He'd written a second, more candid letter to Koch, confessing a few of his exaggerations, though not all. He had considered asking Koch to keep his correspondence a secret, but knowing how unreasonable that would sound he hadn't done it. He'd told Koch he was going to write his father soon. Now he couldn't stop thinking about what that letter might say. It was going to be infinitely harder to write than the ones to Koch. Now he asked Mr. Noe what he thought a father would want to hear.

"Just to hear from you at all would be a gift. Maybe don't say too much. And Harris—"

He looked at Mr. Noe.

"You don't need to lie to him."

That night, he began to write the letter. After a week of crumpling up false starts on thick stationery, he bought a box of cheap foolscap and allowed himself to ramble, writing anything he dreamed of saying, telling himself that this was just a draft, just a trial run. He found that the Gothic handwriting he'd struggled to preserve had indeed deteriorated, and he was somewhat ashamed of the thought of mailing this rough penmanship to his father. He went through dozens of pages, rewording already cautious statements. There were long, hostile rants against his childhood, too, and praise songs to his mother, accusations, insults. The only things he wrote that he considered sending were about the bridge. Even on the coldest days, he loved going up there, day after day. Block by block it rose, and soon it would be the tallest man-made structure in the word. This was the way life should be: gradual accrual amounting to accomplishment over time. He rhapsodized on the techniques of installing bolts, or indeed just the size and beauty of the hardware, the stone blocks, the bridge itself. If only his life showed similar progress and virtue.

He never read over what he wrote, and when he grew tired he burned his pages in the grate. Eventually the idea of an actual letter to his father receded, and he realized he was writing to clarify his own mind. The problem was, his mind kept wandering to the subject of happiness, which meant he thought of Beatrice. He wondered if she'd approve of his handwriting now. But she was even less approachable now than his father.

On Christmas Eve, he took out the box of good letter paper for the first time in weeks, and in a single draft he wrote a very simple letter explaining his present situation to his father. It filled just two pages. He neither lied nor divulged gratuitous, unsavory details of his career in the underworld. He didn't apologize for leaving, just filled in a few details of how his departure came about. It was not all he had to say, not nearly, but it was not shallow either. It was neither dangerously honest nor entirely safe. It was a beginning. He sealed it in an envelope, and the following day it was in his pocket when he paid a visit to the Henleys, bringing a sack of imported oranges he'd bought at Washington Market.

Afterward, he met Sarah Blacksall, and they went out and took water samples for her study, as they did twice a week now, quite routinely entering the manholes with the aid of a sewer gaff Sarah had had made according to Harris's specifications. Technically, this activity was illegal, but they worked with such authority and were so obviously interested in the common good that on two occasions beat policemen had offered to help them by directing traffic away. It made Harris slightly nervous, but Dr. Blacksall was the one who chatted with the policemen, while he did the heavy lifting and collected the samples. They had ten locations they were monitoring, and it took them a couple of hours to get all the samples. Afterward, back at the clinic, Sarah inspected the phials of liquid under the microscope, and they once again found the bacterial counts downstream of the dirt-catchers lower than elsewhere. Harris smiled to think that the work he'd done for the Whyos had been useful after all.

The letter was still in his pocket. It was almost Christmas, but he was in no mood to go home and celebrate the holiday with Mr. Noe. He wan-

dered aimlessly north. He happened to be a few blocks south of the Hippodrome when he found himself stopping, sniffing the air. He smelled cre-
osote, heard alarm bells, several of them. Fires were common enough, but
they turned his stomach, and even more so the crowds that came to watch
them. He decided to avoid this one. Then he glanced up into the sky and
saw the wide arc of the glow. It was more than just some fire; it was an entire block. He turned back and walked toward the blaze.

When the Jimster hadn't shown up, Undertoe had realized his mistake.
He'd told the Jimster they'd be torching the place the next night, but they'd
planned to meet there that evening, just to go over things. Actually, Undertoe's idea was to do the job early and to catch the Jimster off guard. He
didn't know just how the little bastard planned to do it, but Undertoe wasn't
so stupid as to miss the double cross. His problem was, he'd gotten a little
ahead of himself and had already dumped the fuel.

By the time Jimmy got there, the walls were already doused with
kerosene, which he had smelled as he neared the building. It wasn't good,
Jimmy thought. Things weren't set up on his side yet. He was planning to
tip off a cop in the morning based on what he learned tonight, but none of
it was in place yet, and so nothing good could come of his being there
tonight. He had turned and gone straight to the Morgue to fill Johnny in on
the development.

But dupe or no dupe, Undertoe could hardly put the job off now. He
had strolled through the Emporium one last time, smelling the fumes.
Then he lit a cigarillo and tossed the match one way, the burning butt the
other a few paces on. When the smoke began to rise, he ran from the building and toward the nearest alarm box. It was something he always enjoyed,
sending the alarm on his own fires.

Much of what Harris saw was very different from his last Barnum fire:
The Hippodrome was vast compared to the American Museum's work-
manlike structure. He was outside, not inside. And the weather wasn't
freezing, so the building didn't drip paradoxically with ice the way the
American Museum had. But much of what he saw was the same: the fire-
fighters pulling up in their engines, the spectators, the mayhem and, once
again, the animals trapped inside. The place was going fast. Just as the central doorway seemed on the verge of collapse, a group of men ran through

it with heavy ropes. They were doing their best to haul the enormous forms of two elephants through the smoke and fire to safety. The larger one nudged the smaller one ahead of it with her trunk, and both made it out just before the front wall collapsed. Someone was in there, risking his life to save a one-hump camel, but the animal fought and broke the lead. When a vitrine of stuffed pink flamingos caught, they ignited like tinder and the sudden flare flushed the camel, thanks only to luck, into the street. *The elephants are free*, thought Harris, *the camel, that's good.* But the sea lion? The tiger? The bear? He hung his head at the thought of how disasters repeat themselves and, sorry he'd taken part in the gawking, he pressed on toward Fulton Ferry.

But something made him look back one last time when he got to the corner, and as he did he collided with a man who had to have been following him. Or had the man collided with him on purpose? He reached inside his greatcoat to secure his money purse, not that it was very full. Harris backed up to get a look at him, but the man's face was in shadow, the blazing Hippodrome a halo around his head. He braced himself and wished he had a sewer gaff on him, but he was entirely unarmed. Harris took a couple of quick steps to the side, and as he turned, his assailant turned with him, allowing the light from the fire to catch his features: Luther Undertoe.

Undertoe was staring at him, smiling at this good fortune. Seeing Harris—or Geiermeier, as he thought of him—was a strange kind of gift, the sort he hadn't gotten for a while. It seemed like the perfect compensation for the Jimster's bailing out on him: his old dupe, back at just the right time. He reached into his pocket and pulled out a small bottle, which he uncorked and tossed at Harris. Harris dodged it, but it smashed at his feet and the splatter stained his trousers. The bottle, of course, contained kerosene, which Undertoe had planned to use to incriminate the Jimster. This was even better.

"Nice to see you again, George. You know, you really shouldn't play with fire."

George. Harris smelled the solvent and looked at the glass shards. Was Undertoe going to try to light *him* on fire? He decided not to find out, and he ran. Undertoe shouted something Harris couldn't make out—a name, perhaps, because a moment later Harris heard another set of footsteps pursuing him—from the weight and sound of them, a kid's. The kid was pretty fast, but Harris had the added advantage of fear. He made it to the Greenpoint ferry terminal at the foot of Twenty-third Street, the nearest one, just as a boat was casting off, and leapt aboard, barely making it.

"What the Hell?" said the deckhand. "You coulda got yourself killed."

Harris turned and looked back at the dock, but it was too dark to make out the faces of any of the people on the pier. "I know," he said. "Sorry."

He stayed outside on deck, despite the cold, hoping no one would notice the whiff of the fuel. It was a long way on foot from Greenpoint to Fort Greene, but Brooklyn wasn't a place where you could find a cab at that hour. Not that he wanted one, smelling like kerosene as he did. He walked. He got back to his room about two but lay awake till dawn, listening for footsteps.

33.

BEZOAR

A week later, Undertoe oozed his way into his old friend Jones's new office at the precinct house. It was bigger than the old one. He had a window now.

"What rock did you crawl out from under?" Jones said.

"Happy New Year, Jones. I have some news for you," began Undertoe, before telling him he had found Will Williams. He didn't get any further.

"*Who* have you found? And *why* do I care?"

Undertoe didn't mind the tone; it was part of the police culture. He knew Jones would come around when he heard the offer. They always did.

The fact that Harris had jumped a Greenpoint boat had led Undertoe to look for him there first. He had one of his boys redraw the old newspaper image of Geiermeier, add a beard to make him Harris and make copies for the rest. They staked out the East Twenty-third Street dock in twelve-hour shifts for forty-eight hours straight, but Harris never showed. Undertoe's rash had begun acting up then, and he spent the following days watching the ferries—all the ferries, now—and scratching, relentlessly scratching. He'd seen Geiermeier twice now, Goddamnit, after all that time, and he'd be damned if he didn't track him down and send him to the gallows at last.

Finally, he saw him. He'd been scanning a group of passengers at the Manhattan Fulton Street pier when his eyes locked onto Harris's face. He underwent a spasm of excitement and raked his nails so hard across one welt that they came away bloody, but it was well worth it. He'd boarded the boat and shadowed Harris back to Mr. Noe's. He recalled the house from following Fiona the previous summer, and it infuriated him that he'd failed to recognize his man back then, despite watching him come and go for several days. At any rate, now it was indisputable that Harris was working with the Dolan gang. It was tempting just to dispatch him in broad daylight, but Undertoe got a hold on his urges and held out for the greater satisfaction of reeling his man in slowly and delivering him live to the police. He watched the house all night and in the morning saw Geiermeier chatting with a nigger doughnut girl before he went to work. She seemed to know him, so he went over and ordered a coffee just after Geiermeier had left and asked her what his man's name was. She told him.

"Oh, I guess I don't know him. The fellow I was thinking of is German."

Lorraine shrugged and went back to wiping her counter. It surprised Undertoe to find out he was using such an Irish-sounding name, but Geiermeier-Williams-Whateverhisnamewas had thrown a few curves before. That was what made him such a pain in the ass. And it fit in beautifully with the Dolan angle.

Now, as he sat in Lieutenant Jones's office, Undertoe was salivating over the prospect of his lost bounty from the museum fire. He also imagined there might be an excellent incentive related to the Hippodrome conflagration, assuming he could pin that one on him.

Jones didn't react to anything he said, just listened quietly, then sat there silently.

"Surely you do remember Williams, Officer Jones, don't you? Koch was another one of his aliases, and Geiermeier was his real name, George Geiermeier. The American Museum. The girl who burned alive. Back in sixty-eight."

"It's *Lieutenant* Jones."

"Oh. Quite right, *Lieutenant,* but you do remember the suspect, don't you? How he broke out of the Tombs, vanished on us?"

The lieutenant sighed, wondering both why he'd ever taken tips from this lowlife and how the man had managed to weasel his way into his office. He would have to talk to the boys at the front desk. "What I remember is, you pinned the thing on some mysterious Hebrew countryman of yours who you didn't much like for reasons unknown to me, and we were eager to indict him even though it was a setup, because it looked pretty plausible and we were dying for an arrest, what with the papers on our asses because of the dead girl. I also remember the victim turned out to be no one. Someone came in and identified her, but the name probably wasn't right, because no one with that name was missing a daughter, and no one ever came to claim the body. And then you lost your dupe somehow. Barnum collected his insurance money—and from a Connecticut firm, if I recall, meaning it was easy on city coffers. That's about all I remember. I don't remember any evidence. No, I'm afraid no one cares about that case anymore, Mr. Undertoe. It's closed. Excuse me." And he rose from his chair.

"But, officer, I can add something. You see, it's not just an old case—it's a new one, too. I bumped into the guy—Williams, Geiermeier—leaving the scene of the Hippodrome fire, smelling like kerosene and running. I had one of my boys tail him to the ferry. Don't you see, he was the firebug this time, too. He's got something against Barnum, I'll wager. He worked for him back then, you might recall—that's how I knew him. He's working on the Brooklyn Bridge now. What if he tried to burn that down next? Huh, what about that?"

Jones sighed and cast his eyes out the window. It was just a glorified air shaft, no view.

"You think he's going to burn down a couple of stone towers standing in the middle of the river? Why am I not too worried, Lou?"

But Undertoe kept on: "The insurance company's a New York firm this time." Undertoe knew that because he'd shown the inspectors around. "And there's more—he's not working alone anymore. He's with a gang now—or maybe he always was. You know Johnny Dolan and Piker O'Riley, the one that chewed his friend's ear off last year?"

"Let me get this: Your mastermind German pyromaniac's going by the name of Harris now, passing himself off as an Irishman and in league with that bunch of no-count bruisers? I sort of feel sorry for the guy, really."

"They're doing more jobs than you know. And he's working with them. He just works on the bridge as his cover."

Jones looked at Undertoe. The man's information had never been any good. He'd turned in a lot of stooges, just to settle scores, but a lot of the arrests had led to convictions. He had a kind of doggedness that amounted to follow-through—except in that one last case, where he'd blown it. That was why he'd tolerated him. Convictions were good for an officer's career. If the case could really be made, it would be stunning publicity. There wasn't a single lead on the Hippodrome fire, though insurance fraud seemed obvious. But a German arsonist under cover as an Irish laborer? The Whyo gang, that bunch of barbershop musicians? *No,* thought Jones, *I don't think so.* It would make him look like a fool.

"Tell me what you stand to get out of this one, Undertoe."

"I admit I don't like the guy. He screwed me over before. So I'll enjoy it. Otherwise, just the reward money. Although now that you mention it, I wouldn't mind at all if your boys relax the tithe a little. Sir. And a little more latitude from time to time would be nice. Look the other way, things like that."

It was an honest answer, Jones thought. A reasonable set of requests if anything he said panned out, which seemed highly unlikely. But it might be worth a look, just a look. "All right, we'll check into it," he said. "Now get out of my office."

Harris, meanwhile, was in quite a state. Every morning, he woke up wondering if he should go to one of the Whyos and tell them what had happened. It was all the clearer to him now that they really had been protecting him from Luther Undertoe, that Undertoe really had been a threat. But would they still help him now? Could they? Would they just decide to get rid of him themselves, the way he'd feared at the start? There was no statute of limitations on murder, as Beatrice had told him. He ate poorly, went to work and came home. He begged off sick rather than eat with the Henleys or do his sample collections with Sarah Blacksall, thinking it was wiser not to go to Manhattan at all.

Then one morning, a week after Undertoe had gone to see Jones, Harris began to feel a pain in his gut. His stomach lurched at any sudden noise. It felt like something hard and indigestible had lodged in his intestines and was biting into them. It stayed with him until he was up on the tower, but there, in a place so high most people's stomachs would have folded, his anxieties fell away. It was heaven up there, and in addition the top of the tower was an utterly defensible fortress aerie, a place where every approach could be seen far in advance. Where he might have fled to if he ever were pursued to the top of the tower was another matter—there was only one way down—but the stomach is not a rational being. It and he felt safe there, and he came to dread quitting time the way most people dread the beginning of a shift.

For a month, his mind raced constantly with worried questions about how Undertoe had found and recognized him. Which of his blunders had compromised his cover? Had he been tailing him a long time, the same way Fiona had? Was he still? Was Harris endangering Mr. Noe by staying there? He thought of telling Mr. Noe but couldn't bring himself to. And then, well, nothing happened. No one came after him. Undertoe did not show up at his door, nor did the cops. As winter bled uneventfully into early spring, he began to think that he really had dreamed it up—all except for the fact that his coat had stunk of kerosene the next day.

Harris and the crew were mixing mortar on top of the tower one day in March when one of the loads that came up on the crane had a note attached to it. The men on the ground generally communicated with the tower using a semaphore of bells and flags and hand signals, but for anything outside the usual set of messages they resorted to notes. This one said Harris was wanted down at the office. There were a few jokes to the effect that he was either going to be promoted or fired, but no one made much of it. But Harris's stomach was in an uproar. He couldn't go immediately, though, as they were right in the middle of setting a block.

They had already spread the prepared surface with cement, and the bottom edges of the new stone had been trimmed. The stone was fitted into the sling, and Harris was on the guyline. It took several men to hoist each stone in the air, while the men on the guylines kept the stones from swinging wild. Carefully, they brought the arm of the boom derrick around and positioned the stone over the mortar bed. The wind was strong, and the linemen had to use every ounce of their weight to keep the load steady as it was lowered. Finally, the pins set into the top level of the tower were aligned with the sockets cut in the new stone and everything slid into place, just like the latch of a well-hung door clicking shut. They cleaned up the seams and locked the derrick in place, and then Harris headed down.

The footbridge that connected the tower to the ground undulated

under the footsteps of anyone upon it. A sign posted at the bottom read
SAFE FOR ONLY 25 MEN AT ONE TIME. DO NOT WALK CLOSE TOGETHER NOR
RUN, JUMP OR TROT. BREAK STEP! It was far from the most dangerous place
on the site, but compared to the rock-solid tower it was rickety going. Harris slid his palms along the cable handrails as he went and tried to convince
himself there was something good waiting for him below—that promotion
to cutter he'd dreamed of. But when he was halfway down, he saw a group
of uniformed men in the yard near the office, looking in the direction of the
footbridge, the tower and him. Four of them. His stomach began to thrash.
There were black blotches in his vision, and he stopped short on the gangway and gripped the wire rails. A ripple traveled up the boards behind him
and back, like a wave on the sea. He tasted sweet and bitter, saliva and bile,
and a moment later a yellow bolus of Harris's vomit was sailing through the
air—a hundred eighty, a hundred, twenty feet to go—and then it landed in
the river with a tiny splat and was gone. On the pier, the master mechanic
was standing with the police, noticing it all.

"What was that?" asked Lieutenant Jones. "Looked like he dropped
something."

"I'd say that was his breakfast."

Harris stood up. A long string of mucus and saliva trailed from his chin,
and then the wind carried it off. He was light-headed, his knees were wobbly and everything was blurry. He was fully aware of just how easy it would
be to follow his doughnut and coffee to a watery grave. A part of him would
have preferred that to facing judgment, but the greater part of Harris, the
part that had been growing in the time since he'd left the gang, believed
that the truth would prevail. He squatted down, held on and breathed
deeply. Ten seconds later, he was seeing clearly again and slowly picking
his way down the planks to terra firma.

"Feeling ill?" asked the master mechanic. He frowned as if it were a
moral failing.

"Just some stomach trouble, sir."

"Dizzy?"

"No, sir."

"Well then, there are some men who'd like to speak to you, Harris."

The police's strategy was to interrogate Harris in a manner that would not raise alarm in an innocent man. They took him to a room in the bridge office and in the company of one of the master mechanic's assistants told him they were looking into a crime that might have been committed by a man of his name. It was merely routine, Lieutenant Jones insisted, but they were interviewing as many Frank Harrises as they could find, including, he might be amused to hear, a young boy working in the Manhattan caisson. Harris hadn't heard there was another Frank Harris on the bridge, but he knew a kid named O'Hara, he said, feeling a queer surge of gratitude to Dandy Johnny. Hiding in plain sight. They asked him some questions about his career, which he sketched as far back as the paving crew. "That was my first job here," he said. It was the first one he'd put down when he filled out his papers at the bridge office, anyway. He gave the name of the English boat on which the other Frank Harris had arrived, around the same time Georg Geiermeier did, all just as Beatrice had prepared him to do in just this eventuality. He did it all pretty calmly, too, considering the shifty way his stomach had just behaved. But it was easy—it had been drilled into him by Beatrice two hundred times, and he'd used it ever since. They asked his whereabouts on Christmas Eve, and he told them he'd been working with Sarah Blacksall. It all checked out. Jones walked away studying the small, yellowed square of newspaper with the portrait of George "the Torch" Geiermeier. The man looked vaguely similar to it. What with the intervening years and the rigid expression of photographs, it was possible Harris was Geiermeier, except that Harris's English was perfect, his accent undeniably Irish, and he was a skilled stoneworker with a convincing story, reasonable-sounding alibis and no history of criminal involvement. Jones wanted Undertoe to be right, but this was looking pretty far-fetched.

Harris didn't know what to think after they left. The foreman took him aside, but it wasn't over the police matter, which he saw as a mere nuisance. It was the vomiting and crouching down the master mechanic had seen when Harris was on the catwalk. Dizziness was a sure way to get transferred off the top. The bridge company did not want workers falling to their deaths. It was bad publicity. Harris, who had never before shown the slightest sign of vertigo, fit the description. He was grounded.

"It's just a bad turn, sir, I'll be fine tomorrow."

"Two weeks," said the foreman. "Standard rest period for dizziness. And by the way, if you were so queasy, you shouldn't have gone up this morning, Harris. Wait here and I'll see if there's anywhere topside to put you in the meantime. But I'm afraid it may have to be the caisson—that's the only place we're short right now."

Harris sighed. Undertoe, the police and now the Manhattan caisson. The Brooklyn one was complete, but everyone said the Manhattan side was worse. It was deeper, and men were falling ill at an alarming rate and no one understood why. But then the boss came back with a smile on his lips.

"I think you'll like this. One of the yard foremen requested you as a trimmer."

Harris still had the taste of bile in his mouth. He'd been on the verge of collapse, death and incarceration, and just like that he got his dream. He was given the afternoon off to recover from his ailment and joined the crew trimming blocks on the ground the following day.

The granite for the bridge arrived from the quarry already cut to the basic dimensions, but they were rough, and the crews modified each block on site to fit its final location. Most of this work was done on the ground, with just the fine-tuning being left to the men up top. It was simple stonecutting, but every block was as important as those in any church tower. The safety of the countless crowds of passengers that would soon use the bridge to cross from shore to shore relied on those stones. He looked out at the harbor and wondered if the bridge would ever make the Brooklyn ferries obsolete.

When Harris first picked up the tools, he was nervous. But they were much the same as the ones he'd used in Hamburg: the mallet, the spike, the toothed chisel and the straight. No one was doing any carving here, though. The truth was, his skills far exceeded those of most of the men he was working with, and he hadn't forgotten. Within half an hour, a couple of men had remarked at how cleanly and efficiently he did the work. "How long since you worked?" they asked, meaning with stone. But it didn't matter: He still had the feel, and he still loved it, even the pain in his arms that night from the long hours of hammering. After his two weeks were up, Harris was given a new assignment. He'd shown his competence, but he was also obviously well enough to go back up top, where his ability to manage the heights was valued. The difference was that now he would be a trimmer, not a grunt who worked guylines and cranks.

What happened next was proof that you should never let your guard down. You can build yourself a shield, a fortress, a false identity, but it only protects you as long as you keep it up. When danger seems to have passed, that's when it's greatest. Danger has patience; it waits for opportunity. Then it pounces.

It wasn't Jones's fault. Jones had been convinced by Harris's performance—he'd actually pitied the man his stomach ailment and gone easier on the questions than he'd planned. Though when he looked at that picture again, he did decide to leave a couple of men on duty to watch Harris a little longer, just in case he was wrong. They watched him go to work and to and from the Henleys'. They checked the records at the Sewer Division and even found the street contractor he'd worked for before that. It was a pretty large company, and the current secretary didn't remember the man, but he went back to an old payroll ledger and confirmed that there had indeed been a Frank Harris working on one of their crews in the period in question. (That, of course, was the very Frank Harris after whom the Whyos had named him, knowing the chances of sorting the two out were slim.) The whole investigation was becoming an embarrassment for Lieutenant Jones. He'd put half a dozen men to the task of trailing a respectable and uninteresting Irish laborer under the absurd premise, probably trumped up by Undertoe on account of some odd grudge, that the man was a German incendiary. They were laughing at Jones in the department now, and he was angry. He called Undertoe in.

"No," said Undertoe, "I swear it's him. Have you brought him in? Have you talked to him? Do you really believe he's Irish?"

"I've talked to him. He said things like *Oh, aye, that I do.* As Irish as potatoes."

"He's not. He's fooled you." He scratched for a moment. "You see, it's brilliant. There's a hundred Frank Harrises in this city. His name is his disguise."

"Mr. Undertoe, do you think it's a crime to have a common name?"

"It could be useful."

"*Jones,* for example? Listen, Undertoe, just get out of my office and don't return. I don't want to see you back in this building unless it's behind the bars."

Undertoe backed his way out of the station in a posture of disgrace, but the moment he was around the corner he stood up straight and spat twice on the sidewalk. The whole thing made Undertoe's ears roar. When he met up with the little punk who'd chased Harris to the dock for him, he took him straight around the corner for a chat and broke his nose. It didn't cheer him up much, though. Then, on his way uptown later that afternoon—he was going to take a last look at the hulk of the Hippodrome before they knocked it down—he saw an old dog lying in a doorway. It looked half dead, and he kicked it. Unexpectedly, the dog snapped back to life and clamped onto his leg. Undertoe was just on the verge of slitting the thing's throat when its owner emerged from a pub next door and whistled. The dog let go and scurried to the pub.

"I ought to kill you and your mongrel both," Undertoe snarled. He was down on his knee, and his leg shrieked at him through his ringing ears. There were two deep, welling punctures in his calf. He put a finger in his ear and twisted it, but it had no effect on the sound within, of course. It never did.

"You stupid bastard—he wouldn'ta bit you 'less you'd kicked him."

Undertoe would have settled the dispute right then, but the fellow was a bit big, a bit young, and the rioting pain in his leg put Undertoe at a disadvantage. Not to mention that the dog appeared to be quite well trained. He decided just to go home and get off the thing, but on the way he managed to find a vagabond to sharpen his switchblade on. He was sleeping in an empty shipping crate over on the West Side docks, and Undertoe rolled him into the drink when it was done. That made him feel slightly better at last. He always did love to hear the splash.

Harris had missed two full weeks up top—two rows laid down, six feet attained—and the day he returned he could feel the elevation even more intensely than usual. The great thing was, the tower just kept going up. Every time they completed a row of the enormous stone blocks, they casually set about laying the mortar for yet another level, and he was jacked up even higher. Sometimes he wondered whether he'd ever hear back from his father, or if he should try to contact Beatrice to tell her about Undertoe, but neither of those anxieties was all-consuming. Harris felt happy. He loved his work. He had gone back to spending time with his friends on both sides of the river.

For the time being, he just let himself be in love with the top of the bridge. It was maybe the same thing as loving the sky. The air was purer up there. It made the whole world seem reasonable and orderly, although sometimes the gusts there were so remarkable that even the very solid Harris felt he might be blown off his feet. He looked across the water at the tiny world of New York, at nearly uniform thickets of low brown buildings prickling with chimneys, punctuated here and there with something grander. Trinity's bell tower would soon have competition from the secular spire of the new *Tribune* building and the great, tall trunk of the Western Union building that was going up. But even the largest of the city's buildings were small compared to the bridge, and even the busiest thoroughfares were so far off that the city looked quiet. Further uptown, the buildings were sparse and the island was suffused with the bud green of spring growth.

One afternoon that summer, he was up top trimming an edge when heavy clouds rolled in over New Jersey. If they came this way, Harris thought, they'd have to quit early, but he was hoping they wouldn't. It was hot and humid down below, but gorgeous and breezy up above. The crew still was planning to raise several more stones to be set the following day. When the ground team gave the ready signal, Harris left his trimming to help bring the next stone in. The steam winch below engaged, and Harris could only just make out the racket of the engine. Then the cable loop creaked and stretched taut, and slowly the stone groaned into the air. The tower crew landed the block easily enough, and Harris and two others were sliding it along the tracks to the north wall of the tower when they heard a loud crack. Everyone turned in fear to look down at the cable that was going under load again, but it was already bringing up the next stone and inching its way around the turn block. Harris thought, *Thunder?* and looked at the sky. But it wasn't thunder. It was an extra derrick boom that had been tied off in the raised position. The end of the line that fastened it had gotten wrapped around the cable loop and snapped. Now the boom was swinging toward him, right at eye level. Harris bellowed a scatological expletive in German and ducked. It swung over him.

Then he stepped back to get his balance and found nothing beneath his boot heel but air.

NEW WORLD

34

THE FALL OF MAN

Oh, God," he said rather quietly, in English, as he rolled backward in a somersault and into the cool void at the center of the tower. He plummeted slowly at first, like a great ship just setting sail, but soon he was flying freely through the air, his speed limited only by the drag of his windmilling limbs. At one point, his foot struck a piece of hardware set into the interior wall, probably a ladder rung, and he cried out. Then he drew his arms and legs in against his belly, which only made him fall faster.

Where was the jolt of fear that would normally have flung his whole body forward the instant he lost his footing? Where was the impulse toward self-preservation? The fingers that should have shot forth and grasped at anything, anything at all, simply flexed once and conceded their failure. Perhaps it all just happened too fast; perhaps there was a will in him to fall. If he had made a decision, it fell with him as he tumbled through space.

He felt rather than saw the wall rush past, sometimes veering dangerously near. He kept his head tucked and didn't try to reach out and break his fall. Head over heel over ass over elbow he went. He saw black and then a smudge of blue and then black again as the great dark cathedral cavern of the tower rose around him. He thought of his mother, the last thing she said to him. *I'll see you soon, dear. Be good.* He felt cold. He had fallen past the waterline. Outside the tower walls were water, fishes, eels, algae—and somewhere, the body of Waugh. He saw black and a flash of brightness, then black as the bottom rushed toward him, black, and then a small disk of light. Three feet of standing water was all there was to cushion his impact. His spine kissed the bottom. Then the great wave his landing made engulfed him. River-cold rainwater crashed about him as fiercely as North Sea surf. And Harris was dead to the world.

The men on the tower did not gape into the hole. They shrank silently away from it and turned to the outer edges of the tower, where they cast their eyes down at the cresting scallop-edged waves, as if Harris might somehow have been transported outside the tower so that they could see and therefore more easily comprehend his death. Or perhaps they just couldn't bear the blackness of the hole. Then finally (though it was just seconds later), one of them galloped down the footbridge—DO NOT RUN, JUMP OR TROT—shouting, "*Man down! Man in the tower!*" Someone found the orange flag that meant *emergency* and hoisted it on a derrick. But what was the hurry? What was there to do? Harris had fallen. Down below, as people became aware of something wrong, work stopped, machines were shut off and the yard grew silent. There were muttered discussions about whether they'd be able to recover the body. A man who knew Harris was addicted to the tower said, "They ought to let him lie."

"Who is there to tell?" asked the foreman.

"He lives with a man in Fort Greene, in his stable apartment, doesn't he?"

But just a landlord? They wanted to tell a widow, an orphan, an ailing mother. Then someone remembered he had a friend.

"You could ask Henley. He'll know. That Negro blaster. He's over on the Manhattan side now."

So a couple of men were dispatched by ferry to inform John-Henry, thinking that maybe he knew about Harris's family. Meanwhile, the tower crew began to rig a derrick with lines long enough to reach all the way to the bottom. They weren't sure what they'd find, a terrible mess or just a battered body, but there was no question of allowing Harris to have the bridge as his tomb. With Waugh there'd been no choice, but it wasn't the way the company wanted people to think of the bridge. How could the men have gone on with the job, knowing he was down there on his back in the standing water, staring unseeingly, submerging and rising according to the schedule of the microbes and the flies till most of his flesh was gone and a ragged skeleton with a few severe bone breaks at last came to rest on the roof of the caisson, at the bottom of the tower? No, knowing he *had been* down there was going to be bad enough.

When they asked for volunteers to help recover the body, only John-Henry, who'd ridden the ferry across in stunned silence, stepped forward. They drew straws for the second man, and soon the two of them were being lowered on boatswain's chairs. They had a large tarp, a bucket, a rake and two gaff hooks with them. They were wearing headlamps, but as they descended a wind rushed up from below and both their flames died. It was pitch-black all around them and suddenly cold.

"There he goes," said John-Henry with a shudder.

As they neared the bottom, it grew very quiet. They couldn't hear the screeching of the block that was reeling them down anymore. When their feet touched water, they shouted up and sounded the depth of the standing water with their rake. No one knew how much rain and seeped-in river water there would be, but they were a little surprised to find it only waist high. They relit their lamps and began to look around. John-Henry saw it first: a dim hump floating in the water.

"There," he said.

It looked as if he'd ended up facedown, meaning he had surely drowned if he hadn't died in transit. John-Henry moved through the water. The shape was completely still. That was when he heard Harris's voice— gibberish, but definitely Harris. The other man shouted when he heard it, and the sound ricocheted back and forth, trapped by the high, thick tower walls.

"Harris?"

Harris saw one light coming toward him and another going away. He said, "Mutti, I built this tower," or he tried to. He was speaking German if he was speaking at all, but his ears couldn't hear the words he meant his lips to utter.

John-Henry reached out and touched cold, wet wood—a barrel.

"Harris?" he called again, and turned around, peering into the darkness. He thought he heard something moving in the water in the far corner.

And then there were two lights, and Harris saw a face, but not the face of his mother. Two hands clasped his head, but they were not his mother's. He felt a kiss, but not his mother's. John-Henry's. He groaned.

The wave of his landing had washed Harris to a corner and left him sitting propped up, head above the water. He'd smacked the back of his head, lost consciousness briefly, and now he was coming to. Improbable, yes, but it really happened—check and see. He had a very thick skull, Harris. He was carried back to Mr. Noe's some hours later, where he was put up in a first-floor bedroom at the big house and cared for by an excellent team, including the cook, Sarah Blacksall and Mr. Noe's own physician, who declared him the healthiest man he'd ever seen. He had sustained a concussion, but to everyone's astonishment Harris had already gotten some of his wits back the following morning. He refused to give interviews or make a statement, but the intense public interest in death in general and danger on the bridge in particular dictated that his story was a major news event. It made every city paper. The several editors who stooped to giving it a front-page headline sold out their entire editions.

Lieutenant Jones picked up the *Tribune* when he sat down at his desk the next morning and said, "I'll be damned!" Undertoe's dupe had become an instant celebrity. Jones tacked the notice up on the bulletin board himself and braced himself for ribbing from the boys.

Undertoe saw the *Sun*, spat and threw his knife at a fence, where it lodged and vibrated with anger. He didn't know whether to hope that Harris died of his injuries or not. He ate a light lunch of boiled tongue on toast, then went out and took advantage of a pretty little Negro hot-corn girl's carnal wares. For dessert, on an impulse, he smothered her.

Johnny Dolan saw the *Times* and said, "Beanie, trouble. Your boy Harris made the news."

"What?"

"Yeah, you've got to read this. It's worse than Piker's ear. They're liable to write up his Goddamn life story in *Leslie's* or *Harper's*, and who knows where else. I don't trust him to leave us out of it. So why don't you put someone on him and arrange some *complications*—before he gets the chance to talk. Put Piker on it. And bring me another drink, eh?"

Beatrice snatched the paper from Johnny's hand. His grip was soft when he was drunk, and he was indeed well on his way to that, despite the early hour. He'd been backsliding lately. After she'd read the article, she was quiet for a while, then said, "Johnny, why would he talk? What's he got to gain by it? They say he won't even talk to the reporters." But Johnny had left the room to make that drink himself, since she'd ignored the request. He was drinking pretty much all day these days, and Beatrice was doing both their jobs, plus most of the work teaching Jimmy the language, but she wasn't complaining. It brought her greater control.

The following day, Harris received calls at the Noe residence from no fewer than seven more reporters wanting to profile him; a dozen strange women bearing casseroles, pies, cakes and well-wishes; six doctors seeking to examine him for the benefit of medical science; two representatives of P. T. Barnum, who wanted to put him in his own exhibit at the new, 150 percent fireproof edifice of the new, new Hippodrome, due to be completed within the year—and Beatrice. The cook took the food and the names but turned all the visitors away. Harris was doing worse. He was in and out of consciousness and feverish, and it was just family, so to speak, at his bedside: John-Henry and Lila, Mr. Noe, plus Sarah Blacksall and Susan Smith.

There was one other visitor to the Noe place in the days after Harris's fall, a man who didn't leave his card or name, just watched the others come and go. He spent most of Thursday loitering around the crowded yard. When the reporters and curiosity seekers had given up for the day, he stayed around another hour, long past dark, hiding himself in a stand of trees in an undeveloped lot across the street. No one had been over to Harris's usual apartment except a boy who came to feed the livestock at midday. He tried the door and found it open. Then a dog barked, and the man's stomach clutched—he detested dogs. But it wasn't him the dog was bothered by—Undertoe had been lurking in the ligustrum so long that the dog was used to him. It was a girl approaching the house, and Undertoe recognized her: B. B. O'Grady, or whatever her name was, the girlfriend of Johnny Dolan. It was no surprise to him. He watched while she waited at the door and was turned away, then he entered the stable and found his way up to Harris's apartment.

There wasn't much there—some spartan furniture and a few clothes folded on a shelf—but it didn't take him long to find the one thing of greater interest than the rest: a small bundle of letters in a drawer. Some were in English, addressed to Harris, but there were a couple of them in German, too, and when he saw that, he smiled. It was settled then: Harris was Geiermeier.

Undertoe's mother had never taught him German—she considered her Germanness the curse that had held her back—so he had no notion of what the letters said. On top of that, the Gothic handwriting was so diabolically odd he couldn't even make out the name of the addressee, except that he was quite sure it wasn't Harris, Williams, Koch or Geiermeier. Who was he really? Undertoe wondered.

Then he flipped to the end of one of the letters and was able to make out the signature. It looked like it was *from* Robert Koch. How strange, he thought—that was one of Geiermeier's names—but it didn't matter: Whatever the letters said, whomever they were from, they were incontrovertible evidence that Harris was really a German. Undertoe decided to take just one of the letters along with him. He took the first one, the one that described the fire in Fürth, the two bodies in the barn, the funeral; the one that said, *My friend, even if you'd planned to fake your death so you could vanish and never be looked for, you couldn't have done it any better.* In short, it was exactly the sort of circumstantial evidence that could get the Barnum's Museum case reopened, not that Undertoe knew that. He folded it and put it in his pocket.

He decided to study his subject more fully and assemble as complete a body of evidence as possible before he returned to Jones. He was being more cautious, in light of Jones's recent dismissal of him. He followed home several of the visitors to the house, including Susan Smith to Weeksville, way out in Brooklyn, and Sarah Blacksall to her apartment off Gramercy Park. Then he turned his mind to what role the landlord might play in Harris's affairs and tailed Mr. Noe when he left the house, took the ferry across to Manhattan, and then walked to a construction site on Broadway, inspected it and returned home again. Undertoe was baffled. What could possibly link Harris and Johnny Dolan and that crowd to a couple of blacks, an unmarried lady of the better sort and a man who oversaw what appeared to be a mercantile establishment, some sort of factory under construction?

Harris's fever didn't break until the third day.

"Who did you tell me came by again?" Harris was propped up on his elbows and squinting at the cook through a fog.

"Oh, awake, are you? Well, the worst was the agent from Barnum who showed up with a midget in tow—a midget! It's an insult, Frank. To think they'd put you up next to the freaks."

"No, not them, the lady."

"I said a lady *of a sort.* A Miss O'Grabner? Said she was acquainted with you, but really, my dear, I'm not sure you care to remember *every* rendezvous you've made."

"No, bring her in to me, please. I want to see her." He didn't notice Sarah Blacksall and Mr. Noe standing in the doorway, didn't see Sarah blanch nor Mr. Noe put his hand on her arm. Mr. Noe had taken a definite liking to the lady doctor, and he wondered why he hadn't heard more about her from Harris. Obviously, she was smitten, and she was far better than he'd hoped Harris could do for a wife. Sarah held a tray with a phial of laudanum, an envelope of aspirin powder and a pitcher. Mr. Noe was carrying a small crate.

"Well, that wasn't even today, was it?" said the cook. "You were out cold. I don't care to speculate where she might be now. If she wants to see you, she'll come again."

Harris turned to the wall with a groan, but then Sarah made him sit up for his medicines. After he'd taken them, Mr. Noe laid the flat wooden crate on the bed and said, "Frank, my boy, I think this might cheer you up, somehow. I hope so."

It was heavy and about the size of a dictionary or a Bible. There was also a well-traveled letter. Both were covered with foreign franks and bore Harris's name—*Frank Harris,* that is—in an unmistakable Gothic hand: his father's. That was a strange sight, a meeting of two worlds he never thought would converge.

"They arrived yesterday."

He blinked. "Thank you," he said.

Mr. Noe extracted the nails from the crate with a hammer, producing a series of curdling screeches, while Harris fidgeted with the letter.

The letter, of course, was in German, and it was a mea culpa, beginning with the surprising words *My Dear Son, How happy I am to learn you are alive.* The story it told was not as simple as Harris had imagined it. His father wrote of a belated attempt to restore their relationship, apparently sometime around when Harris's uncle brought his apprenticeship to an end. He said he'd sent letters, first to Hamburg, then to Fürth, without reply and concluded his son wanted no part of him. He said Wittold Diespeck had informed him this was true, and that he had respected his son's wishes and desisted. He had, however, continued to send the money to cover the apprentice fees, apparently long after his son had been hauled back from Hamburg—an event of which Wittold Diespeck had neglected to inform him, just as he had failed to pass on his letters. But he acknowledged that the rift was his fault: He had sent his son away. He had neglected him. He was sorry.

Harris felt very little, reading the words. It was as if it were someone else's life that had been ruined by a needless set of mistakes and misunderstandings. The question running through his mind was, *What does this mean to me now?* His father's change of disposition couldn't save him from the ordeals he'd seen or give him a Beatrice disentangled from Dandy Johnny Dolan. It couldn't give him back the life he'd never had. What did it mean? Finally, at a loss, he turned to the box.

Another letter, folded and sealed with blue wax, rested on top of a bundle wrapped in cloth. It had been written the following week—an afterthought, but presumably they had traveled across the ocean on the same boat. *I have realized there are two things of your mother's that should belong to you.* The first was the proceeds of her share of the Diespeck farm, which had been sold off. It was not a great fortune, but it was more than Frank Harris would have made on the bridge in five years, and his father proposed to transfer that value to his son. *A month or more will have passed since I sent this,* his father wrote. *Indeed, many years have passed. But now I urge you to send me the address of your bank in New York by the transcontinental wire. I am an old man now, and I do not wish further delay or accident to prevent this transfer from taking place.* It was the first thing that had really stirred him since he'd opened the letter, this idea that his father might die before they could communicate again. He felt the urgency, too, not for money in his bank account but for an exchange not mediated by months.

If he marveled that he was suddenly the sort of man who had a need to send a message by transcontinental wire, if the idea that he might soon have a bank account full of money was incredible to Harris, the contents of the bundle were far more real. Inside layers of cloth and brown paper, he found a familiar, elaborately tooled leather case. The smell of the old leather and the contours of the thing moved him far more than his father's letters had yet managed to. It was so direct and visceral, so simple, so wanted. He opened the cover of the daguerreotype case and looked into the face of his mother. Yes, her eyes were closed, and yes, she was dead. He'd long since accepted that. The surprise was seeing himself so clearly in the reflection of the polished silver plate, his rather battered, bearded, grown man's face floating just over her shoulder. Before it had always seemed an either-or: her face escaping, his intruding. Now he found they flowed to-gether—viewer and viewed, mother and son. He was part of her, part even of his father, and yet he was also a man his mother could never have imag-ined: a man called Frank Harris who was helping to build a great bridge in a country she had never seen.

Some time later, Mr. Noe knocked. Sarah had gone home. Harris read his landlord and surrogate father parts of his real father's letter, and Mr. Noe shook his head and smiled as he listened.

"Ah, Frank, my boy, that's lovely. But I hope you won't be moving out. The sum he mentions is large enough that you certainly could set up a modest house of your own, but you'll always be welcome here. I'd like it if you stayed on."

"Thank you," Harris said. He hadn't even thought of moving.

"And will you keep your same job? What with the fall and that money, maybe it's time you did a different kind of work? Selling brushes, perhaps, or managing on the factory floor. There's pretty good money in it."

"Thanks. But I want to stay on the bridge—as long as I can work on top." Harris was, in fact, worried he wouldn't be allowed to go back up there, not after falling like that.

"Just so you know, my boy, that I'd like it if you wanted to come to work for me. There's going to be a lot to do to get the new factory up and run-ning. My offer stays on the table, any time you want it."

Mr. Noe was going out that afternoon to inspect the progress of the construction. It was going to be a highly modern factory building and was being fitted out precisely to his rather unusual specifications. The present Noe Brush facility in Brooklyn had been too small for years and was technologically outmoded. It wasn't the first time Mr. Noe had suggested that Harris come and work for him, but he didn't push it—he didn't fool himself that Harris would be as attracted to brushes as he was to stonecutting. *But as soon as he settles down,* thought Mr. Noe—and he was thinking of Dr. Blacksall—*then he'll want a quieter existence.* He smiled and set the daguerreotype of Harris's mother on the bedside table.

35

A NEW ERA

The cook had reluctantly told Harris that she would admit Beatrice the next time she came, but Beatrice did not return. She was fully occupied handling Johnny. She let him believe she'd told Piker what he wanted. To Piker she suggested Johnny had been amused by the news reports—"quite *pleased*," she said, that Harris came off so well.

Piker laughed. Piker laughed at anything Johnny thought was funny. "But doesn't he want me to do him then?" he added. "I thought for sure he'd want me to do him now. He really doesn't?"

Beatrice had been encouraging Johnny's drinking since the Harris story broke. She didn't want him thinking on his feet. At the moment, he was passed out in the living room, in no condition to speak for himself. But she knew it couldn't last. Unless she did something soon, something drastic, Johnny would wake up. If he woke up and went out, he would talk to Piker. And Harris would be dead. She'd be in some trouble, too. She found herself fantasizing about killing Johnny. It would have been so easy—just a blow to the head. But then she envisioned the war for power that would erupt among the Whyos. More people than just Johnny would die, and she would be to blame. If only she had been a man, she thought for perhaps the hundredth, the thousandth time. Then she could have openly taken over.

She left the Dolan penthouse and walked the city till dawn, from the Battery north, all the way past the Restell mansion to Central Park and back. By the time she got home, she'd come up with a plan. It was a long shot, but the Whyos needed a boss. And she needed an ally. She went to see Fiona.

Fiona had come into her own since the Jimster made the gang. In the vacuum left by Johnny's indolence, the two of them had put together a couple of very clever jobs, including a string of robberies based on intelligence about heists other gangs were planning to pull. A small crew of Whyos would arrive at the location first, enter stealthily and abscond with a substantial but exquisitely safe haul of only the most anonymous, fungible, easily pawned goods. It took restraint to leave the jewels and fancy silver behind for the second comers, but that stuff was much more identifiable and riskier to fence. Whoever got caught with it would bear the full responsibility for the job. Yes, thought Beatrice, Fiona had what it took. She understood the principle of subtlety. The only problem was her voice, which wasn't as strong as she'd have wished. But she had an idea of how to handle that. She found Fiona down at the Morgue and arranged a rendezvous at Fulton Ferry that evening.

"Is there something going on? Tell me now."

"*Jesus.* Not here. Just meet me, and bring the Jimster, all right?"

Late that afternoon, after she'd done the report, Beatrice made ready to go out and meet Fiona. Johnny sat up on the couch, polishing and sharpening the blades of his boots. He'd gone out to take a piss and had another drink and an egg sandwich she made him, but he was still in his blue velvet dressing robe.

"See you, Johnny. I'm going out," she called to him from the front room.

"Come in here."

"What? I've got to go out." But she went to the doorway of the living room. She didn't want him to get suspicious.

"You're protecting your old boyfriend, aren't you?" he said.

"What are you talking about?" So it was too late.

"*Aren't you?*"

She realized he'd been listening in when she did the report, to see if Piker had dealt with Harris. Piker didn't generally take two days on an assignment.

"He isn't my boyfriend. *Jesus.* There's a lot of jobs going on, and I'm keeping them all together, not you. Offing Harris isn't my first priority. I happen to think it's totally unnecessary. But I'm leaving for the Morgue right now, and so, if you insist, I'll give Piker the assignment as soon as I find him." It was a weak retort, she knew—there weren't that many jobs going on—but Johnny didn't stop her from going. She tried not to think about Frank Harris. There was no time for mooning, but there might be time to fix things. If she failed—well, she told herself she wouldn't fail. If only Harris weren't such an unlucky guy. Then she went out, not to the Morgue but to meet Fiona.

Undertoe had the German letter, but he knew it wasn't enough to take back to Lieutenant Jones. He was regretting his choice of dupe more than ever—he'd never meant to pick a player, like Harris had turned out to be, just a down-and-out slob with a plausible grudge. The Geiermeier debacle was on his mind as Undertoe walked up the hill from Fulton Ferry to Brooklyn Heights in search of a little short-term satisfaction, maybe a backyard brownstone job that would net him some flatware and candlesticks, maybe just a rich old lady's wallet, jewelry, dignity—whatever came his way. It was just after dark, and he cruised the dead-end alleys at the top of the Heights, one after the other, keeping his eyes peeled for possibilities. He spotted an attractive rear-garden entrance on a narrow tree-lined alley that was dominated by a large church. The casement windows spilled forth the sounds of evensong, chanted by a men's choir, and Undertoe was filled with the sense of promise, of possibility. The sound would make a good cover. One of the problems with Brooklyn as a territory was that it was too quiet; a crash or any sort of unexpected screaming could be heard by everyone in a mile radius, it seemed.

He looked down the alley and saw a young lady standing at the dead end of the street, where it overlooked the harbor. Her slim waist and full skirt were silhouetted by the lingering brightness of the western sky over Manhattan. She appeared to be contemplating the harbor, deeply absorbed in thought. An easy mark. He was planning to come right up and make some remark about the view before he showed his cards. He was close upon her before he saw that she was not alone but engaged in a conversation with two other people who were seated on a bench obscured from his view by the shrubbery and the shadows. Not such a good target after all. As he turned to go, the choir in the church stopped singing and Undertoe picked up the tones of a familiar voice. He turned back for another glance, to see whom he was dealing with. That was when he realized who they were: the Dolan girlfriend, the Jimster and his girl. The rash on Undertoe's neck prickled and he backed out of the alley. He felt angry as he headed back down Hicks Street, the idea of a brownstone job forgotten. It looked, instead, like it was going to be another of those nights on which he earned his nickname.

The three Whyos had taken the ferry across and then they'd verged south, remarking to one another on the flowering shrubbery, just as if they were out for no other purpose than to enjoy an evening stroll on Brooklyn Heights with its views of the city at the end of every lane. The alley they found seemed perfect for Beatrice's needs. The choir rehearsal would mask their voices from anyone—cop, Whyo or civilian—who wandered up the block. They walked to the end of the alley and Beatrice began to talk, starting with how Johnny had collapsed after his mother died. Finally, she bit the bullet and told them the main thing: that she'd been covering for him at every check-in and evening report since. She didn't expect them to believe her, at first, and they didn't. Fiona was just as incredulous as Beatrice had been when Johnny first told her about his mother. The Jimster was a little easier—he'd been her pupil far more often than Johnny's since he joined the gang, and though Beatrice had made sure that Johnny was the one who taught him the private codes, Johnny simply wasn't the legend to the Jimster that he was to the other, full-fledged Whyos. Johnny wasn't impressive these days, the way he used to be.

Beatrice knew from the start that she'd have to prove herself. That was why she'd gone for the cover of the choir. She looked back up the street and, seeing no one, quietly began to imitate his voice, perfectly hitting the strange tenor vibrato of his signature whyo and deploying various secret idioms that Fiona and Jimmy both believed belonged to them and Johnny alone. Of course, she was convincing: It was she they had been talking to every time they reported in, ever since Mother Dolan had died. But it shouldn't have been possible. They looked at each other and then at her, disturbed. They didn't approve. It wasn't right. Beatrice understood. She remembered how she'd felt when Johnny first divulged it to her.

"He can barely do it himself anymore. It takes a lot of control, concentration and thought. God, half the time he can hardly talk straight or stand upright; he certainly couldn't control a situation with his voice. What I'm telling you is, at some point soon, the others are going to see he's weak. He's going to get himself in trouble. And someone needs to be ready to step in the minute he does, because if he goes down and there's no one there, the whole system—the protection, the common till, the freedom of the Why Nots—it'll be gone overnight."

"Jesus," said Fiona. "What are we supposed to do about it?"

"Everything." Beatrice looked from Fiona to the Jimster back to Fiona. "See, you're the ones that can do it. I can't. There has to be a man in front. And if something happens to Johnny, I'll be alone—no one would accept just me. What I propose to do, in exchange for your promise to keep things running fairly and for the benefit of all, is to teach you two what Johnny and Mother Dolan taught me. Then, whenever the time comes, it's going to be your show."

"Beanie, I just joined. There's no way—"

"That's no disadvantage. Everyone knows he likes you, and you're not a half-bad thief, and you can sing. But the main thing is, they'll believe anything I want them to, if we set it up right. Don't you see, I speak for him. *I am him.* But truth be told, Jimster—and no offense—it's not so much you I'm picking as *her.* Or both of you. You'll be the trousers, Jimmy, and the voice. Fiona will run the show."

They were quiet and attentive and seemed nervous, all of which she took as a good sign, and so she went on and explained how it would work: As long as the Jimster could show he knew the myriad individual passwords and code names and as long as he took a strong lead the minute Johnny was down, it would create the illusion that Johnny had chosen him for his heir. There might be a little brawling, but she was confident the gang would accept it. After all, the Whyos liked being Whyos—the security and the income were unbeatable. She explained the rudiments of the secret language and how she ran a report, but she wouldn't teach them the details or all the private idioms until it was really necessary. She omitted one other detail, too: If it worked, she was getting out just as soon as she could, and never going back. They shook hands and then, with the pact made, turned and headed back to the ferry.

Johnny had gotten a queer feeling from Beatrice that night, the way she promised so easily to go find Piker Ryan. She didn't argue half enough, admitted her negligence too fast. It seemed to him she'd been a little too eager and submissive. He didn't trust it. So instead of the squirt of laudanum he was craving, he settled for a jot of rum in his coffee and then went out to the terrace and made contact with Piker Ryan. It felt good to whyo again; he wasn't sure why he hadn't been able to do it for so long.

"So did you find Piker?" he asked Beatrice when she got in.

"It's all set, Johnny, no worries."

"Because he didn't see you down at the Morgue."

"You went out? Well, I guess I saw him after you did. You want a gin?"

"He was just here."

"You know," she said, "you shouldn't worry so much about security, Johnny. It's going to make you look weak. And anyway, I'm doing it all. Everything's under control." But she knew that affecting a breezy manner wasn't going to get her out of this.

"You? You're just a little whore," he growled, and threw his cup at her. "I don't know why my mother was so keen on you." She looked down at her dress, stained with coffee. The cup lay broken on the floor. But that was as far as he went. Then he poured himself a gin, ran himself a bath, hauled out his shaving cup and scraped the razor across his face. He wiped a palmful of pomade through his locks, pared his nails and slipped into his red silk waistcoat and a gabardine suit, carefully sliding the black mourning band around his upper arm. He slammed the door behind him.

When he walked into the Morgue a short time later, swinging his monkey-headed cane, he was looking like the old Dandy Johnny, and he was greeted with bawdy and enthusiastic shouts from the Whyos. They were glad to have their boss back and in a good mood. He bought a round of drinks for the whole bar. Piker Ryan was waiting for him in the back booth, as planned.

As for Harris, the purple and blue bruises that engulfed his backside and half of his face were now beginning to go green around the edges. There was a great nasty lump on his occiput that was still almost unbearably tender, but his mind was fairly clear, and the stitches up his arm and across his right knee were starting to itch. The doctor had told him he'd be back at work in a couple of weeks. The bridge company had told him he could have a transfer to the Manhattan tower if he wanted it, whenever he recovered. Dizziness was never mentioned. He was a bit of a folk hero now, and the publicity of his return would be good for the bridge. The reporters had gone away after a day or two when a better story broke: A disgraced servant girl had leapt from the belfry of Trinity Church and landed on the back of a pony hitched to a baker's cart. Unlike Harris, she wound up dead. The pony had a broken leg and had to be shot as well. The girl's friends and various people who knew her employer were willing to talk to the papers, providing plenty of colorful background. By contrast, what the papers knew of Harris's life had been a bore and Harris himself too squeaky clean.

A few days after the hubbub around Harris subsided, a sizable amount of money was deposited in a bank account under Harris's name via the transoceanic wire. Harris wired his thanks, promising a longer letter, and then began wondering what on earth to do with the money. He thought about sending some of it to the O'Gamhnas, but he was sure they would think it was tainted by some crime. He would have liked to give some of it to the Henleys, but they were proud people. For the time being, he just left it there, untouched, and began composing his letter to his father in his head. But he had trouble concentrating on that or anything else. Writing itself was next to impossible.

There was still a trace of the concussion dulling his mind. He was dizzy, too, in fact. And there was a ringing in his ears. He hid all of this from Mr. Noe's doctors, fearing it would end his career on the bridge, but Sarah Blacksall came by often enough to notice he wasn't quite well. She told Mr. Noe, who was then even more insistent that Harris give up his hazardous work on the bridge. The two of them sat on the edge of Harris's bed and tried to reason with him.

"Haven't you had your adventures, my boy?" said Mr. Noe. "Isn't it time to settle down?" Dr. Blacksall cast her eyes at the carpet. Harris just stared at the wall. His head hurt.

The thing that upset him the most was that Mr. Noe and Sarah Black-sall had gotten John-Henry in on the idea of Harris going to work for the factory. In fact, Mr. Noe had already convinced John-Henry to come and work there himself, once it opened. Mr. Noe was thinking that he'd hardly touched the Negro market at all, and John-Henry was the very man he needed. "Every self-respecting person needs at least three brushes," he explained, "regardless of class, income or even race: A toothbrush, a hair-brush and a clothing brush. And all of them wear out after a time. Therein lies the secret of the industry: repeat custom." John-Henry figured that with Liza to worry about, he really would prefer a safer line of work. He didn't mind the sound of the relatively enormous salary either, or the idea of not working with racist Irishmen and explosives anymore.

Just a week after his fall, Harris was feeling much better. The dizziness and the nausea had passed. His arm was out of its sling. Sarah, Mr. Noe, and John-Henry were all urging him to stay home longer and rest, but he got up, dressed and walked over to the bridge to talk to the master mechanic's assistant about resuming work.

Work and Beatrice were all he could think about, suddenly. It was as if his sense of what mattered had been sharpened by the fall. He knew there was a chance for him with Sarah Blacksall. More than a chance, but he was certain that a life with the kind and intelligent Sarah Blacksall as a helpmeet, selling brushes as a profession, was not what he wanted. He missed the fresh air and the tower, rising ever higher in the air, and he missed Beatrice. On his return from the bridge office, he got an earful from Mr. Noe, whom he had not told where he was going, and then another earful when he mentioned he was going back to work.

"What! When?"

"Tomorrow."

"Harris, that's absurd." Clearly, he was disappointed.

"I'm fine," said Harris. Mr. Noe just shook his head and announced that he was going out—he needed to do a night inspection of the new lighting system at the factory.

Glad for the chance to take an interest in the factory and to divert Mr. Noe's attention from himself, Harris asked why it was necessary to inspect at night.

"Well, my boy, think about it: Winter's a key time of year for manufacturing, but one when many shops are forced to reduce their hours and output for lack of natural light. A December afternoon can be dark as night. Not at the new Noe Brush works, though. It's going to be cutting-edge, just you see."

It was delightful how much Mr. Noe enjoyed his work, thought Harris; if only he wouldn't badger Harris to join him.

"I can't wait to see it," he said. Mr. Noe clapped him on the shoulder and went off.

It was just getting dark when Mr. Noe arrived at the factory. He was thinking that the gas lamps were beautiful. But were they functional? Had he ordered enough of them to ensure the workrooms were brilliantly lit, even on the darkest days? There was no point in half measures, he felt, not if he expected his employees to produce brushes with the highest standards of workmanship. Orders in the past year had exceeded his ability to fulfill them. Scrub brushes, hairbrushes, clothing brushes, curry and saddle brushes, toothbrushes, every kind of brush. With the new space, he expected to triple his output, but he would never sacrifice quality. He had designed the floor plans himself, according to the model of Bentham's panopticon, which he'd come across in an industry journal. It was quite the rage in Europe, the new wave in manufacturing. Each level of the new factory was laid out as a single large workroom with windows all around. The workbenches were arranged radially, and management and supervisors' offices were clustered in central hubs set off by bronze grilles and carved-wood openwork. The hubs would serve as both the brains and the moral seat of the organism that was the factory and its workforce. The idea was to ensure that every worker was at least potentially in constant view of his manager and therefore motivated to exert himself to the utmost. Whether it was his sense of pride, duty or shame that motivated him didn't matter. Quality and productivity were all. The top floor would be devoted to preparing the raw materials, the middle to assembly and the ground level to finishing work, packaging and storage. There were to be six dumbwaiters positioned at regular intervals around the perimeter to eliminate the need for hauling goods up and down stairs. Mr. Noe had great expectations of the system.

The foyer was dark, so he left the front door ajar to let in the last ambient light from the darkening sky while he tapped his way across the floor with the cane Harris had given him. When he found the Lightolier, he touched a match to its oily wick and gained a small circumference of visibility. He stepped up to the first fixture, opened the valve, reached the tall pole to the jet and lit it, throwing the space into a shadowy twilight. He set his cane against the wall and briskly proceeded to light every lamp on the first floor. Mr. Noe smiled. There were enough fixtures, more than enough. He realized how pleased his wife and his son would have been with this place. They had been there with him when he was just dreaming, planning it all, and he wished they could have seen the fruition, but he didn't allow himself to wallow in missing them. It was so unexpected, the way he'd begun to move beyond the grief that had gripped him until Harris first showed up at his door with Bella. Harris had become one of his projects, then something more. Mr. Noe had lost so many things the past few years, but the peculiar generosity of Harris's decision to return Bella to him now seemed to have been a turning point. Harris was such a conundrum, so lucky and unlucky at once. If only he could get him out of the construction business, thought Mr. Noe, the boy might just make it into the realm of respectability.

He closed the front door and proceeded upstairs, lighting the lamps there as well, and then the ones on the third floor. It was delightful how fast and how well the construction had gone. They were nearly ready to move in, ahead of schedule. The dumbwaiters' sliding oak doors were still waiting in a stack to be installed, and he went from shaft to shaft, checking to see whether any of the units were operational yet. The cables had all been dropped through the shafts, but none of the first five had been completed, and none of the cars was in place. But then, in the last shaft, instead of the dark void stretching up and down, he saw a semienclosed box of iron mesh. He smiled. He tested it by putting a little weight on the car, and the bed felt firm. He tried the crank and found it under tension. When he turned it, the dumbwaiter descended, then rose back up easily. It was an excellent design, capable of lifting four hundred pounds under just the power of a hand crank. He set his hat in the center of the bed. It wasn't much of a load for a maiden voyage, but nonetheless, he cranked it down to the ground floor. Then he turned off the gas jets and went back downstairs.

He shut off the second-floor jets as well, expecting that the rows of glass bricks in the floor would allow a sufficient glow to shine up from downstairs for him to see by. But to his surprise, he encountered an unexpected dimness—it seemed the ground floor had gone dark, too. Something must have gone wrong with the equipment, and he felt a jolt of panic that the gas was flowing freely into his brand-new factory. But he was a rational man, and he knew that as long as no spark was struck, the gas would not ignite. He felt his way downstairs. He could just make out the contours of the space. His eyes had gradually adjusted to the darkness, making the most of the crescent moonlight and faint glow of street lamps. It was quiet. He didn't hear the hiss of gas. He reached up to the first fixture and found the jet was already turned firmly off. How odd.

Then an odd glimmer of light caught his eye, off to the right by the stairwell, where no window was, and he turned toward it. He heard heavy steps, saw silver and the twinkling leer of the monkey slashing through the air and down upon him. He raised his arm to shield his eyes and tried to back away, but he was trapped against the bronze grille of the bursar's window at the central hub.

"No—" he said, and then he heard the grunt of the man who wielded the monkey, just before it landed on his skull.

36.

UNDERTOE SINGS

Johnny Dolan woke up scratching. He hadn't been bitten by bedbugs in years, but the Bowery lodging house where Piker Ryan lived was infested down to every mattress. He stepped over Piker's sleeping body, regretting that he'd pulled rank on him—he would have been better off taking the floor himself. He could tell it was going to be a rough morning, after the night they'd had, and there was no point trying to coddle his headache here among the vermin, so he shook out his drawers, put them back on and then slipped into the shirt, vest and suit that lay folded neatly over the back of a chair. If he'd been at home, he would have given the suit a good brushing before he put it on, to freshen it up, but even so hardly a wrinkle showed. Fine clothes were like that, he thought, worth every cent. Last, he pulled on his fighting boots, but not before checking their blades and removing a couple of strands of embedded hair—an old ritual of his, the morning after a wild night, but one he hadn't carried out in some time. He saw that they could also use a rinsing off. He picked up his cane and polished the monkey head on one of Piker's filthy socks, then went downstairs to relieve himself. At the pump in the corner, he stopped to splash off his face and hands and run wet fingers through his hair. He gave a few pumps to his shoes and then walked out to the street, where the haze of the warm, early-summer day was just rising from the gutters.

His early rise paid off. Beatrice was still sound asleep, lying on her back with her arms thrown over her head. He'd arrived in plenty of time to wake her exactly as he'd imagined: with a hard right hook to the center of her face. He felt a definitive snap under his knuckle, heard a grunt. Her eyes flew open, then fluttered closed again. He'd woken her up and knocked her out with one blow.

"You conniving, lying whore," he said, largely for his own benefit.

The first she knew was the tinny taste running down her throat, and then she opened her eyes to Johnny looming over her, blocking out every other sight. She shrank quite reflexively into the corner and clutched the bedsheet about her, but there was no defending herself. She was stunned, he was awake and angry.

"Off your drunk, then, are you?" she finally managed to say. "You gonna kill me? You done with me?"

He snorted. "Went down to the Morgue last night, Beanie, and then Owney's. There were a lot of people there. I heard some things I didn't like."

She closed her eyes. At least she'd done her best, had tried to keep the Whyos alive. But she'd thought she would have more time. She'd underestimated him. Apparently, he had found out her plan. Had it been the Jimster? Maybe even Fiona? Not that it mattered now. She actually smiled a little at the improbable optimism of her scheme. How could she have hoped to pull it off? It was about as ludicrous as her notion of running away with Frank Harris and the Dolans' money, an idea she had abandoned the day before when she looked through Harris's window and saw a dark-haired woman sitting by his bed and mopping his brow more tenderly than a nurse would have done. So Harris had moved on, fallen in love. *Good for him*, she thought. He deserved a normal life.

"You think something's funny, do you?"

It was strange to Beatrice how gorgeous Johnny was when that murderous sneer crossed his face. Cruelty became him like no other emotion. She'd almost forgotten his looks during the period of his dissipation. This was her husband, she reminded herself. She needed to try to keep him from beating her to death. "No, Johnny, nothing's funny. I'm just a little dizzy. Why don't you tell me who you saw at the Morgue?"

"I'll tell you who I saw." He ripped away the sheet she was hiding under, and she cowered, naked. A worm of blood wriggled from her upper lip. She wiped it away, but it kept coming, slow and steady. She let her red fingers mark the sheet, a beautiful snow-white expanse that was bleached to kingdom come every week by her washerwoman. Whatever happened next, she couldn't say that being with Dandy Johnny hadn't raised her standard of living for a while.

"I got talking to Piker," he said. Her eyes darted to his. If he'd *only* talked to Piker and not to the Jimster, she thought, there was a chance she'd get out of this. Although that would mean Piker would be going after Harris, or perhaps he already had, late last night after she'd gone home. "We got to discussing about Harris, see, and why he hadn't dealt with that by now." She closed her eyes, waiting. "Funny thing is, Piker thought I'd changed my mind about Harris." He threw his jacket to the floor behind him, which wasn't like him at all, she couldn't help thinking. Then he rolled up his shirtsleeves and shrugged off his suspenders. "You made me look bad, Beanie. Now Piker knows that my girl is in the habit of opposing me. That makes me look weak. But the thing that really gets my ire up, Beanie, is why. I believe I told you once, *No boyfriends.* Didn't I?" He leaned toward her, and she braced herself. But he didn't hit her; he jerked the buttons of his trousers open. *"Didn't I?"*

"Oh Christ," she said as he reached out and yanked her toward him by the ankles. Her head snapped back and hit the back of the bedstead as he dropped down on top of her. "See, I don't like it when you don't listen to what I say, wife." When she tried to break free, he pinned both her wrists under one hand and used the other to knock her in the nose again. Something moved in it that should have been solid, and she felt sick with pain. She stopped fighting. He sidled his pants down around his ass and pressed her to the mattress. She was his wife, she reminded herself. It could be worse than this. She could be a whore on the street. This could be normal.

"So what we did," he announced, looking at the wall behind her and kneeing her legs apart, "was, me and Piker Ryan, we went out to Brooklyn and took care of the job. Made a real night of it, actually." He jammed himself in with about the same force he'd hit her with. It took her breath away. "So, like you said last night, *everything's under control*—now. No thanks to you."

"What did you do, Johnny? Johnny?" She saw him smile, but he wouldn't meet her eyes and he wasn't talking anymore. The top of her skull smacked plaster in rhythm with the thrusting of his hips. There were bursts of pain in her head, a spreading pain in her face, occasional jabs of pain in her guts. But that was nothing compared to the pain that was general across her, because it was clear she'd been wrong just now: It *couldn't* be worse. They had gone out after Harris last night and finished the job. And she had gone home to bed just when she should have been there to stop him. She closed her eyes and pictured Harris's splendid, slightly lumpy face. Why hadn't she tried to warn him?

Undertoe woke up with blood beneath his nails. His neck rash was a pulsing, violent purple, streaked with fresh, self-administered gashes, but his head was blissfully quiet. He banged his spittoon on the floor for his landlady to bring him his coffee, and after she did the sourness of it settled his stomach. He sat up in bed and counted the money he'd taken in the night before. It had been a profitable, pleasurable evening, and he was feeling well for once. Then he dressed and strolled over to the summer baths along the East River.

He walked out onto the bulkhead and surveyed the great rectangle of floating docks that enclosed the edge of the river there, turning it into a placid bathing area, while beyond the piers the river was choppy with cresting waves. There were several dozen men engaged in their ablutions, but no one was swimming per se. The city had recently begun setting up such baths in the fair months—the fever months—to encourage bathing and cleanliness among the populace. Undertoe squatted, raised his arms like a knife blade over his head, and dove. His form was surprisingly fine, and the spring-loaded force in his legs propelled him into the water so powerfully that every particle of dreck, every sloughed bit of skin, every dried cell of blood, his own or another's, was expelled from beneath his horny nails. His inflamed cuticles were washed clean. He rose with a splash, said *Ahh*, and rolled onto his back. The water was cold but invigorating, and it brought him to a pleasurable realization. He was done with the whole Williams-Geiermeier affair. He didn't need to go back to Jones and prove the case, not anymore. Who cared, really, about that Barnum's bounty when there was so much money and better satisfaction to be had elsewhere?

And Harris?

Harris managed to be boring on a morning when everyone else was embroiled in existential turmoil. He was at work. But the day wasn't a dull one for him: It was his first one back on the job, and he was feeling pretty good. He'd risen early, taken the lunch bucket the cook had left for him the night before and arrived a good half hour early on the Manhattan side. His new foreman joined him for the walk to the top, just to see how he handled the height. Harris was as comfortable and confident as ever, but then they returned to the ground. He was going to put in two weeks of light duty in the yard while he got his strength back.

All morning, men kept congratulating him on his recovery, but he realized he was going to miss working with his old crew. When they broke for lunch, someone told Harris he was wanted in the office. There was no cause for alarm. He walked into the office a common worker and back out a foreman. When he did go up top, he would be the assistant to the head cutter on his crew, in charge of tools and hardware. All afternoon, his head was full of ideas about how they might get things done both more quickly and more safely with just a couple of minor changes in the way the men worked. He looked forward to breaking his news and celebrating with Mr. Noe, Sarah Blacksall and the Henleys that night. Despite their disapproval, everyone would be convening at the house in Fort Greene for dinner. He also thought about the letters he could now write to his father and Robert Koch. He'd actually become what he claimed to be to Koch more than a year before. It now seemed as if it hadn't been pure fantasy, just a bit premature. Harris had no idea that Mr. Noe had not come home. Nor did even the cook until she went knocking on his door, asking if he were quite well.

"Mr. Noe? Mr. Noe, sir?"

But Mr. Noe wasn't there.

He came to on the floor of the factory shortly after dawn, head throbbing, breathing shallow, dazed. He was aware of little more at first than the fact that he was fully dressed, which seemed a strange thing, since he seemed to be awakening from a deep slumber. He struggled to discern where he was and to recall what had made him fall asleep in his clothing, but he couldn't. Nor could he open his eyes; they were crusted shut. With effort, he raised his hand and rubbed the sleep away, but still he could barely see, could focus no further than a foot or two away. Then he touched his fingers together and understood that the sticky, crumbly substance was not the usual eye goo, and that the blotchy, dark vista before him was no landscape but his shirtfront, stiff and black with blood. He wasn't afraid until he found he couldn't raise himself, but then his breaths came faster. His senses were so dulled that he had no knowledge of the flies that fed at the meaty edge of the gash in his scalp and in the thick puddle he lay in. At the outskirts of his limited field of vision, he sensed brightness. He felt a bit of breeze. He mustered what breath he was able and let out a keening, wordless cry.

A ragpicker on her way back from an early-morning visit to one of the East River dumps heard his wail. Why should it be a surprise to anyone that her name was Francie Harris? It was a very common name. She passed this way every day and had monitored the progress of the factory. She'd seen the scaffolding come down and the painting and finishing crews go in but knew the place wasn't occupied yet—and certainly not by families with babies. Yet she'd heard crying. Then it came again, the wail of a baby. Well, Francie Harris had never been married, never had a child, but she'd always loved the wee ones. She couldn't let a baby lie crying in an empty building. The door was ajar, and she opened it wider, peering cautiously inside. Then she heard a dragging sound and jumped with fright—could it be a trap? She fixed her eyes where the sound was coming from and made out a form. It was not a baby, it was a man. He was crawling.

"Are you hurt?" she called. Clearly, he was.

"Who is it? Who's there?" Mr. Noe's voice was a whisper.

She leaned over so he could see her face and said, "It's just me, Francie Harris, sir. I'm going to get you help."

"Oh, Harris, thank God," he murmured. He hadn't seen her face at all, just a pattern: eyes, nose, mouth. He'd heard *Harris* and been glad that his boy, his second son, was there.

In his mind, there was no juncture between that moment and the one half a day later when he roused again, in the bed of his Fort Greene farmhouse, the right Harris now there with him, attending to him in the sickbed that had been set up in the front parlor for Harris. Mr. Noe knew nothing of the simultaneous arrival of the fire department, the police and the newspapermen in response to Francie Harris's alarm. He knew nothing of the doctor at Bellevue Hospital who'd bandaged him and then, after they'd figured out who he was and where he lived, announced that the patient could little be helped and would best be sent back to Brooklyn to die in the comfort of his home.

Both Beatrice's eyes were black when she woke, and her nose sat like a great tumor on her face; it would surely heal with a prominent new hook. But the thing she was concerned about was Johnny. He was dead sober now, and he was sorting and arranging his equipment. She was afraid. Around noon, she was feeling a bit recovered and dragged herself out of bed, but when she dressed and made as if to go out, he told her to take her hat off.

"You're not going anywhere. Fix me some eggs." He was right, of course. She would have run and not stopped if she'd gotten out that door. They had turned a certain corner, and both of them were aware of it.

Johnny spent the day looking through the account books and occasionally whyoing to the gang from the roof. Late in the afternoon, he told her to bring him a glass of whiskey. When she went to the pantry to fetch it, her eye fell on the several phials of hydrate of chloral they kept on hand on a low shelf among the slungshots, bowie knives, gougers and the rest of their gangsters' larder. She mixed it very light, just a drop, then a little heavier on his second round. She was lucky, he was thirsty, and the third one had a lot of the stuff in it. He'd barely touched it before he nodded off, and then she grew bolder: She tipped back his head and dribbled it onto his tongue. That would give her a head start, at least.

She packed a small satchel of belongings, a carpetbag of cash and the keys and papers to their safe-deposit boxes. On the street, she used her quietest whyo to direct the stares of people on the street away from her face, though that was just vanity. The sight of a woman's bashed face was common enough not to draw much attention. She was going to Brooklyn, uncertain of what she would find, but her immediate destination was the public bathing pier on the river. She couldn't face Harris, if he was still alive, without bathing. She was desperate to wash herself clean of Dandy Johnny, to feel the cold, saline harbor water soothe her bruised body.

She passed Undertoe on the street without even seeing him, and he failed to see her either, thanks to the virtual invisibility she'd thrown around herself. She entered the women's side just to the south of where he had exited the men's, changed and lowered herself slowly, carefully into the water, where she clung to a handhold and let the current sweep her. After twenty minutes of hardly moving, she left and walked to Fulton Ferry, trying not to dwell on just how badly Dandy Johnny Dolan and Piker Ryan had ruined the rest of her life.

The crowd in the yard of the Noe house confirmed to her that something awful had happened. There were two police wagons—one from the local Brooklyn station, another from the Manhattan district where the factory was located. Mr. Noe's physician's cabriolet stood parked alongside the buggy of his minister, the good if notorious Mr. Beecher from the Pilgrim church. The horse that was just then being fed a bucket of Mr. Noe's oats belonged to a hack driver getting an all-day rate to take a reporter and a sketch artist from the *Eagle* wherever they had to go to get their stories. At the moment, the two *Eagle* men were canvassing the neighbors. The cook had learned a thing or two about stonewalling the press during Harris's recent crisis.

Beatrice went up to the door and was about to knock when the cook threw it open. "Thank God—oh. Who are you? What do you want?" She was expecting Harris to return any minute.

"It's Miss O'Gamhna. Please, what's happened? Is he all right?"

The cook's body blocked the doorway. She jerked her chin at the crowded yard. "Miss O'Who? Do you think all that would be there if he was *all right?*"

"I called a few weeks ago, after Mr. Harris fell."

"Oh, so you're the one. You look even worse now." She scowled but remembered Harris's desire to see this girl. "Yeah, all right, come on." She stepped back and led Beatrice to the dining room. "Stay out of the way. I'll call for you."

After ten minutes of sitting slumped and blank at the table, Beatrice rose. She had to see him. She thought she heard Harris's footsteps. But it couldn't be. She went to the doorway in time to see him run past.

"*Harris?*" He stopped upon hearing her voice, his name, turned back to look at her and hung there for a moment, squinting, as if she were an apparition.

"Beatrice?" Then he gestured for her to follow, and they both ran toward the sickroom, where Beatrice now realized someone else must be dying. Harris was fine. He had just arrived home. At the closed door, he paused and took her by the shoulders. Perhaps he would have kissed her if her whole face hadn't been so damaged, but he just touched her lips.

"Will you wait for me out here?"

She nodded.

Mr. Noe was awake when Harris got there. John-Henry was already there, standing at the back of the room scowling while the police strove to interview Mr. Noe through his delirium. They weren't making much headway. When Harris entered, they stepped aside and let him go to the bed.

When Harris took his hand, Mr. Noe looked up and said quietly, "Harris, my boy. Where did you go? What took you so long?" But his awareness of his surroundings was transient. After a while, his talk merged back into babble and he slid into unconsciousness. Harris looked around the room for someone to give him some explanation, some information. All he knew was what he'd been told by the messenger who fetched him from work: Mr. Noe was near death.

"We don't know much," said John-Henry. "A woman found him early this morning at the new factory. He must have been lying there all night. Her name's Francie Harris, if you can believe that, so he's got the idea that you were the one who found him."

"Just for the record," asked the policeman, "you're the Frank Harris of bridge-tower fame, I gather?" Harris nodded. "Well, I'm very pleased to meet you. But I do have to ask where you were last night, Mr. Harris."

"I was here. I went to bed early. Ask the cook. It was my last night of recuperation before going back to work. Tell me what happened. Is he going to make it?" Harris felt a queer detachment rather like the one he'd had after falling through the tower—as if every bone in his body had been crushed, but he himself was someone else, somewhere else, just watching it. The policeman said nothing.

"They don't know," said John-Henry. "No idea who did it either. Only clear thing he's said until just now was something about a monkey." John-Henry cast a careful but clearly hostile look at the police lieutenant, who had pursued him with numerous questions after hearing that detail and then instructed him not to leave the premises—as if John-Henry would even have considered leaving, as if he were a monkey and had been implicated, as if Mr. Noe, who'd been a vocal abolitionist, would ever have used such a loathsome piece of slang.

"A monkey?"

Harris was too overwhelmed by the events to recall the gift he had given his friend, which was still lying at the bottom of one of the dumbwaiter shafts where his assailant had thrown it, which was so thickly encrusted with Mr. Noe's dried blood that the leering silver monkey head didn't even give back a twinkle when, later that day, one of the investigating officers lowered a lantern most of the way down the shaft on a length of cord and peered into the darkness. Meanwhile, the police at the Noe house filled Harris in on what they knew and questioned him, but they didn't learn anything that seemed relevant. And no one could think of an explanation for Mr. Noe's statement.

Harris stepped into the hall sometime later, when Mr. Noe lapsed back into his stupor, and saw Beatrice sitting on a bench, head in her hands. Was it really her? She had looked quite horrible, he thought. Why was she there?

"Beatrice?" he said, and she looked up. Her eyes were grotesquely purple. "God—someone tried to kill you, too." He hardly knew what he felt as he sat down on the bench beside her and took her in his arms. "What's happened to you? What are you doing here?"

"Harris, I came because . . . I don't know, really. Who is it in there, your landlord? Is he very bad off?"

"Yes. Mr. Noe. He was beaten very badly, maybe by robbers. He may die. What happened to you?"

"Forget about me. Harris, was it here? Were you here, too? Because they must have mistaken him for you. The reason I came is that . . ." she looked over her shoulder. "I thought something happened to *you*. Johnny told me he sent Piker after you. He figured, what with you being in the papers, you were a risk. And then I tried to stop it, which made him madder."

Harris shook his head. None of that had anything to do with Mr. Noe.

"No, listen—Johnny actually told me they *took care of you*, Harris. That means you should be dead. I don't know why they went after your Mr. Noe instead, but maybe it was a message. Or maybe they were drunk and it was a mistake, in which case they may come back."

"No, this happened to him in the city. I wasn't even there. I've never been to his new factory. Someone followed him in and robbed him and beat him half dead with a stick. Or so the police think. That's not the kind of thing the Whyos do, is it?"

"No, but Johnny was in a vicious mood last night. He still might have done it. What else do they know?

"He hasn't been able to tell them anything, just keeps muttering something about a monkey."

"Really, a monkey head?" Only now did Harris think of the monkey cane and wonder where it was.

"He can't talk much. The doctor said it was probably just a hallucination."

"But a *silver* monkey? Because, Harris, it *was* Johnny then. Johnny had a monkey cane with him last night when he went out on a rampage, and he brought it back home this morning. I watched him cleaning and polishing the head."

Harris looked at her. It didn't make sense. "Johnny has a monkey cane?"

"He bought it at the Hippodrome. He collects canes."

"I bought one there, too. I gave it to Mr. Noe. It has a silver head and big smile."

"So they had the same cane. But Johnny had his with him last night."

"Beatrice, what are you doing here? Do you really think Johnny did it? Does this mean you've broken with him? Can you even do that?"

"Look at me. Clearly, I can't, but here I am."

He looked at her purple nose and terrible eyes, then he looked over his shoulder and, when he saw that no one else was in sight, he leaned forward and gently kissed her.

"Can you tell the police? Can you talk to them? What will happen to you if you do?"

"I'll be all right if they really arrest him, and if they do it fast, and if no one finds out I ratted."

"That's a lot of *ifs*."

"I'm going to do it, Harris. It's the only way to make sure he doesn't come after you next, my only chance to get free of Johnny."

"Let's find Mr. Noe's cane. If it's really the same, we'll show them what it looked like." They stood up and Harris walked to the front door. He picked up the lone umbrella in the stand and looked at it, as if it might sprout a monkey's head. The cane wasn't there.

"It's gone," he said, looking at Beatrice.

"It doesn't matter. Even if it wasn't Johnny's cane, I saw him washing blood off it this morning. We have enough to make it stick."

There she was, really there, and she had left Johnny, had offered to denounce him to the cops. It would have been a dream if only it weren't mixed up with the nightmare of Mr. Noe's crushed skull. Now Mr. Noe was probably going to die and Beatrice was standing there with him, offering to do something so crazy it was likely to get her killed. She had come back to him, in this disaster, but at least she had come. He had no idea what to do, except to take her in his arms. She crumpled against him when he touched her.

It was late in the game, maybe too late to matter, but Frank Harris declared himself to her. In a sense, it went better this time than it had at the Old Bowery. They stayed there together for a long moment. The air around them was fraught: It was made up of roughly 78 percent despair, 21 percent pent-up love and contained trace elements of relief, terror, lust, grief and regret. They weren't happy, not at all, but they found themselves in a desperate kiss. When it ended, they both stepped back, and Harris tripped over a chair leg. She flinched, part on his behalf, part on hers, and touched her nose very gently. Even the kiss had hurt.

He said, "What happened at the bath house, that day before the meeting, that night at the Old Bowery, that time on the pier, before the ferry blew up. . . ." But he couldn't articulate a sentence, much less a question.

She nodded. "I've been in love with you for longer than that, Harris. I really didn't know what was coming at that meeting. But once it happened,

I knew I wasn't allowed to say no, and so I decided to try to make the best of it. I can't tell you I was forced. I chose the power, the money, that whole world. It was all I knew how to do, and I was hoping it would be better for you, too, maybe. You were never going to be a good crook, Harris. You're too nice. Then, by the time I saw you on the pier, everything was crap. I just wish the explosion had been bigger."

She didn't say she was sorry. Both of them had far more things they were sorry for than could be stated in that hallway. They walked side by side back to the sickroom, his arm around her shoulder. The cook was mopping Mr. Noe's forehead, and the cops were once again harassing John-Henry.

Harris said, "She knows something important," and Beatrice talked.

Undertoe stayed in Manhattan that day. At noon, he went over to the Old Bowery to take in a matinee, then headed west across town. He was free and easy till later that night, when he was supposed to meet a newsboy he'd just signed up at Lizzie Fagan's Siren Song, a new place with burlesque dancing and back rooms for hire. Undertoe had made an arrangement with Lizzie to help her dispose of clients who turned uncooperative, something that would benefit both of them equally. As he walked, he fiddled with something in his pocket, a folded piece of paper. He took it out and unthinkingly used the corner to rout the grime that had already begun to collect under his nails since his bath that morning. The paper was nice and stiff. It was Harris's letter, of course. It had been in that pocket for some time now.

That evening, he paid a newsboy he didn't know four cents for the late city final *Sun* and scanned the pages for the item about the Noe Brush factory attack. *Would have been a headline if he'd died,* he thought when he found it. According to the report, the victim was still hanging on but remembered nothing of the crime itself except for seeing a silver monkey-headed cane, which was believed to have been his attacker's weapon. Undertoe laughed at that. Where on Earth would a person go to find a cane like that, now that the Hippodrome had been razed?

He tossed his blond forelock from his eyes with a twitch, drawing a glance of interest from a hot-corn girl who was crooning—*Your lily-white corn!*—though her basket was empty. He paid her, and five minutes later she was grunting on her knees in a doorway, skirts up over her backside. He enjoyed both her options, despite her objection that anything other than standard was extra, then turned her around and told her to open wide.

"That's two dollars more," she said, straightening her petticoat. "And I'm done with you, mister."

"No, it's included," he said, grabbing her by the hair and forcing her back to her knees. He sang her song back to her, just one mocking half tone off-key, as she gagged: "Get your hot corn, your lily-white corn, get your hot corn here, hot corn, hot corn."

He walked away smiling as the woman spat in the gutter and cursed. It was broad daylight, after all, and he was in such a good mood already. There was really no reason to kill her.

37.

RATTUS RATTUS

At the Noe house that evening, the police were gone when Mr. Noe finally woke up again. He was lucid for a few minutes, then faded, and the doctor shooed everyone from the room. Harris was painfully aware, as he followed the corpulent preacher into the hall, that although Mr. Noe had treated him like family since he'd come there, to the world he was just a lodger, a part-time stablehand who had traded work for room and board. Or worse: He had been welcomed by Mr. Noe, been helped by him, and then had brought trouble to his vicinity, the result of which being that Mr. Noe was now near death.

The preacher and the lawyer went into the study and closed the door behind them. Harris, John-Henry and Beatrice filed awkwardly into the dining room to wait, and the cook returned to her kitchen. Soon, the cook returned with Sarah Blacksall. She had come as soon as she got word. She recognized Beatrice immediately and looked her over while Harris did what propriety required—even among social reformers and members of the Manhattan underworld—and made the introductions. If this was her competition, thought Sarah Blacksall, there was little she could do but accept it.

"Miss O'Gamhna, I do believe you need a pack of ice for that nose." With that, Sarah Blacksall turned for the kitchen. She was a practical woman. She saw what she saw, and what she saw was that Harris was in love with the girl with the broken nose. It was, at least, an explanation for why she had never managed to get closer to him, despite all their mutual interests and her attentions. She also saw, however, that the situation was complicated. The girl was clearly in trouble, which might mean that Harris was, too.

Beatrice took the ice-filled dish towel. "Thank you, ma'am."

That was when the somber-faced lawyer came to the door.

"He's going, we think." And they all returned to the bedroom, where Mr. Noe's eyes were open but glazed over. His hand was hot but flaccid in Harris's.

"Mr. Noe fancied himself a kind of paternal figure to you," said the lawyer. "And since the Lord in his infinite wisdom has seen fit to separate him from his family and you from yours, he made certain provisions for you in his estate. I don't believe he had time to inform you of that before this occurred."

Harris peered into Mr. Noe's face, but there was no sight in his eyes, just a quivering of the irises. Then Mr. Noe coughed and seemed to want to speak himself. Everyone in the room drew to his bedside, but Mr. Noe's mouth just hung there, gaping the way dead mouths gape.

A few moments later, Mr. Beecher said a short prayer, and the doctor drew the sheet across Mr. Noe's face. But Harris couldn't stand that. He sat down beside his friend and pulled the bedclothes back down, then took his hand one last time. It was still so warm it seemed it wasn't dead, so heavy Harris knew it was. He took Mr. Noe's slack face in his two hands and whispered quietly, "Forgive me." Then he settled Mr. Noe's features in such a way that his lips and eyes were softly closed. The skin was already distinctly less warm than a living person's. *Maybe it's the radiating heat that carries the spirit from the body,* he thought, in which case Mr. Noe wasn't entirely gone yet. Maybe there was something left of him that could perceive Harris's gratitude, his loyalty, his love, and so Harris stayed there by the bedside while, one by one, the others left. He waited till all the heat was gone from Mr. Noe's body, hours, before finally pulling the sheet back over his face. As he did so, he felt strangely absolved, as if Mr. Noe had released him, as if he had said, *It's enough. Now bury me and go on.*

When Sarah got up to go, she made a point of asking Beatrice if she had somewhere to go that night and offered her a place to stay.

"No, I'm fine, thank you, ma'am." Sarah winced—she didn't think herself that much older or more respectable than Harris's little friend—but certainly she was relieved.

As for Beatrice, her night had just begun when she left the Noe house. She tried not to think about Harris's girlfriend. She had no right to mind. And she had much to do to ensure that Harris didn't become Johnny and Piker's next victim. She'd told the policeman who interviewed her, a Lieutenant Jones, that she would make sure Johnny was at home and off his guard at ten o'clock. Of course, Jones could have found Johnny at home and off his guard right then, too—he'd be out for several more hours, she figured—but she needed time to get back there herself and tie up a few loose ends as well as to prepare Jimmy and Fiona to step forward rather sooner than expected. It was going to take a major effort to ensure the Jimster performed well enough that the Whyos accepted him as their boss.

She was relieved that it was quiet when she turned onto their block—so they hadn't jumped the gun on her, thank God. But then a Whyo kid who lived nearby nodded to her and said that Piker was upstairs with Johnny. She mounted the creaky stairs with a fluttering terror in her chest, but as soon as she entered the apartment she saw that she was safe. Piker was out, too. He must have come in and helped himself to some of the doctored rum. She redosed them both with another bottle from the larder, just in case, and then went out onto the roof to think. She was going to have to give Jimmy a crash course in Johnny's lingo, but that could start tomorrow. For tonight, she was pretty sure she could get away with teaching him just one short sequence that would prove to the others he knew Johnny's codes and thus that he was Johnny's appointed lieutenant. The major trick was that she couldn't allow Jimmy and Fiona to know that she had set Johnny up; she couldn't be sure they'd go along with her if they knew. And so she would have to wait till the cops had come and gone to start teaching him.

At ten to ten, she went downstairs and made a point of saying hello to an old lady sitting on her stoop. Beatrice was going for a growler of beer. Could she bring another one back with her? She surely could. At ten sharp, Lieutenant Jones arrived. Indeed, Lieutenant Jones kicked the door down himself, though he could well have assigned the job to one of his underlings. All six men on his squad had their pistols drawn. They were wearing

headlamps, lit but shaded. Johnny Dolan's monkey-headed cane was gri-
macing in the darkness from the corner by the door rather than the umbrella stand where it belonged, and when the wood of the lintel splintered
and the screws popped from the brass lock plate and the door banged open
into the dark apartment, the cane slid—slowly at first, with just a scraping
sound, then clattering to the floor in a silver and mahogany explosion of
noise. Jones fired first. He shot into the darkness that was the kitchen—and
killed the icebox. Cold water burbled from a hole in its side. The man that
had aimed down the side hall took out a wardrobe, putting holes through
two of Beatrice's shirtwaists. There was no return fire.

They shone their lights around and made their way cautiously through
the apartment. They found them under the kitchen table. Lieutenant
Jones's bullet had whistled across the tabletop at the level of the gut of anyone seated there, but Johnny had keeled off his chair and onto the floor
long before the cops arrived, as had Piker Ryan.

When Piker had got there, Johnny was sitting in his chair with his head
tipped back. "Johnny?" Piker said. "Oh fuck, that far gone already? Don't
you want to spiffy up, man, and go out? We got a little business we was
wanting to take care of, don't we? Come on now." But Johnny was in no
condition, so Piker Ryan had sat down with him and polished off Johnny's
drink. Then he poured himself a little more. A half hour later, he'd been
blowing bubbles in a puddle of drool of his own. Beatrice had told Lieutenant Jones he'd find Johnny and Piker out cold, but Jones didn't trust her
that much. He had been expecting an ambush.

When Beatrice returned, two police wagons were parked out front. She
delivered the old lady's beer and then approached the penthouse cautiously, not sure if she would be dragged off to jail, too, by association. From
out on the roof, she watched the police moving through her house. She
didn't feel violated at all. She had removed the few things she wanted hidden from the police. The rest of it was theirs to do with as they pleased.
Mainly, though, they were interested in Johnny and Piker. It seemed no
amount of nudging with nightsticks nor even several sharp blows could
wake them. Eventually, four of the six cops dragged the two weirdly smiling, conked-out gangsters past her to the stairwell and down five flights by
their arms, heels whomping with every step.

Lieutenant Jones was twirling the monkey-headed cane like a baton, while his second in command struggled behind him on the stairs with a crate containing most of the contents of the Dolan family larder. The eye-gougers in particular impressed them. There were a number of unsolved murders on the books in which the victims had been missing their eye-balls—their very neatly excised eyeballs. This could be the beginning of something, Jones was thinking, like a promotion to commander.

"What do you say, Lieutenant?" asked the shirtwaist shooter. "We bring-ing the wife in, too?" Beatrice was still out on the roof, watching and lis-tening. It was a crucial juncture. If it sounded like they were going to arrest her, too, she planned to jump to the next roof over and follow one of the Dolans' long-established escape plans. She had little to lose.

"Bring her in? I don't think so," said the lieutenant. "I was thinking, send posies. It was easy pickings, thanks to her. She drugged those boys to half an inch of their lives. You know, what amazes me is, I've watched the Points for years and never saw what those two was. Just brawlers, just croon-ers, I thought, nobodies."

"Yeah, people'll surprise you, won't they?"

And then they drove the two Whyos to the Tombs.

For the initial alarm, Beatrice used her own voice. She let forth with a yowl of a rutting tomcat in C-sharp, followed by the first two verses of "Willy the Weeper"—a song that was never sung by Whyos except to call secret meetings at Geoghegan's. Beatrice didn't normally call meetings (at least not in her own voice), so the urgency of the message was obvious. A short time later, Fiona and Jimmy met her at the penthouse, worried and pale. She told them she didn't know anything other than that the cops had broken in and carted the men away while she was out. "But we don't have time to think about how it happened right now," she said. "We have less than two hours." And then she began, quietly, to teach Jimmy the song he would need to sing.

Where's Johnny? The Whyos were furiously whispering among the cop-per fermenting vats when Beatrice stepped forward with Jimmy at her side. She told herself she wasn't nervous, she was excited. She knew that calling the meeting for Geoghegan's would put the Whyos on edge, and she was right. People were already starting to get ideas. Obviously, something had happened to Johnny. They were thinking of the power that Johnny had had and seeing opportunity, wondering what jobs they could get that Johnny'd never let them do, whose boss they could be, what girls they could run and imagining how much richer they might be if they didn't have to pay the fucking tithe practically every other night at the Morgue. Beatrice was right about at least one thing: The collective was fragile. People weren't thinking about what they got back from the gang or all the times their weekly cut of the tithe had kept them afloat when they were otherwise broke or the times when the gang had worked together to get them out of some trouble or jail. What do you expect of a bunch of criminals? She could already feel the riot starting in their minds as she picked up two lanterns, one in each hand, and raised her arms. Fiona had made sure all the other lights in the brewery were extinguished.

"I have a message from the Tombs," she said, though Johnny probably wasn't even there yet. A murmur went through the assembly. *So it was true.* "Johnny has asked me to let you all know he's been *temporarily inconvenienced.* Him and Piker. But not to worry. He's provided us with a way to carry on uninterrupted in his absence. He asked me to introduce the man who's going to command us till this gets sorted out." And then she passed the Jimster the lanterns, and he sang her song.

A half hour later, Beatrice O'Gamhna slipped out of Owney Geoghegan's alone and went home to the penthouse, where she slept dreamlessly in Johnny's bed. It had worked. Order was restored before it had even broken down.

The following morning, she kept her ears open, listening for sounds of discontent in the gang, but as far as she could tell, no one had figured out what she'd done, not even Jimmy and Fiona. They came by at ten, while she was out on the roof again with a cup of tea, and told her that so far the Jimster had been welcomed with surprise and a certain amazement by the gang. Then they got down to work. Tomorrow was the biweekly report, and the Jimster wasn't nearly ready. Beatrice reminded herself that the Jimster didn't have to impersonate Johnny's voice, which meant even a fairly stumbling performance would probably impress them. It was nothing like her own debut, which had had to be perfect. She went over the book with both of them, spent an hour coaching Jimmy on all the standard phrases, then sat down with Fiona and cracked a brand-new account book. She carried over the balances from a sheet of paper she'd prepared but didn't show Fiona the old book—she didn't want her getting ideas about the kind of graft the Dolans had benefited from. When the time came the following afternoon, she stood next to Jimmy and prompted him whenever he needed it, while Fiona recorded the figures. It went pretty well, she thought.

As for what Piker Ryan and Dandy Johnny thought when they came to at the Tombs, it wasn't what you might have expected. Johnny was so self-confident and Piker so confident in Johnny that neither of them could imagine such a thing as Beatrice turning rat. Of course, they could taste the hydrate of chloral on their tongues, but the fact that she'd doped Johnny's whiskey wasn't so out of line. He'd just broken her nose, after all. It had cracked pretty loud and looked like Hell the next morning, he thought. She had reason to be mad. And he had always encouraged her feistiness. It was only the terrible timing of it all that made him want to kill her. From what Johnny and Piker had heard in the joint, they were being held for something totally random. Some fool shopkeeper'd gotten himself killed, and when the murder weapon was announced in the papers, it happened to be a cane just like the one he'd bought at the Hippodrome and had been carrying that night. It was all in the paper, and someone who had seen him with the cane had told the cops.

In fact, what Piker and Johnny had really done that night was amuse themselves with a drunk businessman they ran into down on South Street. They rolled him for his money, and that would have been that, but the guy tried to fight back. Piker had whacked him with a slungshot. Johnny did the kicking. Then they rolled him again, under a cart, but he wasn't even dead. It was really Goddamned unfortunate, thought Johnny, that the one night his girl doped his whiskey out of spite, the only night in recent memory that he'd actually used the blades in his boot tips, was the night the cops had happened to come after him on a case of mistaken identity. It was maddening, and it was very bad luck. Johnny planned to teach Beatrice a lesson when he got the Hell out of the joint, but he never suspected that she was the rat. On the contrary, he trusted her completely, especially with managing the report and the gang in the meantime. She was a bit of a genius with the whyoing, that girl. She would figure something out. His mother had picked a winner.

And the more Johnny thought about how Beatrice was out there somehow saving his Dolan ass, the fonder he started to be of her. She was willful, and she was skinny, but she could be sexy, too, the way she hissed when she was mad. Piker asked him what he was going to do to her when they got out. Johnny thought about it.

"You know, maybe nothing, because in a way I like her more in the wake of this."

Piker squinted at him.

"You think that's stupid?" he said. "I should probably just kill her. Normally, anyone who even thought of doping my jug would be dead."

Piker rolled a booger between his fingers, popped it in his mouth and crunched it like a louse. "Nah. She's your girl. If you still like her, don't get rid of her. Just show her some respect. First thing you do when we get back, Johnny, is break her other nose. Then see how she looks. If you still like her, then sure, let her live."

The Whyo rules of stealth strictly precluded jail-cell visits, but after a week Johnny was surprised Beatrice hadn't bent that just a little. She was good enough at whyoing to have pulled off something without much risk.

Another week later, he did get a visitor, Maggie the Dove.

"Hiya, Dandy boy," she said through the heavy grille of his cell door. "How you holding up? Don't let them pin nothing on you, all right? But how could they? No jury'd ever believe you hurt a fly, my sweet."

"Nothing to pin and nowhere to pin it, Dove. I never met the poor man, apparently a manufacturer of brushes." And he laughed because it was true, he was innocent. Not that it mattered. The Whyos were quite capable of fixing any jury in the world from a distance of one hundred yards. Then he laughed again because he was so glad to see her. He thought about Beatrice as he looked at Maggie. They were awfully different women. Maggie knew how to talk to a man. He'd never had to break Maggie's nose. What was it about Beatrice, then? He couldn't put his finger on it.

"Tell me, Dove, how's life outside?"

She took the cue. "Jimmy's doing great at his new job, you know. I never would of knew he had it in him. Otherwise, nothing much, we're just all missing you."

Johnny coughed. "Jimmy's new job's going well, eh?" He smiled like he thought it was quite a clever way of putting it, but the truth was that wasn't at all what he'd expected to hear, and he wasn't sure he liked it. "The Jimster," he said. "So he got the job, did he? That's good news. Glad to hear it. You'll let me know if he blows his lines, won't you, Mag?" She winked and smiled and pressed herself up against the door grille, and they kissed until the warden came along, banging his nightstick on the doors and dislodging one woman after the next, like leeches, from their criminal lovers' lips.

After she left, Johnny sat on his bunk for a while, trying to figure out what Beatrice was up to. Surely she'd sent Maggie as a messenger, and he decided he had to give her credit for her subtlety there as well as with the Jimster. He could only imagine that she was now doing the Jimster's voice the way she'd done his, letting the Whyos think the Jimster had been his well-trained lieutenant all along.

It wasn't a terrible plan—pretty clever, really—but it did surprise him, because Beatrice liked the Jimster, and she knew Johnny liked him, too. He was Fiona's boy, after all, and Fiona was like a sister to her. Beanie was a smart girl. She must have seen the conflict, must have known he'd have to deal with the Jimster, maybe both of them, the moment he got out. Apparently, she'd decided that sacrifice was worth it to keep the gang rolling on while he was in the joint. It was quite a sacrifice, and it was going to be a bit of a pity, he thought, but he liked the way it showed both her loyalty and her ruthless side.

He was just lying there looking at the ceiling and thinking about Beanie and Maggie, wavering between the two of them in his mind's eye—Beatrice or Maggie, feisty or bawdy, bony or soft—when he spotted the gray rat staring at him brazenly from the foot of Piker's bunk. "Get the fuck out of here, varmint!" he said, and whipped one of his defanged boots at it, hitting it, quite to his surprise, and actually knocking it over. It lay on its side with its eyes open and its soft, light-colored belly heaving fast. *Odd*, he thought. *It must be sick to be so slow.* The rat twitched. He squinted at it and saw its complexity: soft belly and devious nature, sharp teeth and smooth tail. He had to admit, he kind of admired rats. Then he used his other boot to knock the carcass to the floor, and when the rat had fallen, he spat into his palm and reached down his pants.

38

PROFIT SHARING

Beatrice barely saw Harris those next two weeks, just twice on the street when she contrived to intercept him on his way to work. She feared the Whyos would perceive her disloyalty if she saw him more, but those few minutes were enough for her to find out what she had to—that he wasn't in love with Sarah Blacksall—and to tell him what he needed to hear: She was working on her exit from the Whyos.

In the meantime, she was helping Fiona and Jimmy. She was also arranging for a lawyer for Johnny and Piker and doing innumerable small bits of damage control, massaging tempers, showing Fiona how to do the accounts. When she felt she had done enough to keep the gang on its feet, she intercepted Harris again on his way home from work.

He smiled widely just at seeing her and would have taken her hand, but she backed away from him. It was a dangerous step she was about to take. A casual indiscretion could put a grim end to it. "I'm ready to get out, Harris," she said, "but I need to decide where to go. I can't go back to my aunt's."

"Well, there's Mr. Noe's. It's going to be my place now, and it's huge." Harris had just learned the terms of the bequest in a long letter from Mr. Noe's lawyer—there were so many things he wanted to tell her—but Beatrice cut him off. It was imperative, she explained, to keep the Whyos from noticing a connection between Harris and the man Johnny Dolan was accused of killing. So far, no one had, but she couldn't very well fall into his arms and move in with him and get away with it.

"You have to realize, I'm married to Johnny Dolan, Harris. Actually married to him. If I just went off with you now, the gang would find out what happened and hunt me down and kill me. You, too, maybe. I was thinking I could stay at that women's hotel in Brooklyn Heights, the Margaret, but really I should go further."

The line she'd given Fiona and Jimmy was that she wanted to lie low before the trial, for Johnny's protection, to disassociate him and her from the rest of the gang as much as possible—just until he got off. They still believed that all of this was temporary. Johnny would be boss again, Beatrice would still be First Girl, and they would be their lieutenants. They had no idea she was praying he would hang.

"Sarah came by this week," he said. "She was concerned about you, and she had an idea about where you might stay."

"Sarah?" She nearly lost her composure at the mention of the lady doctor. She damn well wasn't going to go live with Harris's old girlfriend, that was for sure, no matter what sort of do-gooder she was.

"She's a very good person. That's all. She knows that. She mentioned that her partner's family has a big house in Weeksville. They've offered to take you in."

"Weeksville? Where is that?"

"It's further out in Brooklyn, a black neighborhood."

"Really, a black neighborhood? I don't know."

"Dr. Smith is black, a black woman doctor."

"A black woman doctor?"

"Come on, why don't you go meet her? It would be perfect. The gang would never find you . . . and maybe I could see you somehow." He gave her the clinic address.

"All right, Harris, I'll talk to her." And then she melted into the crowd. She went to the clinic late that afternoon, rather hoping to have arrived too late, but both the doctors were there.

She felt terribly awkward with Sarah Blacksall. Dr. Smith she found surprisingly articulate and intimidating, at first, but Beatrice quickly warmed to her. She learned that the house in Weeksville belonged to Dr. Smith's parents, but that Smith and Blacksall stayed there two or three nights a week, when they were holding office hours in their Weeksville clinic. Dr. Smith invited her out there for dinner and to spend the night, to see what it was like before she decided. She wasn't very comfortable with the idea, but how could she say no?

And so, the following night, Beatrice returned to the clinic, took the ferry across to Brooklyn and rode out to Weeksville with the two doctors in their rig. She went mostly just because Harris had asked her to. She was thinking that hotel in Brooklyn would be more convenient while she waited for the trial and, hopefully, freedom. She didn't need to be put into the midst of another family—and a black family at that—that would disapprove of her life. Plus, the two doctors were obviously such do-gooders. She was fed up with them before she'd even heard their lectures. But then they surprised her. Mr. and Mrs. Smith were warm and not the least bit nosy about why she needed their help. The doctors neither pestered her nor lectured her about the life she'd lived nor proselytized their hygienic theories nor otherwise dispensed advice. The dinner conversation was dominated by talk of the doctors' more interesting cases and how they'd met at the Women's Medical College. They made what they did sound almost as exciting as being a Whyo: solving a different problem every time, inventing new ways to do the same job better, knowing when it was worth it to risk a great deal on a grand and outrageous possibility, when to be conservative and cautious. They held power over life and death, she saw, and clearly it was exhilarating. Smith and Blacksall were perhaps the first women Beatrice had known whose lives weren't either illegal or desperately boring. Even Sarah Blacksall wasn't half as bad as she'd expected. For her part, Susan Smith was like no other Negro woman she'd ever known, Beatrice thought. Then she corrected herself: She'd never really known one at all before.

The Smiths showed her the room she could have, which had its own back door, and told her she'd be free to do whatever she wished with her days, welcome to dine with them or not. It was ideal, and she was grateful. She accepted the invitation that night. Long after old Mr. and Mrs. Smith had gone to bed, the three women stayed up talking over a bottle of sherry until the fire had died in the hearth. When the doctors asked Beatrice about the medical problems of girls in the Five Points, she said, "Oh, you don't want to know," but in fact they did. They already knew quite a lot, but they fervently wanted to know more, especially the worst of it, and what help the women there would want, what they thought they needed.

"Lemons," Beatrice said, thinking she was being cryptic. "Free lemons all year round would be a help."

To her astonishment, they knew what she meant, and they told her there existed a device made of rubber that could serve the same purpose but more effectively, if only it were legal to manufacture and market widely.

"But in the meantime, you're right, we might as well give out lemons," said Dr. Smith. "I don't know why we never thought of that, except that I'm afraid it sounds a little old-fashioned. But I guess there's no point believing we're *not* in the dark ages when we surely still are."

Beatrice had never imagined she could be friends with such people, but *very* quickly she was. And she felt something she hadn't felt for years: admiration.

The next day, she returned to the penthouse apartment to pack up some of her things. She was going back to Weeksville that night. But first, she would be seeing Harris. He had invited her to dinner. She was fairly terrified as she rode the ferry back to Brooklyn and walked up to Fort Greene with her carpetbag of clothes. The prospect of seeing him alone had her far more nervous than she'd ever been.

The cook let her in through the kitchen door and shouted into the yard for Harris. The cook knew well enough that the house had been passed to him, but she didn't quite see her way to treating Harris as master of the house, especially not as he was still living over the stable and acting like a stablehand, too. It was fine with Harris. He wasn't eager to become anyone's master and didn't want to move into the big house, not in the least. He found it too sad, too strange without Mr. Noe.

He was struggling to lace his shoes when the cook shouted. He was nervous, too. He'd had a good day on the tower, but now he was a wreck. That was the way his life felt lately: uneven. At the moment, between the loss of Mr. Noe, the surprise of suddenly owning most of Mr. Noe's worldly goods and the enormous anxiety of this meeting with Beatrice, he didn't know whether to laugh or cry or throw up.

She was waiting in the parlor for him when he finally came over. It was an unbearably odd setting for the two of them. For a young man of means in Fort Greene to invite a young woman to his house alone was unthinkably scandalous. He should properly have had a whole party of people to diffuse the sexual tension. But this was Harris. This was Beatrice. They'd slept on adjacent mattresses in the same room for more than a year at the O'Gamhnas', had heard each other fart and snore. Not to mention their night in the sewermen's bath hall. There was no reason to be coy. But all that was a long time ago now. They stood at opposite ends of the room, facing each other.

"Hello."

"I'm glad you came."

"How are you?"

"Fine, you?"

The parlor itself seemed to demand this ceremony. Beatrice couldn't stand it.

"Jesus Christ, I can't make small talk with you, Harris."

He agreed, but he was confused by her. He was afraid she would leave. "But what else can we do?" he said.

It made no sense, so she laughed. "How about you show me around?"

It was better when they were walking. Things occurred to them to say.

She told him how she'd left Fiona and the Jimster in charge. How she thought it would be okay as long as Johnny was in jail. He didn't ask about after.

"Are you going to miss it all?" he asked.

"No, God, no, I'm glad to be out. But then again—yes. I guess I'm sorry in a certain way, about some of it. I was good at being that. What will I do?"

They went through the whole house, and then, in what was the most egregious breach of social protocol yet, he asked her if she'd like to see his apartment in the stable. They stood at the top of the rough stairway, looking in at his spare living quarters. There was nothing much there for him to show her but the picture of his mother, but suddenly he realized that the apartment was dominated by his bed and how inappropriate this must look. He blushed.

"Sorry," he said, and they turned around. Going back down the stairs, he followed closely on her heels. His leg brushed the fabric of her dress. Then she stopped, and his leg bumped hers, beneath her skirts.

"Harris," she said, and reached out for him, but he wasn't prepared and was knocked off balance. He sat down hard on the stairs, pulling her with him, and then they slid down several more stairs, kicking and bumping and clutching each other. It was not a very proper seduction.

"Oh—" she cried. "Ow, my nose!" which started him laughing, and then her, too, though it did hurt. Then, rather slowly and carefully, he came at her face from the side, kissing her cheek, her cheekbone, the corner of her lips. The way they were tangled in her dress within the narrow, boxed-in stairwell, there seemed to be no getting up again, so they scootched to the bottom together and then ran back up the stairs to reconvene their embrace on the more stable ground of Harris's bed. They didn't talk. Their clothes began to loosen and come away.

I can't think of a single thing that could have stopped them from consummating something then and there—except for the cook, calling that their supper was ready, which it wasn't, but she had her eyebrows up at the manner in which they were carrying on. *Showing her his apartment, indeed*, she thought.

They straightened themselves up and went inside, though, and after a half hour standing around the kitchen stove waiting for dinner, they ate not in the dining room, where the cook had laid the table, but in the kitchen, where Harris said he preferred it. Afterward, they tried out the parlor again, this time with fewer inhibitions and less monitoring from the cook, who was occupied with the dishes. Before long, they were sitting right beside each other on the horsehair sofa. He looked into her face. The black eyes were fading, but she still looked pretty beaten up. Her nose was red and swollen. It was going to be a lot more Roman than before.

"Harris," she said, "I'm really sorry I punched you with the knuckles that time." He touched the side of his own face, where she'd hit him. "But we didn't know what to expect from you. It's not so simple, two girls jacking a big man like you—you might have been tough. You might have fought back. But never mind that. I'm just sorry."

"Don't be. That turns out to have been a good day."

They talked about the beginning: the fire at Barnum's, the way the Whyos had heard of Harris on the street through the Jimster and Undertoe, and why they'd been so convinced he was Undertoe's collaborator, starting with the German connection and the aliases. That conversation brought Harris to ask her something he'd been wondering a long while.

"I just couldn't let him kill you, Harris. I knew you could keep your trap shut. But also, I don't think Johnny was capable of being threatened by you. That made it easier."

"I hated you then, but maybe I should have been grateful." He told her how he first came to live with Mr. Noe. "It was right after the post-office job and that letter you sent me. I was out of my mind—I didn't know what to think."

"I'm so sorry, Harris—"

"I am, too."

"He must have thought so highly of you, Harris, to leave you this house."

He told her Mr. Noe had left most of his money to the missionary fund of the Pilgrim church, Lincoln University in Ohio and the S.P.C.A., but that the house and the business had gone to him. "I don't know what to do with the brush company. I can't run it. I don't know anything about it."

"Isn't John-Henry working there?"

He looked at her. "Maybe I'll just give it to John-Henry. He's excited about it, and that way I can stay on the bridge. Mr. Noe should have thought of that. He was all for the uplifting of the Negroes."

"Harris, you can't just give an entire factory to John-Henry; he won't take it, for one. It's yours."

"Well, Mr. Noe just gave it to me."

"That's different. He died. It's a matter of pride, and of a lot of other things, too."

"You know, the only thing I ever gave Mr. Noe was that cane. I picked it because he liked animals. It had such a smile on it. But I still haven't been able to find it. What if it wasn't Johnny's cane he was beaten with, what if it was his?"

She clamped her eyes shut. "It's a coincidence, that's all. They may have had the same cane, but Johnny's cane was found with traces of blood on it. There was hair in his boots. He killed someone. Mr. Noe was killed. It doesn't mean a thing that they had the same cane."

"Yeah, it's just a coincidence."

"Did you look hard?"

"I looked everywhere."

"Harris—"

Both of them were thinking it through. If Johnny wasn't guilty, they were the ones who could prove it. They could weaken the case against him by telling the police about the second cane. But if he went free, he'd surely do his best to do away with both of them. Harris didn't know what to do with the feelings that roiled within him. Someone had killed Mr. Noe. Wasn't the actual killer the one who should hang? But letting Johnny hang would solve so many of their problems. He looked down at her. She was beautiful, even with the broken nose.

"Even if Johnny didn't do it," she said, "I'm going to make sure he hangs. I'm never going back."

"What about the real killer?"

"Shhh."

Harris got up and went to close the parlor door. When he came back to the couch, he slipped his arm around her. For a long time, he just explored the contours of her waist. Finally, she pulled away and turned her back to him.

"Help me with these." As he began to work the hooks and buttons of her dress, unwanted images of Maria flashed in his mind, the last woman he'd been with. But beyond the buttons and the stays, Beatrice was not like Maria. She had her own ideas. She said, "No, not like that—like this." And the surprise of that—or when she flipped him over, pushed him to a different angle and, once, simply leaned forward, buried her face in his chest and breathed him in—was the fulfillment of the fantasy that had remained beyond reach for so long, the one in which he was confident she wanted him, too, loved him, too. It was a half an hour before Beatrice gripped her toes and writhed. Harris saw flashes of carmine red, magenta and deepest blue. They had known this once and then lost it. How could they have lost it? he wondered. But of course, he remembered. They might lose it again, too, and more.

"Harris," she murmured, but she couldn't formulate her thought. It was the second time now he'd made love to her without beating her up. She was amazed to realize that maybe that was the way it would always be with him.

"I wish I were the only man you ever knew," he said.

"Don't. It doesn't matter now."

He tried to smile, but it came out strained.

"Don't keep thinking of Johnny, Harris," she said, as if she knew his thoughts. "We're going to be rid of him for good soon. It never amounted to anything between him and me, just business, a very strange sort of business. He never even liked me, just liked to keep me in my place."

Harris sat up. Something had dawned on him. If Johnny wasn't in love with her, if it hadn't been his cane and he wasn't jealous, then someone else had truly killed Mr. Noe. And Harris suddenly had someone in mind, someone as irrational as Johnny, as ruthlessly efficient in his violence, someone who had been plaguing him almost since he arrived, someone who appeared able to hold a grudge for years: Undertoe. There was no evidence for it except the strange theft of the letter, but Harris was suddenly certain that Undertoe had killed Mr. Noe. He didn't believe it could have been random.

"Beanie—"

"Harris, don't call me that. It's what *they* all call me, Johnny, the Whyos. Just say Beatrice, like you always do. It's hardly any longer, you know."

He thought of his own real name, what he might ask her to call him, but the question was so wide and hopeless, and the thing he'd wanted to say so much more pressing, that he let it pass.

"What about *Bea*?"

"All right, *Bea*," she said. "My ma called me that."

At which point, Harris's desire to explain his insight to Beatrice was suddenly dwarfed by another one: He thought to ask her to marry him. He braced himself and was on the verge of saying it when he remembered she was already married, and he blushed deeply. He twisted his lips around and managed to tell her what he'd been thinking about Undertoe.

She agreed with him that it made sense—but not about trying to prove it. "Does it help Mr. Noe?" she asked. "No. And think what it would mean if Johnny went free. I'm going to have a hard time preventing that anyway."

"Can you let him hang for something he definitely didn't do? He's your husband."

"Harris, come on, don't remind me of that. I can't help that. He's an evil bastard."

"Can I let Undertoe go free if he's the one who really did it?"

"Johnny's killed so many men, Harris. Who cares if he hangs for the wrong one? If Johnny gets off, we're next."

"But Undertoe?"

"Undertoe I can handle. Or the Whyos can. I'll make sure you get your justice, Harris. The Jimster'd probably enjoy doing it." Beatrice was quiet for a moment, then got up and stepped into her petticoat and her dress and turned her back to him.

"Yes, I think I've got an idea," she said as he did up the buttons.

He drove her to her new home in the buggy, and at the very end of the ride, when he took her hand to help her down, he managed a watered-down version of the question he'd stumbled over earlier: He told her that as soon as she could do it without the Whyos knowing or minding, she must come to Mr. Noe's house and live with him. She opened her eyes wide in mock horror.

"I'd like that, but what would the cook say?"

"The cook? Who cares? But I think she'd get used to it. There are a lot of rooms. You can have your own."

A week later, Beatrice returned to Mr. Noe's. It was just Harris to welcome her—he had given the cook the day off so she wouldn't be scandalized again so soon. Harris and Beatrice went through the bedrooms of the big house one by one, and finally chose for her a large and sunny one in the rear.

"It's your room, whenever you want to stay here, as often as you want."

"Where's your room going to be?" she asked, and he told her he preferred the stable. And thus it was that Beatrice had the pleasure of inviting Harris to stay in his own house.

In the morning, he got up and said good-bye to her, not knowing when she would be back—they had agreed she would keep her visits irregular and err on the side of caution if she thought she'd been observed by a Whyo—but he was certain that she would be back before too long. At work, he was almost afraid to go up the footbridge, he was so giddy. His mind swung from the ether of love to the abysmal recollection of all that had had to take place to congeal his affair with Beatrice. And in between that high and that low, there was still the very real anxiety that Undertoe or Johnny or the Whyos would somehow interfere and end it all before it had truly begun. He tried to occupy his mind instead with the work at hand and with the concept of profit sharing, which Beatrice had described to him as the principle that distinguished the Whyos from other gangs, though not enough. He was captivated by the idea. He went home that evening not expecting her to be there, but she was, and not just she but the Henleys and Sarah Blacksall and Dr. Smith. She had invited them all over, and the cook had produced a chicken pie in spite of herself, though she was none too pleased about the trollop who was acting like the mistress of the house or the quality of the company, blacks and nobodies and loose women. She was thinking of moving on. Then Harris put his head through the kitchen doorway and asked her to set herself a place and join them.

"Well, I never," she objected, but a short time later she emerged with a place setting and sat down.

Over dinner, Harris told the others a little of what he'd learned about Mrs. Dolan's vision of a collective gang. Smith and Blacksall nodded. They knew all about communes and collectives. But no one knew what to say when Harris explained that he wanted to turn Noe Brush into a collective. It was a radical idea but in keeping with Mr. Noe's politics, that much was clear.

"Not a corrupt collective, a real one, right?" Beatrice asked. "Where you really give everyone their share of the take?"

They all laughed, but she was serious. So was Harris. He said he was planning to meet with Mr. Noe's banker and his lawyer to see if it was possible. "I don't want to run the company. I don't know how. This way, I won't have to, but I won't have to sell it either. We'll work out a system so the people who do run it and do work there really share in the profit of the business."

Harris asked John-Henry, who'd been there for just a couple of weeks, who the most important people in running the plant were. Beatrice suggested giving each of the floor managers and the general manager shares in the company and described the way that profits had been divvied up among Whyos.

When Harris approached the lawyer about the idea, the man was surprised at how well Mr. Noe's otherwise rather ignorant-seeming heir appeared to understand so much about industrial economics, in particular the radical new profit-sharing model, which had recently been tried at several well-known progressive factories. Apparently, Mr. Noe had taught this man more than the lawyer realized, and from then on he granted Harris increased respect. It was just as well that the lawyer didn't realize one of the major partners was a black man until the day they all showed up in his office to sign the papers, for he might have been more reluctant to arrange it, but by then it was too late. There was no legal barrier to allowing a black into a white business, and the deal was made.

Beatrice came to Harris's just a couple of nights a week, usually unannounced, often late at night. But every night he waited hopefully in the room they both still called her room. It turned out he'd spent his last night in the stable, for even when she wasn't there he loved sleeping in her bed, just for the whiff of her that dwelled in the sheets.

One night, shortly after the factory had been reorganized, Harris suggested that she should go to work at the company, maybe in accounting. They needed help, and she had devised the whole plan, after all. She laughed.

"Working at the brush factory was too boring for you, Harris. You think I'm going to like it?"

He had to admit he did not.

"But aren't you getting bored doing nothing? I don't want you to get so bored you miss the Whyos."

"I'll still have some work to do when the trial starts," she said, but the truth was, he was right. Earlier that week, she'd arranged for a part-time job working at the Smith-Blacksall clinic. And there was something else: "I was hoping to work full-time, but Sarah and Susan encouraged me not to." Instead, they had urged her to apply to Erasmus Hall, an academic high school that catered to immigrant and unconventional students in particular.

"Really, school?" Harris was thinking of her old insistence that she hadn't come to America for education.

"I told Susan I wished I was a doctor. I didn't mean anything much by it, but she said, 'What are you talking about, *wish*? You're not paying *rent*, are you? To Harris or my folks. What do you need a job for? You want to be a doctor, all you need is an education.' " Beatrice blushed as she described it—and Beatrice never blushed. "So, what do you think?"

"I like it. *Dr. O'Gamhna.*"

"One step at a time, Harris."

She was accepted on a rolling basis and began classes in the middle of the term. For six weeks, Harris took the ferry to the Manhattan side of the bridge every morning and Beatrice copied down grammar rules and mathematical formulas. Some nights, she went home to him, but mostly, out of caution, she went all the way back to Weeksville. On weekends, she worked in the clinic. Beatrice was neither the oldest nor the unlikeliest student at Erasmus Hall. She was largely ignorant of history and literature, but she was good at math and languages. She already knew how to do complicated bookkeeping and was fluent in Gaelic, Whyo and English, after all. German wasn't hard, with Harris as a tutor. Latin was worse, but she applied herself, since it was the language of medicine.

When she spent the evening with Harris, she read aloud to him, and she encouraged him to do the homework with her, so that he got a thinned-out version of her education. He liked the math and physics, especially. He was eager to understand exactly how the improbable bridge he was building could stand. On those nights, they usually fell asleep together over her books in the parlor. Then, sometime in the middle of the night, they awoke on the Turkish carpet in front of the dying fire and stripped off their clothes, pushed the books to one side, and made Dandy Johnny Dolan a cuckold once again.

39

EXTREME UNCTION

eatrice made it all the way to the trial, two months from the date of
Piker and Johnny's arrest, without missing a day of school. It was a pretty
good attendance record for a gangster's moll, but she was saving up, since
she planned to be entirely absent during the trial. Her life and Harris's were
riding on what she did or didn't do there. She sent word to her teacher that
she'd been taken ill, and in a sense it was true: It did turn her stomach, all
of it.

The first morning, she met Harris at the ferry and traveled across with
him. Before they parted, he pulled her very tightly to him, leaned down as
if to whisper something but merely pressed his mouth against her ear. The
anxiety and turmoil so overcame her that she actually spit up her tea in the
bushes outside the court building before she could bring herself to enter.
But then she thought of Harris, his lumpy, benevolent face, his black eyes,
his naïvely guilty conscience, and she gathered herself and went to take her
place in the gallery beside the Jimster and Fiona. She didn't know what was
harder, seeing Johnny across the room after having received Harris's silent
kiss, or sitting next to Fiona, lying to her while hoping her husband and fellow Whyo would be hanged. It was strange to be with the Whyos again, like
coming home. Their community, their laughter, their collective manner
were all incredibly seductive to her. She didn't want it back, exactly, but
yes, she missed it.

From that same seat, she looked at Dandy Johnny hard, continuously, all day, day after day, all week. She had a one-quarter view of his face most of the time — the jawline, the cheekbone, the tip of the nose, the edge of the brow — but if he shifted slightly, she could see his eyes. She did not respond to his one or two attempts at subvocal communication, rebuffing them with a very low frequency emanation of her own, something between a protracted exhalation and a hum. No Whyo could fault her for that. It showed she was in control, and control, as they all knew, was essential. Control was what they wanted from their leader and his First Girl. In the brief moments they had alone with Beatrice, Fiona and the Jimster told her they were doing fine. All the Whyos were confident that everything would work out; Johnny would get off on what would seem to the world at large to be a surprise jury decision. She tried not to think about what would happen if they were right. Some mornings, the absurd riskiness of what Beatrice was trying to pull brought on stomach cramps. Once, she actually had to be sick into her handbag.

What the Whyos in the courtroom — including Dandy Johnny — knew about Beatrice was that she had gone inactive since Johnny and Piker were taken in, which seemed reasonable and cautious. The wife of a murder suspect might, after all, fall under extra police scrutiny. They also knew that Beanie had informed Fiona that Undertoe had actually committed the murder and set Johnny up. It made sense to them, whether it was vengeance for the Barnum's job or the Old Bowery drunk dump or both — especially considering the way that the Noe murder had affected Harris. The word on the street was that Undertoe had specifically selected a cane that matched one of Johnny's and had made a point of using it in a murder, then tipped off the police. Some members of the gang, especially Maggie, had been in favor of meting out a little swift Whyo justice to settle that score, but the Jimster and Beatrice had made it clear that they wanted Undertoe left alone so Johnny could have the pleasure of doing it himself when he got off. Among the things the Whyos did *not* know were that Beatrice was sleeping with Frank Harris again and that she dreamed farfetchedly of becoming a doctor. They also did not know the great subtlety and range of her whyoing. She had concealed the full extent of her abilities from even Fiona and the Jimster. But there was one thing the Whyos — and the Why Nots in particular—did know that Beatrice did not: She was pregnant. They could see it, and they could smell it. The girls were excited at the idea of Dandy Johnny having a baby, and there was talk of other girls wanting to have babies, too, now, so their daughters could grow up to be First Girl to Dandy Johnny's boy.

On the last day of testimony, the defense attorney introduced a surprise piece of evidence: a second cane. He didn't much like John Dolan or Peter Ryan or the trashy little wife who had hired him, but the case was purely circumstantial. He'd gone out several times to search the city for another, similar cane, merely to illustrate his point to the jury, and at the last possible moment he had stumbled upon one in the shop window of Marm Mandelbaum's, a vast pawnshop on the corner of Clinton and Rivington. It was no more the cane that killed Mr. Noe than the one that had been entered into evidence already—the true weapon was still entombed in the shaft of dumbwaiter number 3 at the Noe Brush works. But the cane matched the first one in evidence—Johnny's—in every detail. The attorney told the jury that the emporium at Barnum's had had six dozen of the monkey-head models, half of which had sold by the time the Hippodrome burned. The judge admitted it to evidence, though it proved only how little the first cane had proved. Several character witnesses, all Whyos, were called to buttress the defense's arguments. The police and medical experts described Mr. Noe's wounds and also the bits of hair and flesh that had been found under the blades in Piker's and Dandy Johnny's boots. The fact that both defendants had clearly kicked *someone* in the head repeatedly on the night of the crime was the most damning fact of all.

When the defense rested, despite the second—or rather the third—cane, there were only four people in the courtroom who still believed Johnny and Piker were innocent: the defendants, the perpetrator and Beatrice. Even the Whyos believed the case had been made. But they weren't worried about a little detail like that.

As the jury received its charge, the Whyos and Why Nots began their work, each one transmitting his or her message to a specific jury member via signals that were barely audible, barely even distinguishable from their breath. It was silent, but it created such an air of agitation in the room that the judge banged his gavel for order. Undertoe, who had arrived early and taken a seat in an obscure corner of the upper balcony, shrank into the wooden backrest of his chair, agitated by the familiar vocalizations. He remembered the feeling all too well from Mother Dolan's funeral and began to wish he had passed up the spectacle of the trial's final day. He had never learned the important lesson that gloating is unwise.

Beatrice sat stiller than any of the Whyos, transmitting so subtly that none of them even realized she was doing it, and yet she cast her voice more loudly and intently than any other Whyo. She was leveling the messages of the Whyos, so that what reached the jury, which had been dismissed to an adjacent deliberation chamber, was just empty sound, void of content, indistinct from the distant sound of the actual wind, the rustling of real skirts, the grinding of genuine carriage wheels outside or the buzzing of true flies against the window. All the Whyos' work she reduced to white noise. Beatrice's plan was to allow the jury to come to their own conclusion. She felt confident enough of the verdict not to do anything more active. The case against Johnny and Piker may have been weak, legally, and possibly the extra cane should have introduced reasonable doubt in the minds of the jury, but Beatrice was no lawyer—she was just an average New Yorker—and she knew without question that to the men of the jury, Johnny and Piker were vermin who had killed an upstanding citizen in cold blood; they deserved to die. And so as long as she could pull off this final feat of whyoing, she knew which way it would go.

The Whyos quickly understood what was happening, and they thought they knew its source. To put it mildly, they were baffled. One after another, their jaws lolled in dismay and they fell quiet, truly quiet. They ceased their whyoing as if they'd been commanded to do so. For Beatrice was doing more than just negating their voices—she was doing it in Dandy Johnny's own voice, using his signature vibrato and his most secret codes. She was casting her voice across the room in such a way that it seemed for all the world to anyone who knew how to whyo to emanate from him. She was using every trick Mother Dolan had ever conceived of to keep control of both the sheepdogs and the sheep.

Johnny had turned in his chair and was staring straight at Beatrice. What the Whyos saw was this: Dandy Johnny, sweating and intensely agitated for the first time during the trial. They saw love in his eyes. They saw pain. They saw him look longingly at Beatrice and sacrifice himself for the good of the gang. A few times he seemed to waver in his resolve—almost to speak in two voices, at once joining in and negating their message to the jury—but not for long. What they heard was their leader committing suicide. They could never have guessed what only Johnny and Beatrice understood: that she was faking this suicide, impersonating him, while overriding the control the gang could have had over the jury. And then, after a few protests, it really was suicide—he let her do it.

Above all, Beatrice had feared a duel with him. She knew that her voice was in practice, whereas his was out of it, but she had thought it through and was aware that Johnny's urge for self-preservation might lend him some decisive power, sufficient either to drown her out or expose her fraud. But she needn't have worried. To the gang, she now sounded more like Johnny than he did. She was the one they'd been talking to, beginning when the *Westfield* blew all the way till Johnny's arrest. It's a complex business to debunk a competent imposter. There was something else that constrained Johnny, and this she had been counting on: his ego. For to expose her fraud would be for Johnny to admit that Beatrice had been speaking for him all that time. It would abnegate all his authority, amounting to just another, slower, more painful kind of suicide. He saw this, and he didn't even try.

Piker Ryan sat at the table next to Dandy Johnny in a state of shock. There were *two* lives on the block, after all. He gaped as all the other Whyos first whyoed in desperate confusion and then gradually fell silent. Finally, he spoke—in English.

"Johnny, what are you doing? What the Hell are you doing, Johnny?"

He asked it again and again, but Johnny wouldn't look at him. Johnny couldn't take his eyes off Beatrice's expressionless face—Beatrice, whom he'd come increasingly to admire and then, quite irrationally, to adore during his incarceration, Beatrice, whom he'd kept hoping would finally relent and come to see him, to tell him she wasn't mad anymore, Beatrice, who, from her new plumpness and her spitting up in her bag, even he'd begun to think might be carrying his child. He had plans for making it all up to her, how rough he'd been, what he'd done to her nose. What had happened to Johnny was this: He'd fallen in love with her while he languished in the Tombs, but it was late for that. Now he watched her put wordless words in his mouth, words that would hang him, and he cried like a child, because he knew that somehow, indirectly, he really was their author after all.

The verdicts came back quickly, based on the preponderance of the evidence. There had been doubt in some jurors' minds at first. The matter of the two canes, exhibits A and Q, was puzzling. But exhibits E and F, the two pair of ax-tipped boots belonging to Ryan and Dolan, respectively, had convinced them that even if no one had seen the accused men kill Mr. Noe, they very probably had. At the very least, they'd killed someone. In the end, it was unanimous: guilty and guilty. John Dolan and Peter Ryan were sentenced to hang.

Beatrice was given a brief private audience with Johnny before he was taken away. She was his wife. He could have said a lot of things, but what he did was reach out his hand, which was in shackles, and touch the side of her nose. It hadn't healed very elegantly this time.

"Forgive me, Beanie," he said.

She felt compelled to brush away a drop of sweat that was beading on his forehead before it could roll into his eyes, but she didn't have to brush away her own tears, because she wouldn't admit to herself that she was crying. She looked at him and saw an incredibly handsome man who was obviously in love with her. She had sent him to his death. She could almost have kissed him, have taken it all back.

"What is it, you want to run them all by yourself now? Is that it—modern times, women's suffrage?"

"No, Johnny, I'm getting out. I'm sorry. I'm sorry about everything." Then the lump in her throat met the one that was rising from her stomach, and she ran from the room.

The Whyos streamed down the white marble steps of the courthouse. They were so distraught, so disarmed by what had happened that they'd abandoned even the vestiges of their usual discretion about gathering overtly in public. They were crying on the street, hugging and talking to one another, drawing undue attention to themselves. They were struggling to find an interpretation for what had just happened, and the only thing they could come up with was that it was a noble sacrifice: Johnny's refusal to let them bring notice to the gang by forcing an unexpected, implausible acquittal. At the same time as they wept, they rallied around the Jimster as

Johnny's chosen successor. Beatrice came out a little after the others and couldn't stand to watch them. It was a queer, solitary feeling, not having anyone but a soon-to-be-dead man understand what she'd just done: the enormity of the feat and of the betrayal. She wanted Harris—she could tell Harris everything. But the truth was, even Harris would never really understand. And first she had one last important task to do, for Harris, for Johnny, for herself, and above all for a man she'd never met: Mr. Noe. She found Maggie the Dove in the crowd and drew her attention to Undertoe as he slunk along the far edge of the wide courthouse steps. Maggie would have the right amount of fury, she thought.

"Johnny can't take care of it himself now," she said. "Let's do it." That was all it took. Then she slipped away from the Whyos and headed for the Manhattan yard of the bridge to find her man. He was at work, waiting to hear the verdict. She would tell him, and they would go home. She could go home with him now. And then she had a week's worth of neglected homework to do. She was thinking, *Boring is fine, boring will be wonderful, give me boring, please.* She was imagining Harris's remarkable arms.

No Whyo saw her go. Maggie the Dove spread the word, and soon everyone understood what had to be done. No one gave an order, but the gang functioned with one mind, as if it was possessed of a collective consciousness. They desisted their un-Whyolike behavior. They fell quiet. They dispersed. They fanned out across the plaza and into neighboring streets. No one had a plan, but they might as well have rehearsed it, they were so efficient.

Just two men were tailing Undertoe as he turned north onto Chatham Street, but they made sure the others knew their location. Undertoe didn't even realize he was being followed yet, but the net of Whyos was so tight around him that there was no corner around which he might have turned to escape. When he made to walk up Bowery, a populous street, they herded him east instead. He began to feel nervous as they pushed him even further toward the river, to Oliver. His ears were ringing. He heard again the whispering that he'd come to understand was something much more than trees or birds or carriage wheels on Belgian block. He'd known something about what he had been hearing in the courtroom; now he knew it in a different way. He realized it was directed at him, and he tried to resist but was unable. He looked behind him and saw no one, nothing, but nevertheless he was afraid. Even when Luther Undertoe broke into a trot, even when he ran, he was not free—his very feet moved under direction from the Whyos. Finally, he found himself almost at the river. There were livery stables on either side and a narrow passage between them that opened onto the docks, which at that latitude were taken up entirely by the East Side Manure Depot, a complex of piers where stables and street-cleaning carts dumped the solid waste of every horse in that quadrant of the city. Undertoe darted through the gap between buildings and found himself up against a mountain of fly-swarmed dung as tall as he was. *What am I running from?* he wondered as a chill coursed his spine. He turned three hundred and sixty degrees in place. *Strange,* he thought, *there's no one around.* But of course it was not strange at all if one happened to know that the Whyos had purposely cleared the area. And then there were people all around, people with faces he recognized—the men and women from Mother Dolan's funeral, from Billy's, from the Morgue—and there was no doubt that they were working in concert. He saw men he'd known vaguely, years ago at the Newsboys Lodging House. He saw the Jimster—the Jimster had been his boy once. Then someone kicked a rooster tail of dung in his direction, and they fell upon him.

In all his years, Undertoe had never thought twice about any of the people he'd killed, and, no, he didn't start to do so now. He felt no redeeming pang of remorse. What filled his mind as the Whyos surged toward him was the very same thing that had always filled it when he was on the other side of a crime, dealing blows: the image of his mother, Lola Unterzeh, the Pomeranian Soprano-Contortionist, P. T. Barnum's early great hope and even greater flop, the fizzled precursor to the star act that followed, the woman the world called the Swedish Nightingale. Undertoe's mother had had a voice even sweeter than Jenny Lind's, but her act, while squarely up Barnum's alley, was too much of a hybrid to catch on. She sang arias while standing on her hands, with her legs over her shoulders and her derriere exposed; she crooned lieder while performing a flashy one-hand backbend in a sequined chemise. It was sheer genius, really, how she managed to project her voice in those postures, but he hadn't promoted her right, and when ticket sales faltered Barnum had shunted her off to the sideshow, while

Jenny Lind's American tour had made her famous and him a world-class impresario. Loopy Lola, as some people called her, began to feel ill one evening when Luther was a boy, just after a flawless execution of her pièce de résistance, a Mozart aria that ended with a high C she belted out in the standing double-lotus position. An audience of four saw the act: two woozy sailors, an Indian on break from another exhibit and her son. Lola had had to excuse herself afterward to go throw up. For three days, Lola Unterzeh had writhed in pain and watched her stomach bloat. She couldn't eat a thing. It wouldn't have helped her much to know what it was: an impacted bowel, triggered by an unlucky constellation of small disorders, including constipation from her little laudanum habit, an exacerbation of the chronic inflammation that she suffered as a low-grade carrier of typhoid, and then, of course, the unfortunate angulation of the knot she'd tied herself in that afternoon. Luther had never forgotten the fecal stench of her vomit toward the end, his helplessness, her final words: "Luther, my pea, my sweetest pea, if I don't get well, go to your father. He'll take care of you."

Undertoe had always known who his father was but had never really known him. Mr. Barnum, as he called him, kept his distance from all but the gold-medal acts, and Lola Unterzeh hadn't panned out. He'd given Undertoe a lousy job selling trinkets and a bunk to sleep in, in the stable, just to shut him up, but the day the boy came up to him in front of half a dozen others and dared to say *father*, he'd slapped him in the face without compunction.

"Excuse me, boy, is that something your opium addict of a mother told you, or is it just your own little dream?"

Undertoe had landed his boy's flyweight left hook in Barnum's grandiose gut—to no particular effect—before being dragged away by a couple of the freaks. He'd started to dream of fire that very night. Fire was a fine kind of revenge for a boy, one with a potential impact far surpassing the incendiary's personal strength. That was what had hooked him, really: the exponential growth of it from the first small flickering match to something that seemed like the end of the world. It had made him, who was no one, just as powerful—or more so—than Barnum, for a while.

Someone landed a slung-shot squarely on the whorled cup of Undertoe's right ear, and he heard an angelic sound: the trill of a perfect high C.

His ears hadn't rung so purely since before he caught the mumps. Many of the Whyos had clubs and bowie knives. The first two who got to him with gougers prized out his eyes. Maggie the Dove got the left, slightly astigmatic one. Before five minutes had expired, it was over, and there was no body anywhere in sight—just a freshly turned spot on the festering pile and half a hundred average-looking Irishmen and -women fading back into the streets, tucking in their shirts, straightening their skirts, discreetly wiping their hands on the insides of their pockets. From the top layer of the pile of shit beneath which Undertoe lay, maggots went on bursting into horseflies, almost like popcorn, just as they'd been doing all day long and the day before and the day before that, ad infinitum. And then, one by one, they flew off—green-eyed, buzzing and hungry for the cycle of their procreation to begin again.

40.

WORLD WITHOUT END

angings at the Tombs were not public; they were held in the building's fully enclosed courtyard. But because of the relative height and prox-
imity of the surrounding buildings, whenever the gallows went up the
adjacent rooftops transformed the area into an amphitheater, with elbow-
to-elbow balcony seating for the spectacle below. All the residents of Five
Points converged upon the area. Bowery theaters stayed dark, knowing no
one would come. And then there was always the smattering of upper-class
rakes who donned shabby jackets and risked joining the fray just to feel the
thrill of watching a healthy man jerk and die, just to be able to say they'd
seen what their acquaintances only read about in the *Sun* or the *Trib*. It was
almost as adventurous, to them, as going to sea or to war, but the war was
long over and sea voyages were notorious hells. Going down to the Fourth
Ward to take in a hanging demanded only a single night; they'd be home
for lunch the next day.

The revelry began around dusk the night before and went on till hours
after the rope was finally cut down. Vendors who otherwise sold their wares
on the streets by day made their way up to the rooftops at sundown and did
a brisk trade walking from building to building through the wee hours.
Eventually, just before dawn, every square foot of roof space was so thick
with people that the vendors returned to the streets below, which at least
were still navigable, though even then they were thronged with latecomers

who'd failed to find perches with views onto the action. The crowds being as thick as they were, a hanging was also a great opportunity for petty thieves and pickpockets. Beatrice and Fiona and the rest of the Why Nots had gone out with baskets of corn and profited handsomely from many a hanging in the past.

This time, as the soon-to-be widow of one of the condemned men, it was going to be different for her. Beatrice received an invitation from the warden himself to witness the event from a balcony within the courtyard; the letter came some two weeks in advance of the date. It arrived at the old Dolan penthouse, where Fiona and the Jimster lived now, and was delivered to Dr. Smith's house in Weeksville by a girl she didn't know—a new Why Not, she presumed. So business was going on without her. After she'd read it, she tore the heavy sheet to shreds. Newly law-abiding or not, author of his death or not, she damn well wasn't going to stand beside the cops while a couple of innocent Whyos were strung up to die. But it did raise the question: Would she go at all? Join the rollicking crowd? Accompany the other Whyos, some of whom had dreams of an eleventh-hour rescue? She didn't think she belonged there anymore.

"I don't know what I want to do, Harris. Maybe I shouldn't go at all. And yet I feel I have to."

She didn't expect him to have an answer. It was a bit of an awkward subject for him, but after a minute he said, "Well, it wouldn't be a great view, kind of far away, but unobstructed, away from the crowds."

"What, the bridge?"

He nodded.

"It's not allowed, is it?" She was almost smiling. She'd wanted to go to the top of the bridge for some time, but he hadn't offered. The company had banned all ladies from the footbridges, thanks to a couple of scandalized newspaper articles the month before, after an assistant engineer brought his young daughters on a tour and they had both been so paralyzed with fright that they'd had to be carried down.

"I seem to remember you playing the part of a boy rather convincingly, the morning I first met you. You and your brass knuckles."

"*Harris.*"

"Well, you did."

"I'm well aware."

It was something of a problem for her, actually, how he managed to be both sensitive and funny, and then, just when she was sick of what a goody-goody he was, he would want to break some rule, do something wrong, go far enough afield to keep her interest. He was too perfect.

That week, she'd found yet another matter to preoccupy her. She couldn't believe she hadn't realized it before, but she had finally gone to the Smith-Blacksall clinic one day, after school—as a patient.

"Lord, girl," said Dr. Smith, who was on duty. "What about school, your plans, haven't you learned a thing at this clinic?"

Beatrice was silent.

"Well, are you planning to marry that Harris boy? You're going to need to think a few things out."

Beatrice coughed. "To start with, I'm still married to the other."

"Oh—so you are. But you don't mean to tell me . . . it's *his*?"

Beatrice could see her counting backward in her head.

"I don't know. I thought maybe you could help me figure that out. If it's Harris's, see, I think I'd feel different."

It turned out the window of opportunity spanned the time when Dandy Johnny had last raped her and she'd first taken up with Harris. There was no way to know. Maybe it was the hormones, circulating wildly irrespective of paternity—because no matter how big a mistake she'd made, Beatrice was normally anything but a blubberer—but now she burst into tears.

Dr. Smith said, "I'm sorry, Beatrice. I'm awfully sorry for you. You have to figure this one out. But I'll tell you, if you stick to school, if you work hard, you really could be a doctor. It only takes determination, studying, time . . . or all that plus a strong stomach, which I know you have. There's a lot of girls out there who need caring for. You could go back to the Five Points and help those girls, show them what's possible. There are even fewer women than Negroes in medicine, you know. They're needed. You could make it if you didn't quit."

"But what if I love him, Harris, and it's his? What do I do then?"

"I don't know. You have to choose."

She couldn't bring herself to go back to Dr. Zhang's, nor did she ask Dr.

Smith for more help, nor did she even tell Harris. She told herself she would wait until Johnny was dead, although why she felt that gory milestone would make things any clearer even she couldn't have said.

For the next week, she bounced from morose ill humor to clinging adoration of Harris, from impatience with him to insatiable lust. He was pretty patient, considering, but he was anxious, too. Great, unpredictable changes were bound to occur in their lives. And then the eve of the day arrived. When it grew late, they climbed into bed. He reached around and embraced her from behind. He seemed to weigh the flesh of the stomach in one hot hand, a breast in the other. He seemed to know what she hadn't told him, and she imagined he was waiting for her to confess. It was reasonable, perhaps, but she resented it.

"You know, don't you?"

"Know what?"

"You know, Harris—" she said, and then he got it.

"What, really?" He sat up and looked at his hands and then at her in amazement, happy amazement, as if he had built something wonderful. Then he leaned over her and covered her with himself, kissing her face while she lay flat and unresponsive. She wasn't kissing back. It was so warm and humid out that his skin made a damp, sticky sound on releasing from hers. She looked at him. He was still smiling, a little thickly. He hadn't even begun to imagine the problems. Sometimes he seemed like such a fool to her.

"But it's good, it's all right, Beatrice," he said and reached out to her again, but this time she rolled away.

"You don't understand, Harris. It's not as easy as that."

"You don't want a baby? Or it's me?" His face crumpled a little, and he looked away from her.

"I don't know, Harris. The first problem is, it could be *his*. What if it's a gangster's baby, would you like it then?"

This next bit was one of Harris's better moments so far: Instead of backing up and saying, *Oh. Oh no*, he looked at her in a way that said he didn't care. He'd already understood the risk. He reached out and put his fingers against her waist in the gentlest way and said, "We could handle that. It'll just be a *baby*. And maybe it's mine, right? I don't mind if it isn't, but I feel lucky now." Which made her bury her face in the pillow. He was as good as he could have been, and it still didn't answer her questions.

"I'm not even married to you."

It sort of made him fill with joy to hear her say that. She was obviously miserable, angry, too, but he heard the glimmer of promise, of possibility.

"Well, Bea, as soon as you aren't married to someone else, maybe . . ."

She gave him a look, a setback. "Is that how you're asking me, like that? Harris, I don't even like the idea of marriage."

"Oh." He was starting to feel bad again.

"I've got plans. You might not believe it, but I'm really going to go to the medical college."

"I believe it."

"And I've got some money of my own. A lot. I could do it alone. I don't need you."

"Oh."

"You've got no idea how much I can do."

"Maybe I do. Maybe you could do even more than you think. You could do both."

She growled with frustration and turned away. There was something about his kind, supportive rebuttals that oppressed her and made her want to be free, never have to think about him or some child, whoever its father was.

"*Ich liebe dich.*" He said it in German because there was a sense in which it still meant more to him in his own language, even after all this time. It somehow seemed realer to him, but it didn't touch her.

"What?" she said. "Why are you suddenly speaking German now?"

"I love you, just so you know."

"I'll take it into consideration." And they talked no more that night.

The next morning, Beatrice and Harris got up very early. She dressed in a suit of Bobby Noe's clothes: trousers, a vest, a boy's cap, a short coat. She was still a remarkable chameleon: He hardly would have recognized her, except that he remembered this boy she'd become. "Shut up and get moving," she had demanded of him once. There was much that was different about it now, walking through the streets with her in a boy's garb, but now as then he was afraid. On the ferry, the fact that he couldn't reach out to guide her elbow nor she take his arm (it would have been most inappropriate, given her costume) was at once painful to him and titillating.

Harris being a foreman now and because of his connection to the Dolan murder case, it was generally expected at the bridge site that he'd be going up there that morning to take in the spectacle from the safety and remove of the tower. He introduced Beatrice as Ben O'Gamhna, a relative, to a couple of men in the yard, and she shook their hands like a boy who hoped to be respected as a man. She was very good at characters. Then they made their way to the footbridge. He sent her up in front of him so he could rush to her aid if she grew dizzy or slipped, but her step was firm. She held one wire rail in each hand and walked steadily in the direction of Brooklyn. Up and out, away from Manhattan, toward the open river, looking past downtown Brooklyn to the unspoiled farms and villages further out. He turned back to look at Manhattan briefly. It gave him a crowded feeling. Brooklyn was where he belonged, he thought—not Germany, not Manhattan. Out on the Heights and beyond, past Fulton Ferry, there was room to breathe, room to build, room enough to cope with trouble and to make a new life. If only she would join him, he could be happy there. But after last night, he was less sure than ever that she would. It wasn't exactly a surprise to him to realize he was about to miss another near chance at being happy. That's the way it had always gone with him. He looked at her slim legs in Bobby Noe's knickers and sighed. He would just keep on working. It would be enough.

The Manhattan tower was about three quarters finished. When she reached the top, she turned around and held out her hand to him. It was funny, her helping him, when he was the one who came here every day, but he realized he needed it. Harris was reeling, not from dizziness or height but love. She hadn't said much all morning, but it was her way of silently breaking the distance between them. He tried to give her a smile that was warm but not happy, something that showed loyalty but did not stake a claim. It wasn't a very large terrain he was trying to chart with that smile. Between the event they were there to witness and their conversation last night, he was on delicate ground. But the sight of her with her legs in those trousers, standing wide for balance in that high place, was very nearly more than he could bear. He bit his lip. It was a grim moment for her, a complicated one. For the love of God, they were up there together to watch her husband be hanged by the neck till he died. Yes, and though he told himself it was loathsome, insensitive, crass, Harris couldn't stop thinking that as soon as Johnny Dolan was dead, she would be his. It wasn't true, of course. She had never been a chattel to be transferred from one man to the next, not Beatrice O'Gamhna, not even when Johnny had claimed her. He knew now, from the past months, from the bumps in her nose, from her role in bringing about what they were there to see, that she had never succumbed to that. But Harris could not deny that he was looking forward to seeing Dandy Johnny kick, gasp, dangle and finally go slack, leaving Beatrice free at least to choose.

He was, of course, far more jealous even than he admitted to himself. It would be harder than he could imagine if he ended up the father of a *gangster's baby*. He and Johnny did not resemble each other, meaning it would very likely be possible to tell. It would be hard, but he had an especially compelling reason to make the effort. That reason leaned toward him, one hand still grasping the terminal bolt of the railing stanchion, the other mingling her fingers with his, and pulled him up off the wavery catwalk onto solid rock. They walked around the central pit to the northwest edge and sat down on a couple of barrels to watch what was taking place at the Tombs.

"That's where you fell, down that hole in the center?" It was deep and dark.

"Yeah, but not that one. On the other side."

"God, Harris." She put her hand on his thigh. He told himself not to overreact.

The people below seemed tiny and unreal, but as with watching ants, once Harris and Beatrice had been looking at them for a while they adjusted to the scale and were able to make out the movements of individuals as well as the larger patterns of flow and stasis. From the streets all around, people were converging upon a space that was already so crowded it seemed unable to accommodate more. In the ring of packed rooftops there was one anomaly: a building with a roof that was not crowded at all but held just a few dozen onlookers, as if it were some kind of private box at the opera. It was also some two stories higher than those on either side of it, which kept the traffic from adjacent buildings from flowing across it. Beatrice knew the building; it was a burned-out warehouse that was sometimes used by the Whyos for meetings and stashing loot.

"You see that building there, with the charred windows? That's the Whyos."

At the center of this arena there lay, like the yolk of an egg, the Tombs itself, and the bloody strand in the yolk, the center's center, was the double gallows, its pale new wood gleaming in the early-morning light.

Part of the curious remove of Beatrice O'Gamhna and Frank Harris's vantage point was the silence. There was no noise from the street, just the slightest hum, which lent an unreal quality to the tableau below, as if it were an enactment, a trial run, a figment of their dual imaginations, perhaps. The world down below was loud and tawdry and desperate—just this side of a riot, in fact—but up there it was so calm as almost to be boring. After a while, Harris noticed that Beatrice wasn't even looking down at the Tombs but out at the harbor. And just then the distant scene began to change.

"Bea," said Harris. "Look."

A small phalanx of buglike figures had come into the courtyard. They spread out and took up places at and around the gallows. One of them walked beneath the raised structure, and a moment later first one and then another black square appeared on the light wooden platform. For a moment, they seemed to be the blackest spots in the universe, holes deep enough to suck every living creature into them. Then the trapdoors shut again and the holes disappeared. One of them was the hole through which Dandy Johnny would fall. Of course, it wouldn't be the hole itself that killed him. The condemned man's own weight would release the latch. Then the rope loop over the crossbar would tighten and, depending on the suddenness of the action, either snap Johnny's neck or more slowly stop his breath.

"I'm the one that's killing them," Beatrice said as two figures finally emerged from a small doorway. But which was which? It hadn't occurred to Harris the height would be so great as to obliterate the difference between them. They ascended the platform, but before stepping forward to have the noose secured around his neck, one of the figures paused. He turned slowly around in a circle, scanning the crowd, it seemed. So that was Johnny, on the left. Beatrice knew he was looking for her and, though sound couldn't possibly have carried so far, she perceived that he was why-oing. Cold sweat rose everywhere on her body. Her hairs bristled. He was free to communicate with the Whyos, free to tell them anything, free to accuse her of any crime he could think of, free to set them on her. *What was he saying?* She focused intently, trying to make it out through the wind.

"Oh, no," she said. "Oh, God."

"What?" Harris asked her, but she didn't answer.

A few minutes later Dandy Johnny refused the hood that was offered him by the executioner, choosing to die open-eyed. He didn't fight while the rope was placed around his neck. All that remained was for him to step forward and plunge to his end. Harris held his breath and reached for Beatrice's hand, waiting for everything to be over, but before that could happen, Beatrice jumped up from the barrel and turned to him. Her face was wet and blotchy.

"Don't get so close to the edge, Bea—"

"This was your plan, wasn't it? To get me up here and wait till he was hanged and then ask me to marry you. Isn't that it? Isn't that basically what you told me last night?"

It wasn't really true that he'd planned it like that, not at all, but neither could Harris quite defend himself against the accusation. He tried, not very successfully, to shake his head, but she was gripping his jaw in her hands.

"Goddamnit, Harris. A hanging is a Hell of an unromantic moment to start a life. I can't even bear to watch it. I'm going. I don't know why I came."

She turned from him and made for the footbridge, choking and wiping her eyes, but Harris caught up and firmly pulled her to him. He didn't want her out on that footbridge, not right now. She was stiff in his arms, but she didn't buck away. They were each looking out past the other's shoulder, he up the river, she down it, neither of them at the Tombs. He said softly into her ear: "It doesn't start here—it started years ago. A couple of months ago it changed completely. Now it changes again."

He wasn't watching, he didn't know the perfection of his timing, but at just that moment their lives had indeed changed. Dandy Johnny Dolan's body had ceased to jerk. Instead of a notorious gangster, there was just a terrible pendulum swinging at the end of the hemp loop.

"I thought I heard him whyoing, just now," Beatrice said. "I thought I heard him saying that he loved me."

"Not like I do."

"I know," she said. And then, after a pause: "So are you going to do it?"

"You mean, ask you?"

She nodded.

"Do you want me to?"

"Goddamnit, Harris."

He swallowed, not knowing what to do. She had rejected him any number of times. She had more or less just told him *not* to do it. Did she want him to?

"Oh, Christ, all right. *I'll* do it then." And then she asked him, which somehow made everything all right.

Just as they began to kiss, one of the young men from Harris's crew came onto the tower platform. He did a double take and then swore loudly in astonishment at the sight of his foreman embracing a teenage boy.

Harris and Beatrice turned to him, and Beatrice pulled off the cap into which her hair had been tucked.

"This is my good friend Miss O'Gamhna," Harris said, "so don't go spreading funny rumors. And have some respect."

Then they turned back to the gallows. Piker and Johnny were dangling. They had missed the execution after all. They walked out onto the footbridge, into the atmosphere above the harbor.

There they were—just them, no impediments that they knew of.

The city was different from how it had been when they reached the tower an hour before, and the city would never change. Deals had been made for tens of thousands of dollars and breakfast had been eaten by hundreds of thousands of mouths. Several bloody babies had been born, and all of them were crying, and five New Yorkers had died: two in sickbeds; one of a heart attack on the floor of a law office, soiling his pin-striped trousers and a Persian rug; the other two there in the yard at the Tombs. But for everyone who died, another entered, if not two, to vie for the open position.

There were still the same number of mothers and babies and bankers and bakers and crooks in the world. No single man, woman or child was needed to define the whole. The city was so big, even then, and there were so many people in it that someone was always there waiting in the wings to cover for those who fell away. Maybe it wouldn't be the Jimster and Fiona who would dominate organized crime in the Five Points in the following decade—they weren't that ruthless, really—but someone would. That's how the city made its citizens free: free to defy expectation, free to spit at fate, free to work the chaos in the system, free to fail. And so were Frank Harris (if that's what you choose to call him) and Beatrice O'Gamhna free.

A baby's born shrieking in the night. A sullen child matures to better temper. A family arrives at the Port of New York unable to imagine the misery and joy that await them. A man learns who he is. A woman leaves a life of crime. And over on the West Side, at the Barclay Street ferry pier, a girl who's just been tapped to join a secret gang tosses aside a stripped twopenny ear of fresh, sweet, lily-white summer hot corn and licks her lips. She flexes her fingers and steels her nerves, and a few brief minutes later she reaches as deftly as she can into a pocket, hoping to come away undetected with something of value in her fist, imagining that if only she accumulates enough such stuff she'll be able to revise her life according to her dreams. That girl doesn't know the first thing about the currency of happiness, yet. And whether she ever learns it or not, the waves of the harbor will take the same scallop-edged forms, ever changing, never varying, capping endlessly white against the wind that fans her hair, that girl's, then gusts past Harris and O'Gamhna on their transit back to solid ground, swirls between the two outrageous towers of the great bridge and blows the whole way across Brooklyn, over Staten Island, out to sea and beyond.

AUTHOR'S NOTE

Many actual historical details shaped the writing of this novel: A Bengal tiger really leapt from an upper story of P. T. Barnum's burning American Museum on the corner of Broadway and Spring on March 2, 1868, and was shot by a policeman. There really was a gang called the Whyos with a boss named John Dolan, known as Dandy Johnny, who was hanged in the Tombs for a murder resembling the one that takes place toward the end of this book. The Whyos were said by Herbert Asbury in his marvelous (if not always rigorously factual) folk history *The Gangs of New York* to have gotten their name from a call they used to communicate with one another while they worked. There are a few mug shots of Whyos in that book, including one of a supremely stupid-looking brute named Piker Ryan, whom I couldn't resist making into a character. In general, though, the Whyo gang is not very well documented, which I saw as an opportunity to invent freely to suit my tale.

My stableman's childhood was inspired by the life story of the German histologist Jacob Henle, who was a mentor to the pioneering microbiologist Robert Koch, and who was by all accounts a much nicer man than the stableman's father in the book. Back in the United States, the character Susan Smith is based on an actual black woman doctor who practiced progressive medicine and provided safe abortions and other medical care to indigent women; her colleague in the book, Sarah Blacksall, is based in part on Elizabeth Blackwell, who was a professor at the amazingly radical Women's

Medical College, where black and white women not only dissected cadavers in the anatomy lab but did so side by side, in an integrated setting.

The East River did in fact freeze solid several times in the late nineteenth century, which has been called by climatologists and historians a "mini–ice age." A ferry called the *Westfield* did blow up at the Whitehall Street terminal, a disaster that remains, as of 2004, the most lethal ferryboat accident ever to take place in New York harbor. Finally, a workman named Frank Harris did in fact fall from the tower of the Brooklyn Bridge while it was under construction, and, incredibly, he lived.

Such people and events were the true-life framework around which I constructed many other aspects of my fictional metropolis, including the culture of the sewermen and their custom of washing up after work in a city-run bath hall; the language and skewed utopian vision of the Whyos and the existence of the Why Nots (though there were several girl gangs in operation in 1870s New York, notably the Forty Little Thieves, affiliated with the male gang called the Forty Thieves); the extent to which the nascent New York City sewer system could have been navigated underground; and the blowout in the Brooklyn caisson (though a somewhat similar accident did occur on a Sunday, when no one was working below, caused simply by a confluence of low tide and high internal air pressure).

I drew from many books and other sources in researching *Metropolis*. Among the most important to me were *The Great Bridge* by David McCullough, *Paris Sewers and Sewermen* by Donald Reid, Asbury's *Gangs of New York*, *Low Life* by Luc Sante and *Gotham* by Edwin G. Burrows and Mike Wallace. Some of my favorite sources were contemporary: old technical volumes on subjects ranging from street construction to lighting technology to sewerage, the annual corporation manuals of the City of New York, George E. Waring's 1886 *Report on the Social Statistics of Cities*, period travel guides and directories and, crucially, daily and weekly newspapers, especially *Frank Leslie's Illustrated*, *Harper's Illustrated*, the New York *Sun* and the Brooklyn *Eagle*. (The full-text archives of the *Eagle* are now available online, in fully searchable format, through a marvelous project of the Brooklyn Public Library.)

For those curious for more detail about what in the book is true (and what isn't), I have posted a hypertext map of New York in 1870, with links to images, documents, websites and various facts relating to New York and the novel, on my website, at www.elizabethgaffney.net.

. . .

Much of this book was written while I was in residence at the Blue Mountain Center, the MacDowell Colony, the Medway Institute and Yaddo. Thanks to all the people who keep those wonderful places going.

For their generosity, encouragement and sound advice to me while I worked on this book, I am enormously grateful to Andrea Barrett, Emily Boro, Michael Chabon, Andrea Chapin, Amanda Davis (1971–2003), Jeffrey Eugenides, Brigid Hughes, Jonathan Lethem, Rick Moody, George Plimpton (1927–2003), Elissa Schappell and Ayelet Waldman.

For their tireless efforts on behalf of *Metropolis*, I am indebted to my agent, Leigh Feldman; to my editor, Kate Medina; and to Frankie Jones, Kristin Lang, Ros Perotta and Danielle Posen.

And profoundest thanks to my family: Ann Walker Gaffney, who taught me her love for the city; Walker Gaffney, who saw the view from the top of the tower; and Alex Boro, the best man I know, for everything.

METROPOLIS

ELIZABETH GAFFNEY

A READER'S GUIDE

Question: What was the inspiration behind *Metropolis*? How did you come up with this particular story and these characters?

Elizabeth Gaffney: My first two decisions were to write about a time different from my own and to take up a male character as a protagonist. I wanted to learn something while I was working on the novel and to get away from the limitations of my own point of view. Where I stuck close to home was in the setting—New York City. I was born here and have lived here most of my life. In fact, I was interested in the idea of using the city as one of the main characters right from the beginning. The title was one of the first things to come to me. I chose a young, unlucky, struggling immigrant character for my hero because I think everyone can relate to the difficulty of creating an identity. It's the biggest job we human beings have during that trying period of puberty and adolescence—that's why coming-of-age novels are so universal. By picking the 1870s as my time period, I was trying to make the book a coming-of-age novel for the city and for the nation, too. This was a time of grand infrastructure projects that still shape our urban landscapes and allow us to sustain the population density that we do. I chose an inspirational and very public structure that was built around this time—the Brooklyn Bridge—to symbolize my character's aspirations and chose a hidden and generally unmentioned one—the sewer system (also largely built in this period)—to represent the dark underbelly of experience that my character would have to traverse and overcome to achieve his goals. The late nineteenth century was also a time when a great wave of immigrants came into our country, which necessitated the eventual opening of Ellis Island as an immigration center. Immigrants have always been at the heart of New York's culture, and this whole country's culture—we're almost all descended from immigrants, after all, except for Native Americans. So I knew I would be writing about an immigrant. I decided to make him German because I had spent time living in Germany and I knew the country well. I made the other main character, Beatrice, Irish because Ireland is a large part of my own heritage, and also because the Germans and the Irish were the two largest immigrant groups during the period I chose to write about.

Q: You use the same title as the great silent film by Fritz Lang. What sort of connection do you see between your book and Lang's *Metropolis*?

EG: I find Lang's *Metropolis* to be a quintessential urban social drama, and I was greatly inspired by it. For me, a futuristic vision like Lang's is not all that far from a historical narrative—both step away from the here and now, but in so doing are capable of commenting on the present perhaps more strongly than a story set among all the familiar features of our everyday existence. Lang's *Metropolis* combines the personal coming-of-age story of its protagonist, a scion of the ruling class, together with a love story, a story of social revolution and a story of a mad Frankenstein-like scientist's botched automaton—there are so many things going on. Like Siddhartha, the hero is born into privilege and is at first entirely unaware of the poor laborer class that makes his world possible. But once he learns that it exists, he chooses to descend into that underground world, where he finds terrible suffering and injustice, and he makes sacrifices to set things right. He devotes himself to serving truth and justice, not the status quo. I can't say any of my characters are quite so saintlike or revolutionary, but I did partly base the structure of my book—Harris's being born to privilege and descending into an underworld before he can rise up again—on that of Lang's *Metropolis*.

Q: What attracted you to this particular period in New York's history? How long did you research this book? What were some of your more interesting or unexpected sources?

EG: The biggest things that drew me to the period (roughly the 1870s) were the sewer system, which underwent a major renovation and expansion then, and the Brooklyn Bridge, which was under construction at the time. For me, those two elements of the city's infrastructure were symbolic of the unsavory hidden underworld and the highest possible intellectual and artistic achievement of American society. Both were opportunities to look deep into the lives of ordinary workingmen and women of the period and what their lives were like. I chose not to write about the engineers or the powerful politicians and financiers; rather, I wanted to take up the unsung common people as my characters. The research was a lot of fun and I was constantly discovering new facts throughout the seven years I spent writing *Metropolis*. Sometimes what I found made me introduce substantial plot changes into the book, so I could add interesting new details I had just come across. For instance, when I read about the women's medical college, I knew I had to include it. That gave rise to two new characters who are both important: the white doctor, Sarah Blacksall, and the black doctor, Susan Smith—a real figure by the way, who practiced medicine for many decades in Brooklyn, and elsewhere, after she married and moved away.

Q: The line between truth and fiction is blurred in *Metropolis*—many of the people and places are real, while others are fictional and still others seem somewhere in between. How did you decide what to use from history and how did you make it your own creation? Who were some of the real people from history that became characters in your book that the reader might not have known?

EG: Aside from Susan Smith, there are many real characters in the book, but not many famous ones, since I was seeking to document the other side of society. A few well-known people, like P. T. Barnum, have walk-on roles, but I was more captivated by stories like John Dolan's, and that of the brush manufacturer Mr. Noe. The murder that occurs towards the end of the book is based on reality, and some of the details, including the monkey-headed cane that was the murder weapon, are drawn from contemporary newspaper accounts or from books like Herbert Asbury's *Gangs of New York*. Piker Ryan, one of the Whyo gang members, was also a real person. I saw a mug shot of him, and he was so dumb-looking and just so plain ugly that I couldn't let him lie. In general, I tried to use real stories I felt I could adapt freely to my own, keeping a line of real material running through the narrative, while not being too bound by facts. The balance I sought was one that allowed for both a realistic portrayal of the times and a rollicking good story.

Q: Why did you decide to have two villains, Dandy Johnny and Luther Undertoe?

EG: I am interested in seeing how various people with similar backgrounds can evolve differently. I suppose it's a way of studying character. At any rate, if you examine Johnny's early childhood and compare it with Luther's, you will find that they were similar; both lost their fathers at an early age and grew up in the rough world of the Five Points with morally compromised immigrant mothers. But as villains, they are quite different. Luther is pretty much a sociopath, while Johnny is a player, a criminal who has charm and charisma to mask his dark side. I think having characters who are variations on a theme is an interesting way of exploring the human psyche. For that matter, Harris had a lot of the same setbacks as Johnny and Undertoe, and is certainly led toward a life of crime, but he resists it, despite some missteps, and remains a fundamentally moral, promising human being. You could look at the central women characters and see similar patterns among them, too. But each person reacts differently to the circumstances, and that's how you know what sort of person each is at her core.

Q: There are many strong women characters in the novel, but your hero is male. How did you decide to go with a male main character? Was it difficult to write from a male point of view?

EG: I set out to use a male protagonist as a sort of exercise, to get away from my own point of view and limitations. That's also why I chose to write a historical novel. I wanted to learn something new and to expand my own horizons. It turned out to be fascinating and illuminating. I wouldn't have had half as much fun or have learned nearly as much if I'd written about a thirty-something aspiring writer who lived in New York City. The way I see it, if I was having fun as a writer, then there was a chance I could give some of that same energy to my reader, so it was about keeping it interesting. That said, I could easily borrow a line from Flaubert and say about Harris: "He is me." I relate to him on so many levels. That's true of all the characters in the book, bad and good. I'd never do what Undertoe does, but I have had impulses to be cruel and destructive. I've been tempted to take my frustrations and troubles out on others. I tried to tap into the full range of emotions I could imagine and play them out to their extremes where they suited the story.

Q: Were the Whyos and the female counterpart gang the Why Nots based on real gangs from the period? Is the Whyo language your creation?

EG: The Whyos was a real gang, and there were real girl gangs affiliated with some New York gangs—including a group called the Forty Little Thieves, who worked with a gang called the Forty Thieves. But I made up the Why Nots. As for the Whyo language, it is based on the record—the Whyos did have some form of covert communication, but I couldn't find anything at all about the specifics of it, so all the particulars are my invention.

Q: Your style seems to borrow from some of the traditions of the nineteenth-century novel, and yet in other ways *Metropolis* seems very modern. Which writers have influenced you, particularly in the creation of *Metropolis*?

EG: I wanted to tap into the form of nineteenth-century novels by doing certain things, like having short chapters with cliff-hanger endings, leading the reader from one chapter to the next. It seemed to suit the material. Some of what I do in the book, such as my use of a somewhat intrusive omniscient narrator, is both quite old-fashioned and quite postmodern. You see that kind of voice governing the earliest novels, from *Don Quixote* to *Tristram Shandy,* and then again in much more recent and contemporary-seeming fiction. I wanted the novel to straddle the past and the present, and for some of its issues to speak to present-day issues. As I see it, the social injustices of the nineteenth century are still with us, just in different forms and particulars. By having my narrator be aware of modern genetics and that sort of thing, or about social statistics such as the rate of abortions among various demographic groups, I wanted to suggest how little the world has changed. There are still a lot of diseases that afflict the poor much more often than they afflict the middle and upper classes, for example. I was trying to make a book that had some of the pleasures of escapism that a good novel can give, but I didn't want the book to exist only on that level. And I didn't want it to be a mere costume drama. I always appreciate it when there's some substance behind a story, and this was my way of trying to provide that.

Q: *Metropolis* has very strong female characters, and some of the themes are very forward thinking for the time period (the women's medical college, women running gangs). Who were the historical women that inspired these themes?

EG: Susan Smith was real, as I said. She graduated from the first class of the Medical College for Women. Her friend Sarah Blacksall is based loosely on the director of that institution, Elizabeth Blackwell, who was a generation older. I mention briefly a famous fence named Marm Mandelbaum, who really existed, as well as a real-life abortionist and charlatan who called herself Madame Restell (though she was not the least bit French). The late nineteenth century was a time of visionary thinkers and social change. Women were asserting themselves in any number of social contexts. Margaret Sanger and a rival of hers named Mary Ware Dennett were promoting women's health care and contraception. There were colonies that practiced free love, the communal raising of children, and open marriage. The suffrage movement was well under way. The thing that struck me over and over as I did my research was how advanced the society was in its thinking, and how we haven't come quite as far as we think we have, given where society was then. Certainly not half far enough. Or maybe the point is that progress itself is not inherently good.

Q: There's a good deal of nineteenth-century medicine and science in the book, including women's health issues, a number of references to epidemic diseases such as typhoid, a fairly graphic account of a heart attack, and several characters who are doctors. What role do medicine and science have in your story?

EG: I am fascinated with how the whole world works, from how a city is built to how a body functions to how a person thinks and acts. I was interested in placing the physiology of a society, or of a city, side by side with the physiology of its component parts, great structures and individual flesh-and-blood human beings in their most bodily manifestations and in their behavior. I see all sorts of interesting parallels between infrastructure, physiology and the psyche. We are all alive, after all, and our physical bodies are such a great part of our lives. I am surprised more writers don't focus on this part of the human experience. For me, it makes a death more understandable, more manageable, to know about the medical causes behind it. It can also reveal things we wouldn't otherwise know about the narrative of a person's life.

Q: You include a lot of technical information about engineering, street construction, and that sort of thing. Why was that important?

EG: Again, the whole world is a stage for a novelist. I see my task as one of exploration, and that means looking in the closets and under the counters and down the manhole covers, not just eavesdropping on conversations that take place in living rooms and parlors. I am especially interested in terrain that is commonly overlooked or avoided, especially for reasons of social propriety. Very few writers go into the bathroom with their characters, but often I find that important things transpire in the bathroom (or indeed the sewers) and see no reason to look squeamishly away.

Q: What are you working on now?

EG: My new book is called *The War Effort*, and it is set in the period between the end of World War II—V-J Day, in fact—and the Vietnam War. The action all takes place in New York, once again, and to a great extent the book is focused on the effects of war on the home front. The issue of a good war versus a bad war comes up, as does the civil rights movement, and some scientific and mathematical discoveries that were taking place in that era. One of the main characters is an aspiring myrmecologist—an ant specialist. Her mother is a depressed housewife who enters into a sordid love affair. Under the same roof, her invalid husband lies in bed, suffering from late-stage polio while his contemporaries go off to war and win honor and die with glory. Another character is a Marine who comes back from Vietnam badly damaged. Overall, the book centers on the ongoing relationships of two families, one white and one black. I'm excited to delve into a whole new set of social and emotional situations, and to get a chance to research the more recent past.

1. The hero of *Metropolis* remains nameless for the first part of the book; later, he tries on different names, which he then rejects, each in turn. Why are names important, and why do you think Gaffney chose to complicate her main character's identity in this way?

2. Beatrice O'Gamhna does not initially appear to be the nicest heroine when we first meet her; she is involved in pickpocketing and kidnapping. How did you feel about her character, as you read? What is her appeal?

3. Although the main character is a man, the strongest characters in the book are arguably the women: Mother Dolan, Beanie, Fiona. The issues of women's suffrage, violence against women and women in traditionally male professions such as medicine also come up in the story. What sort of point is Gaffney making? How much do you think society has changed in its attitudes toward women since the nineteenth century?

4. Harris is dogged by bad luck in the book, but he also has his share of very good luck, and there are any number of serendipitous or coincidental events that occur. What role does luck play in the story? Are characters held responsible for their actions?

5. Harris did not commit the particular crime of arson that he is suspected of, but he is not purely innocent either. Is his sense of guilt appropriate? Is he responsible for the things that happen after he is conscripted into the gang? Does old unresolved guilt carry over into his present?

6. Most of the characters have complicated moral situations: they are good people, and yet they are criminals; or they are criminals, but there is some explanation for how they fell into a life of crime. In certain cases, characters appear to be good, but they are in fact deeply corrupt. In what sort of moral universe do the characters of *Metropolis* live? Are any of the characters strictly good or evil?

7. There are two main villains, Dandy Johnny Dolan and Luther "the Undertaker" Undertoe. Why do you think Gaffney wanted two villains in the story, and how do they differ?

8. The Whyo gang has a complicated secret language and uses a profit-sharing scheme where funds are collected according to ability and distributed according to need. They treat women considerably better than do other gangs of criminals; at the same time, the gang is also extremely violent and corrupt. What did you think of the Whyos, in the end, and why? Is it possible to imagine a "good" gang?

9. Several of the characters in the story—Harris, Beatrice, John-Henry, and Luther—lost their mothers early in their lives, and Johnny grew up without a father. How do these formative events affect them, and how does each character handle the difficulty of growing up with this loss?

10. There is a large cast of secondary characters in *Metropolis*, as well as many side stories and digressions from the main narrative, on topics such as street paving, sewer building, underwater caisson excavation, women's health and bacteriology. Why did Gaffney choose to include all these characters and themes, and how do you think they contribute to the main story?

11. Do you think that the city of New York is more than just the setting for the novel? Could the city itself be seen as a character in *Metropolis*?

12. Occasionally, the narrator's voice intrudes on the story to comment on the action. How does this change the experience of reading the story? Would you say *Metropolis* feels like an old-fashioned novel, or are there aspects of it that mark the book as a product of the twenty-first century?

PHOTO: © DAPHNE KLEIN

ELIZABETH GAFFNEY is a native of Brooklyn,
New York. She is Editor at Large of the literary
quarterly *A Public Space* and was staff editor of
The Paris Review for sixteen years. In addition to
teaching writing at New York University, she has
translated from German *The Arbogast Case*,
The Pollen Room and *Invisible Woman:
Growing Up Black in Germany*. Her short
fiction has appeared in many little magazines.
Metropolis is her first novel.

ABOUT THE TYPE

This book was set in Electra, a typeface designed for Linotype by W. A. Dwiggins, the renowned type designer (1880–1956). Electra is a fluid typeface, avoiding the contrasts of thick and thin strokes that are prevalent in most modern typefaces.

Printed in the United States
by Baker & Taylor Publisher Services